MORE THAN 30 YEARS OF THRILLS!

New York Times

bestsel

P9-DFO-844

J.A. JANCE

Praise for *CLAWBACK*

"Series fans will enjoy this highly personal case."

—*Publishers Weekly*

"Readers will find themselves on the edge of their seats as they move through the story. This is J.A. Jance's eleventh Ali Reynolds book, and each installment has gotten better or has been just as good as its predecessor."

—*Bookreporter*

"This is a fast-paced addition to this beloved series, and drew me in a little closer to the characters. . . . I don't think you will be disappointed."

—*The Book Review*

COLD BETRAYAL

"Incredible. . . . This is a gem by a winning author. . . . Yet another terrific book by Jance that fans and readers will absolutely cheer about."

—*Suspense Magazine*

"Lively. . . . Jance knows how to tell a story . . . series fans won't be disappointed."

—*Publishers Weekly*

"Ali's good heart and sense of justice combine with well-paced suspense to create a satisfying whole."

—*Kirkus Reviews*

"It's about time that Jance got props from literary as well as thriller readers. . . . Jance's plots are less about violence, more about family, problem solving, and individual character. They are always page-turners."

—*Examiner.com*

MOVING TARGET

"Jance adroitly combines well-rounded characterizations and brisk storytelling with high-tech exploits, arson, kidnappings, and a shootout for an entertaining and suspenseful addition to this solid series."

—*Booklist*

"Crisp plotting, sharp characters, and realistic dialogue carry *Moving Target* through its many surprising twists."

—*South Florida Sun-Sentinel*

"Engrossing. . . . Jance provides enough backstory to orient readers new to the series, and longtime fans should enjoy insights into B.'s and Leland's pasts."

—*Publishers Weekly*

DEADLY STAKES

"Jance melds elements of the thriller and police procedural with a touch of romance to carry readers swiftly to an unexpected conclusion."

—*Kirkus Reviews*

"Jance's story is well-crafted and keeps one's interest to its final word. . . . The rapidly moving story makes it a fascinating mystery, full of multiple suspects and numerous possibilities."

—*Bookreporter*

LEFT FOR DEAD

"Jance at her best . . . engaging, exciting, and fast-paced."

—*Tucson Citizen*

"A truly thrilling case with red herrings, characters coming out of the woodwork, backstories that will make you gasp, and a conclusion that you will not see coming!"

—*Suspense Magazine*

"Entertaining on all counts."

—*Booklist*

"Loyal fans and newcomers alike will be glad to join feisty Ali in her latest adventure."

—Kirkus Reviews

FATAL ERROR

"The plot never stalls."

—Publishers Weekly

"An entertaining mix of sleuthing and human relationships."
—Booklist

"Jance continues to delight with her detail-filled suspense stories that capture so much of life."

—Library Journal

TRIAL BY FIRE

"Fast pacing, surprising plot twists, and a strong, principled heroine."

—Booklist

"Fans will not be disappointed with this new novel. It's a page-turner."

—Green Valley News and Sun

CRUEL INTENT

"Compelling . . . satisfying."

—USA Today

"A fast-paced read with as many twists and turns as a county fair roller coaster."

—Seattle Post-Intelligencer

"Jance has honed her talent for writing entertaining, accessible mysteries that readers can zip through."

—Booklist

ALSO BY J.A. JANCE

CLAWBACK

AN ALI REYNOLDS NOVEL

J.A. JANCE

POCKET BOOKS

New York   London   Toronto   Sydney   New Delhi

The sale of this book without its cover is unauthorized. If you purchased this book without a cover, you should be aware that it was reported to the publisher as "unsold and destroyed." Neither the author nor the publisher has received payment for the sale of this "stripped book."

Pocket Books
An Imprint of Simon & Schuster, Inc.
1230 Avenue of the Americas
New York, NY 10020

This book is a work of fiction. Any references to historical events, real people, or real places are used fictitiously. Other names, characters, places, and events are products of the author's imagination, and any resemblance to actual events or places or persons, living or dead, is entirely coincidental.

Copyright © 2016 by J.A. Jance

All rights reserved, including the right to reproduce this book or portions thereof in any form whatsoever. For information, address Touchstone Subsidiary Rights Department, 1230 Avenue of the Americas, New York, NY 10020.

First Pocket Books paperback edition January 2017

POCKET and colophon are registered trademarks of Simon & Schuster, Inc.

For information about special discounts for bulk purchases, please contact Simon & Schuster Special Sales at 1-866-506-1949 or business@simonandschuster.com.

The Simon & Schuster Speakers Bureau can bring authors to your live event. For more information or to book an event, contact the Simon & Schuster Speakers Bureau at 1-866-248-3049 or visit our website at www.simonspeakers.com.

Manufactured in the United States of America

10 9 8 7 6 5 4 3 2 1

ISBN 978-1-5011-1079-5
ISBN 978-1-5011-1076-4 (ebook)

*For all the people who gave me
500,000 reasons for writing this book.
Whoever you are; you know who you are.*

Clawback: Proceeds from an investment that is found to be fraudulent are confiscated and then redistributed to all investors on a proportional basis.

Prologue

After years of running Sedona's Sugarloaf Café, Bob Larson was enjoying the fruits of his labors and one of the most enjoyable benefits of retirement—the opportunity to sit at the kitchen counter, linger over a second cup of coffee, and watch the morning news. Short-order cooks in diners never see the news at that time of day. They're always too busy dealing with the morning rush.

His attention had drifted momentarily to an Anna's hummingbird delicately sipping nectar from the blooming paloverde just outside the living room window, but the words "Ocotillo Fund Management" penetrated his consciousness and drew his attention back to the screen. Realizing he'd missed the first part of the story, he grabbed the remote and ran the footage back to the beginning of the segment, so the sweet-faced, blond-haired news anchor could take another crack at it.

"Yesterday, employees at Phoenix-based Ocotillo Fund Management were sent home early with the doors chained shut behind them and the company out of business. Late yesterday afternoon, the Securities and Exchange Commission announced that they are launching a full investigation into allegations that monies invested with the company have gone missing. An unnamed source who is also a former employee of the firm said that the move came as a complete surprise to all concerned. This morning, we've left several messages for the company's founder and CEO, Jason McKinzie. So far those messages have gone unanswered."

Bob could barely believe what he was hearing. Ocotillo Fund Management? *That* Ocotillo Fund Management—the very company Bob and his wife, Edie, had chosen to manage their retirement funds? How could it be? With his heart hammering in his chest and both hands shaking, Bob set down his coffee mug and pulled his cell phone out of his pocket. He scrolled through his contacts list until he found Dan Frazier's number—numbers, actually—work, home in Sedona, home in Paradise Valley, and cell. He tried the cell as well as both home numbers. Those calls all went to voice mail. The last one—to the work number—didn't go through at all. Instead there was a tuneless three-toned signal followed by the standard notification.

"The number you have reached is not in service at this time. If you feel you have reached this message in error, please check the number and try again."

Bob Larson did not try again. He ended the call and slipped the phone into the pocket of his worn khaki shirt. That was only to be expected. If the office's doors were in lockdown, most likely the phones would have been turned off as well. So it was frustrating but hardly a surprise that there was no answer—no answer on the phones and no answers to his questions and no answers to his fears, either. All the while he'd been trying to call, a clutch of dread had grabbed his gut and twisted it, turning that last half-drunk cup of morning coffee into pure acid.

Abandoning both the TV remote and his coffee cup on the kitchen counter, Bob staggered over to one of the pair of easy chairs he and Edie had bought new when it came time to furnish their newly rented two-bedroom unit at Sedona Shadows. He was grateful Edie wasn't there with him and hadn't seen the news. She had gone off an hour earlier for her morning water aerobics session. She was still down at the pool, doing whatever it was the ladies did for an hour or more every morning. He could imagine her chatting away with her pals, blissfully unaware of the financial calamity that had just befallen them, but Bob was fully aware. He understood it completely.

Their nest egg was gone. Wiped out. The safety net he and Edie had carefully put aside for a rainy day had evaporated. Much as Bob wanted to unknow the extent of what had just happened, he couldn't. He also knew it was his fault. Not his alone, of course—damn Dan Frazier anyway. That was the thing that was causing that white-hot knot of anger to form in Bob's gut. He and Dan were friends—at least that's what he had thought— friends first and clients later.

They'd known each other since their early twenties. When Dan's dream of becoming a CPA had come to grief, he'd gone to work in his father's property and casualty insurance agency right there in town, where Bob and Edie Larson had been among his first customers. They'd stuck with him through the years as Dan's insurance business grew and prospered. Over time he had added an alphabet soup of official designations after his name, enough incomprehensible letters to choke a horse—Chartered this and Certified that.

Somewhere along the way, Dan had hit the big time, partnering with Jason McKinzie, a young hotshot financial wizard specializing in wealth management who had taken central Arizona by storm. Eventually Jason had invited Dan to join Ocotillo Fund Management, and where Dan Frazier went, Bob and Edie inevitably followed.

Once on board the OFM juggernaut, Dan had continued to maintain his Sedona office, running the insurance part of the business with underlings, while he spent most of his time operating out of the corporate office in Phoenix—the very one where the doors had been locked and the phones were no longer in service.

Dan had been a regular at the Sugarloaf, back when Edie's mother had still owned it. He and Dan had worked several community service projects over the years, and when Dan was able to go to a Barrett-Jackson auction and acquire a fully restored 1966 Mustang convertible, he had come to Bob looking for advice on the care and feeding of it.

Through the years, Bob and Edie had faithfully salted money away for retirement, stashing it in Ocotillo-managed accounts that Dan had recommended. When Bob reached age seventy-and-a-half and had to start taking annual distributions, they'd still been running the restaurant and hadn't needed the money, so they had plugged those funds back into non-tax-deferred accounts with Ocotillo as well. When they had finally decided to sell the diner, Dan had used his connections to help locate the business broker who had effected the transaction. Since their unit in Sedona Shadows was essentially a rental, they'd had to pay a deposit, but they hadn't needed either a down payment or a mortgage. That's when they decided to put the proceeds from the sale of the restaurant into an Ocotillo account as well.

"Are you sure about this?" the always practical Edie had asked. "Isn't it a lot like putting all our eggs in one basket?"

"Dan's a good friend," Bob had replied. "He wouldn't steer us wrong, would he?"

That was the problem. Obviously Dan Frazier had done exactly that—steered them wrong. Bob remembered every detail about their discussion that day, shortly after the sale of the restaurant— every single word. Dan had told him everything would be fine—that their money would be perfectly safe. Only it wasn't, and now all their retirement eggs were shattered, lost beyond repair.

The news reporter had mentioned that the SEC was now involved, and Bob had no idea what that meant or what would happen next. Bankruptcy, maybe? Lawyers? All of that was above his pay grade, but Bob did understand that if lawyers got their grubby paws on the process, whatever happened next was bound to be expensive. If he and Edie were lucky—very lucky—they'd maybe get pennies back on the dollar from an amount that, with the sale of the diner as well as the accompanying living quarters, had risen to a total of over a million bucks.

When they sold the Sugarloaf, they had splurged on a new Buick for Edie—her toes-up Buick, as she called it—and on some new furniture for their unit at Sedona Shadows, but the rest of the money had been handed over to none other than Ocotillo Fund Management!

When Dan had first urged them to move their IRAs and defined benefit accounts to Ocotillo, he had brought them a shiny, full-color prospectus delineating the various funds and their expected returns. There had been all the CYA stuff about "historical returns are no guarantee of future results," and Bob had wondered about that.

"How can Jason McKinzie make these returns happen?" Edie had asked, after reading through one of them. "How is it possible for him to beat everyone else's earnings by two to four points?"

"By being smarter than the average bear," Dan

had replied with an engaging grin. "He's bright enough to spot market corrections coming in advance. That way he unloads underachieving properties before things go south, giving him cash to reinvest while prices are still low. That's what you have to do in this business—be ahead of the curve."

In the end, though, having voiced her opinion, Edie had left the final decision up to Bob. "I'm the one who knows everything there is to know about flour and yeast," she told him. "You're the one with the head for business."

Armed with Edie's somewhat grudging agreement, Bob had gone along with his old friend Dan, and signed on the dotted line. Ocotillo had three separate funds for him to choose from, and Bob had opted for the most conservative of the three. Two points above the market was one thing. Four points or six? That sounded like too much of a good thing, so he had settled on the lowest one.

But now even that fund had been wiped out. Ocotillo was out of business. The office was locked, the phones were off. As for Jason McKinzie? Bob realized that McKinzie was most likely in the wind, but what about Dan Frazier—Bob's good friend, his old pal? What was he doing right about now? Did he have the good grace to at least feel guilty about what had happened? Was he ashamed of himself for not warning people in advance?

That was the thing Bob could hardly stomach. Dan must have known this was coming. The "unnamed source" the newscaster referred to, the one who said all this came as a "complete surprise," was maybe low enough on the totem pole that he'd had no idea about what was happening, but Dan was another story. Supposedly Dan had been part of upper management in the firm—at least that was how he'd presented himself as far as Bob and Edie were concerned. If the venture was about to implode, he must have had some inkling in advance that something was wrong.

And yet, a few weeks earlier, when Bob and Edie had run into Dan and Millie Frazier at the annual Kiwanis Mother's Day Pancake Feed at the high school, Dan had been his jolly old self, glad-handing everyone who came within reach and giving the ladies, Edie included, discreet pecks on the cheek. It irked Bob now to realize that, the entire time, Dan must have been putting on a show and pretending that everything was A-OK. He hadn't said a word to Bob that day that had hinted that anything was amiss—nothing to warn his loyal clientele of the oncoming train wreck.

Dan had been a businessman in town for decades, so it stood to reason that he was well known in the community, but today Bob couldn't help wondering how many other folks attending that pancake breakfast had been duped out of their life savings in the same way he and Edie had. How many poor rubes had that low-down snake in the grass greeted that morning with his firm handshake and misleading smile? Remembering that breakfast, Bob blinked back to the memory of introducing him to Betsy Peterson, one of Sedona Shadows' most recent arrivals and the grandmother of his grandson's wife, Athena.

Betsy was still in the process of selling her properties in Minnesota, and Bob had intended to introduce her to Dan with the recommendation that she might consider putting her funds under Dan's management. At the time, Betsy had responded with a firm "Thanks, but no thanks." Bob had been a little put off by that, but now he was supremely grateful that she had. At least Bob had dodged that bullet.

Glancing at his watch, Bob realized that Edie and Betsy would soon be finishing up with water aerobics and might return to their unit any minute. To everyone's surprise, after arriving at Sedona Shadows, eightysomething Betsy had taken to Edie Larson and to water aerobics like nobody's business. The two women were fast friends now, relishing their daily sessions in the pool along with a shared interest in a set of mutual great-grandkids. And once the aerobics session was over, they often returned to Bob and Edie's apartment for what Betsy and Edie both referred to as "forenoon coffee."

Right that moment, Bob wasn't ready to face either one of them. It was going to be hard enough to tell Edie about the situation. Doing so in front of a third party was utterly unthinkable. Besides, what Bob really wanted to do was track down Dan Frazier and punch the guy in the nose—or, at the very least, give the jerk a piece of his mind.

Standing up, Bob grabbed his keys off the

table by the door, and headed for the vintage '72 Bronco that—due to his skill as a mechanic—still ran like a top. Bob's aging Bronco and Dan Frazier's recently purchased Mustang were only six years apart in terms of model years, but no one would mistake Bob's workhorse vehicle for a showpiece. The Mustang was a low-mileage, highly polished, spoiled brat of a car, best used in fair-weather conditions only. The Bronco, on the other hand, dented but dependable, was a one-owner, four-wheel-drive beast that had gotten Bob out of more than one tricky off-road situation. If the odometer—the one thing that didn't work—had still been functioning, Bob estimated it would have turned over for the fourth time well before this.

Not wanting to encounter the women on their way into the building, Bob double-timed it down the hall in the opposite direction and let himself outside through a side entrance near his assigned covered parking spot. As he drove the few miles and many roundabouts on his way to Dan's place on the far side of town, Bob realized this was probably a fool's errand. Jason McKinzie had most likely run for the hills well in advance of the collapse, and Dan Frazier might have pulled a similar stunt. Still, going to Dan's place gave Bob a good excuse for not facing Edie right then and there and having to give her the bad news.

Dan Frazier's Sedona residence on Elberta Drive was modest in terms of Sedona's current real estate market, which tended toward the Mc-Mansion end of the housing spectrum. The house dated from an earlier time in his career, from when Dan had just started working for his father's insurance agency, and from an earlier era in terms of housing design. The in-town location meant it was long on convenience and had reasonably good views. Still, this one was little more than humble pie when compared to the spectacular hillside residence Millie and Dan occupied in Paradise Valley. That one came complete with a four-car garage. The one in Sedona was two cars only.

Once Bob turned off onto Elberta Drive, he stopped two houses short of the recently installed rolling gate at the bottom of Dan's driveway. For a time—a period of several minutes—Bob simply sat there with the car windows open and the engine running, trying to consider what the hell he was going to say to this man who had once been his friend: How could you do this to us? How dare you do this? What the hell kind of friend are you? None of those seemed adequate to the situation at hand.

At last, having had time to cool his temper and resolving to remain civil, Bob finally put the Bronco in gear and moved forward. Arriving at the end of the driveway, he was surprised to see Dan's rolling gate standing wide open. It was one of those that required the use of a remote. Installed after the purchase of that prized Mustang, Bob never remembered seeing it left open before—day or night.

As Bob crested the driveway and jammed the Bronco into park, one of the two garage doors began to rise. Once it was open, Bob saw that two cars were parked inside—Dan's Mustang and Millie's Volvo XV60. He more than half expected that one or the other of the vehicles, unaware of Bob's presence, would slam into gear and come speeding out of the garage. Realizing that any resulting collision was bound to be harder on either of Dan's upscale vehicles than it would be on the aging Bronco, Bob braced for a crash.

Except nothing happened. Neither of the two vehicles moved. The backup lights didn't come on, and there was no sign of life inside the garage. After waiting for the better part of a minute for someone to emerge, Bob finally gave up, shut off the engine, and exited his own vehicle. Only when he entered the garage did he hear the low rumble of the Mustang's idling V-8 engine, but no driver was visible behind the wheel.

"Hey, Dan," Bob called. "Are you in there?"

For a time there was no answer, then, over the hum of the engine, he heard a faint call. "Help me. Please."

The call for help seemed to be coming from the car, so Bob sprinted forward. Only when he was even with the Mustang's driver's side door did Bob realize there was a lone occupant inside the vehicle. Dan, seated behind the wheel, was slumped over onto the passenger seat in an unnatural position that left none of his head showing over the seat back. Both of Dan's eyes had vivid bruises around them, standing in sharp contrast to the pasty gray coloring of his face. His lips were cut and swollen. Someone had clearly beaten the crap out of the man. Then Bob's eyes were drawn to the bright scarlet stain spreading up and down a once spotless white shirt. Dan held one hand tightly against the wound, as if trying to stem the flow, but it wasn't working.

Bob had served as a corpsman in Vietnam. He knew his way around bloody wounds, and he knew way too much blood when he saw it. He pulled his phone out of his pocket and dialed 911. "We need help!" he barked into the phone when an emergency operator answered. "Man down and seriously wounded. Can't tell if he's been gunshot or if it's a knife wound."

"Knife," Dan managed weakly through clenched teeth. "They both had knives."

"Make that a knife wound," Bob corrected. "And there were two of them."

With his phone still on speaker, Bob spat out Dan's address. Then, with the call still active, he slipped the device into his shirt pocket, freeing both hands so he could reach inside, hoping to help apply pressure on the wound even though he already suspected that the damage was too severe. The wound was bleeding profusely. The stain was spreading at such an alarming rate that Bob doubted it was survivable.

"Do you know who did this?" he asked. "Where are they? What happened?"

"Tried to go for help," Dan mumbled weakly, batting away Bob's suddenly bloodied hand. "Go check on Millie," he urged. "Please!"

"Millie?" Bob asked. "Where is she?"

"House. She's in the house."

"Help is coming," Bob assured Dan as he backed away. "I'll go check on her."

After first switching off the Mustang's engine, Bob raced into the house through a door that opened from the garage directly into the laundry room. There were bloodied footprints staggering from side to side and leading from the kitchen into the garage, and there were bloodied smears across the faces of both the washer and dryer as well as on the opposite wall. Most likely Dan had come this way, in a desperate attempt either to escape the carnage or to summon help. Bob registered the stains on the floor and reflexively tried to dodge them, but he was too focused on moving fast to avoid them entirely.

Once through the laundry room, he came to an abrupt halt and stood aghast and unmoving in the kitchen doorway. Millie Frazier lay facedown in the center of the room in a rapidly expanding pool of blood.

Horror-struck, Bob didn't know what to do first. Should he check for a pulse that most likely wasn't there or simply retreat the way he had come? Then, in the sudden silence, a tiny voice spoke to him from his pocket. "Sir, are you still there? Emergency units are on the way."

"There are two victims," he said. "The one in the garage, a male, is a stabbing victim, and the one in the house is a woman. She's been stabbed, too. The man's still alive. I think this one's already dead."

That was the moment when Millie Frazier shuddered. Until then, Bob had been sure she was dead. Darting across the room to where she lay, he slipped in pooled blood and fell forward. When he came to rest, he was lying facedown on the injured woman's back. Appalled that he might have exacerbated her wounds, he heaved himself off her and scooted to a spot where his face was near hers, close enough so she could see him.

"Can you hear me?" he asked.

Her eyes blinked open, but they were dazed and out of focus.

"It's me, Millie. Bob Larson. I've called 911. Help is on the way. They'll be here soon. Who did this to you?"

For a moment her eyes seemed to register recognition. "Bob?" she mumbled. "Where's Dan?"

"Out in the garage," Bob answered. "He's still alive."

"He's a good man," she whispered. "Tell him I love him. Be sure to tell him that."

The focus faded from her eyes. Her impossibly shallow breathing became even more so.

"Stay with me," Bob pleaded, taking her hand and willing her to live. "You've got to hang in here. Help will be here soon."

He could see, though, that it was already too late. After a moment, eyes that had blinked open at the sound of his voice stared emptily into space. Bob checked again for a pulse. This time there wasn't any. Scrambling to his feet, he slipped and fell to his knees. He had to grab hold of the countertop to pull himself back upright. Once on his feet, he dashed out of the room the same way he had entered.

In the garage, he leaned into the car and then stepped away once more. The wail of oncoming sirens cut through the silence, but Bob knew the EMTs would be too late twice over. Millie Frazier was gone, and so was her husband. The tiny voice of the emergency operator was still speaking to him from his pocket, demanding an update. Reaching for the phone, he simply ended the call, paying no attention to the bloody prints his fingers left on the face of his phone.

With sickening clarity, Bob Larson understood that once the cops arrived, they would find three bloodied people at the residence. Only one of them would be alive—the guy who had called it in—and he was the one who would most likely turn into the prime suspect.

1

As the sun came up over the Mogollon Rim to the east, Haley Jackson lay in bed, still tossing and turning. The day before, her Sedona-based insurance agency where she was the office manager had been shut down by agents from the Securities and Exchange Commission. Her boss, Dan Frazier, had given her no advance warning that the raid was coming. In the hours since, she'd tried reaching out to him over and over—to no avail. He wasn't taking her calls, and as far as she knew, he hadn't tried calling her, either. Without hearing from Dan or having some kind of direction from him, she had no idea what she was supposed to do next. What was she supposed to tell her employees, to say nothing of the firm's anxious clients?

Try as she might, Haley still couldn't make sense of what had happened. Late in the afternoon, a group of men in suits had walked into the Frazier Insurance Agency and paused in front of the receptionist's desk. Although Haley didn't recognize the new arrivals, at first nothing seemed amiss. She assumed they were new in town and in the market for some kind of insurance coverage. As they continued to speak to Carmen Rios, the receptionist, however, Haley noticed the young woman growing more and more agitated. Finally, sensing something out of the ordinary, Haley left her own desk toward the back of the room and walked up to Carmen's.

"I'm the office manager here," she said, focusing on the man who seemed to be in charge. "Is there something I can do for you gentlemen?"

"They claim they're from the SEC," Carmen whispered, sounding worried. "They say we have to close the office immediately."

"The SEC?" Haley asked. "You want us to close the office? What's this all about?"

The man standing directly in front of Carmen turned to Haley and extracted an ID wallet from his pocket. When he held it up for Haley's examination, she saw that it belonged to one Donald Ferris, a senior agent with the Securities and Exchange Commission.

"All right," she said. "I see that you're with the SEC, but I have no idea what that means or why you feel it's necessary to shut down my office. What's going on?"

"My understanding is that Daniel Frazier Jr. is the owner of this establishment. Correct?" the guy asked.

Haley nodded. "Yes, but he isn't in right now. If you'd like to leave a card . . ."

Ignoring her objection, Agent Ferris continued. "Mr. Frazier is also a duly registered representative of a firm called Ocotillo Fund Management, right?"

"That's true," Haley began, "but . . ."

"Ocotillo Fund Management initiated bankruptcy proceedings earlier this afternoon. We've been directed to shut down this office and take custody of any and all applicable files. Since some of your insurance customers are also investment clients, we'll be taking them all."

"You're taking our files?" Haley echoed. "As for Ocotillo Fund Management filing bankruptcy? This is the first I've heard anything about it. Besides, you can't just walk in here like you own the place. Do you have a warrant?"

"Funny you should ask," Agent Ferris said, producing a document from an inside pocket of his suit jacket and handing it over. "You and your employees are to clear the premises at once. You may take personal items—purses, cell phones, tablets, and such, but all company files and equipment are to remain here. If anyone attempts to remove files via something like a thumb drive or other device, they will be found and confiscated as you exit."

When he said the words "thumb drive," Haley remembered briefly that Millie Frazier, Dan's wife, had stopped by the office on Friday morning. She had seemed exasperated and more than a little put out. "I had two appointments down in Paradise Valley later today, but Dan insisted that I cancel both of them and drive all the way up here to put this in the safe-deposit box," she had grumbled, holding up a postage stamp–sized object.

"What is it?" Haley had asked.

"A kind of thumb drive," Millie said. "I forget the real name—micro something or other. A memory card, maybe. Dan says he has an adapter here that'll make it work in his dinosaur desktop. As for why he needed this little item to be in the bank this morning rather than later today or maybe even tomorrow morning? I have no idea. Anyway, you know how Dan is. Once he gets an idea in his head, it's 'my way or the highway.' So that's my next stop—the bank."

"I didn't know thumb drives could be that small," Haley said, "but it must be important."

"Something to do with work, I expect," Millie allowed. "Something he doesn't want falling into the wrong hands. How are things here?"

"Fine," Haley had told her.

"Glad to hear it," Millie had said, then she was gone.

Standing there facing down Agent Donald Ferris, Millie Frazier and her tiny memory card were the least of Haley's worries.

"Before you or your people touch a thing," she said, reaching for her cell, "I need to check with Mr. Frazier."

"Sorry," Agent Ferris insisted. "This warrant says otherwise. Now if you and your people will gather all your belongings and clear out, we'll be able to get started."

"This is outrageous. You can't just shut us down."

"Yes, we can."

"For how long?"

"For as long as it takes—maybe indefinitely. We'll be sorting through the material tonight and deciding what's to stay and what's to go. We'll send a truck here tomorrow to pick up what's going. In the meantime, I've called a locksmith."

"You're changing the locks?"

"Yes, ma'am. Once you leave here, no one's allowed back inside until we give the go-ahead. Presumably, you're in charge, so I'll need your contact information."

With the phone pressed to one ear, Haley listened as her call to Dan's cell phone again went unanswered. "Call me," she said when the voice mail recording came on.

"It's time," Agent Ferris said. "We need to get started."

It had taken only a couple of minutes for the eight office employees—Haley included—to gather up their goods and be herded into the parking lot, with all purses having been thoroughly inspected on the way out. Naturally everybody was upset, and a couple of the girls were crying. What was going on? Did they still have jobs? What were they going to do?

Haley had done her best to be reassuring to the others, but that was a tough act to maintain, especially when a locksmith showed up in a van and proceeded to change the locks on the doors, both front and back, rendering Haley's prized master key useless.

While the locksmith worked, Haley had continued to try to reach Dan. There was still no answer at any of Dan's numbers, but she finally left brief messages on all three. "Please call me. Agents from the SEC came by and shut down the office. I need to know what's going on. Call me when you can. I'm worried." As a last resort, she tried Millie's cell phone, too. There was no answer there, either, and Haley left yet another message.

Gradually the other women drifted away to their cars. Haley stayed on, watching through the windows as a crew of workers dismantled the office. Computer terminals and keyboards were removed from desks and left in a heap near the front door. She was horrified to see the files from her superefficient wall-mounted and color-coded filing system be summarily tossed into a collection of empty Bankers Boxes and carted over to the door in no particular order. Had Agent Ferris allowed Haley to participate, she could have pointed out that files with blue tabs indicated investment clients only. Green and blue meant the customers had both investment and insurance accounts, while files with solo green tabs indicated insurance customers only.

Watching the haphazard way things were stuffed into boxes and stacked in random piles left Haley sick at heart. Once the files were returned, it would take days to sort them and put things back to rights. If ever.

What if the files never did come back? What if the demise of Ocotillo Fund Management spelled the end for the Frazier Insurance Agency as well? What if, rather than being a temporary measure, the office ended up being shut down for good? What would happen to her and to the other women who had worked there? During a mostly sleepless night, while fruitlessly checking her phone for incoming texts from Dan or Millie, Haley had wrestled with that question both for herself and for the others. What would become of them?

As far as Haley was concerned, the Frazier Insurance Agency was the only place she had ever worked. Like little Carmen Rios at the reception desk, Haley had gone to work for Dan Frazier straight out of high school. Almost two decades later, she was the office manager and the beneficiary of a business continuation plan that would allow her to buy the business outright in the event of either Dan's retirement or death. But what if the business was wiped out completely? Where would she go then? With her experience and with professional designations to back it up, she supposed some other insurance company would hire her, but working for someone else wasn't something to look forward to.

Haley's childhood had been chaotic at best. She had seldom ended a school year in the same school or even the same district where the year had started. The best thing her druggie mother ever did for her was to leave. As an awkward seventh-grader, Haley had been dumped into the care and keeping of her grandmother, Carol Hotchkiss. Not only was she an outsider in her new surroundings, she was also terribly behind as far as academics were concerned. Nonetheless, under her grandmother's tutelage Haley had come into her own.

Carol had spent her adult life working as a secretary for a local attorney, and she had deemed that what had been good for her would be good for Haley as well. Carol had insisted that Haley learn to type, teaching her at home on an aged Toshiba laptop. She had also taught Haley the intricacies of shorthand—something that was no longer offered in high school.

Once out of high school, those basic but increasingly rare secretarial skills had been enough to get her an entry-level job with Dan Frazier. Eighteen years later, nearly forty, Haley was married to her job. At Dan's insistence, Haley had earned her CLU, CPCU, and ChFC designations, and those had been sufficient for Dan to promote her to office manager. For years her duties had also included many of the functions more in line with those of a personal assistant. Once Dan had joined forces with Ocotillo Fund Management, however, Haley's PA duties had been passed along to corporate hires down in Phoenix.

Jason McKinzie had insisted that, as an executive with the firm, Dan have a full-time PA in Phoenix rather than a part-time one ninety miles away. The latest of these was Jessica Denton, someone Haley regarded as little more than a BBB—blond, bombshell bimbo—words Haley never uttered aloud. Jessie, as she liked to be called, may have been long on looks, but she seemed to be short on everything else, including shorthand and typing skills. Her occasional telephone conversations with Haley reeked of condescension.

It hadn't taken long for Haley to resent this latest unwelcome addition, but thank goodness, Jessie was Phoenix-centric. She seldom ventured far from the city, and when Dan was back home in Sedona, it was easy for Haley to ignore Jessica's existence entirely and fall back into the comfortable old ways of doing things—and running occasional errands when needed. Regarding Dan's Sedona-based clientele? At this point Haley knew his local customers far better than he did.

But was that enough? Haley wondered. If Frazier Insurance had come to the end of the road, would her intimate knowledge of the business and her years of faithful service make it possible for her transition to a comparable job somewhere else?

Although Haley was wide awake and had been for hours, she started when her alarm went off. Scrambling out of bed, she realized that, by now, the failure of Ocotillo Fund Management was probably not only public knowledge but a hot topic of conversation all over town. Even though the office would be closed, Haley's sense of responsibility prodded her to dress for work. After all, someone needed to be there to provide a company presence not only for concerned customers but also for whoever the SEC was sending to retrieve the Bankers Boxes packed with files.

Dressed and with her makeup on, Haley headed for the kitchen, where she turned on the coffeepot and prepared to make the oatmeal that Gram insisted on having for breakfast summer and winter. While waiting for the water to boil, Haley switched on the television set in the living room, coming into the news broadcast just as someone mentioned Ocotillo Fund Management. By the time the segment was over, Haley was frozen in her grandmother's recliner and on the verge of hyperventilating. The broadcast moved on to a commercial break, but Haley stared unseeing at the figures on the screen with a storm of questions flashing through her mind. How had this happened? And would her office be able to weather the storm?

By the time Haley staggered back into the kitchen, the water in the saucepan had mostly boiled away. As she started over on the oatmeal, she recalled one bit from the broadcast that had hit her especially hard—the quote from an unnamed source, reportedly a former OFM employee, who claimed that the bankruptcy proceedings had come as a complete surprise to everyone.

That couldn't be true, Haley realized. Dan must have known. Had to have known. She had worked with the man long enough that she understood his moods, both good and bad. It seemed to her that he'd been in a dark place recently—for the past several months, anyway. Now with the bankruptcy issue out in the open, she thought she understood why. He must have realized that there was trouble brewing with the SEC. Still, it hurt more than Haley could fathom that this man she had trusted so completely—someone who had been the only thing close to a father figure in her life—hadn't confided in her or given her so much as a single word of warning that disaster was looming. It was one thing for him to do that to relative strangers, but how could he do that to her?

The oatmeal was almost ready to serve when she heard the click, click, click of her grandmother's walker coming down the hall. Haley reached for the remote to silence the TV set.

"Morning," Gram said, easing herself onto her chair and placing her walker off to the side. "Don't bother turning it off," she added. "I was watching the news in my room before I came out. Have you heard from Dan?"

Haley shook her head. "Not a word."

"Asshole," Gram muttered as Haley placed a cup of coffee and a bowl of steaming oatmeal in front of her. "You'd think he'd at least have the decency to call you back."

"You'd think," Haley agreed, taking her own seat.

Despite whatever pitfalls the coming day might hold, Haley couldn't help smiling at her grandmother's plainspoken opinion, but then, Carol Hotchkiss had never been one to hold back. Two years ago, Haley's mother had dropped by for an unexpected and unwelcome visit, making her first appearance after an almost thirty-year absence.

"You don't give a rat's ass about either one of us," Grandma C. had told her errant daughter.

"You may think you can show up after all these years and hope to hang around long enough for me to die so you can pick my bones. Well, my dear, you've got another think coming. Haley and I are doing just fine without you, thank you very much, so get the hell out of here and don't let the door hit you on the ass on your way out."

Haley's mother had left and hadn't come back. A few months later Gram had suffered a stroke. She had made what her doctors said was a remarkable recovery for someone in her mideighties, but ongoing mobility issues made the walker a must. Without Haley there to look after her, Carol would have had to go into some kind of assisted care situation. Had Haley been married with kids, it might have been a different story, but as things stood, she didn't begrudge the fact that their caregiving roles—that of guardian and ward—were now totally reversed. It was a debt Haley was happy to repay. After all, Gram had been Haley's safe harbor once, and now Haley was hers.

"Looks like you're dressed for work," Gram observed a few moments later. "I thought you told me that the office would be closed today. Are you still going in?"

Haley nodded. "Someone needs to be there."

"Dan's the one who should be putting in an appearance, not you," Grandma C. groused. "After all, he's the one who went overboard for Jason McKinzie in the first place. Where do you suppose Dan is? And where's Jason McKinzie, for that matter? According to what they said on the news there's a possibility that he's fled the country. For all we know, somebody may have slapped Dan's ass in jail. From the sound of it, deservedly so."

The thought of Dan's being in jail somewhere had occurred to Haley as well. That would explain why Dan hadn't called her back, but Millie hadn't returned her calls, either. Why not?

Haley's phone rang just then. Hoping it was Dan, she answered on the first ring, but the caller turned out to be Carmen Rios.

"Have you heard anything?" Carmen asked anxiously. "Are we supposed to come to work today or not?"

"I haven't heard otherwise," Haley said, "so I'm assuming the office is still closed."

"Do you want me to call and change the message on the answering machine?" Carmen asked.

"Good thinking," Haley said. "Say that the office is temporarily closed and that messages left on the machine will be returned as soon as possible. Can you monitor the messages from off-site?"

"Sure, why?"

"I'm afraid that the voice mail box will be overwhelmed. If you could keep track of messages—writing them down if not necessarily replying to them—I'd really appreciate it. That way we'll be able to get back to them eventually. If people keep getting messages that the mailbox is full, it'll be that much worse."

"Sure thing," Carmen said. "I'll be glad to. I saw what they said on TV," she added. "It sounds bad."

"Yes, it does," Haley agreed. "We just have to keep the faith. I'll call you if anything changes."

Leaving half her oatmeal uneaten, Haley stood up and began clearing the table. "The fact that people have lost their money isn't your fault, you know," Gram said, "so don't hold yourself responsible."

"But I am responsible for some of them," Haley countered. "Over the years I've sent plenty of Frazier Insurance customers over to the investment side."

"It's still not your fault," Gram insisted. "You're not the one who ran the company into the ground. Somebody else did that."

With tears springing to her eyes, Haley hurried across the room to give her grandmother a quick hug.

"Thank you," she whispered. "You're the best."

Realizing that television crews might be present at the office, once Haley finished loading the dishwasher, she went back into the bedroom and changed into something dressier. It was while she was taking another crack at her makeup when Haley thought again about her conversation with Millie Frazier on Friday morning, the one about the memory card that was probably, even now, hidden away in Dan and Millie's safe-deposit box.

Haley remembered the part about it containing something from work that Dan didn't want to fall into the wrong hands. When Agent Ferris had shown up at the office, issuing orders and laying down the law about the search, he had mentioned thumb drives specifically, but presumably the ones in question had been thumb drives on the premises rather than somewhere else. And whose hands exactly constituted the "wrong" ones? Maybe Agent Ferris himself was on the wrong side of that equation.

Finished retouching her makeup, Haley reached for her purse and key ring. And there it was—the third key to Dan and Millie's safe-deposit box. Dan and Millie had given her the key when they had named her to be the executrix of their wills. They had entrusted her with the key along with the expectation that she would faithfully carry out their wishes. For right now and until she heard otherwise, that memory card was safe with her as well.

2

It was hot in the backseat of the patrol car—unbearably, ungodly hot. At first the car had been parked in the shade, and the windows were cracked open, but it was June in the high desert. With the car now in full sunlight, Bob felt like he was imprisoned in an oven.

He hadn't argued with the two cops who had arrived on the scene first and in separate patrol cars when they cuffed him and locked him inside. After all, they were young guys, still wet behind the ears. Bob suspected that when it came to dealing with homicide scenes, both of them were newbies.

As a consequence, they tried to do everything by the book. They knew from the 911 call—a call Bob himself had placed—that they were being summoned to a double homicide. And he, of course, was the very first person they laid eyes on at the scene, someone with blood on his clothing and on his hands. They took one look at him and ordered Bob to get on the ground, which was no easy accomplishment for a guy in his seventies who had spent all his working life standing on his feet, hour after hour, while running a commercial kitchen.

At that point, Bob had known that handcuffs would come next, and they did. After that, though, he figured they'd at least talk to him and give him a chance to tell them what had happened. He expected them to ask a question or two, and listen to his side of the story. Nope, not them. Instead, they hauled him to his feet like a bag of potatoes and then half dragged, half carried him to one of their two patrol cars.

When it came to television, Edie tended to watch *48 Hours* and *Dateline*. Bob preferred *Cops*. He loved watching how patient officers talked their way around guys with no driver's licenses who claimed that the stolen car they were driving belonged to a good friend of theirs and that the drug paraphernalia in the glove box or under the driver's seat wasn't theirs, either, and they had *no* idea how it got there.

Bob had watched all those programs, so he thought he knew what to expect. He was anticipating a period of casual de-escalating chitchat on their part: Do you have any weapons on you, sir? Anything in your pockets that might hurt me? Any drugs in your possession? What seems to have happened here today?

But these young whippersnappers weren't experienced enough to do de-escalation. They patted Bob down, relieving him of his Swiss army knife, his wallet, and his bloodied cell phone in the process. Bob thought all of this was an overreaction on their part, but again he tried giving them a break. With his hands still behind his back, they ducked his head to clear the door, chucked him into the backseat of the patrol car, and slammed the door shut behind him. Then they started toward the garage.

"Wait," Bob called after them through the bars welded to the frame. "Don't you want to know what happened?"

"I think we have a pretty good idea of what happened," one of them said, and away they went.

Time slowed to a crawl. The fire truck and ambulance came and went. More patrol cars, some marked and some not, arrived on the scene, and so did the medical examiner's van. Bob's hands were still cuffed behind him, and periodically they fell asleep, stabbing him with needles and pins. There was no way to sit comfortably. Sweat poured off his face. Flies and wasps, attracted no doubt by the scent of the blood on his clothing, found the partially opened window and flew in for a visit. As for the coffee Bob had consumed much earlier? That proceeded to run its course. He needed to pee in the worst way. For guys of a certain age with enlarged prostates, when you gotta go, you gotta go.

After what seemed an eternity, one of the younger uniforms reappeared and climbed into the driver's seat.

"Hey," Bob said. "Can you let me out for a minute? I need to take a leak."

"Sorry," the cop replied. "That'll have to wait until we get back to the department."

They entered the police department complex through the sally port. By then it was too late in the "take a leak" department, making Bob Larson's humiliation complete. He was led into what he assumed to be the booking room with a very visible dribble of urine running down the inside of his pant leg.

The cop removed the cuffs. "You want to use the restroom now, before we take the photos?"

"You're a complete jackass," Bob growled at him. "And no, I no longer need a restroom. As you can see, that ship has sailed. You said you wanted photos? Go ahead. Let's get this the hell over with."

They took photos of him in his bloodied clothing. Once they finished with that, he was directed into a room to strip off his outer clothing—shirt, belt, pants, shoes, socks, and watch. To Bob's dismay, everything—including the urine-soaked pants—were handed over to a very young woman, an evidence clerk, whose name badge said CARLOTTA SIMS. She stowed each item in clear evidence bags which she carefully labeled and sealed. In the meantime, Bob was handed an orange jail jumpsuit and a pair of plastic sandals. He could tell by simply looking at the sandals that they were far too large for his feet.

Minutes later, when Bob shuffled out of the restroom dressed in his orange jail togs and clumsy sandals, he was relieved to see that the pushy young cop was gone. The evidence clerk then used a digital camera to photograph his arms, neck, and face. *Probably looking for signs of a struggle or scratches*, Bob surmised. Of course there weren't any of those. Surely, sooner or later, someone would finally figure out that he wasn't responsible.

Once the photos were taken, Carlotta ushered Bob down the hall and directed him into what was clearly an interview room—a Formica table attached to the wall; three plastic chairs; a mirror that was obviously a two-way; a video camera mounted to the ceiling; an immense wall-mounted clock, like the ones that used to be in school classrooms, complete with a sweeping second hand.

"Can I get you anything?" Carlotta asked.

"A telephone so I can let my wife know where I am."

"Sorry," she said, "no can do."

Bob had slurped water from the faucet into his mouth by hand while he'd been in the restroom changing. But after baking in the car for so long, he was still dehydrated. He was also hungry. "A bottle of water, maybe?" he asked.

"Sure," she said.

When she closed the door, the automatic lock clicked shut behind her. She returned in less than a minute—according to the ticking clock—bringing bottled water.

When the door closed for the second time, he glanced at the clock again—1:05. That's when he realized that lunchtime at Sedona Shadows was almost over, and he had failed in his mission—

Wanda Farmer's birthday cake was still in the bakery at Safeway.

"Edie's going to kill me," he muttered aloud to himself.

Someone listening in on that derisive comment might have assumed that Bob was talking either about his losing his retirement funds or else ending up in a jail interview room. All he was really talking about right then was the damned birthday cake, because Bob knew Edie would be fit to be tied.

3

"Crap," Alberto Joaquín muttered to Jeffrey Hawkins, his partner in crime. "Coming away without that damned SD card means we blew it big-time. What the hell do we do now?"

Alberto may have gotten the gig in the first place, and he was the one at the wheel of their parked pickup truck, but as far as Jeffrey Hawkins was concerned, Alberto was definitely not the brains of the outfit. They had stripped off their bloodied latex gloves and paper surgical gowns before leaving the crime scene. Jeffrey was the one with enough presence of mind to have pitched his knife in through the back window of the crappy old Bronco that had shown up unexpectedly in the middle of everything. With a little luck, maybe the cops would think the guy in the Bronco was the one responsible.

Everything else, including Alberto's knife, had been shoved into the black trash bag Jeffrey had been smart enough to bring along for that very reason. After leaving the crime scene, they'd used one of the shovels from the back of the landscaping truck to bury the bag two feet deep in the soft sand of a wash just off General Crook Trail south of Camp Verde.

As far as Jeffrey could see they had managed to avoid bringing any blood evidence back into the truck with them, although he worried there might be a few invisible blood smears on the floorboard. If they were there, however, they were also invisible to the naked eye.

The job had been simple enough. Alberto's job as a landscaper had made it easy enough to collect the victim, detain him, and try to convince him to hand over a microSD card that evidently contained something Dan wasn't supposed to have. Except it had taken far more convincing than either Alberto or Jeffrey had anticipated. When beating the crap out of the old guy hadn't done the job, Jeffrey had suggested they track down the wife and use her as a bargaining chip. That hadn't worked very well, either.

"Mrs. Frazier was a nice lady," Alberto said. "I felt sorry for her."

Jeffrey had noticed at the time that Alberto had a weak spot for the woman. Jeffrey was the one who had held the knife to her throat, thinking that a tiny pinprick of blood would be enough to bring the husband to his senses. What he hadn't expected was that a furious Dan Frazier would somehow lurch to his feet and launch himself into the melee. By the time it was over, Frazier and the woman were both down for the count. By then,

Jeffrey didn't give a damn about the SD card. His only thought was to get the hell out of there.

"Frazier was a hell of a lot tougher than he looked," Alberto said. "Who ever would have thought an old guy like that would have balls enough to tackle both of us at once? Now two people are dead, and we've got nothing to show for it."

"Maybe not," Jeffrey said.

Alberto gave his partner a quizzical look. "What do you mean maybe not? We were supposed to bring back that damned card, and we don't have it."

"That doesn't mean we can't get one," Jeffrey countered. "It won't be *the* SD card, but it will be *an* SD card. It's simple. We go to a drugstore, buy ourselves a brand-new one, and take it to the meet. We give the guy the card, he gives us our money, and we go on our merry way. By the time he figures out he's got the wrong one, we'll be long gone and so will his money. After all, since he's the one who ordered the hit, he won't be able to send the cops after us."

Alberto had to chuckle at that. "I guess not," he said.

"And if he tries anything at the meet," Jeffrey continued, "what say we shoot the bastard right then and there? Two to one, buddy. You lose."

Years earlier, when Alberto Joaquín and Jeffrey Hawkins had been assigned to the same cell in the Mohave Correctional Facility, a private prison near Kingman, numerous bets had been placed about which one would outlive the other. At the time, both of them had been new to the place. Hawkins with his blue eyes and dirty-blond hair was rumored to be a white supremacist, and Joaquín was thought to have connections to one of the Hispanic gangs. Much to everyone's surprise, the two men had hit it off and sorted themselves into a two-man gang all their own. They were tough enough and mean enough to hold out against all comers, and in the long run, no one had dared cross them. Now that they were both out and back on the streets, the same held true.

"So where do we get one?" Alberto asked.

"The camera department of a drugstore," Jeffrey said, nodding his head back in the direction of the town they'd already passed. "Camp Verde must have at least one of those."

"What if there are security cameras inside?" Alberto asked.

"So what?" Jeffrey asked. "We show up at the meet empty-handed, we get nothing. With the drive in hand, we're cool. Up against a chance of walking away with another ten K apiece or walking away with nothing, I say risking being picked up by a security camera at a drugstore in some out-of-the-way burg in central Arizona is well worth it."

Alberto thought about it for a moment before nodding. "You're right," he agreed. Then he glanced at his watch. The payoff meet was scheduled for three o'clock in a deserted gravel pit a few miles off the 303 north of Sun City.

"We'd best be doing it, then," he added. "If we're going to pull this off, we can't afford to be late."

Half an hour later, Jeffrey emerged from the

drugstore with his purchase in a plastic bag. Once they finally extricated the drive itself from its plastic packaging, Alberto was amazed. "That tiny little thing?" he asked. "What the hell could be on something like this that would be worth dying for?"

"Beats me," Jeffrey said. "You're right. It doesn't look like much from here, but we're not the ones calling the shots and paying the fare. Now, what say we stop off and have a burger before we get back on the freeway? It was a long night, and I'm starving. Besides, we need to keep up our strength. I'm thinking we have another long drive ahead of us later tonight."

4

Ali Reynolds held the phone away from her ear as the woman droned on. "As I already told Ms. Fletcher yesterday, her sister's children cannot and will not be admitted to schools in our district."

During Ali's years in the television news business, first as a reporter and later as an anchor, she had dealt with plenty of recalcitrant mid-level bureaucrats. Now in her fifties and long retired from her television newscast days, she currently performed administrative and PR duties as well as occasional investigative work for her husband's cyber security company, High Noon Enterprises. Most of the time, unfailing courtesy and a bit of humor could break through bureaucratically enforced barriers. On this occasion, however, those remedies didn't seem to be working.

It didn't help Ali's frame of mind that Adele Harris, the woman drawing lines in the sand, was speaking to Ali in an archly superior manner that suggested her listener was something less than all there. "We are unable to enroll any children whose

parents don't present properly certified birth certificates. A notarized photocopy of a page from a
family Bible simply doesn't cut it as far as district
policy is concerned. No exceptions."

Ali sat back in her ratty, definitely nonergo-
nomic desk chair, closed her eyes, and did her best
to keep from grinding her teeth. An old-fashioned
electric clock hung on the far wall of her grim little
office. As the hour hand landed on eleven, she
realized she had spent twenty minutes waiting on
hold to speak to this faceless school district official
located several hundred miles away most likely in
an equally grim office in far-off Albuquerque, New
Mexico. Once Ms. Harris came back on the phone,
Ali had wasted another twenty minutes while attempting to explain, in great detail, why the three
Johnson children—ages seven, five, and three—
had no officially issued birth certificates. None of
the children from The Family, the polygamous cult
from which the Johnson brood had been liberated
some three months earlier, had been given officially sanctioned birth certificates. Records of live
births in The Encampment had been kept in family
Bibles and nowhere else.

Despite plenty of evidence to the contrary, Ali
continued to hold herself almost wholly responsible
for the fact that Christine Johnson and her now fatherless brood had been cast out into the cold, cruel
world and into a twenty-first century that they were
ill-prepared to face.

In the aftermath of the bloody massacre that
had put an end to The Family's lucrative human

trafficking business, Ali, along with numerous others, had devoted countless hours trying to aid the survivors. The bloody shootout on a cold March night on the outskirts of Colorado City had displaced approximately thirty separate polygamous families. The death toll left behind at least a hundred women bereft of husbands along with two hundred or more fatherless children. All of the survivors had been deprived of home and hearth. They had lost everything familiar. With almost no preparation, they were thrust out into a strange new world which, from the survivors' points of view, might just as well have been another planet.

Ali had done her best to explain all of that to Ms. Harris, but her detailed recitation of the facts had left the school official unmoved and unfazed. "As I said before, our district policy requires that we must have proper documentation for all our—"

Ali hit end on her phone, cutting the woman off in mid–bureaucratic doublespeak. Then, after scrolling through her recent calls list, she pressed one of those. The phone rang twice before being answered by a pleasant-voiced receptionist.

"Governor Dunham's office."

"Ali Reynolds here. Could I speak with the governor, please?"

"She's on another line right now, Ms. Reynolds. I don't know how long she'll be."

"That's all right. I'll hold."

While Ali waited, she checked the computerized list that contained the names of all the women and children who had been dispossessed by what people in the media still persisted in referring to as the Dunham Massacre. What Governor Virginia Dunham had intended as a bloodless preemptive strike to recover evidence of The Family's human trafficking had been anything but bloodless. It had, instead, turned into a slaughter that left more than two dozen dead and the governor herself gravely wounded.

Working out of a repurposed utility room turned office, Ali spent two to three days a week as a volunteer trying to iron out some of the thorny reentry issues faced by The Family's dispossessed women and children. In the meantime, the governor was working on locating the funds Bishop Richard Lowell, The Family's charismatic former leader, had hidden away for his own benefit in any number of offshore accounts. Governor Dunham was intent on tracking down the funds so they could be used to meet the ongoing economic, educational, physical, and emotional needs of the cult's traumatized survivors, many of whom could barely read and write and who had few, if any, marketable job skills.

As for the children? The cult's so-called homeschooling had been appallingly deficient, leaving the kids completely at sea in grade levels commensurate with their ages.

Having lost patience with only the most recent of several unhelpful school functionaries, the one in Albuquerque, Ali had resorted to bringing out her big gun—Governor Dunham herself.

"Hey there, partner in crime," Virginia Dunham said cheerfully, coming on the line. "How are we doing in the exploding microwave department? Any more electronic casualties to report?"

Exploding microwaves weren't exactly a laughing matter among The Family's struggling refugees. As the women moved first into emergency housing and now into more permanent facilities, coping with modern appliances had become a major problem. There were no electrical appliances back home at The Encampment, and the women were at a loss as to how to use them. Microwaves in particular had been a problem. To date four of them had been lost—three to meltdowns caused by overheated tinfoil and one to a very messy six-egg explosion.

"No," Ali said with a laugh. "The microwaves are all fine as far as I know. This is a school enrollment problem."

Governor Dunham sighed. "Another of those? I'm guessing that means we're up against the old missing-birth-certificate bugaboo."

"Yup, that's it," Ali replied.

Governor Dunham's tone went from cordial to all-business. "Who's the client?" she asked. "And where's the school district?"

"Christine Johnson is the client. The school district in question is Albuquerque Unified, and the woman dragging her bureaucratic high heels is one Adele Harris."

Ali heard the governor keying information into her computer. Ali and the governor worked with a shared Dropbox file devoted to The Family's refugees. It contained the names and current addresses for all the affected women and children. It also included medical, dental, and vaccination records. Getting all the kids vaccinated had been another roadblock to enrolling them in schools. Once Ali had seen to that, she thought they were home free, but the missing birth certificates had proved to be an equally pressing issue.

"Okay," Virginia Dunham said. "Got it. Christine Johnson. It says here that she and her children, ages seven, five, and three, were taken under the wing of an older sister, Edith Fletcher, who somehow managed to escape from The Family several years ago."

"That's correct," Ali said. "From what I can tell, the sister landed on her feet and is now pretty squared away. She's made arrangements to have learning assessments done on both of Christine's school-age kids. She's also arranged for private tutoring this summer to bring them up somewhere close to appropriate grade levels."

"Are we paying for that?" Virginia asked.

"I offered," Ali answered, "but Edith said there was no need—that she would handle it."

"Getting back to Ms. Harris, it sounds like I'll need to find a way to go over her head, then," Virginia observed.

"I was hoping you would," Ali answered. "Thank you. But before you go, can you tell me what's happening on the financial front? Any news on that?"

Governor Dunham had personally taken charge

of overseeing the untangling of The Family's complicated financial situation. "Not much," she said. "We're still working the problem. With the help of your husband's firm, we've managed to locate many of the offshore accounts, but getting the money back from those and then sorting out the distribution of funds to the proper heirs and beneficiaries is a mess that will take years."

Ali's husband, B. Simpson, and High Noon Enterprises, had been involved in the problem from the get-go. Ali and B. had been together in Governor Dunham's Sprinter the night of The Family's bloody shootout. Since then, B. had devoted plenty of the company's pro bono time and effort toward tracking down the cult's purloined funds.

Finding the money had proved to be the easy part. Figuring out who should inherit was another issue entirely. In a polygamous community, the question of who was related to whom and how wasn't always clear-cut. The records from the family Bibles weren't always complete, either, since daughters who ran away or even attempted to do so were simply stricken from the record. Several of those supposedly errant daughters may have been disavowed by their families, but the rule of law outside The Family's compound meant that, in the absence of properly drawn wills, they were still legitimate heirs.

"When it comes to sorting that stuff out," Ali said, "better you than me. Besides, my total focus right now is making sure all the school-age kids are enrolled in suitable situations by the time September rolls around."

Ali's phone buzzed in her ear. A glance at the screen identified the incoming call.

"My mom's calling," she said into the phone. "I need to take this."

Governor Dunham laughed. "You have one of those, too? While you talk to her, I'll tackle the governor of New Mexico."

"Fair enough," Ali replied. She ended the call and switched over to the other line. "Hi, Mom."

"Hello yourself," Edie Larson said. "Have you heard from your father?"

"No, why? Has he gone missing?"

Ali intended her comment as a joke, but for Edie this wasn't a laughing matter.

"He and that rusty bucket-of-bolts Bronco of his were MIA by the time Betsy and I got back from water aerobics first thing this morning," Edie complained. "He went off in such a hurry that the TV was still on and the remote was on the kitchen counter along with a half-empty coffee cup, which he didn't bother to rinse out, by the way."

Ali's parents had run the Sugarloaf Café together for years with very little squabbling. Now that they were retired and living in a small two-bedroom unit at Sedona Shadows, Ali had noticed that, on occasion, they tended to get on one another's nerves in what B. referred to as a perpetual case of cabin fever.

"I'm in charge of this month's birthday list,"

Edie Larson said, continuing her rant. "Bobby was supposed to pick up Wanda Farmer's birthday cake from the bakery at Safeway and have it here before lunch. So here it is, almost lunchtime. Bobby's nowhere to be found and neither is the cake. I've been calling and calling, but he doesn't answer. I finally called the store to check. Turns out the cake is still there. That means I'm going to have to fire up the Buick and go get it myself. You'd think I'd know better than to trust a man to do a woman's job."

Ali knew that her father served as the self-appointed guardian to a homeless enclave in the Mogollon Rim woods halfway between Sedona and Flag. Many of the guys who lived out there were veterans with medical and or mental issues. Ali understood that if one of "my guys," as Bob Larson liked to call them, was in some kind of difficulty, her father would move heaven and earth to fix it. Considering how long her parents had been married, it shouldn't have come as a complete surprise to Edie that on Bob's list of what was and wasn't important, a scheduled birthday cake delivery might easily have fallen to the bottom.

"One of his pals is probably in some kind of difficulty and he's up on the rim helping out with that," Ali suggested. "I know from personal experience that cell phone service up there is mighty spotty."

"Right," Edie grumbled. "And the old fool probably drove that rattletrap Bronco of his straight up Schnebly Hill Road to get there. For all we know, he might have driven off a cliff somewhere, and he's lying out there dead in a spot where only the buzzards will find him. Wouldn't you think he'd have brains enough to leave me a note telling me where he's going? I swear, sometimes I think that man is going to drive me to drink."

"After fifty-odd years of marriage, I doubt that's going to happen anytime soon," Ali observed, saying the words with a smile she was glad her mother couldn't see.

"No," Edie agreed. "I suppose not. I'd better head out and pick up that blasted cake, but if you hear from your father before I do, you tell him from me that he's in hot water."

"I will," Ali agreed. "I'll let him have it with both barrels."

"Good," Edie said. "He might just listen to you."

When Edie ended the call, Ali glanced at her watch and saw that it really was almost noon. After being shut up in a dreary, windowless space all morning long, she decided that a brisk walk was in order. She stopped off in the break room long enough to pick up the egg salad sandwich her majordomo, Leland Brooks, had made that morning and sent along for her to have at lunch. With sandwich and a Diet Coke in hand, Ali left the building and stepped out into the warm sunshine.

It was June. There were no clouds dotting the bright blue sky overhead. How did that almost forgotten old poem go? Ali recited part of it aloud as she marched along, not caring if passersby thought she was nuts and talking to herself. It didn't matter:

"And what is so rare as a day in June?
Then, if ever, come perfect days . . ."

As far as Ali could see right then, it seemed like a perfect June day, and it kept right on being perfect—until the moment it wasn't.

5

Delayed by countless phone calls, it was late midmorning before Haley finally arrived at the office. By then the strip mall's parking lot was already loaded with cars, including two separate media vans, one from a television station in Flagstaff and the other from one in Phoenix.

A disorganized crowd of people had gathered on the sidewalk outside the front door, milling restlessly on either side of an unmarked delivery truck parked directly in front of the agency's main entrance. The door itself had been propped open. Under the direction of Agent Ferris, two men in matching coveralls were busily carrying armload after armload of Bankers Boxes out of the office and packing them into the truck. It was all Haley could do not to break down and weep. In no small way, those boxes represented her life's work.

As Haley moved through the crowd, people began hailing her by name and shouting angry questions in her direction. She knew most of the hecklers by sight. Some were insurance customers only, worried about what would happen to their coverage if Frazier Insurance went out of business. Several of them, folks she knew to be OFM customers, had arrived in full protest mode, carrying handmade placards that said, "HEY, DANNO. SAY IT AIN'T SO!"

Frank Merrick, one of the placard-bearers, waved his sign directly in Haley's face, forcing her to retreat.

"What's the matter?" Frank demanded. "Is Dan Frazier such a coward that he can't come out and talk to us himself? He had to send you?"

Haley had never liked Frank Merrick. Because he was a customer, she forced herself to tolerate his frequent bouts of rude behavior. She often ran interference for the other girls in the office by handling Frank's visits herself rather than subjecting other employees to his routine boorishness. Even under these difficult circumstances, she did her best to be courteous.

"Good morning, Mr. Merrick," she said. "I'm here because I'm supposed to be here. This is where I work."

Unfortunately, by then Merrick had succeeded in getting the crowd's undivided attention. The people gathered around him fell unnervingly silent, listening to Haley's reply.

"Where's Dan?" Merrick insisted.

"Not here at the moment, as you can see," she said mildly. "How can I help you?"

"How come the office is shut down?" The question came from someone near the back, someone

Haley couldn't see. "Who are these people? Why are they emptying your office? Are you leaving?"

"We're closed today, and I'm not exactly sure when we'll reopen. No doubt you've all heard about the situation with Ocotillo Fund Management. The files are being removed, temporarily, as part of an ongoing SEC investigation. We should be back up and running in a day or two. In the meantime, for those of you who have insurance coverage, please be assured that there will be no lapses in your coverage."

"I wouldn't be so sure about that," Frank interjected. "If there was cheating going on with the investment side, what are the chances the same thing was happening on the insurance side? What if we all think we have coverage but we really don't? And what about you, Haley Jackson? Are you being paid to be here? If so, is your paycheck coming straight out of our money? You're part of all this mess. Dan cheated us, and I'll bet you did, too."

Haley's face flushed with shame. In her heart of hearts, she knew it was true. She hadn't knowingly cheated anyone, but she had sent some of her insurance clients to OFM. If their investment money was gone, she was certainly partially responsible.

"As I said before," she insisted. "There is nothing wrong with your insurance coverages. Ocotillo Fund Management is an entirely separate entity."

There was a jostling in the crowd. A moment later, Julia King, a client who also happened to be Dan Frazier's across-the-street neighbor, appeared at Haley's elbow. "Something's wrong," Julia whispered urgently in Haley's ear. "You need to come with me."

"Excuse me," Haley said back to the crowd. "I need to attend to something."

That wasn't an end to the matter. Frank Merrick was still shouting insults in Haley's direction as she followed Julia through the crowd.

"What is it?" she said. "What's wrong?"

"Something bad is happening at Dan and Millie's house."

"What?"

"I don't know. There are cop cars everywhere and ambulances, too. They've blocked off the street."

"I'll go get my car," Haley said at once.

"No, that won't work," Julia insisted. "You need to get in mine. They're allowing residents through at this point, but no one else. The only way you're going to get there now is to ride with me."

Haley did as she was told. Approaching Elberta Drive, Haley noticed that the media vans she had seen earlier in the parking lot outside the office had been redeployed and were now on either side of the entrance to the cul-de-sac. Stopped at a roadblock, Julia had to pull over to allow a white van with flashing orange lights to drive by. When Haley saw the lettering and logo on the side of the van—YAVAPAI COUNTY MEDICAL EXAMINER—her heart constricted. "If the ME's here," she breathed aloud, "someone must be dead."

The cop manning the roadblock tried to turn them back, but when Julia showed him her driver's license with an Elberta Drive address, the officer waved them through. Haley's whole focus was on the driveway leading up to Dan's house. It was crowded with cop cars surrounding an aging, faded red Bronco with old-design plates—white letters on a red background. She recognized that vehicle at once because it belonged to one of her clients— Bob Larson.

As Julia turned down her own driveway, Haley looked back toward Dan's house in time to see a cop car come barreling down the hill. Hopping out of the car, she hurried back to the top of Julia's driveway, just as the patrol car swung on to Elberta and raced away. Haley arrived in time to see Bob Larson's unmistakable profile in the backseat.

"Hey, lady," another cop farther up the driveway called out to her. "We're dealing with a double homicide here. You need to go back down the hill and mind your own business."

A double homicide? Haley was aghast. That could only mean one thing: Dan and Millie Frazier were both dead. And she had seen Bob Larson being driven away from the scene in the back of a patrol car. Could that nice old man be the one who had done it?

Blinded by tears, Haley stumbled back down the steep driveway, where she fell, weeping, into Julia's comforting arms.

"They're dead," she sobbed brokenly. "Dan and Millie Frazier are both dead."

6

Governor Dunham was good to her word. By the time Ali returned to her office there was a message saying she should give Adele Harris a call. Ali did so immediately.

"Evidently I was mistaken," Adele said in an aggrieved tone Ali's mother would have referred to as "snippy."

"It seems the superintendent of schools has received a call from the governor's office saying that in the case of the Johnson children, records from the family Bible will be considered sufficient," Adele continued. "That does not mean, however, that we will be waiving the requirement for each child's vaccination record to be up to date."

"That's easy, then," Ali said. "I just happen to have those records at my disposal. If you'll give me a fax number, I'll send them right over."

"Usually parents are the ones who supply shot records," Adele objected.

"Not in this case," Ali answered.

Ali downloaded the necessary documents and fed them into the fax machine.

"Yay," she said aloud as the last one was sent.

"Yay what?" Sister Anselm Becker asked, slipping quietly in through the open door to Ali's makeshift office.

Sister Anselm was a tall, spare woman with iron-gray hair and steel-rimmed glasses. She was dressed in her customary fashion—a navy blue pantsuit paired with a crisp white blouse complete with a button-down collar. Only the crucifix she wore on the outside of her blouse hinted that she might belong to a religious order. A Sister of Providence, Sister Anselm was based at St. Bernadette's Convent in Jerome, Arizona, where she acted as an in-house counselor to nuns dealing with personal and/or mental health issues. She also devoted much of her time to traveling the state and functioning as a patient advocate for seriously ill or badly injured indigent folks who needed help navigating complex medical issues.

Ali and Sister Anselm had met years earlier at the bedside of a badly burned woman who subsequently died. Since then, they had become good friends. They had also both been caught up in the drama surrounding the Dunham Massacre. In the aftermath of that, Sister Anselm had devoted almost as much time and effort to helping The Family's dispossessed victims as Ali herself had.

"Governor Dunham just brought another foot-dragging school district official to heel," Ali answered with a smile. "Christine Johnson's kids' lack of birth certificates is suddenly no longer a barrier to their being enrolled in Albuquerque public schools. I just finished sending over their vaccination records, which was the last 't' that needed to be crossed. You'd be surprised how fast things move when one governor picks up the phone and calls another one."

"No I wouldn't," Sister Anselm answered, smiling too. "I wouldn't be surprised at all."

"What brings you to town?" Ali asked.

"I had a meeting at the hospital earlier this morning," Sister Anselm answered. "Before heading back to Jerome, I stopped by to see how our girls are settling into their new digs."

Ali's main focus had been two-pronged—finding employment for the women and getting the children enrolled in schools. Initially, emergency housing issues had been handled with help from a local domestic violence shelter, Irene's Place. Now, though, when it was time to find permanent housing, Sister Anselm had applied her considerable organizational skills to the problem.

Weeks earlier, with the help of her benefactor down in Phoenix, Bishop Francis Gillespie, Sister Anselm had scored an amazing deal on a run-down rental property near the NAU campus. The place had been in such bad shape that she'd been able to negotiate a favorable long-term lease in exchange for doing an extensive cleanup and rehabbing whatever needed fixing. An army of volunteers had tackled the project, and the last city inspector had signed off on the rehab work the week before.

Now Sister Anselm had a relatively low-cost four-bedroom home that The Family's refugees could cycle through as needed.

Because the first tenants would be coming directly from emergency housing with little more than whatever clothing they could carry, much of Sister Anselm's weekend had been devoted to furnishing the place with donated and secondhand goods. The kitchen was stocked with dishes, pots and pans, silverware, and utensils as well as a new microwave while Ali and B. had personally seen to it that both the fridge and pantry were generously supplied with groceries.

A day earlier—move-in day—Sister Anselm and Ali had accompanied the new tenants on their goggle-eyed initial walk-through. For them the mismatched secondhand furnishings seemed like heaven itself, and the colorful Bed Bath & Beyond artwork decorating the walls constituted incredible luxury.

One of the four, Enid Tower, was a sixteen-year-old with a three-month-old baby whose father had died in the massacre. The ground-floor master bedroom, large enough to accommodate a crib, had been designated as Enid's and Baby Ann's. When Ali ushered them into the room, Enid was nothing short of astonished. She ran her fingers along the smooth surface of the crib rail and then touched the arm of the well-used but highly varnished wooden rocking chair with something close to reverence.

"All of this is just for us?" she asked in wonder. "You mean we don't have to share it with anybody else?"

"It's just for you," Sister Anselm had assured her.

When it came time to tour the kitchen and the women discovered that both the fridge and the pantry were brimming with food, another of the women, Agnes Gray, simply burst into tears. After a failed attempt to run away from The Family, Agnes had been designated as a Brought Back girl, The Family's version of an untouchable pariah. As such, she and another would-be runaway, Patricia Glenn, had been forced to live in squalid conditions in an unheated Quonset hut where they were required to look after a herd of pigs and survive on near-starvation rations that consisted of a single meal of table scraps grudgingly passed to them at the kitchen door after everyone else had eaten their evening meal.

"I never knew there could be this much food," Agnes had sobbed. "Food we can eat whenever we want."

Ali and Sister Anselm had shared a knowing nod at that comment. The other two roommates, Donna Marie and Christina Gray, were Agnes's half sisters. Sold into a human trafficking ring and shipped to Africa, they had somehow managed to stick together. Stranded in Nigeria, they had survived for years without passports or papers by working for free in the orphanage that had initially taken them in. Inseparable, they preferred to share a single room rather than having rooms of their own.

With the exception of Enid, who was still nursing the baby, all the other roommates had jobs that made paying the rent feasible. Agnes had been hired as a hotel maid. Patricia worked for a local animal shelter, while Donna and Christina had found employment at nearby daycare centers. The rent was divided four ways, while Enid, the youngest, would earn her share by serving as housemother and handling the cooking and cleaning. It was a communal style of living with which they were all accustomed.

"How are our five ladies doing today?" Ali asked.

"A little of the initial giddiness has worn off," Sister Anselm observed wryly, "but after lives of utter deprivation, they're still on top of the world. I suggested that they might want to throw a housewarming party as a way of thanking the volunteers. I could just as well have been speaking in a foreign tongue. Not one of the five has ever attended a party, much less given one, so they'll need a bit of direction on that score."

"No parties?" Ali echoed. "Not ever?"

"Not a one," Sister Anselm said.

Ali's cell phone rang just then with her mother's name showing in caller ID and with the clock registering 2:05. "Hi, Mom," she said into her Bluetooth. "How's it going?"

"Where are you, Ali?" her mother demanded.

"I'm still in Flag, why?"

"I need you to come home."

Ali had seldom if ever heard outright panic in Edie Larson's voice, but there was panic now. She also sounded close to tears.

"What's wrong?"

"It's your dad," Edie answered.

Ali's heart went to her throat. Her father was in his midseventies. As far as she could tell, he was in good health, but still . . .

"What's happened?"

"That's just it. I don't know what's happened," Edie replied. "Like I told you earlier, he took off right after breakfast, and I haven't seen or heard from him since."

"He's still not back?" Ali did a quick calculation. Her mother's earlier call about Bob going AWOL had come in just shy of noon. It was now two hours later. A dozen scary scenarios began playing out in Ali's head. No doubt her mother was imagining the same things.

"No," Edie answered. "He's still nowhere to be found."

Ali tried to compose herself before she answered, willing her voice to sound calm and reassuring. "He probably just had car trouble and is having to hike out from wherever he happened to get stranded. B. keeps trying to tell him that he needs a newer SUV, one that's more dependable."

"You know your father," Edie grumbled. "He'll never give up that stupid Bronco no matter how old and decrepit it is. He says he has to have a car he can fix himself, not one that operates on some kind of computer chip."

Ali was relieved to hear a little of the customary impatience come back into her mother's voice. Under the circumstances, impatience was preferable to panic.

"You've tried calling his phone?"

"Do you think I'm stupid? Of course I've tried his phone—every fifteen minutes on the dot. My calls go straight to voice mail."

"Did you call B.?"

Years earlier, when Ali had been the victim of a kidnapping, B. had managed to ride to the rescue by tracking her cell phone. Since then, Ali's technophile husband had seen to it that the cell phones and devices of all family members were equipped with a tracking app that allowed for following and locating the device—regardless of whether it was turned on or not. In addition, it contained a mapping service that showed where the device had been.

"I thought about it," Edie admitted, "but I didn't want to bother him with this. If your dad is stuck out in the boonies someplace with a busted transmission or just out of gas, he'll be embarrassed to death if we call in the cavalry."

"B. isn't the cavalry," Ali said. "He's my husband and Dad's son-in-law. That means he's family. He'll be glad to help."

"What should I do in the meantime?"

"Where are you?"

"At home. Betsy's here with me."

Betsy, a woman in her eighties, was Ali's daughter--

in-law's grandmother. She was also eminently sensible.

"I'm glad you're not on your own," Ali said. "The two of you stick together and stay right there, I'm on my way. I'll also call B. and let him know what's happened. I'll stop by as soon as I get to town."

"Thank you, Ali," Edie said in a surprisingly small voice. "I don't know what I'd do without you."

7

Julia King escorted a shaken Haley into the house and settled her on a sofa in the living room. Haley was humiliated to be bawling like a baby in front of someone who was not only a client but also a near stranger. Still, she couldn't help herself.

When Julia returned with a box of tissues, Haley took one and used it to mop her face, removing most of her carefully applied makeup in the process. "Sorry to make such a fool of myself," Haley murmured.

"Don't apologize," Julia said. "You've had a terrible shock. We all have. The idea that something this awful could happen right here on our street is unbelievable. I saw the piece on the news this morning about the whole bankruptcy thing. Is it possible one of Dan's clients went off the deep end?"

Haley nodded but said nothing. With Bob Larson locked in the back of a patrol car, that wasn't just possible—it was likely.

Across the room from the sofa, a floor-to-ceiling window offered an unobscured view of what was happening up the hill and across the street. Haley and Julia watched in stricken silence as not one but two gurneys bearing what looked like body bags were rolled out of the house. One was placed in the van bearing the medical examiner's logo while the other was loaded into a waiting aid car that had evidently been temporarily commandeered by the ME's office.

"So both of them, then," Julia said softly as first the van and then the aid car came down the driveway and turned on to the street. There was no need for flashing lights or sirens. It was already far too late for those.

"Yes," Haley agreed softly. "Both of them."

Officially Haley had worked directly for Dan, but in actual fact, for years she had worked for both of them, functioning as Dan's and Millie's personal assistant and doing whatever needed to be done, including running errands like picking up dry cleaning and prescriptions.

Haley regarded Dan and Millie as an unstoppable team, both personally and professionally. Dan was easygoing and gregarious—a glad-hander—who was the perfect front man for the business. Millie was more reserved and seemed content to operate in the background, but that didn't mean she wasn't involved. If one of the girls in the office was having a birthday, you could count on Millie to show up with a gaily decorated cake. Or if someone was getting married or ended up pregnant, Millie hadn't organized the showers, but she had always shown up with thoughtful and beautifully wrapped gifts in hand.

"They were such nice people," Julia said moments later, wiping away tears. "I wasn't that close to Dan, but Millie was someone who brightened every room she entered. I can't believe someone could possibly hate them enough to murder them."

Haley and Julia sat in stunned silence for a time, grieving together for two people who had suddenly been wiped off the face of the earth. They were startled out of their reverie by a sharp knock on the door. Leaving Haley where she was, Julia hurried to answer.

The man standing outside was a uniformed cop, and Haley was relieved Julia didn't invite him to enter. She didn't want to have to explain to anyone what she was doing there right then, but because she knew someone would be around to question her sooner or later, Haley listened in on the conversation. After introducing himself and noting Julia's name, the officer started by explaining Dan and Millie were dead before he launched off on a series of questions.

"Did you see any unusual activity in the neighborhood this morning?"

"None at all," Julia said. "I was out in the backyard having breakfast and working on my pots. I didn't notice anything unusual. The first I realized something was wrong was when I heard the sirens as cop cars and ambulances poured into the neighborhood."

"No strangers hanging around, then?" the cop asked. "No one who looked or acted out of place?"

"No."

"What about unusual vehicles? Did you see any of those?"

"That red one," Julia answered, pointing up the hill in the general direction of Bob Larson's vehicle.

"The Bronco parked in the driveway?"

Julia nodded. "I've seen it before now and then, but never this early in the morning, and never on a weekday. That one usually showed up on weekends."

"How well did you know the Fraziers?" the cop asked.

Haley shivered, noting the officer's deliberate use of the past tense—"*did* you know"—not the present tense—"*do* you know."

"Fairly well, I suppose," Julia answered. "We've lived across the street from them for close to ten years."

"What about their relationship?" he asked. "Any marital difficulties that you know of?"

"None," Julia answered definitively. "None whatsoever."

The interview ended soon after that. Haley assumed that this was little more than an initial canvass. An interview with a detective would most likely entail a lot more detail.

Julia closed the door and returned to the living room. Julia gave Haley a sad smile. "I think I could use a cup of coffee," she said. "How about you?"

"Please," Haley said.

There was something infinitely comforting about that small gesture of hospitality—a tiny piece of normal in the midst of chaos. Somehow it helped Haley pull herself together.

8

Bob Larson sat in his orange jail jumpsuit and concentrated with every fiber of his being on not looking at the clock on the wall. He could hear it ticking, but he did his best to keep from watching it.

He knew from all the true-crime shows on TV exactly how guilty suspects behaved when they were left cooling their heels in interview rooms for an indeterminate period of time. They fidgeted; they looked at their watches; they studied the ceiling tiles; they cracked their knuckles. Bob tried his best to do none of those. If anyone was watching him through the two-way mirror on one side of the room or on screens fed by the video cameras mounted on the walls and ceiling, they would see a man sitting quietly in a corner and doing absolutely nothing.

He'd gulped down the bottle of water right after Carlotta had brought it to him. Now he was starting to regret that. Once again he was building up to needing to take another piss. If someone didn't come open the door soon and let him use the restroom, he'd end up peeing his pants for the second time that day.

He glanced down at his hands. He'd scrubbed them as well as he could in the bathroom. There was nothing lingering under his nails because Carlotta had taken scrapings of all of those. Nonetheless, there were still traces of blood here and there—Dan's or Millie's or maybe both—lingering in the nail beds on both hands.

Bob remembered that old Shakespearian play they'd studied long ago in Mrs. Fitzsimmons's high school English class. He wasn't sure if it was *Hamlet* or *Macbeth*. It had to be one of those, but he recalled with chilling clarity how the old woman, whoever she was—the murderer—went nuts because she couldn't wash the guilty blood from her hands. Now, even though he'd committed no crime, he understood how she felt, minus the guilt, of course.

He considered holding up his still-bloodied hand, waving at the mounted video camera, and asking for a restroom pass, but he didn't. He held off. He was too damned old to have to ask someone for permission to go relieve himself.

The whole while he'd been sitting there, Bob had done his best to tamp down the anger he now felt toward those two young officers, the first ones who had arrived. He understood that their initial focus had been to take control of the crime scene, but once they had, why hadn't they listened to any of what he had to say? As to why he was sitting here waiting hours later? That probably had something to do with their initial assessment of the situation.

On the other hand, Sedona PD probably didn't have much of a history when it came to double homicides. Bob didn't know the exact statistics on the Sedona Police Department. He estimated it had maybe a total of thirty sworn officers, about that many support staff, and probably no more than a couple detectives. No doubt all hands had to be on deck at the crime scene and were probably still there—securing the scene and gathering evidence. All of that meant that, like it or not, Bob had to wait his turn until someone finally got around to talking to him and letting him go.

What was stressing him right now, more than anything, even the critical need to take a leak, was thinking about Edie. He'd left the house just before nine without leaving her so much as a note saying where he was going or what he was going to do. It was two o'clock now. Bob had been AWOL for five whole hours. He knew that by now she was no doubt worried sick—worried enough that she might even forgive him for messing up on Wanda's birthday cake, but probably not enough to forgive him for losing all their money. Without thinking, he reached for his cell phone to call, but of course it wasn't there.

Somehow, not having the phone available when Bob needed it most was the final straw to an already unbelievably bad day. That was when despair and helplessness finally overwhelmed him. He leaned over the table, buried his face in his hands, and wept while the unblinking eyes of the camera continued to watch his every move.

He had barely managed to pull himself back together when the door to the interview room clicked open. Detective Hank Sotomeyer entered the confined space wearing a blue sport jacket and tan pants along with a white shirt and tie. Bob recognized the detective at once. In his mind's eye, however, the Hank Sotomeyer Bob remembered was an eleven-year-old kid in a freshly pressed brown uniform, standing at attention to receive his Tenderfoot badge.

Hank's mother, Linda, was a war widow whose Marine Corps husband had perished in Desert Storm. After her husband's untimely death, Linda had come home to Sedona with her seven-year-old son to live with her parents. Over the next few years, in both Cub Scouts and Boy Scouts, Bob had been honored to take the boy under his wing and be there as a stand-in when it came time for overnight campouts and other designated father/son occasions. After Linda remarried, Hank had dropped out of scouting. Bob knew Hank had hired on with the local police department, but until that moment, he had no idea that he'd been promoted to detective.

"How's it going, Mr. Larson?" Hank asked.

Obviously their old relationship as Boy Scout and scoutmaster still held sway in Hank's head as well as in Bob's. That was a relief.

"Not so great," Bob admitted.

"For us, too," Hank said. "Sorry to leave you here so long, but . . ."

"I get it—a double homicide, a messy scene, people you know. It's tough on everybody."

"I'll be recording this interview," Hank said.

"Before you do, you might want to take me down the hall to a restroom," Bob warned him. "Otherwise I'm going to piss all over this chair."

9

"What's going on?" Sister Anselm asked as soon as Edie Larson's call ended.

"It's my dad," Ali explained. "He took off earlier today—much earlier—without telling my mom where he was going or when he'd be back. He's still among the missing, and my mother is worried sick—enough so that she just asked me to come home."

"You do that, then," Sister Anselm said. "I'll be glad to sit in for you and 'woman the phones,' as it were. Before you go, tell me if there's anything pressing that needs handling, and I'll do my best."

Ali flashed her friend a quick smile. "I'm guessing that your best will be plenty good enough."

Once in her Cayenne, Ali called B. Most of the time her calls tracked him down in some distant corner of the planet. This week, however, he happened to be at home, or close to it. He was spending most of his days and parts of his nights in Cottonwood at the corporate headquarters for High Noon Enterprises.

At the moment, he and his newest recruit—Lance Tucker, a teenage computer hacking prodigy hired straight out of juvenile detention—were putting together a copyright application for Lance's latest piece of coding genius, something he had developed on the side while he was supposed to be working on his freshman-level computer science classes at UCLA.

"I promise I won't be late for dinner tonight," B. said when he answered his phone. "Leland is making meat loaf, and I'd never be late for that."

"I wasn't calling about dinner," she said, "although I'm glad to know you'll be home at a reasonable hour. I was really calling to ask you to do something for Mom. Dad has gone off everybody's radar since sometime this morning. He's not answering his phone, and she's worried sick. I was hoping you could turn on the device tracking app on Dad's phone and find out where he is. My best guess is that he's had car trouble in that old jalopy of his. He's probably broken down somewhere out in the back of the beyond."

"No problem," B. said. "I'm doing something else right now, but I'll put Stu or Cami on it right away."

Stu was Stuart Ramey, B.'s second in command at High Noon, and Cami was Camille Lee, Stuart's relatively new assistant.

"Where are you?" B. asked.

"On my way home from Flag," Ali said. "See you when I get there."

A few minutes later, Ali was on I-17, headed

south. She considered trying to call her father's number in case the only calls he wasn't answering were ones from his wife, but then she thought better of it. As Ali accelerated to highway speeds, she still considered that what she had said earlier to her mother—that Bob had gone off to look after one of his "guys"—was the most likely scenario. But it wasn't until she saw the highway sign saying SCHNEBLY HILL ROAD EXIT ONE MILE that she decided to do something about it and go see for herself.

Ali had been to the homeless encampment on many occasions over the years, often accompanying her father when Bob went there—especially on Thanksgiving and Christmas, when he handed out food and clothing, served with a side of holiday cheer. Obviously she knew the way.

After turning off the freeway and leaving the exit behind, she left the bright June sunshine behind as well. Within a few hundred yards she was under a gloomy canopy of ponderosa pines and driving a confusing maze of narrow dirt tracks. There were road signs designed to keep her on Schnebly Hill Road itself, but none directing her toward the camp, which she knew was perched on the edge of the Mogollon Rim not far from where Schnebly Hill Road plunged off down the mountainside into the valley below. Fortunately, Ali's father had taught her to read the secret codes left in subtle small mounds of rocks stacked along the shoulder on either side of the road. For those in the know, the rocks were as good as street signs.

Even here on what was relatively flat terrain, the road surface was washed out and rough enough to make Ali grateful for having four-wheel drive. How bad conditions would be farther down Schnebly Hill Road was anybody's guess.

A few stray spots of dappled sunlight alerted Ali to a piece of blue tarp or maybe part of a tent off to her left that indicated she was nearing the camp. At a tiny wide spot in the road, she pulled over and parked. She had exited her vehicle and was turning to click the door lock when she heard the distinctive racking of a shotgun directly behind her. The hair rose on the back of her neck. A spike of adrenaline shot through her body, leaving her fingers tingling as she spun around, hands in the air. She turned just as a huge man materialized from behind the trunk of a nearby tree.

He was large enough that his arms seemed to dwarf the twelve-gauge, making it look like a child's toy in his meaty paws. If ever there was a mountain man, this guy was it. Wild red hair, ten inches long and sprinkled with gray, stood out from his head in a wild, tangled afro. The explosion of hair, combined with an equally unkempt two-tone beard, added to the effect, making him even more giantlike and that much less human. In addition, he was missing several front teeth.

He wore a faded plaid flannel shirt, ragged around the cuffs, and a pair of threadbare jeans. Layers of duct tape were wrapped around the soles of his boots, literally holding body and sole together. The fact that both boots lacked shoelaces of any kind meant that they flopped loosely on his immense feet with every step. Even from ten feet away, Ali could smell the rank stink of sweat, grime, smoke, and rough living.

"If I was you, missy," he growled, waving the shotgun in her direction, "I'd get my ass back in that fancy-shmancy vehicle you're driving and get the hell out of here."

Ali stood for a long moment, peering down the barrel of what she had no doubt was a fully loaded weapon. She forced herself to take a deep breath before attempting to speak. "I'm here looking for my father," she said, hoping her voice sounded steadier than she felt.

"If your daddy is up here with us," the mountain man told her, "then there's a pretty good chance he ain't interested in being found. Now get going."

"You don't understand," Ali said. "My father doesn't live here. His name is Larson—Robert Larson, but he goes by Bob. He comes here to help out sometimes. He's been gone from home for several hours. Since we can't reach him, my mom and I were wondering if maybe he came up here."

The effect of her words was instantaneous. The barrel of the shotgun lowered. "Sorry, missy," the man said at once. "My sincerest apologies. I had no idea you were Corpsman Bob's daughter. I been out here keeping watch on the road for three hours now, and I ain't never seen him. He might of come up the back way, though—up Schnebly Hill. He does that sometimes, you know."

The adrenaline that had been holding Ali
upright receded as quickly as it had come. For a
moment she felt a little weak in the knees. Not
trusting her ability to stand on her own, she leaned
against the car door for support.

"Yes," Ali agreed, when she found her voice.
"He does like to come up the back way."

"Want me to check for you?"

Rather than reaching for a cell phone that
probably wouldn't have worked anyway, the man
pulled a walkie-talkie out of his shirt pocket.
"Hey, Tom-Boy," he said. "It's Luke. Anybody seen
Corpsman Bob around here today?"

"Nope, neither hide nor hair," came the scratchy
reply. "He generally checks in with me first thing."

Ali thought about the eleven cliff-hugging
miles of Schnebly Hill Road between the homeless camp and Sedona. Her adjustable-ride-height,
four-wheel-drive Cayenne was nimble and respon-
sive, but even in it, the switchback riddled trip
down from the Rim would be a challenge. Depending on road conditions, the descent might take as
long as two and a half to three hours. A glance at
her watch told her it was already going on three.
If she drove that way and left immediately, she'd
be lucky to make it back to civilization by evening
when herds of elk would be on the move. And if
she happened to find her father's crashed Bronco
somewhere along the way, what would she be able
to do about it? Most of the trip she'd be out of cell
phone range. No, given the circumstances, the
freeway was probably her best bet.

"You think Corpsman Bob's lying out there dead or hurt bad somewhere down on Schnebly Hill?" Luke asked.

Ali bit her lip before she answered. "That's what we're afraid of. I could try driving that way, but I'm worried about it taking too long."

"Likely it would," Luke said, "so don't you be thinking about doing such any thing. One guy here, Owen, went through a hell of a divorce. All he got out of the deal was his Jeep, which he owns free and clear. He don't have no insurance on it and no license, neither, so he don't take it out on the highway. But if Corpsman Bob's life is on the line, he'll head down Schnebly Hill Road in a heartbeat."

Ali handed over one of her business cards. "If Owen finds anything and wants to be in touch, here are my phone numbers."

Luke took the tiny card in his huge, grimy paws and held it up to squint at it for a moment before stuffing it into his shirt pocket right along with the walkie-talkie.

"Will do," he said.

"Thank you, Luke," Ali murmured as she opened the door of the Cayenne. "Thank you very much."

10

The gravel pit was deserted when Alberto and Jeffrey arrived at five past three. "He stiffed us," Alberto fumed. "The asshole stiffed us. He isn't even gonna show. And why here? This place gives me the creeps."

It didn't help that on the way down from Sedona there had been a Silver Alert posted for someone driving a white Ford F-150, which happened to be the same kind of vehicle they were driving. The plate license didn't match theirs, of course, and it was unlikely that someone who was the subject of a Silver Alert would be driving around in a company truck loaded with landscaping equipment. Still, anything that sent additional scrutiny in their direction was worrisome.

"Come on," Jeffrey told him, getting out of the truck. "Have a cigarette. Don't get yourself all worked up. He'll be here. Maybe he's just running late. Maybe there was traffic on I-17 or an accident."

Standing outside in the triple-digit temperatures in the gray expanse of gravel pit wasn't fun, but standing in the heat was better than working in it, Alberto told himself. With his skills as a landscaper, he knew he could get a job almost anywhere, no questions asked and no papers needed, either. This time, though, wherever he ended up, he was determined it would be someplace a hell of a lot cooler than Phoenix.

They were a long way off the freeway, but the low rumble of traveling semis carried across the raw desert. Gradually, the steady noise seemed to settle Alberto's frayed nerves. Once they had the money in hand, that's what they'd be doing—hitting the road. As for the truck? It was Alejandro's, of course, but maybe one day Alejandro would forgive him. After all, isn't that what big brothers always did? They forgave you no matter what.

Ten minutes later, a dusty tan minivan nosed its way into the gravel pit. "See there?" Jeffrey said triumphantly. "I told you he'd be here, and now he is."

"But is he gonna fall for it?" Alberto whined, as if one solved problem had instantly been replaced by another. "What if he has a computer along, plugs in the drive, and figures out we've brought him a blank?"

"Will you please just shut the hell up?" Jeffrey demanded. "If you're so worried about all this, maybe you'd better let me handle it."

They waited, standing side by side, until the van stopped with the sliding passenger door directly in front of them. It was a nondescript older-model Dodge Caravan that someone had taken the time and trouble to turn into a wheelchair-accessible vehicle. Slowly the rear door rolled open. Next a silver-haired man, seated in a wheelchair and wearing cataract-style sunglasses, appeared in the doorway. When he pressed a button, a heavy-duty metal plate emerged from the floor of the vehicle and then gradually lowered both man and chair to ground level.

"Are they dead?" he asked.

That had been part of the deal. Even if Dan Frazier had told them exactly where the SD card was and handed it over, the contract had stipulated that neither Dan nor his wife would live to tell the tale.

Jeffrey stepped forward, assuming the role of spokesman. "They're gone," he said. "We saw to it."

"No witnesses?"

"None. We did it right."

"Weapons?"

"Knives," Jeffrey said. "We got rid of them along with the gloves and the gowns."

"Great. Where's the drive?"

"Got it right here, sir," Jeffrey said deferentially as he pulled the tiny device out of his shirt pocket. He was relieved to see that the man was empty-handed. There was no laptop visible. He wouldn't be able to check on the drive until after Alberto and Jeffrey were well on their way.

Jeffrey studied the other man's face as he stepped forward and dropped the drive into the man's waiting palm. There was no hint that the guy had any concern about their playing him or deceiving him. Alberto was doing the same thing—watching the man's face. Neither of them noticed as the figure of a shooter materialized around the edge of the minivan's passenger door. Neither of them heard the bark of a firearm as two carefully aimed shots echoed off the walls of the gravel pit.

Alberto and Jeffrey didn't hear the gunshots for one very good reason—they were both already dead.

11

Utterly astonished, Jason McKinzie could only sit and stare at the bloodied fallen bodies. Jessie had shot them both front and center before either man had a chance to react. Yes, they'd talked about the fact the guys she'd hired for the job were most likely expendable, but Jason sure as hell hadn't expected her to gun them down in cold blood right there in front of him. That was the whole appeal of white-collar crime. No blood.

Jason had read about the pink spray in novels and seen it occasionally in particularly violent movies, but never in real life. As for Jessie? He'd been warned before he'd hired her that underneath that helpless-blond-bimbo façade lurked a vicious attack dog, but this was more than Jason had bargained for—way more.

He watched as she walked over to one of the bodies and placed the weapon she'd used—a handgun of some kind—in the hand of one of the dead men—the Hispanic one—before pulling his fist closed around the handle. After peering briefly into the parked pickup truck, she turned and walked back toward Jason, nonchalantly peeling off a pair of latex gloves as she did so.

"I told them to make it look like a burglary," she said. "Looks like they got that right. There's quite a haul in the back of that crew cab."

Overcoming his initial shock, Jason finally found his voice. "Did you have to do that right here and right now?" he demanded.

Jessica glanced around at the empty gravel pit and then shrugged. "Seems like as good a place as any," she observed. "Besides, letting them go didn't seem like an option. Neither did paying them. Isn't that what you meant by the word 'expendable'?"

"Yes, but . . ."

"But nothing," she said. "Now come on. We need to get the hell out of here."

The wheelchair had been intended as nothing more than a disguise, but right that moment, Jason doubted his ability to stand on his own. He sat there, unable to tear his eyes away from the two fallen victims.

"Shouldn't we bury them or something?" he asked. "And when they're found out here in the open like this, won't the trail lead right back to us?"

"No," Jessica said. "It won't. That trail will lead right back to Dan Frazier and nobody else. I used Dan's .38, by the way. It'll have his DNA and fingerprints on it, and now it has Alberto's. There's nothing out there in the electronic world that links you and me to them—no e-mails, no texts, no cell phone calls or GPS trails, either. As far as the authorities are concerned, your phone went dark last weekend somewhere in Mexico City. Mine's at home in Phoenix. What that means in law enforcement terms is that we're not here."

"Okay, then," Jason said, feeling somewhat reassured.

He got out of the chair and reentered the van, leaving Jessie to load both the chair and lift back into the van. "But are you sure they did it?" he asked, once Jessie was back behind the wheel. "They said Dan and Millie are dead, but are you sure it's true?"

"I'm sure," Jessie replied. "I've been monitoring my scanner, and that's what they're saying. There's all kinds of chatter about two unidentified homicide victims found in Sedona—one male and one female. There's also word that a suspect has been taken into custody, which means the cops are looking at someone else entirely. Couldn't be better."

Jessie started the van and drove out of the gravel pit the same way they had entered, leaving behind the abandoned pickup as well as two newly dead bodies.

"Aren't you worried about leaving tracks?" Jason asked.

"Not in the least," Jessie answered with a confident smile. "That's why I set the meet for here. A gravel road leading to a gravel pit means we're leaving behind no usable tracks."

Jason couldn't help being taken aback by her calm demeanor. She had just gunned down two people with what seemed like utter indifference, and now she was as calm as if it were a completely ordinary set of circumstances. Perhaps for her it was.

Jason reached for the leather case that held his laptop. Pulling it out, he booted it up and then inserted the card. A moment later he exploded in anger. "Damn it all! The drive is empty!"

"What do you mean?"

"Just what I said. There's nothing on it. It's completely blank. Either Dan gave them a dud, or those incredible assholes were trying to rip us off!"

Jason heard the rising panic in his voice and wished it weren't there, but with the drive still out there loose in the world, he understood that everything he'd worked for was at risk.

His long-unsubstantiated suspicions about Dan Frazier had finally come to a head on Friday morning. He'd watched the whole thing play out on the security footage. Late Thursday night, 10:39 p.m. according to the time stamp, one of the members of the cleaning crew—someone with access to Jason's private office—had allowed Dan inside. He had walked over to the desk as though he owned the place. He'd had zero trouble unlocking the desk and then had gone straight to the drawer containing the laptop. Within seconds, Dan had booted up the computer, inserted the drive, and started the download. He'd been in and out in a matter of minutes.

Jason often left his computer in the office, in the mistaken belief that it would be better off in his locked office than entrusted to the parking valets at his many evening social engagements.

Obviously he'd been mistaken about that, but having seen Dan in action, Jason drew the only sensible conclusion. Dan Frazier had most likely gone rogue and was attempting to gather incriminating information against him, probably in advance of going to the feds.

If Jason McKinzie had been any less OCD, he might never have been any the wiser. In this case, however, his obsessive-compulsive disorder operated in his favor. Despite the fact that he had never used a fountain pen in his life, Jason nonetheless kept a plush leather-bound desk-blotter on his desk. The last thing he did each night, after clearing and locking the desk, was to align the blotter perfectly with the edge of the desk—a desk all cleaning ladies were forbidden to disturb in any way. Friday morning, when Jason had noticed the blotter was slightly out of alignment, he'd gone directly to the security footage.

For months Jason had worried that Dan Frazier had become his weakest link. That was the whole reason he'd hired Jessica Denton in the first place—to keep an eye on Dan. Once Jason knew it for sure, he and Jessie had set about pulling the various triggers designed to make both the business and Jason disappear in a puff of smoke. Unfortunately, many of the pieces of Jason's well-thought-out exit plan were now loaded onto that missing microSD card, the one Alberto and Jeffrey had failed to retrieve. Some of the files Dan had stolen were merely password protected. The most sensitive ones were encrypted, of course, but they were still out there, and Jason was frantic to get them back. Naturally he had turned to Jessie, his right-hand man, as it were, for help.

Jason had hired her initially as a monitor for Dan. In the months since, however, the woman had wormed her way into both Jason's heart and his bed, making herself damned near indispensable in the process.

She had used some of her underground connections to help create the complex network of safe houses they'd be able to use when it was time for them to go bye-bye. When Jason had explained the need of trashing OFM's financial records in advance of a possible raid from the feds, Jessica had used her dark web contacts to find an IT guy capable of doing the job. She'd also located the Jason McKinzie look-alike who had flown out of Sky Harbor to Mexico City, on Friday night, using Jason's own valid passport and taking his cell phone along for good measure.

Those were all strategic measures Jason appreciated having in place. On Friday morning when he'd been in a blind panic, Jessica had been dead calm. "Don't worry," she had said. "I'll handle it, but I'll need to use some of the cash you gave me to get everything done."

"Get what done?"

"It's clear that Dan's about to turn state's evidence. That means he has to go and so does Millie. It's as simple as that."

Jason was stunned. "You mean go as in permanently?"

"Exactly," she said. "And I already have someone in mind for the job."

"But can this person be trusted?" Jason asked.

"Enough to get the job done," Jessie had answered.

The guy who had first recommended Jessica to Jason had hinted that she wasn't afraid to handle what he called the "rough stuff," on occasion, but today in the gravel pit was the first time Jason had glimpsed what must be the real Jessica Denton. She had trusted her hired killers enough for them to do the job, but not enough to let them walk away afterward.

"So where's the real drive?" Jason asked.

"I'm betting Dan hid it somewhere and gave Alberto and Jeffrey the blank. They would have had no way of knowing if it was real, and I don't think either one of them would have been smart enough to make the switch themselves."

"Damn Dan Frazier anyway."

"I'll find it," Jessica assured him. "By now both of Dan's residences are most likely locked down as crime scenes, but I happen to have keys, remember? I also have the combinations to their in-house safes. I'll check out both places tonight and have a look-see."

"Is that a good idea?" Jason asked. "What if you get caught?"

"I won't," Jessica replied. "I'll be in and out without anyone being the wiser. If it turns out the drive can't be found either place, there's always another possibility."

"What's that?"

"Dan might have handed it off to his office manager up in Sedona."

"I didn't even remember there was an office manager."

"Believe me, she exists," Jessie said. "Her name's Haley Jackson. He always raved about how dependable she was and how he could always count on her in a pinch. Just to be sure, while I'm up in Sedona, I'll see to it that she and I have a chat."

It took the better part of forty-five minutes to get from the gravel pit, over Loop 303, and then back to the 60, giving Jason plenty of time for reflection.

"What if they were going to do more than just rip us off?" he asked.

"There you go, then," Jessie responded. "Better them than us."

That was true. For right now, Jason was incredibly grateful to have Jessica Denton in his life. He suspected that from here on out, he'd be dealing with situations where having an ever-present bodyguard—one with her particular skill set—would be a lifesaving necessity rather than an option.

The first scheduled way station for Jason's disappearing act was an anonymous rental property on a golf course in Peoria. The neighborhood was upscale enough to be comfortable, but it wasn't the kind of area where people were likely to stand around chatting back and forth over backyard fences.

Although it wasn't officially a 55+ kind of development, there were enough retirees hanging around the area that an aging, nondescript minivan bearing a handicapped sticker wasn't at all out of place. People glancing inside would have noticed that the silver-haired gentleman riding in the passenger seat wore a pair of oversized cataract sunglasses, making him somewhere close to older than dirt. That also meant that the young woman at the wheel of the van was most likely a paid caregiver of some kind. All those things taken together rendered Jason and Jessica not only completely uninteresting but also invisible.

As for the cookie-cutter house with the red tile roof where they were staying? It was the kind of place where the old Jason McKinzie wouldn't have been caught dead, and that was the whole point. No one would think of looking for someone like him in a run-of-the-mill housing development. At least no one had so far. The prospect of sitting around watching TV for what seemed like days on end may have been boring as all hell, but being bored was preferable to being caught.

Besides, being stuck here wasn't exactly a life sentence. This was only the first of his hidey-holes. The next one was scheduled to be at a secluded oceanfront condo in Belize.

Once they reached the house and in order to maintain the fiction, Jason used the wheelchair to lift himself out of the van and onto the floor of the garage. "You're sure there's not enough time for a roll in the hay?" he asked plaintively as Jessie walked past him toward the relatively new, bright yellow VW Beetle parked in the second stall of the two-car garage.

"Not if you want to see that drive anytime soon."

"All right, then," he agreed reluctantly. "But when will you be back?"

"When I have that drive in hand," she answered, "and not a moment before."

"And I'm supposed to sit here and wait until then without so much as a single phone call?"

"That's right," she told him. "No incoming calls and no outgoing ones, either. Maintaining radio silence makes us that much harder to track. But knock yourself out. Watch all the on-demand movies you want. By the time the bill comes due, we'll be long gone."

He sat in the garage and watched her reverse down the driveway, then, as the garage door closed, he rolled himself into the house.

Jason McKinzie had known plenty of women in his life. As one of the Phoenix area's most eligible bachelors, he'd been a staple on the charity ball circuit, spending years squiring dim but beautiful women to one sumptuous event after another. He'd also been active on any number of dating Web sites.

As far as Jason was concerned, the women he'd found along the way had proven to be arm candy—great as subject matter for the steady stream of photo ops that kept his name and face front and center. A few of the women were somewhat amusing for a time, although eventually he had tired of them all.

The thing was, none of them could measure up

to Jessica Denton. Yes, he'd been warned she was dangerous. After today he knew firsthand that was inarguably true, but being dangerous was also a big part of Jessica's appeal—better dangerous and smart than safe and dimwitted.

It tickled Jason's fancy to think about entering some fabled room—like the Monte Carlo Casino for instance—with Jessica on his arm. Everyone else would see just what they were supposed to see—a somewhat older gentleman accompanied by a beautiful and much younger woman. What they wouldn't grasp was that Jessie, in addition to being young and beautiful, was also a lethal weapon.

12

Back in the interview room after visiting the rest-room, Hank placed another unopened bottle of water on the table in front of Bob. "As I said earlier, I'll be recording this interview, Mr. Larson," the detective said.

Bob nodded. For a fleeting moment it occurred to him that maybe this was the moment when he should ask for an attorney, but he didn't. The guys who were guilty were always the ones who lawyered up. Besides, Hank was from his old Cub Scout pack and his Boy Scout troop, for Pete's sake. How bad could it be?

Once the recording equipment was activated and Hank had supplied both his name and Bob's, the detective kicked off the interview.

"Why don't we start by your telling me exactly what happened this morning and how you happened to be the first one on the scene?"

"Edie and I . . . ," Bob began. "My wife and I were clients of Dan's and have been for years. When he suggested that we move our IRAs to a different company, over to Ocotillo Fund Management, that's what we did. It's an outfit that has an office—had an office, that is—down in Phoenix. They billed themselves as a wealth management company.

"This morning, while I was watching the news, I saw that the company had suddenly gone belly-up—that the SEC had come in and shut the place down. I could barely believe my ears. Not only were Edie's and my IRAs there, so were the proceeds that came from the sale of the Sugarloaf. After all, we'd been with the company for years, and we were getting good returns—on paper, anyway—so when we sold the restaurant, we plowed most of the money from that over into OFM as well."

"You say you were getting good returns," Hank said, "so what kind of money are we talking about?"

"Twelve percent, maybe," Bob answered.

"No, I meant how much did you put in?"

Bob sighed before he answered. While he'd been sitting there all that time, he'd been mentally adding it up. "One point two million dollars," he said. "Give or take."

Hank whistled. "That's a lot of money."

"Yes," Bob agreed ruefully. "Yes, it is."

"Okay, so you saw this disturbing piece on the news," Hank continued. "Then what happened?"

"I wanted to talk to Dan about it—to hear straight from the horse's mouth about what was really going on. I figured he owed me that much, anyway. I tried calling all his numbers, including the office number down in Phoenix, but that one had already been disconnected, and he didn't answer any of the others. That's when I decided to go to his house instead, not the one down in Paradise Valley, but the one up here."

"You just stopped by, even though there was no answer at his residence?"

"It's easy to not answer a phone," Bob said, "especially if it's someone I don't want to talk to. When someone shows up on your doorstep, that's a lot harder to ignore."

"What was the purpose of your visit?" Hank asked.

"Like I said, I wanted to find out what was really going on," Bob answered. "I wanted to ask Dan Frazier face-to-face and eyeball to eyeball exactly what had happened to our money and find out where the hell it went, even though I already knew it was no use— that the money was probably long gone. I still wanted to hear what he had to say about it in his own words."

"You drove there right after the news broadcast?"

Bob nodded.

"What time was that?"

"I was watching a station with local morning news—probably the local Fox affiliate. I think that newscast ends somewhere around nine. I left a little while before it was over, so it must have been around nine or so."

"You drove straight there—to the Fraziers' place?"

"Yes."

"It takes what, twenty minutes or so to get from your residence to theirs?"

"About that, I suppose," Bob agreed.

"You say you left your house about nine, but the call didn't come in until 9:52, almost an hour later. Did you stop off somewhere along the way?"

"No stops," Bob said. "I drove straight there."

"What took you so long, then?" Hank asked. "Was there highway construction along the way or traffic congestion, maybe?"

"No, nothing like that. When I got there—to his street, I mean—I stopped a couple of houses away for a while to think about what I was going to say, trying to figure out if I was going to talk to the guy or just walk up and bust him in the chops."

"So you were angry?"

"Damn straight—was angry and still am. Wouldn't you be?"

"Angry enough to kill him?"

Bob looked at Hank and shook his head sadly. "Don't you know me better than that?"

The detective ducked his head and cleared his throat before he asked the next question. "When you arrived at the house, did you see any other vehicles nearby?"

Bob thought about that for a moment before he answered. "I believe there was a landscape truck parked across the street at the next house up from Dan's—a crew cab white Ford F-150. A nice enough truck, recent but not brand-new and not a Platinum model, either. I'm not sure how landscape guys can afford new trucks like that, but they do."

"You're sure it was a landscape truck?"

"Of course. It was loaded with all kinds of gear—

a mower, trash cans, rakes, shovels, the whole nine yards."

"Did you see anyone outside working?"

"Nope," Bob answered. "They could have been out back."

"Did you see anyone in the yard at the Fraziers' house?"

"No. The only thing that struck me as odd was the fact that when I finally drove up to the house, the gate at the bottom of the driveway was wide open. Maybe a landscaping crew or delivery guy left it open, but Dan would have raised hell about that. Once Dan scored that Mustang of his, he kept the driveway locked up tight. He and Millie both had remotes, of course, but visitors had to be buzzed in or use the code on the keypad. As I drove through it, I remember wondering why it was open."

"So you're familiar with that gate? You've seen it before and know how it operates?"

"Yes, I'm familiar with the gate," Bob said. "I was Dan's client, but we were also friends. I've been to his house on numerous occasions."

"Recently?"

"The last time I was there was a couple of months ago, just after he brought the Mustang back from Scottsdale."

"Did you go inside the house that day?"

"Nope, we stayed in the garage so he could show me his baby."

"But you've been in the Frazier house before."

"Yes, definitely."

"Back to this morning, then. What happened next?"

"Like I said, I sat there for a while trying to figure out what I was going to say to the low-down cheat. Then, just as I parked at the top of the driveway, one of the garage doors rolled open. Both cars were there—Dan's Mustang and Millie's Volvo—and I expected one or the other of them to shift into reverse, back out of the garage, and maybe slam into me, but nothing happened.

"At first, I didn't see anyone in either of the cars. Finally, I got out of my Bronco. I heard someone call for help, so I walked into the garage. That's when I realized that the Mustang was running—idling—but I still couldn't see anyone sitting inside, at least not at first. It wasn't until I was right next to the open driver's window that I spotted Dan. He was seated behind the steering wheel, but he had slumped over at an angle onto the passenger seat so his head wasn't visible from the rear of the car. His face was pretty beat up. Then I saw the blood on his shirt. At first I thought he'd been shot, but he told me it was a knife—that he'd been stabbed. And he said there'd been more than one assailant. Two at least. He said they'd used knives. Plural."

For a moment Bob stopped speaking, thinking about the bloom of blood spreading across Dan's shirt and pants and leaking out between the dying man's fingers as he tried to hold back the tide. Sitting in the interview room Bob could almost see the blood again and smell it, too.

"Go on," Detective Sotomeyer urged, drawing Bob out of his momentary reverie.

"Okay," Bob said. "Let's see. The convertible top was open and the driver's window was down. At that point, although Dan was badly injured, at least he was still alive. I called 911 right away, then I reached inside the Mustang, thinking that if I helped him apply pressure to the wound, Dan might last long enough for the ambulance to arrive. That's when he asked me to go check on Millie."

"He was conscious when you got there? He spoke to you?"

Bob nodded.

"Did he tell you anything about who had done it—who was responsible?"

Bob shook his head. "Just that there were more than one of them. He begged me to go check on Millie, so that's what I did."

"While the perpetrators were still inside the house?" Hank asked.

"I never gave that a moment's thought," Bob answered. "I left Dan right where he was. I went in through the garage door that leads through the laundry room into the kitchen, and that's where I found Millie—on the floor in the middle of the kitchen, lying facedown in a pool of blood."

Once again, Bob paused to collect himself before continuing.

"Just looking at the blood, I figured Millie was already a goner. I was about to leave her where she was and go back to the garage to help Dan, when she moved a little—this tiny shudder you could barely see. I was amazed. With all that blood it didn't seem possible that she was still alive. I hurried over to see if I could do anything to help. In the process I slipped in the blood and fell. I landed right on top of the poor woman." He paused again and put his hand over his eyes as if to shut out the memory.

"You're saying that's how Mille's blood got on your clothing—when you fell on her?"

"Then, and later, too, when I was trying to get up. I slipped and fell again. The blood was so damned slick it was like skating on ice."

"But she was still alive when you fell on her?"

Bob nodded. "Barely," he said.

"Did she say anything to you about who her assailant was?"

"I asked, but she didn't tell me. All she said was that Dan was a good man and that I should tell him she loved him. Those were her last words. 'Tell him I love him.' A moment later she was gone."

"What happened then?"

"Since I couldn't do anything more for her, I went to help Dan, but there was blood all over the tile in the kitchen. That's when I fell the second time. I ended up having to grab hold of the counter just to pull myself up. By the time I got back to the garage, Dan was dead, too. Somehow or other through all that, I had stayed connected to the 911 operator. I told her then that I was sure they were both dead. That's about the time the first patrol car arrived on the scene."

"Dan didn't give you any hints about who was responsible, either?"

"I already told you, all he said was for me to check on Millie."

"Is there a chance that this is a case of murder/ suicide?"

Bob thought about that for a moment before he answered. "No," he said. "I don't think so. Dan said he was trying to get help—that's why he was in the car. The problem is the Mustang's a stick shift. He somehow got the thing started, but I think he was hurt too badly to be able to operate the pedals and the gearshift."

"But why go for help?" Hank asked. "Why not pick up the phone and dial 911? As badly injured as he was, wouldn't that have been a lot easier than attempting to operate a standard transmission?"

"I have no idea why he didn't call," Bob said. "Maybe he was so badly hurt that he couldn't think straight."

"What happened next?"

"Like I said, I was still on the line with the 911 operator when the first patrol car showed up. Two cops got out. I was covered in blood, so naturally they assumed I was responsible. I can hardly blame them for that. They took everything—my phone, my wallet, and my knife. Then they hand-cuffed me and locked me in the back of their patrol car. That's where I was when the fire truck and aid cars arrived. I sat there burning up for damned near forever before they finally brought me here.

They took photos and swabbed my hands, then they had me strip off my bloody clothes. That's how come I'm dressed like this," he added, gesturing toward the jumpsuit. "They said they needed my clothes as evidence, so I had to change. Then they brought me to the interview room and left me here."

For what felt like hours on end, Bob thought, but he didn't say that aloud.

"You had a weapon with you when you came to the house?"

"A weapon?" Bob asked. "I had my pocket knife with me—my Swiss army knife is all, and it's more of a tool than a knife. You can check it until hell freezes over. There's nobody's blood on it, except maybe a little of mine on occasion."

"You already told me you hold Dan responsible for losing a big chunk of your retirement money," Hank ventured. "Do you know of anyone else who might have a grudge against him or Millie and want to hurt them?"

"Edie and I sure as hell aren't the only ones who lost money on this deal," Bob said, "not by a long shot. I'm guessing there are a whole bunch of people from around here who are in the same boat. I wouldn't be surprised if everybody else is just as pissed as I am."

"I doubt many people lost more than a million bucks, though," Hank interjected. "That many dollars sound like a lot of reasons to be pissed off. I've seen cases where murders happened over far less money than that. The problem is, of all Dan's customers, you're the only one who showed up at the crime scene with blood all over your clothing."

"How many times do I have to tell you?" Bob demanded. "I did not kill Dan Frazier. I didn't kill Millie, either. I tried to help them. I went to their place with one purpose and one purpose only—to ask Dan face-to-face what the hell was going on and what had they done with my money. The only reason I went inside the house was to help Millie, and that was because Dan specifically asked me to check on her. Check on the 911 tape. You might even hear her voice."

"Okay, then," Hank said, closing his notebook and ending the interview. "I guess that's all for right now."

"Does that mean I can go home?"

Hank shook his head. "Soon," he said, "but I believe someone else wants to talk to you first."

"If I could just call my wife . . ."

"Sorry, Mr. Larson," Hank said. "That's just not possible at the moment."

Hank stood up, collected his note pad, and left the interview room. The lock clicked home as he shut the door, leaving Bob Larson trapped inside. Once again he was alone in the room—alone, frustrated, and needing to pee. Again. Damn that Flomax anyway!

13

While Julia prepared the coffee, Haley pulled out her phone and scrolled through her recent calls. She wanted to be the one who told her employees what was going on. Even though Haley didn't have all the details about what had happened across the street, she wanted to be the one to deliver the bad news to her girls, even though, in a politically correct world, she wasn't supposed to call them "girls."

Since Carmen Rios's number was the last one on the list, she was the first one Haley called. "I'm transcribing messages as fast as I can," Carmen told her. "Over a hundred so far, and the mailbox fills up again within a matter of minutes. But is it true?"

"Is what true?"

"That Mr. and Mrs. Frazier are dead?"

Haley sighed. That meant she was already too late in delivering the news. This was a small town after all. Rumors were obviously flying thick and fast.

"What are you hearing?" she asked.

"That they're dead," Carmen answered. "I also heard that someone has been taken into custody. What's going to happen now, Ms. Jackson? Will we still be in business when all this is over?"

"I hope so," Haley said. "With OFM out of business the investment side is gone, but we'll still have the insurance lines."

"But what if the clients go away?" Carmen objected. "I can tell from the messages that people are upset. You should hear what they're saying on the phone. Some of the messages are really ugly. They're saying Dan was a crook, and we're all crooks, too."

"Try not to take the messages personally," Haley advised. "When things settle down, we'll do what we can to mend fences."

As Haley finished the call with Carmen, Julia returned with a mug of coffee. "Will you be taking over the business?" she asked.

Haley nodded. "I hope so," she said. "That was the intention, at least, but with everything that's happened . . ."

"I'll leave you alone," Julia said. "You sit right here, make yourself at home, and do whatever calling you need to do."

Taking Julia at her word, Haley spent the next forty-five minutes making one difficult phone call after another, letting her other employees in on what had happened. Walking each of the stunned women through their shock and disbelief was no easy task. Only when she was finished with the last of the girls did Haley dial her grandmother's number, but it turned out Gram was already totally up to speed.

"I heard," Carol Hotchkiss said. "I called down to the pharmacy to check on a prescription, and Sylvia told me about it. I didn't want to bother you because I was sure you were busy, but how are you holding up? Are you okay?"

The question made Haley falter slightly. "I think so," she said. "I'm coping. It's a lot to take in. I've just been calling the girls from the office to give them the news."

"That's got to be tough," Gram said, not bothering to hide the concern in her voice. "Come home when you can. I've thawed out that mac and cheese casserole you made last week. Once you're here, we'll have a nice supper, just the two of us."

Another piece of normalcy. "Thank you, Gram," Haley said. "That sounds perfect."

Finished with her calls, Haley stood up and looked across the street as a final patrol car eased out of Dan and Millie's driveway. Putting the vehicle in park, the officer exited his vehicle and manually pulled the gate shut. Then, after stringing a strip of crime scene tape from one side of the gate to the other, he returned to the patrol car and drove away.

The utter finality symbolized by that tape hit Haley hard. Managing to stave off a new set of tears, she went looking for Julia, who was in the kitchen starting to make dinner. "The last of the cops just left," Haley said, "and I should probably be going, too. If you're too busy to take me, I can probably get someone to come pick me up."

"You're sure you don't want dinner?"

"No, thanks. It's sweet of you to offer, but I live with my grandmother. I need to get home to make dinner for her."

"All right, then," Julia said. "And of course I'll take you. After all, I brought you here. I wouldn't think of your having to ask someone else for a ride back."

The drive from downtown Sedona to the office in the Village of Oak Creek was mostly done in silence. Haley was too strung out to make idle chitchat, and Julia seemed to understand and respect that.

As they neared the office, Haley feared the parking lot would still be as jammed with cars and people as it had been when she'd arrived there hours earlier. Instead, the lot was virtually deserted. Her own car, a humble years-old Honda, looking lost and forlorn, was parked three rows back from the front entrance in an otherwise empty row. The SEC truck was gone. The door that had been propped open for loading earlier that morning was now shut and locked. What took Haley's breath away was the mass of flowers that completely covered the sidewalk and banked up against the front door.

One glance at that display of flowers was enough to make Haley cry again. She couldn't help it. Carmen had told her about all the angry, disgruntled clients out there, but it turns out there were plenty of other people in town who were willing to give Dan and Millie Frazier the benefit of the doubt. That profusion of flowers was one way of showing they cared.

"Are you sure you'll be all right now?" Julia asked, as Haley exited the car.

"Yes," Haley said. "I will be. Thank you for everything—for coming to get me so I'd know what was up, and thank you for giving me a private place to stay long enough to pull myself together."

Julia smiled. "Think nothing of it," she said. "That's what friends are for."

Haley stood transfixed, watching as Julia King's silver Lexus pulled out of the parking lot and drove away. Shaking her head, Haley couldn't help but marvel. On this terribly appalling day, something entirely unexpected had happened. Life had handed her a precious gift—a brand-new friend.

14

When the interview door opened the next time, the person who entered was Sedona PD's chief detective, a guy named Eric Drinkwater, and not necessarily one of Bob Larson's favorite people. Drinkwater had hired on as a city cop after serving as an MP in Desert Storm and after working for the sheriff's department in either Maricopa or Pima County—Bob wasn't sure which.

When Eric first came to town and before he married, he'd been a regular at the Sugarloaf Café— a regular with a reputation for being a stingy tipper. Finally, after he'd stiffed the waitstaff of their tips once too often, Edie had called him on it. Much to everyone's relief, he'd stopped coming by the restaurant altogether after that, something the café's employees regarded as a personal favor. Bob hadn't minded having Hank Sotomeyer ask him questions, but he wasn't thrilled to see Eric Drinkwater.

Drinkwater activated the recording equipment and made the required announcement before addresing Bob directly.

"Ever hear of a guy named Charles Ponzi?" the detective asked, grabbing one of the two chairs on the far side of the table from Bob. He may not have been physically present in the room during Hank's interview, but clearly he'd been following what had been said, word for word.

"Who?" Bob replied.

"Charles Ponzi, of Ponzi scheme fame," Drinkwater said. "He conned people into investing with him by promising them huge returns. For a while he delivered. Early investors made out like bandits, because he paid them the large returns he'd promised. The only problem was, he siphoned a lot of the money into assets for himself. Then, when things started going south, he used funds from later investors to pay large returns to the early ones. The whole deal worked just fine right up until the money ran out. Which is why, when later investors came looking for their money, it wasn't there."

"You're saying that's what happened to Edie and me—we got caught up in a Ponzi scheme?"

"Textbook case," Drinkwater said. "I just got off the phone with the SEC. According to them, Ocotillo Fund Management has been a Ponzi scheme from beginning to end. There's no telling how big it is at this point. They're guessing it'll end up amounting to several thousand investors, a fair number of whom were clients of our homicide victim Mr. Frazier."

"They're probably as upset as I am."

"I'm sure that's true, Mr. Larson, but as my colleague Detective Sotomeyer just pointed out, of all those disgruntled customers, you're the only one who happened to show up at the crime scene with blood all over your body and with a possible murder weapon in the back of your vehicle."

"A what?"

"A possible murder weapon, Bob—a bloody knife."

"And you found it where?"

"In the back of your Bronco."

"Is this some kind of joke?" Bob demanded.

"Believe me, this is no joking matter," Drinkwater replied. "So maybe you and I should take another crack at this. How about if you tell me again exactly what went on this morning?"

"My car was unlocked and the windows open," Bob said. "The AC quit working years ago. Whoever did it must have tossed the knife inside as they were leaving."

"So you believe that the killer or killers were still at the residence while you were there?"

"They had to be."

"But you saw no one."

"I was looking out for Millie and Dan," Bob said.

"There were no signs of a break-in at the residence," Eric continued. "Millie and Dan Frazier opened their door and let the killer into their home. That suggests their assailant was someone they knew, most likely someone they knew well and maybe someone they had known for years. Someone like you, perhaps?"

"I already told Hank all of this," Bob insisted.

"Yes, that's true," Eric allowed, "but how about if you tell the same story to me, then, from the very beginning."

Bob took a deep breath. The last thing he wanted to do right then was rehash the whole ugly story, but he could see that he didn't have a choice.

"It all started this morning," he said. "I was sitting in Edie's and my apartment drinking coffee when I saw the piece on TV about Dan's investment company, Ocotillo Fund Management, going belly-up . . ."

15

It took time for Ali to make her way back to I-17 through that tangled, forested maze. The moment she hit enough bars on her cell, her phone rang. "Ali!" her mother exclaimed. "Are you almost here? I was worried before, but now I'm downright frantic."

"I'm still up on the Rim and just now getting back on the freeway," Ali answered. "I went up to the homeless camp off Schnebly Hill Road to see if Dad might have stopped by there."

"And?" Edie asked eagerly. "Had he?" There was such naked hopefulness in her mother's questions that it made Ali's heart hurt.

"No," she answered. "No one up there had seen him, but what's wrong now? You sound upset."

"I just heard from someone here at the Shadows who got it off some kind of Internet news feed that there's been a double homicide here in town today. In Sedona, no less. They're not releasing any information pending notification of next of kin and all that, but I'm beside myself with worry. What if Bobby somehow got himself in the middle of it?"

"Why on earth would Dad end up in the middle of a double homicide, Mom? It's just not possible."

"Then why won't he answer his phone?"

"There are a number of possibilities that don't include a double homicide. Maybe he forgot to plug his phone in and it ran out of juice. Maybe it got turned on silent, and he doesn't know it's ringing."

And maybe, Ali thought, *he turned it off so he could have a few moments of peace and quiet.*

"And maybe he's lying dead in a ditch somewhere," Edie fumed. "I've got half a mind to get in the car and drive around looking for him."

"Going out looking for him is the last thing you should do right about now," Ali cautioned. "Is Betsy still there with you?"

"Yes."

"Stay there with her, then," Ali said. Call-waiting buzzed in Ali's ear. "Look, Mom," she said. "I've got another call. Believe me, I'm coming as fast as I can."

"Just so you know," Edie said, having the last word. "Once I find Bobby Larson, if he ever pulls a stunt like this again, I'll kill him myself!"

Cami Lee's name appeared on the screen, and Ali switched over to the other call. "What do you have for me?" Ali asked. "Have you found him?"

"I'm not sure," Cami replied tentatively. "I've got a lock on his cell phone. Right this moment it appears to be somewhere inside the headquarters for the Sedona Police Department."

Ali's heart skipped a beat. There had been a double homicide in town. If her father's phone had been located somewhere inside the police department, did that mean her father was there, too?

"At Sedona PD?" Ali asked. "Are you sure?"

"I'm sure."

"Have you heard anything about a reported double homicide in Sedona?"

"I haven't," Cami said. "There might be something on Stu's police scanner, but he's been busy, and so have I. Do you want me to go check?"

"First tell me about Dad's Bronco. It's possible he may have been in an accident of some kind."

"I've located no information on his vehicle," Cami continued. "And there have been no reported MVAs involving a Bronco. I remember Mr. Simpson saying that he was going to put a GPS locator on your dad's SUV, but that must not have happened."

"It didn't," Ali said. In fact, her father had bristled at the very idea. "No way you're putting one of those gadgets on my baby," he'd declared. "If you can follow me around, so can the government. Where I go and what I do is none of their business or yours, either, for that matter."

The GPS "gadget" stayed off.

"B. said we were gathering all this information for your mother," Cami continued. "Would you like me to call it over to her?"

"And tell her that my father may have been connected to a double homicide?" Ali demanded. "Absolutely not!"

She pressed the gas pedal all the way to the floor, and the Cayenne shot forward.

"Do not call my mother about any of this," she continued. "And if she calls you, do not answer, understand? If you end up having to speak to her, tell her you've been too busy to check on this yet. Got it?"

"Yes, ma'am," Cami replied. "Loud and clear."

"But do tell B.," Ali added. "I want him to know everything that's going on. Also, you might try calling the nonemergency number at Sedona PD, and see if they'll give you any information."

"Will do."

With a white-knuckled grip on the steering wheel, Ali drove on, disregarding all posted speed limits as she raced for Sedona. She had told her mother that there was no way on earth that her father would be involved in a double homicide. Now she wasn't so sure. If he was involved, how involved was he?

The Sedona Shadows Internet source had reported a double homicide in Sedona. There was a chance, of course, that her father was one of the two victims. If he had died—if he was already dead—Ali knew that her mother would be utterly devastated. They had worked hard for all those decades, running the Sugarloaf day after day, seven days a week, telling themselves and anyone else who cared to listen that they'd be kicking up their heels once they hit their "golden years." But what if Bob and Edie Larson's golden years had just come to a screeching halt? That idea was more than Ali could handle right then.

On the other hand, if her father wasn't dead,

was there even a remote possibility that he was the perpetrator?

"Geez Louise, Dad," she said, speaking aloud as though Bob Larson were right there with her on the front seat of the Cayenne. "What in the hell have you gotten yourself into? If you're not already dead, I'm pretty sure Mom is going to kill you. And if she needs any help getting the job done, I'll be right there giving her a hand."

16

Driving at top speed on the freeway was one thing, but once Ali turned on to Highway 179, all bets were off. The posted limit was fifty-five mph, but the lumbering RVs and gawking tourists didn't drive anywhere close to that fast, and the long stretches of no-passing zones made getting around slower vehicles impossible. It didn't help matters that it was after five. Rush hour in and around Sedona was the same as rush hour anywhere else—glacial.

Ali was going through the first roundabout in the Village of Oak Creek when Cami called back. "I found something on the Internet. I googled 'double homicide in Sedona' and came up with a bunch of photos someone had posted on Facebook."

"Photos from the scene?"

"That's right. The house in the background is an address on Elberta Drive. My records show the owners of that property are Dan and Millie Frazier. Do either of those names ring a bell?"

"Of course the name rings a bell. Dan Frazier has been Mom and Dad's insurance and financial advisor for years. But what exactly do the photos show? Are they the victims?"

"That's not clear, but that address is where the cop cars and emergency vehicles were earlier, although they're probably not there now. One police cruiser, parked in the driveway, was of particular interest. When it came down the hill, a bystander managed to snap a photo. The photograph was taken from a fair distance away, but you could see the profile of someone in the backseat. I had to enhance the image some before Stu could get a reading on it, but when we ran the image through our facial rec program, it came back as belonging to your father."

"My father—in the back of a police car," Ali muttered. "As in locked in the back of a police car at the scene of a double homicide? Did you tell B.?"

"I didn't have to. Mr. Simpson was right there watching the screen when Stu got the hit. He said to tell you not to call him right now. He says he's going to be on the phone locating a defense attorney. He'll meet you at the police station."

For the second time that day, needles and pins shot through Ali's fingertips.

"Is there anything else I can do for you, Ali?"

Several weeks earlier, a case involving black market LEGOs had taken Ali and Cami to Bisbee in the southeast corner of the state where Cami had come close to losing her life to one of the conspirators. There's nothing like going to war with a stone-cold killer to create a lasting bond of friendship, which was where Ali Reynolds and Cami Lee were now. When it came to Ali, the "Ms. Reynolds" part had been x-ed out of Cami's vocabulary. B., however, was now and most likely would always remain on the far more formal level of "Mr. Simpson."

"Is there a time stamp on any of those photos, especially the one of the police cruiser?"

"Just a sec." There was a momentary pause before Cami spoke again. "Yes, the one of your dad in the patrol car is time-stamped 11:43 a.m."

Ali glanced at her watch. The side trip from the freeway back and forth to the homeless camp had taken longer than she expected. It was almost 5:30. That meant that her father had been in police custody of some kind for almost six hours—six hours during which he'd not been allowed to make any calls. That combined with his being locked in the back of a patrol car was enough to convince Ali that Bob Larson was being treated as a suspect rather than a witness. If B. was in search of a defense attorney, he'd come to the same conclusion.

When Ali pulled in to the lot at Sedona PD a few minutes later, B.'s Audi was already parked in a visitor's slot. By the time she stopped her Cayenne next to B.'s Audi R8, he was standing there waiting to open her door.

"You must have talked to Cami," he said. He glanced at his watch. "What took you so long? I was starting to think you'd come to some kind of grief out on the highway."

"Sorry to worry you," she apologized. "At the last minute I stopped by the homeless camp up on the Rim, just to make sure that Dad hadn't been there. He hadn't, of course. From what Cami tells me, he's been right here in Sedona most of the time."

"Not only in Sedona, but also in police custody," B. added.

Gauging her husband's mood, Ali was glad she hadn't mentioned her close encounter with Luke and his twelve-gauge. With everything else that was going on right then, it was best not to add any more fuel to the fire.

"Should we go in?" she asked.

"Not yet," B. replied. "We're waiting for Dash."

Ali knew that Dash—short for Dashiell—Summers was a local defense attorney. He and B. had struck up a friendship when they purchased neighboring homes on a golf course in the Village of Oak Creek and later discovered that neither of them actually played golf. Dash and B. were the same age. Dash's wife, Kitty, was ten years younger than her husband, which made her twenty-five years younger than Ali. Kitty had far more in common with Ali's daughter-in-law, Athena, than with Ali, so the two couples seldom did things as a foursome.

But the two men had a lot in common. Both were successful and outgoing, and both had spent lifetimes dealing with complex name issues. As a kid named Bartholomew Quentin Simpson, B. had endured years of "Bart Simpson" name-calling and bullying before he had dropped everything but the first letter of his first name. Dash, the son of a woman who loved Dashiell Hammett's books beyond bearing, had ditched the name Dashiell for just plain Dash for much the same reason—due to constant ribbing from classmates.

"Dash said he's tied up in a meeting, but he doesn't want us going in without him. That's all right, though. It'll give me a chance to catch you up with what's going on."

"You mean about the double homicide?"

B. nodded.

"Cami told me some of it," Ali said. "I also know that Dad and Mom are longtime clients of Dan Frazier. Is there more?"

"Unfortunately, there's a lot more," B. said grimly. "You ever hear of a company called Ocotillo Fund Management?"

"Sure," Ali said. "That was the investment arm of Dan Frazier's business. I'm pretty sure the folks had several accounts with them, all of them placed through Dan."

"That's very bad news," B. said, "because Ocotillo Fund Management declared bankruptcy yesterday. Whatever money your folks had invested with them is probably wiped out."

"Wiped out?" Ali echoed. "Everything's gone? Their IRAs, the money from selling the Sugarloaf, and everything?"

"All of it," B. said with a nod. "Does your mom know about that?"

"I doubt it," Ali said. "At least, if she did, she

didn't mention it. But is that what this is all about? My parents lost money with Dan, and the cops think Dad went after him because of it?"

"How much money are we talking about?"

"I'm not sure," Ali said, "probably quite a bit."

"If your father held Dan responsible for those losses, that would certainly give him motive."

"My father is not a killer," Ali declared, "no matter what the provocation."

A Cadillac CTS pulled in to the slot next to Ali's Cayenne. As Dash Summers exited the car Ali and B. stepped forward to greet him.

"Thanks for coming," Ali said.

"Glad to help," Dash said. "Has anyone heard from your father?"

"Not that I know of," she answered. "I certainly haven't, and if he'd called my mother, I'm sure she would have phoned us immediately."

"Well, then," Dash said, "we'd best go on in and see what's up. Just remember, I'm here representing your father, and I do the talking."

"I'll keep that in mind," Ali said.

Dash led the way inside. The public lobby of Sedona PD looked more like a small-town credit union than a police department. The civilian support staff worked behind a wall of bullet-resistant glass barriers with slots underneath for passing paperwork back and forth and lip-level screens that allowed for speaking without shouting. At the far end of the room, seated behind a counter, sat a uniformed cop—the desk sergeant. Behind the counter somewhere was a button that opened the security door behind him, the one marked NO ADMITTANCE that led to the nonpublic part of the operation.

This particular desk sergeant—Al Kronnan—happened to be someone Ali knew. When her parents had announced that they were selling the diner, Al had been one of the most vociferous in worrying that Sugarloaf sweet rolls would immediately vanish from the planet. He was also someone who had reached his Peter Principle high point early on and had clung to it like lichen to a boulder ever since.

Ali was surprised to discover that Sergeant Kronnan and Dash seemed to have a reasonably cordial relationship. "Hi there, counselor," Al said. "What can I do you for?"

"I'm here to see my client Bob Larson."

Upon hearing Dash's request, a slight frown flitted across Al's broad features. "He's in an interview room right now," Al said hesitantly. "I'm not sure I should interrupt."

"Is Mr. Larson under arrest?"

"Bob under arrest? No, of course not. He's just talking with Detective Drinkwater," Al said.

The cordiality disappeared from Dash's voice. "It's my understanding that they've been in that interview room for an extended period of time. I wish to see my client, and I wish to see him now. Is that clear?"

Al seemed taken aback by the sudden change in Dash's body language and demeanor. This was an order, not a request.

"Let me go check," Al said at last, pushing his stool away from the counter. He set out a preprinted BACK IN A MINUTE sign and then used a keypad to let himself through the security door behind him.

Once Kronnan was gone, Dash turned to B. "This Cami person you mentioned earlier. Can she tell us exactly when Bob's cell phone first turned up at this location?"

"Let me check."

While B. pulled out his phone to check with Cami, Dash turned back to Ali. "What do you know about your parents' financial situation?"

"Just generalities," Ali said. "I know they've done business with Dan Frazier for years and years, both for insurance as well as investment purposes, but when it comes to the specifics about how much money they had invested with him, I have no idea."

"This bankruptcy thing is all very unfortunate, and no one would blame Mr. Larson for being upset over such a serious financial setback. Even so, I do need to ask. Has your father ever been known to be a hothead?"

"My father?" Ali replied. "No, absolutely not. No matter how much money he lost, he wouldn't go off the rails and murder someone over it. My father is not a killer," Ali added, repeating the same words she had used with B. only moments earlier. How was it possible that she'd even need to say such a thing?

"You can say that, but how you see things and

how the county attorney will see them are probably worlds apart," Dash told her. "If your father
suffered a major financial loss on Dan Frazier's
watch, we'll probably have to prove to a jury that
he wasn't and isn't a killer."

B. was just ending his call. "Okay, Cami, thanks,"
he said. Slipping the phone into his pocket he
turned to Dash. "According to the phone records,
the first ping from this location came in at 11:43."

"In terms of being in police custody, arrested or
not, that's a long time," Dash Summers observed,
glancing at his watch. "And from a defense attorney's point of view, I'm afraid it's a very long time
indeed."

17

The security door behind the counter clicked open. When two men emerged, Ali recognized them both. The first was Al Kronnan. The other was Detective Eric Drinkwater—someone Ali knew and most definitely didn't like.

Al hoisted himself back up on his stool while the detective came around the counter to speak to them.

"How can I help you folks?" Drinkwater asked.

"I'm here to see my client Bob Larson," Dash said. "I have reason to believe he's been here at the police department for the better part of six hours. Since he's not been allowed to get word to his family, I'm assuming he's most likely in police custody. I demand to see him."

"What makes you think he's here?"

"Excuse me, we already know he's here," Dash countered, "so please don't pretend he isn't. Sergeant Kronnan already told us as much."

The detective shot a scathing look in Al's direction before he answered. "Mr. Larson is currently a witness in a double homicide. We're in the process of interviewing him. Once we're finished, you'll be able to see him."

"In the course of a six-hour interrogation, I'm pretty sure he's already told you everything he knows. Is he under arrest?"

"I just told you, he's a witness, not a suspect. This is an interview process, not an interrogation."

"Cut the crap, Eric," Dash admonished. "You can claim he's a witness or a person of interest until hell freezes over. All that really means is that you haven't gotten around to reading him his rights. I'm here to represent him. Either arrest Mr. Larson or release him. One way or the other, I want to see my client now!"

Ali could tell from the stiffening of the detective's shoulders and the sudden appearance of a nervous tic in his cheek that Eric Drinkwater didn't like being challenged. By anybody.

"Let me remind you," Dash continued. "My client is a man of a certain age and possibly not in the best of health. If he were to suffer any ill effects due to this extremely prolonged interview process, I promise you, this department will be held accountable, and you'll be looking for a job."

Ali knew that instances of police misconduct were big news in the media these days, but if her father ended up adversely affected by being detained by the cops, she doubted people would be taking to the street to protest in his behalf. Still, Dash's threat of legal consequences seemed to have some impact. The tic in Drinkwater's cheek twitched again. Ali certainly noticed it and, most likely, so did Dash Summers.

"So," Dash proceeded after only the slightest pause, "with all that in mind, are you going to allow me to see my client or do I need to go before a judge and get a warrant? Remember, Detective Drinkwater. This isn't Chicago. There's no place for a Homan Square–style police black site here."

The detective took a small step back, physically conceding defeat rather than replying directly.

"Open up, Kronnan," he muttered.

Al pushed the security code and the door clicked open. As Dash stepped around the counter and started through the opening, Ali made as if to do the same, but Drinkwater held up an arm, barring her way.

"The attorney goes in. Nobody else."

Ali started to argue, but B. took her arm. "Come on," he said. "Let's have a seat. We'll wait here in the lobby."

Ali reached for her phone. "I need to call Mom."

"No," B. said, "not yet. Not until we know what's really going on."

"But she's worried."

"She'll be even more worried if she knows your dad is a suspect in a double homicide. Let's wait until we hear what Dash has to say. Besides, what would happen if you told her?"

"She'd come down here on her broom and rip Detective Drinkwater a new one," Ali answered.

"Exactly," B. agreed with a terse smile. "And the

next thing you know, she'd be under arrest for assaulting a police officer."

B.'s words had merit. Ali put her phone away. "Tell me more about Ocotillo Fund Management."

"They're dead as a doornail," B. said.

"Then my folks may have lost everything."

"That's a possibility," B. said, "but don't worry about your parents. If they need help, we're both in a position to do so. They'll be fine. We'll see to it."

Grateful for the reassurance, Ali grabbed B.'s hand and squeezed it. "Thank you," she said.

B. took up his iPad. Ali suspected he was searching for information about what was happening with Ocotillo Fund Management. She could have done the same, but right then she didn't have the heart. Instead, she closed her eyes and leaned her head against B.'s shoulder.

Lost in thought, Ali also lost track of time. More than half an hour passed before the door behind the counter clicked open again. Dash came out first, smiling in their direction and letting them know that he had succeeded in his mission. He was followed by Detective Drinkwater who, upon laying eyes on B. and Ali, delivered a firm warning.

"Just because Mr. Larson has a bigwig daughter and son-in-law who both have access to private jets, I want you to make sure that your client understands that, as a person of interest in this case, he's not allowed to leave town."

"Yes, yes," Dash said impatiently. "I can assure you Mr. Larson won't be going anywhere."

The third person through the door, the one trailing far behind the detective, was a man who looked vaguely like Ali's father, but at first glance she barely recognized him. Bob's thin white hair stood on end like a ghostly fright wig. His normally ruddy face was a pasty gray. Dressed in an orange jump-suit, he shuffled along on a pair of ill-fitting rubber sandals as though he could barely find enough strength to put one foot in front of the other.

Ali had intended to jump forward to greet him, but the shock of seeing him like that left her im-mobile. He seemed smaller somehow, as though the body of this formerly robust man had, in a matter of hours, somehow collapsed in on itself. He looked lost, frail, and uncertain—bewildered, almost. It was enough to break her heart.

"Dad," she managed, finally moving forward. "Are you all right?"

He opened his arms then. She ran headlong into his embrace, but this time something was out of kilter. The strong arms that had comforted her for as long as she could remember no longer seemed as strong as they had once been. Ali's father had been her rock no matter what disaster had befallen her. She'd always been able to turn to him, fall against his seemingly massive chest, and spill out her latest heartache. That didn't happen this time. Instead, Bob Larson buried his head in his daughter's hair and sobbed like a baby.

"Oh, Ali," he moaned. "I've lost everything—all our money. What are Edie and I going to do, and what am I going to tell your mother?"

For a time, they stood there oblivious to everything and everyone around them, while Ali's father continued to weep—something he had never before done in her presence. Because the big issues seemed far too complex to deal with right then, Ali focused on the small ones, allowing herself to build up a case of outrage.

"What in the world have they done with your clothes?" she demanded when Bob finally straightened up long enough to wipe the tears from his eyes. "Why are they sending you home dressed like a common criminal?"

"They took everything away," Bob answered with a shrug. "My pants, my shirt, my belt, even my underwear and shoes. Since there's blood on them, they're holding them as evidence. They've also impounded my Bronco."

Aiming a fierce glare in Eric Drinkwater's direction, Ali took a step back along with a deep breath. "Come on, Dad," she said, taking him by the hand and leading him toward the front door. "Let's get you home."

"Home?" Bob echoed, looking down at the offending jumpsuit. "I can't go walking through the halls at Sedona Shadows dressed like this, can I?"

"Of course you can't," Ali agreed. "We'll take you back to our place. Have you had anything to eat?"

Bob frowned. "I don't think so, not since breakfast."

Ali shot a withering look in the detective's direction. "He's been here for hours and you didn't even have the common decency to feed him?"

Drinkwater shrugged. "If he was hungry, he should have asked."

"Like hell!" Ali told him. Then, tightening her grip on her father's hand, Ali led him toward the door.

"That's settled, then," Ali said, making up her mind for all of them. "Leland was making meat loaf for dinner tonight. I'm sure there'll be enough to go around. While he's putting food on the table, we'll make arrangements to get you a change of clothing."

Leland Brooks, Ali's aging but still very capable majordomo, liked nothing better than rustling up a quick but suitable dinner for unexpected company. It was one of his strong suits. He was also someone Ali could count on in a pinch. She called him on their way to the parking lot, putting him on notice.

"But what about Edie?" Bob objected. "We can't leave her out of all this."

"And we won't," B. said. "I'll stop by Sedona Shadows. I'll pick up Edie along with a batch of clean clothes. She's been worried sick about you, Bob," B. added. "She's spent the whole afternoon thinking you were lying dead in a ditch somewhere. She needs to be brought up to date."

"Go ahead and tell her that I'm safe, but don't go into any of the rest of it," Bob cautioned. "This is a mess of my own making. I'm the one who needs to tell her face-to-face exactly what's happened. As for my being dead in a ditch somewhere? I only wish I were. I'd probably be better off, and so would Edie."

"That's no way to talk," Ali admonished, opening the car door, helping him in, and then making sure his seat belt was properly latched. "Once you've changed into clean clothes and had something to eat, things won't look as bleak."

That's what Ali said, but she wasn't at all sure she believed a word of it. On her way around the car to the driver's side, Dash pulled both B. and her aside.

"If you can," he advised, "you should probably avoid discussing any of this amongst yourselves."

Ali stopped short. "What do you mean not discuss it?"

"If Bob reveals anything incriminating, Edie can't be compelled to testify against him, but you and B. can."

"Does that mean you think he did it?" Ali asked.

"All I'm saying is that if he reveals any details to you or to any member of your family besides your mother, you can be compelled to testify about it. Your mother? No. But the rest of you? Absolutely."

"We'll take that under advisement," Ali said, but she didn't mean it. "Like hell," she muttered under her breath as she got into the car and slammed the door shut behind her. If Dash Summers thought they were going to let all this pass without discussing it as a family, he was dead wrong.

"What did you say?" Bob Larson asked. "I didn't quite catch that."

"Nothing," Ali reassured him. "I was just talking to myself."

She buckled her own seat belt, started the engine,

and then sat for a moment with her eyes closed. When she opened them again and glanced over at her father, he was staring straight ahead.

"How am I ever going to tell your mother about what happened to our money?" he asked brokenly. "How can I tell her we're dead broke?"

"You'll find a way," Ali said reassuringly. "Maybe it's not as bad as you think."

"It's bad, all right," Bob replied grimly. "Worse than you can possibly imagine."

"Well, then," Ali said with as much confidence as she could muster. "We'll cross that bridge when we come to it."

That brought her up short. Those words were one of the many platitudes her parents had used on her over the years. Now here she was spouting them right back.

Shaking her head, Ali put the Cayenne in gear, backed out of the parking spot, and then drove out of the lot.

What goes around comes around, she thought ruefully. *And so much for my perfect day in June.*

18

In the end, there was nothing more for Haley to do, so she went home. When she arrived at the house at the end of Art Barn Road, she was surprised to see an unfamiliar car parked in her customary spot. The last thing she needed right then was an unexpected visitor. Letting herself in through the unlocked front door, she was astonished to find Jessica Denton seated in the easy chair next to Gram's recliner.

"Haley," Carol Hotchkiss said. "I'm so glad you're home. As you can see, we have company."

Haley felt the smallest twinge of guilt. In addition to her office employees, Jessica was the one other person who should have been informed about what had happened to Dan and Millie. From the wad of used Kleenex in her lap, someone else—Gram, most likely—had already handled that issue.

"I still can't believe they're dead," Jessica wailed. "It's incomprehensible that something so awful could happen to such nice people. I didn't mean to just drop in on you unannounced like this, but I didn't know where else to go. I needed someone to talk to—someone who at least cared about them—and I know you do."

Moved by Jessica's obvious anguish, Haley patted her on the shoulder. "Yes, I did care and I still do. And I'm so sorry. I should have thought to call you earlier, and I didn't."

"I'm sure you've had your hands full, what with the SEC coming in and pushing people around," Jessica said, seeming to get hold of herself. "I had been trying to get hold of Dan for hours. When I started hearing rumors about the double homicide up here, something made me think that Dan might have been involved, and I had to know what really happened. I tried calling the police department, but they wouldn't tell me anything. 'Pending notification of next of kin' is what they said."

"They didn't tell me anything, either," Haley said, "at least not officially, but it's true all the same. I saw the cops carrying bodies out of the house."

"You saw it? You were there?"

"I was across the street."

"When will they release the names—officially, I mean? As far as I know, Dan and Millie didn't have any next of kin."

"Some cousins, I believe," Haley answered, "and maybe an aunt or uncle or two back home in Missouri where Millie's family came from originally, but no kids. No grandkids."

"Would you care to stay for dinner?" Gram asked suddenly, inserting herself into the conversation. "It won't be anything fancy—a reheated mac and cheese casserole and salad is all, but on a day like this, it's easy to run out of fuel. You're welcome to join us."

"Are you sure you wouldn't mind?" Jessica asked. "I don't want to intrude."

As much as Haley wanted to dislike Jessica Denton on sight—as much as she wanted to send her packing, she couldn't bring herself to do so. Jessica was far too distraught to go driving anywhere by herself right then. She seemed to be almost as grief-stricken by what had happened as Haley herself was. In the end, Haley's innate sense of kindness won out.

"Of course we don't mind," Haley said. "Gram is right. We've both had a terrible shock today, and we need to eat. All I'm going to do is heat up the casserole and make some salad."

"Can I help?"

"The kitchen's too small for two people," Haley said. "If you'd like to, why don't you go freshen up while I put the food on the table."

"That's probably a good idea," Jessica said with a nod. "I've been crying my eyes out for hours on end. I'm sure I look a fright."

Mentally Haley took exception to that. There was no way someone like Jessica Denton could ever look bad.

"The bathroom's down the hall on the left," Haley said. "Help yourself."

19

As Ali pulled in to the garage, the aroma of meat loaf and freshly baked bread wafted through the air. Entering the kitchen, she saw Leland, knife in hand, at the cutting board working on salad makings while Bella scampered around them in ecstatic, welcoming circles while the tags on her collar jingled like so many tiny bells.

"The table's set," Leland announced, "and there's plenty of meat loaf to go around."

"I'm not hungry," Bob muttered as Ali bent to greet the dog.

"You will be," Ali promised, leading her father toward the guest suite. "First off, I want you out of that jumpsuit. While you're taking a hot shower, I'll find a robe for you to wear until B. and Mom get here with some clean clothes."

Bob was already in the shower when she returned with a robe. Tossing it onto her dressing table chair, she and Bella returned to the library. Ali hadn't wanted a dog, but the little waif—found abandoned in a casino parking lot—had, in a matter of months, wormed her way into both B.'s and Ali's hearts. Now, seeming to sense Ali's disquiet, the dog asked to be picked up and then settled, contentedly, on the chair next to her. Sitting there, stroking the dog's smooth fur, Ali tried to prepare herself for dealing with her mother. As distraught as her father was, Ali feared her mother would be even more so.

When B. drove up, he stopped in the front driveway rather than pulling in to the garage. Bella leaped off the chair and raced to the front door, barking a full-scale alert. By the time Ali opened the door, Edie Larson stood on the front porch, carrying a loaded clothes hanger as well as a paper grocery bag that also contained items of clothing. One look at her mother's face told Ali that rather than being distraught, Edie Larson was downright furious.

"Robert Larson has been in the police station all afternoon and no one bothered to pick up the phone and let me know?" she demanded. "What in the world were those people thinking? What were *you* thinking? Obviously you found out a lot sooner than I did. You should have called me. Immediately!"

Ali agreed that her mother had a point. Still, recalling the way her father had looked as he shuffled out into the lobby, Ali didn't second-guess her decision. Seeing her father like that had been hard enough on her. It would have been devastating for her mother.

"Sorry, Mom," she said, leading her mother inside and back toward the cozy library at the end of the house. "I wanted to have some real information from Dash Summers before we notified you."

"Dash Summers, the attorney?" Edie repeated, stopping in midstride. "This is unbelievable. You saw fit to call Dash Summers about all this but not me? How could you? I'm Bobby's wife, after all."

"I didn't call him, B. did," Ali answered. "Dash met up with us at the police department. Once inside, Dash went back to the interview room to find out what was going on. My plan was to wait until we had solid news before I called you. When Dash and Dad came out, he swore B. and me to secrecy, insisting that he wanted to tell you about all this himself rather than having anyone else do it. Dad and I came straight here while B. went to get you."

"Well, I'm here now," Edie railed, "and thanks to B. I still don't know one single thing. He's been acting like he's operating under some kind of court-ordered gag order."

"He is," Ali said. "We both are because that's the way Dad wants it."

Clearly offended and still holding on to her load of clothing, Edie plopped into the love seat. "Does that mean you're not going to tell me anything, either?"

"That's right," Ali answered. "I'm not. Come on, now. Let me help you with all that stuff."

Rather than handing over her load of clothing, Edie held on to it for dear life, hugging it to her chest. "I'm perfectly capable of carrying my husband's clothing, thank you very much," she said. "Now, where is he?"

"In the guest room, taking a shower and cleaning up."

"I'll clean him up, all right," Edie declared determinedly. "I'll also give him a piece of my mind!"

Ali knew that right then Bob Larson would need the full armor of God to deal with his outraged spouse.

"Please, Mom," Ali said, once more reaching for the clothing. "At least give him a chance to be dressed in his own clothes before he sees you. Right now he's most likely wearing one of B.'s robes, which will be a foot too long at the hem and six inches too short around the middle."

B. approached from behind, interrupting a blazing mother/daughter stare-down. "That's right, Edie," he said, gently removing the clothing from her hands and passing them over to Ali. "Why don't you and I wait here while Ali takes Bob his clothes. In the meantime, I'll ask Leland to bring us some tea."

"This is utterly ridiculous," Edie huffed. "I've been married to the man for more than fifty years. I've seen him stark naked plenty of times. There's no need for him to be dressed before I lay eyes on him."

"There's a need this time," B. told her, "both for his sake and yours."

On her way through the house, Ali glanced inside the bag. It contained shoes, clean underwear, and socks. Unfortunately, Edie hadn't brought along a second pair of suspenders—the indispensable piece of equipment Bob Larson required to keep his pants in place.

Arriving at the guest room door, Ali tapped on it. When no one answered, she let herself in. Her father, shoulders hunched, stood by the window, staring dejectedly out into what was now deepening darkness. Just as Ali had suspected, the robe he was wearing was at once both too big and too small, and it made him look ridiculous.

"Dad?" she asked tentatively.

He started in a way that told Ali he hadn't registered her earlier knock.

"Thank goodness it's you," he said. "I was afraid it would be your mother."

"She's waiting in the library," Ali advised, handing over the clothing. "Finish getting dressed. That's where we'll be whenever you're ready to face the music."

"As far as that's concerned," Bob muttered. "I'm not sure I'll ever be ready."

"Don't worry, Dad," Ali said reassuringly. "You'll see. Mom will be fine."

Ali entered the library in time to see Leland hand his mother a cup and saucer. "There you go, Mrs. Larson," he said kindly. "A cup of tea will do you a world of good."

Leland's sense of propriety meant that he would never presume to call either of Ali's parents by their first names. Or Ali and B. by theirs, either, for that matter.

"Would you care for a cup of tea?" Leland asked when he saw Ali.

"Please," she said, sinking into her customary chair and gratefully accepting her own cup and saucer. "Where's B.?" she asked.

"Mr. Simpson is in the kitchen tending to something," Leland answered. "He'll be right back."

"If this is about that old girlfriend of Bobby's from high school," Edie said, "the one who contacted him through Facebook, I know all about her."

As far as Ali was concerned, her mother's automatic assumption that this was all due to some old romantic entanglement would have been laughable had the situation not been so much more serious than that.

"Please, Mom," Ali pleaded. "Let's let Dad do the telling."

"All right, then," Edie grumbled. "Have it your way."

Bob came into sight just then, pausing in the doorway long enough to get the lay of the land. His hair was combed. He was wearing clean clothes and socks and a pair of regular shoes. The lack of suspenders meant he had to keep tugging at his pants. He entered the room as if uncertain of his welcome. The unmistakable look of utter defeat about him instantly dissolved Edie's anger.

"Oh my," she said, springing to her feet and hurrying toward him. Taking his hand, she pulled him into her arms. "Bobby, you look like you're at death's door! What in the world has happened to you? Come in here and tell me all about it, mister," she added, dragging him toward the love seat. "You're going to tell me every single thing."

"Our money's gone, Edie," he whispered hoarsely. "Everything we set aside for our retirement is gone—wiped out."

Edie took that news with seeming equanimity. "I heard something about that OFM situation earlier this evening. Once we talk to Dan Frazier, he'll be able to straighten things out."

"But he can't and he won't," Bob said brokenly. "Dan and Millie Frazier are dead—both of them—murdered."

Edie was horrified by the news. "I knew two people had died. Everyone was talking about that earlier during afternoon coffee, but I had no idea it was them. Who would do such a thing?"

"Don't you understand?" Bob continued. "That's the whole problem. The cops think I did it. Detective Drinkwater believes I held Dan responsible for losing our money, and he thinks that's why I killed them."

"You?" Edie demanded. "Are you kidding? That jerk Eric Drinkwater went so far as to blame you for what happened?"

Bob nodded. "And that's where I've been all afternoon, down at the police department in an interview room being grilled first by Hank Sotomeyer and later by Eric."

"This is absurd—utterly and completely absurd."

"It's not absurd, sweetheart." Bob Larson seldom used endearments. The fact that he had used one now wasn't lost on any of the people in the room.

"I can see where Drinkwater's coming from," Bob continued. "I was at Dan and Millie's house just after it happened. I'm the one who found them."

"You were at their house? How come?"

"I heard about the bankruptcy things on the news. I wanted to talk to Dan about it, and I went there. He and Millie were terribly wounded, but they were both alive when I called 911. I tried to administer first aid and ended up with blood all over me. That's why I needed clean clothing. When the cops dropped me off at the station, they took all my clothes away to use as evidence."

"Evidence that you did it?"

Bob nodded. "I was the last one to see them alive, and I'm the one who called it in. Naturally they think I'm responsible."

"Naturally nothing," Edie declared. "I have half a mind to go down to the police department right this minute and give that young jackass Eric Drinkwater a piece of my mind."

"You're saying there was blood at the scene?" Ali asked her father.

Bob nodded. "Lots of it," he answered.

Ali was relieved. "That's probably a good thing," she said.

Her parents looked at her in horror. "How can that be a good thing?" Edie demanded.

"Because the killer's footprints are bound to be there, too."

During that exchange, B. had appeared in the doorway between the living room and the library. Completely focused on one another's faces, neither Bob nor Edie seemed to notice as B. slipped into the high-backed chair across the coffee table from Ali.

"I still don't understand why Eric Drinkwater would think you did this," Edie continued.

"Because I was there," Bob said.

"Oh, for goodness' sake," Edie said. "You would never in a hundred years do anything of the kind."

Her heartfelt declaration left Bob momentarily speechless. At that juncture Leland reappeared in the doorway. "Dinner is served," he announced. "Would you care to eat in the dining room, or would you rather I served the meal on trays in here?"

As usual, Leland's instincts were spot on. Ali shot him a grateful look. "In here please," she said. "If it's not too much trouble."

"No trouble at all," Leland murmured, melting quietly out of the room. "It'll be ready in a jiff."

Both Bob and Edie had fallen silent. When Leland left, Edie turned to her husband.

"You heard about the bankruptcy first thing this morning and then went traipsing off to Dan's house without mentioning a word of it to me?"

"You were still at aerobics with Betsy. And I didn't have the guts to face you right then. I needed to know for sure what had happened before I told you about it. Instead I drove over to their place to ask Dan face-to-face. I found him out in the garage, sitting in his Mustang. Millie was on the kitchen floor. They'd both been stabbed. I called 911 right away, but they were both gone before the EMTs got there. And then . . ."

He broke off, unable to continue.

"And then what?" Edie urged.

"The cops found what they believe to be the murder weapon in my Bronco," he said. "The windows were wide open. The killers must have tossed a knife inside on their way past."

"You're saying the killers were there at the same time you were?"

"They must have been. Whoever did it must have walked out the front door while I was in either the garage with Dan or the kitchen with Millie."

"Oh, Bobby," Edie said as tears sprang to her eyes. "It's a wonder you weren't killed, too."

"But you didn't see anyone?" B. asked.

"No," Bob answered. "I never saw anybody, but as I turned up the driveway I noticed another vehicle was parked in front of the house next door."

"What kind of vehicle?" Ali prompted.

"A white Ford F-150 loaded with landscaping equipment."

"But you didn't see any workers."

"No, they were probably on the far side of one of the nearby houses."

While they'd been speaking, Leland had made several trips in and out of the room, each time carrying individual trays laden with plates, napkins, and utensils. Each plate held a hunk of meat loaf, a helping of salad, and a thick slice of freshly baked bread, already slathered with butter. Ali's tray held a small ramekin with ketchup, and the others had both mustard and ketchup. When the last tray was delivered, Leland made a discreet departure, closing the French doors behind him.

"So did the person toss the knife into your Bronco just to get rid of it?" B. asked.

Bob shrugged his shoulders. "I have no idea."

"Or maybe the killer put the knife there in a deliberate effort to frame someone else," Ali suggested.

"It's possible, I suppose," Bob agreed.

Edie took a deep breath. "Exactly how much money did we lose?"

Put on the spot by her direct question, Bob's face burned with shame. "About one point two mill, all told," he answered at last. "You tried to warn me about putting all our eggs in one basket. Now, because I didn't listen, it's gone."

"All of it?"

"Yes."

After a brief silence, Edie asked, "What day of the month is this?"

Her seemingly sudden change of subject caught everyone off guard. Glancing at the date on his watch, B. answered before anyone else. "It's Tuesday," he said, "June sixteenth."

"All right, then," Edie said, turning back to Bob. "When we moved into Sedona Shadows, we paid the first and last month's rent, and our move-in date was on the first of the month. That means we have until the end of August to find a new place to live."

"Mom, please," Ali interjected.

"No," Edie said, "no arguments. If we're left living on nothing but social security, there's no way we can afford Sedona Shadows. We'll have to move, no question. And it's likely one or the other of us will have to go back to work. Since I'm five years younger, I'm the one who'll need to find a job. Maybe I can get hired on as a cook in one of the school cafeterias. Or maybe we can find a snowbird who will let us do some kind of caretaking work in exchange for a place to live."

Now it was Bob's turn for outrage. "Edie Marie Larson, you are not going back to work—not if I have anything to say about it!"

"Sorry," Edie said. "After fifty years of marriage, you'd think you would have figured out by now that bossing me around was not in the contract. If I want to go to work, I will. End of story."

"Wait a minute, both of you," Ali said. "B. and I have already talked about this. We're more than happy to help out, and we'll be glad to make up any shortfall that will make it possible for you to stay on at Sedona Shadows without either of you having to go back to work."

"Not on your life," Bob declared. "This is not happening! I didn't work this hard or come this far to end up having to count on charity for my daily bread." His voice softened a little. "As for Dash Summers? I appreciate your having him show up to bail me out tonight, but don't think you're the ones who'll be paying his bill. One way or the other, Edie and I will manage. If I have to have a public defender, so be it. And if we have to move into a shed somewhere out in the Verde Valley, that's what we'll do, too. Edie and I have always lived within our means, and we're not changing now."

"All right, then, Bobby," Edie said, "now that all that's settled, tell us what happened today—all of it."

20

With a sigh, Bob Larson launched off into his story, telling it from beginning to end for perhaps the fifth or sixth time that day. In the course of the afternoon he'd lost track of the number of times he'd been asked to repeat it. He talked nonstop for the better part of an hour, telling them everything he could remember, from the time the story had first appeared on the morning news until Dash Summers had collected him from the interview room. Just as he seemed to be finishing up, a phone rang. Ali recognized her mother's distinctive ringtone, although it took Edie a moment to unearth the device from somewhere in the depths of her purse.

"Hello," Edie said. "Oh, why hello, Bridget." Her voice had brightened for a moment. "Yes, Bobby seems to have misplaced his phone, but you've reached mine. What can I do for you?"

Ali recognized the name. Bridget Wagoner was the young woman who functioned as the nighttime desk clerk and receptionist at Sedona Shadows.

Edie's brightness was replaced with concern. "No way!" she exclaimed. "That's so not happening!"

"What?" Bob demanded in the background. "What's going on?"

"Bridget said the cops showed up in the lobby a few minutes ago," Edie replied, holding the phone's mouthpiece away from her face. "They came with a search warrant. Bridget says she's sorry, but since they had a warrant, she had to let them into our unit. She tried calling your cell phone first, since yours is the one they have listed as our emergency contact. Then she called Betsy and got my cell number from her."

Bob rose to his feet. "We need to go," he urged. "Now."

"I can see why you'd want to be there," Ali interjected, "but don't speak to the officers, and, whatever you do, don't interfere. Getting into a pissing match with cops who are in the process of executing a search warrant is the last thing you should do."

"Yes," B. agreed. "If they have enough probable cause to obtain a warrant, that means this is very serious. It's also way beyond the point where you should settle for the services of a public defender. I'm going to call Dash Summers right now and let him know the latest. And before this goes any further, both of you are going to agree to my paying for Dash's services. Understood?"

Defeat registered on her parents' faces as first her father and then her mother reluctantly succumbed, accepting their son-in-law's terms.

Much as they wanted to fight their own battles, they knew they were in over their heads, and that knowledge diminished them both.

When Bob rose to his feet and made for the door, the worrisome, uncertain shuffle Ali had seen earlier was back. Even in his own shoes he walked with the same pained gait Ali had observed at the police department and attributed to his ungainly footwear.

It shocked Ali to realize that in the course of a single day her father had somehow changed into a frail and tired old man.

B. must have arrived at the same conclusion. "If you're ready to go now, I'll be glad to take you home, but only if you agree to leave the police officers alone, and only if you'll let me call Dash and have him meet us there."

"What do you say, Edie?" Bob asked.

Nodding, Edie reached out and took her husband's hand. "Ali and B. have a lot more experience with these kinds of difficulties than we do, Bobby," she said kindly. "If they think we need the help, then we probably do. I agree that it's important for us to stand on our own feet, but right now isn't the time. As for Eric Drinkwater? If he thinks we'll go down without a fight, he's got another think coming. Now come on. Let's go home and see what kind of a mess those cops have left behind. I'll probably be up half the night cleaning up after them."

Ali smiled as the old can-do attitude came back into her mother's voice. This version of Edie Larson was the one her daughter knew best—the one who always refused to take no for an answer.

Standing in the doorway, Ali watched her parents walk hand in hand down the flagstone-covered pathway toward the gate. Clinging together with their heads bowed and shoulders slumped, they were a picture of utter despair.

Suddenly Ali was propelled back in time to her seventh-grade classroom. On the first day of school she had discovered that a surprising summertime growth spurt had made her not only the tallest girl in her class but the tallest kid as well. When she fell into the habit of slouching, her mother had taken her to task and given Ali a code Edie used in public to urge her daughter to stand up straight. "Knockers up," Edie would whisper under her breath.

At first, Ali had believed the word "knockers" was just another way of saying shoulders. Later on she realized that knockers didn't mean shoulders at all, but when you straightened your shoulders, you straightened other things as well.

When Aunt Evie, her mother's twin sister, died, she had left Ali her extensive collection of records. Most of them had been original cast recordings of Broadway musicals, but among them was an LP by Rusty Warren, who had, in the sixties, taken the sexual revolution onstage and on the road in the form of music with unrepentantly bawdy lyrics. Ali's mother and aunt had shared a love for Rusty Warren's work, and "Knockers Up" had been one of the artist's signature songs.

"Hey, Mom," Ali called after her parents. "Don't forget about Rusty Warren."

Edie turned around and looked at her daughter for a moment, and then a miraculous transformation occurred. Ali's father's shoulders may still have been stooped and bent, but at once her mother's back shifted to ramrod straight. Still holding her husband's hand, Edie walked on to B.'s car with her shoulders thrown back and most definitely with her "knockers up."

It looked for all the world as though Edie were leading her beloved Bobby into battle. Whatever was coming, the two of them would face it together.

21

While Ali waited for B. to return, she bustled around, taking the dinner trays back to the kitchen and loading the dishes into the dishwasher. It wasn't that late, but Leland was an early-to-bed-early-to-rise kind of guy, and he had evidently decamped for the night to the privacy of his fifth-wheel residence on the far side of the garage.

Sedona is located in high desert country, an area with huge temperature differences between daytime highs and nighttime lows. As the house cooled, Ali felt a chill, but she realized it might have far more to do with emotional exhaustion than it did with whatever showed on the thermometer. Given that, she lit the gas log in the library and brought out a bottle of Cabernet along with a pair of glasses. She opened the bottle to let it breathe and then settled down with James Joyce's *Finnegans Wake* open on her lap.

She had embarked on a self-imposed effort to tackle the classics, reading them because she could and wanted to, rather than because a teacher or English professor was standing over her with a threat to her GPA if she didn't get the job done. She had been making good progress in that regard, but she had pretty much stalled out with James Joyce. Whatever was going on in *Finnegans Wake* had the unerring ability to put her fast asleep within no more than a couple of pages. And that's what she was doing when B. returned an hour later—sitting with the book open in her lap but with her eyes shut and her chin resting on her breastbone.

She stirred when he came into the room and clinked the neck of the bottle on the rim of one of the glasses. She glanced at her watch. It wasn't that late, just a little past ten. Still she felt as though she'd been asleep for hours.

"After today, the last thing I expected was to find you asleep," B. observed, handing her a glass of wine.

She replaced her bookmark and closed the book.

"You don't seem to be making much progress."

Ali held up the book and studied the position of the bookmark. She'd barely made a dent in the pages. "If somebody could bottle all these words, they'd make a terrific over-the-counter sleep aid."

B. smiled and raised his glass in a toast. "Then here's to James Joyce," he said. "On nights like to-night, sleep is a good thing."

"How are the folks?" Ali asked, setting the book aside.

"Your mother was in a state of high dudgeon by the time I left to come home. From what I could see, the cops executing the warrant were leaving quite a mess."

"Cops in general or one cop in particular?"

B. nodded. "That would be Detective Drinkwater. There didn't seem to be much love lost between him and your mother."

"You called that shot. He's the kind of guy Mom absolutely despises. You know the type—ones who come into a restaurant with a group but who don't bother asking for separate checks until after the food has been served. If the group ends up dividing the bill so each one pays cash, those guys always manage to short the waitress's tip on his part of the bill. Drinkwater pulled that stunt over and over, and Mom finally called him out about it."

"You're thinking Drinkwater is coming after your dad because he has a major chip on his shoulder."

Ali shrugged. "It could be," she said. "Not only that, I wonder how much homicide experience he has. Probably not much, and this one is a double to boot. If he's looking to clear it in a hurry, Dad might seem like an easy target."

"Yes," B. said, "but from what your father said, there must have been bloody footprints all over that house. If the killer went out the front door while Bob was in the garage and kitchen with Dan and Millie, those footprints will tell the tale plain as day."

"Let's hope that's true," Ali said.

"And just to be on the safe side, Dash showed up at Sedona Shadows not long before I left to come home. He brought along all the paperwork needed authorizing us to handle the costs of whatever legal fees your father's case entails."

"Did he sign?"

B. nodded. "On the dotted line."

"I don't believe it."

"We must have caught him at a weak moment. Your mother disapproved, of course, but as Dash reminded her, Bob's the one with his life on the line here, and he has to have the final say."

"Good," Ali breathed.

"On the way out," B. added, "I let Dash know that High Noon stands ready to undertake any investigative work he deems necessary and that we'll do so on a pro bono basis."

They fell quiet then, both of them sipping their wine. "Do you think they're actually going to arrest him?" Ali asked finally.

"I'm not sure. If the CSIs do a decent job, it won't come to that, but the local CSIs are probably pretty green in the homicide department, too."

"Probably," Ali agreed.

"With Dash looking after the case, our next big hurdle is going to be your folks' housing situation. With their lives totally upended at the moment, the last thing either one of them needs to be worrying about is moving away from Sedona Shadows, a place where they're already settled in and comfortable."

"But you heard what Mom said," Ali objected. "They want to pay their own way."

"It doesn't matter," B. said. "Here's what we're going to do. Tomorrow morning, first thing, you're going to show up at Sedona Shadows with a cashier's check in hand that will cover their rent for a year in advance. With an additional year plus their first and last month deposit, that gives them fourteen months to get through whatever legal process has to be handled before they even consider making a move."

"They'll never agree to that."

"We're not going to give them a choice," B. explained. "Rather than asking permission, we'll present them with a fait accompli. It's always better to ask forgiveness after the fact than it is to ask permission in advance."

"What kind of income tax ramifications would a gift like that have?"

"Believe me, your parents are going to be in such a low income tax bracket from now on that it won't even cause a bump. Not only will they not be receiving whatever income they were previously receiving from Ocotillo, most likely whatever funds they received previously will have to be paid back."

"Paid back?" Al echoed. "Are you kidding?"

"I wish I were," B. said. "Have you ever heard the term 'clawback'?"

"What's that?"

"In the aftermath of a Ponzi scheme like this, anyone who has received payments before everything went south is required by the bankruptcy court to pay back those previous distributions so the resulting funds can be distributed equally among all of the scheme's victims."

"The bankruptcy court confiscates the funds? Is that even legal?"

"Unfortunately, yes."

"So my parents get hit twice, first by the Ponzi scheme itself and then by the bankruptcy trustees—insult to injury."

"That's about the size of it."

"And when the bankruptcy proceedings come to an end? What happens then?"

"Most likely those won't conclude until years from now," B. said. "When they do, Bob and Edie will be lucky to get pennies on the dollar."

"What about Jason McKinzie, the guy who started Ocotillo Fund Management? What does he get?"

"If they catch him—*when* they catch him—he'll serve a few years in a federal prison for security violations and/or fraud, and then he'll walk away and pick up where he left off, probably living off money he's been squirreling away for himself all along."

"You think he has money stashed somewhere where the authorities can't touch it?"

B. nodded. "That's what those guys usually do."

"Will the bankruptcy trustees make any effort to find his stash?"

"Probably not. They'll be more focused on the low-hanging fruit—the assets that are easy to find and liquidate."

"Maybe *we* should."

"Should what?"

"Go after McKinzie's money," Ali said. "Maybe

we should initiate a little clawback maneuver of our own. After all, you've achieved some pretty good results in finding the monies Richard Lowell hid away."

"If we were to do that and managed to find anything, remember that whatever funds we retrieved would have to be turned over to the trustees."

"Of course," Ali said. "That's only fair. After all, if there's enough of it, maybe all McKinzie's victims can get a few more pennies back on their lost dollars. If we were to attempt this, where would we start?"

B. thought about that for a minute. "Let me talk this over with Dash tomorrow morning. If we're working on the case and take the position that the Frazier murders are connected to the OFM mess, that gives High Noon a reason to go poking around into all kinds of things."

"The Fraziers' murders are connected," Ali asserted. "And if we can link them back to McKinzie, he'll be doing hard time for murder rather than hanging out in Club Fed."

B. smiled. "Sounds like you want to turn this into a crusade."

"I do."

"Okay, then. Tomorrow morning I'll put Cami and Stu to work data-mining everything there is to know about Jason McKinzie and Dan Frazier, too. Combing through a mountain of material, looking for some helpful nugget is going to be a massive job."

"Right," Ali said. "And I know just the person to do it. We're not going to coerce my parents into accepting rent money from us. That would kill them both, but nobody said we can't give one or the other of them a job."

"As in, turn your parents into our in-house researchers?"

"I can't think of anything my mother would rather do just now than get the goods on the guy who stole their money, especially if there's a chance of getting some of it back."

"Maybe you're right," B. said, after a pause. "Whether they turned up something or not, it would at least give them something to focus on besides sitting around worrying. It also gives us a way of putting cash in their pockets without getting their noses out of joint." He put down his glass, then glanced at his watch.

"Okay, Bella," he said. "Let's go. Time to get busy and go to bed."

22

Immediately after dinner, Jessica took her leave, launching off on her two-hour drive back to her apartment in Phoenix. Once she was gone, while Haley put the kitchen to rights, she and Gram talked together in a way that hadn't been possible earlier with a third party present. On a day when the unthinkable had happened, Haley needed a safe place to unburden herself, and she did so, sparing nothing. Carol listened, saying little until Haley finally ran out of steam.

"What happened to Dan and Millie is appalling," Gram said when Haley finished, "but your real responsibility now is to the girls who work for you. If you want them to be able to keep their jobs and be able to support their families, it's up to you to make sure the business doesn't go down the tubes."

Haley nodded. "You're right."

"You said earlier that Carmen spent the whole day fielding a barrage of angry voice mails. No doubt some of those came from disgruntled clients—especially the ones who got burned by the OFM scam. Many of those will go away forever, no matter what you say or do, but in order to keep the business afloat, you're going to have to find a way to hang on to as many of your customers as possible. You need to keep that trickle of outgoing clients from becoming a flood."

"How do I do that?" Haley asked. "The girls and I do the work, but it was always Dan's name on the door and his face and voice on the commercials."

"From now on you have to be that face and voice, starting tomorrow when you personally return all those calls. Now, tell me about the business continuation plan," Carol went on. "Is it a formal arrangement, presumably with insurance to fund it?"

Haley nodded.

"Then as soon as a death certificate is issued, you'll need to initiate the death claim process."

"At this point I can't even think about filing a claim. It's way too soon."

"No it's not," Carol told her granddaughter. "This is business, Haley. You have to set your emotions aside."

"How can I?" Haley asked. "Right this minute the whole thing seems utterly overwhelming, but you're right. All the paperwork for the business continuation plan, including the policy itself, is in Dan's and Millie's safe-deposit box, along with their wills. I have a key. I'll stop by the bank tomorrow."

"Even with a key, you may still need a death certificate."

"I didn't know that," Haley said.

"I didn't spend all those years as a secretary in a law office for nothing, you know," Carol told her. "Now let's get to bed. It's way past my bedtime, and I know you're exhausted."

"Yes," Haley said. "This was probably the worst day of my life."

"I have a feeling your days may get a lot worse before they get better."

23

Sedona's Crystal Inn was at the far low end of Sedona's upscale tourist industry. This was summertime in Sedona—a peak travel season. Most of the upper-crust places in town had their NO VACANCY signs visibly posted. The Crystal Inn still had rooms—and for good reason. It was a grim throwback to first-generation motels, complete with a drive-up window in the office.

Jessica paid cash for her room, using a phony driver's license in the name of Barbara Toomey as photo ID. The place was old enough to have tiny garages next to each room. The one allocated to room 108 was big enough for Jessica's VW, but just barely. After checking to be sure there were no nearby security cameras, she ducked inside carrying only a backpack, her purse, and a box of cold pizza she'd picked up from another drive-up window on her way north from Peoria.

Switching on the light, Jessica surveyed the stifling room. It was exactly what she'd expected—a sagging queen-sized bed covered with a faded floral bedspread; a stained orange-and-brown plaid sofa; two Formica-topped bedside tables, as well as a tiny round wooden table and two rickety wooden chairs. She deposited the briefcase and pizza on the tables. When she switched on the under-window AC unit, it immediately filled the room with the unmistakable odor of mildew.

Shaking her head, Jessica opened the briefcase and went about setting up her equipment. Depressing as the place might be, it came with one huge advantage: it was less than a mile away from Haley Jackson's house on Art Barn Road. Once Jessica's listening station equipment came on line, the droning voices of Haley Jackson and her grandmother filled the room.

Listening to them talk, Jessica couldn't help blaming herself for the fix she was in. The listening devices she had planted in Dan's homes and cars had given her plenty of advance warning that Dan was in the process of reaching out to the feds. Had she passed that information along to Jason? No, she had not. Jason was intent on stealing other people's money, and Jessica was intent on stealing his. She had assumed, correctly, that once Jason was under the pressure of closing up shop at OFM and bailing, he would be at his most vulnerable. By then he'd have no one else to rely on but her. What she hadn't anticipated was that Jason would be stupid enough to leave his computer in a place where Dan could access it.

As for Dan? Nothing she had overheard on the listening devices she had planted in his cars and homes had alerted her to the fact that he intended to target Jason's supposedly secure computer. Who had given him that idea? She doubted Dan was computer savvy enough to have come up with that one on his own, to say nothing of pulling it off. On Friday morning when a frantic Jason had called to tell her what had happened, Jessica had realized at once that the stolen files spelled disaster for her plans every bit as much as they did for Jason's.

The feds were focused on reeling in Jason McKinzie, but Jessica didn't want anyone taking too close a look at her, either.

"Don't worry about this," she had told him. "I'll handle it."

And she had, from beginning to end, to the very best of her ability. The previous evening, during her visit with Haley Jackson, Jessica had used her trip to the bathroom as a cover to reuse some of the devices she had retrieved from Dan's home in Paradise Valley. She had inserted one into the landline phone on Haley's bedside table. Pretending to have spilled her purse, she had managed to plug a second one into a wall receptacle behind the living room sofa and had dropped a third one—with a newly charged three-day battery and sporting a black matte case—into the bottom of Haley's purse. And on her way out of the house, she'd affixed a GPS tracking device on the inside of the wheel well on Haley's aging Honda.

Knowing she could monitor her target's every move and word, Jessica was confident that if Haley was indeed the person in possession of the damned drive, Jessica would be able to get it back well within her self-imposed twenty-four-hour deadline. She couldn't afford to leave Jason on his own any longer than that for fear of his going bonkers.

All of which explained why Jessica was spending the night in this grim hotel room. While the noisy AC unit labored under the window, Jessica munched cold pizza and listened in on the feed from the device planted behind the living room sofa. Every word was crystal clear, making Jessica thankful that she'd sprung for the high-priced models with state-of-the-art mics.

Jessica listened in on the two women for more than an hour without hearing a single mention of a missing SD card. When Haley and her grandmother finally called it a night, so did Jessica. If they were going to be up and out early, Jessica would need to be, too.

24

Bob and Edie sat in the lobby until the search of their apartment was complete. Dash Summers stayed with them until Eric Drinkwater and his crew finally departed the premises. Only then did Bob and Edie return to their unit. As expected, the place was a shambles. The kitchen especially had been torn apart.

"They took the knife block," Edie observed, assessing the extent of the damage. "But why did they have to leave things in such a mess?"

"It doesn't matter," Bob told her. "We'll work on this in the morning. Come to bed."

"No way," Edie responded. "I'm not spending the night with the prospect of having to clean this up tomorrow hanging over my head. I wouldn't sleep a wink."

So Bob went to bed by himself—to bed but not to sleep. He lay awake, listening to Edie bustling around in the other room, first in the kitchen and eventually in the combination living/dining room as she put things to rights. Eventually, he realized that she was humming under her breath as she worked. Edie had always done that—while she was baking or sewing or cleaning house. It was one of the things he loved about her, but tonight hearing her hum was like a knife wound to his heart.

The fact that Bob was a suspect in a homicide investigation was one thing. It was a serious matter, true, but Bob knew he had done nothing wrong, and even tonight, while the cops were conducting their search, he had felt in his heart of hearts that eventually Dash or someone would be able to prove his innocence. It was the other problem that was tearing him to pieces—the one that wouldn't be going away. That was the one that demanded his complete focus.

Edie was happy here at Sedona Shadows—content in a way she had never been before. They both were. And now, because of his bullheadedness in insisting on going with OFM, they were about to lose this haven. Yes, B. and Ali had generously offered to help out, and even though they could probably easily afford to do so, the idea of being dependent on them was anathema to Bob.

He had been shocked when he caught sight of himself in the mirror as he was getting ready for bed. An old man had stared back at him—an undeniably old man. There was no trace of the guy who, only a matter of months ago, had been tripping the light fantastic in cruise ship ballrooms. In fact, they'd already made a nonrefundable deposit on a cruise for next year. Now there would be no more cruise ship ballrooms because there would be no more cruise ships. They couldn't afford cruising anymore. Life in retirement as they had planned to live it was over.

Lying there staring up at the ceiling, Bob realized that there was an answer to his dilemma—an answer that led straight back to Dan Frazier. A short time later, the lights in the front room clicked off. Realizing that Edie was finally coming to bed, Bob rolled over on his side and pretended to be fast asleep. She came into the room and went through to the bathroom to undress and brush her teeth. A few minutes later, he felt the weight of her body as she sat down on her side of the bed. Then, moments later, as she lay down beside him, he felt the light pressure of her hand on his shoulder as she snuggled up beside him.

Knowing it was the last time, Bob lay there beside her, forcing himself not to sob while silent tears dribbled into his pillow.

25

With B. and Bella off to bed, Ali decided to stay up a while longer—long enough to finish her wine and take one last crack at James Joyce. She had barely opened the book when her phone rang and Dave Holman's name appeared in the caller ID window.

Dave, a Yavapai County homicide detective, was one of Ali's longtime friends. For a while there had been some romantic sparks between them, but that affair had ended amicably. After both Ali and Dave went on to marry other people, there had been some initial awkwardness between the two couples, but Ali was grateful that had evened out enough that the friendship remained intact.

"Hey, Dave," Ali said when she answered. "What's up?"

"I'm down at the bottom of your drive. I've been hearing a lot about what went on here in town today, and I thought you might be in need of some moral support."

"You called that shot," she said. "Hang up so I can open the gate and let you in."

Knowing that the sound of the doorbell would set off a barking frenzy, Ali opened the front door just as Dave stepped up onto the porch. He walked over to her and gave her a hug. "Tough day?"

"Very. Come on in," she said, ushering him into the house. "I was just finishing my wine. Would you like some?"

"Sounds good, but I'd better not," he said. "I'm off shift but still driving a company car."

"What's your pleasure, then?"

"A soda would be fine. Any flavor, diet or not. I'm not fussy."

"Ice or not?"

"No ice," Dave said, "and just the can works for me."

When Ali returned moments later with a frosty can of root beer, she found Dave seated close to the fire in B.'s customary chair.

"Nothing like a double homicide to get the gossip mills in town running at warp speed," Dave said with a rueful smile as Ali handed him his soda. "How are you people holding up?"

"I'm fine," she said.

"And your folks?"

Ali knew that Dave was on shaky ground. A double homicide inside the city limits was outside Dave's jurisdiction, but she knew that discussing an active case with the family of a person of interest in that case meant Dave was crossing a line most cops wouldn't cross.

"Mom's holding up fairly well, I think," Ali answered. "As for my dad? This has hit him hard. He's someone who's never had so much as a single speeding ticket in his life. To be taken into custody the way he was and treated like a common criminal when all he was doing was providing first aid and trying to save Dan and Millie's lives . . ." She broke off for a moment.

"Had to be tough," Dave offered.

Ali nodded. "They had him locked in an interview room for hours on end," she continued. "By the time we figured out where he was and could do something about it, Dad looked like he'd aged ten years. Not only that, they sent him home in an orange jumpsuit. You know my mom. If someone from Sedona PD had bothered to call her, she would have been there in a blink with a change of clothes."

"With E.D. as the lead investigator, that's to be expected," Dave observed.

"E.D.?" Ali asked with a frown.

"He's a jerk," Dave said. "E.D. may be Eric Drinkwater's initials, but when people call him that behind his back, they're referring to something else entirely, because he's your basic limp dick in every sense of the word."

Ali spluttered on a sip of wine and ended up laughing and coughing.

"There are real cops and there are ninety-day wonders," Dave continued. "Drinkwater got himself fast-tracked out of patrol. Now that he's a detective, if he runs true to form, he'll be looking for a quick close since I already know he's got feelers out to other departments. When it comes to transferring, clearing a double homicide would give him a lot of currency in that direction. E.D.'s big problem right now is that the blood evidence doesn't support your father as the doer."

"It doesn't? You know that how?"

"Because I'm friends with some of the city CSIs," Dave answered. "They've got three different sets of bloody footprints, two of which exited through the front door. The whole search warrant thing at your folks' place tonight was mostly for show. That was E.D. hoping to get some kind of lead on your father's so-called accomplices."

Dave paused. "And speaking of searches," he added. "The house had been ransacked. The killers were searching for something. There's no telling what they were after, but the search evidently happened first. The two sets of bloody prints lead from the scene in the kitchen and out the front door, most likely because they realized your dad was coming up the driveway."

"Anything distinctive about the footprints?"

"Yes and no. The killers were both wearing booties—paper booties like you see in operating rooms. That means this was clearly premeditated. They came prepared to kill somebody and they did."

For the first time since she'd seen her father shuffling along in his jail jumpsuit, Ali took a real breath—a deep breath. Dave hadn't just crossed that line. He had jumped over it. She reached over and touched the back of Dave's hand.

"Thank you for that," she murmured.

"You're welcome, but don't think that means this is over," Dave continued. "As I said, Drinkwater's going to do everything in his power to make the evidence match his theory. And oh," Dave added with a grin. "None of this came from me."

"Absolutely not," Ali agreed.

"As for the Ponzi scheme guy? Jason McKinzie seems to have disappeared into thin air. I've heard he was last seen boarding a plane for Mexico City sometime over the weekend. That's where he cleared customs. The federal marshals do a good job. They'll grab him eventually, either inside the U.S. or wherever he comes to rest. They'll lock him away for a few years—probably not for nearly as long as he deserves—and then he'll walk."

"And spend the rest of his days living it up on what's left of other people's money—on money he stole from people like my parents," Ali said.

"I heard about that," Dave said. "How badly did Bob and Edie get hit?"

"Somewhere around a million two, give or take," Ali answered.

"Whoa," Dave said. "That's a bundle. And Dan Frazier was their advisor?"

"Yes."

"If he weren't already dead, sounds like Dan Frazier may have deserved some jail time, too."

Dave glanced at his watch. "It's late," he said. "I need to get home."

Ali followed him as far as the door. "Thanks so much for stopping by and for letting me know some of the inside dope."

"You're welcome," Dave said, giving her a quick hug. "And, when you see your dad again, be sure to tell him that I'm in his corner, and I'm not the only one, either—not by a long shot."

26

Once Edie was finally settled, Bob waited until she was snoring softly beside him before he crept out of bed. He dressed in the bathroom without turning on the light and walked back through the bedroom in his stocking feet, carrying his shoes. He felt silly, tiptoeing around in the living room while he searched for a wallet that wasn't there. When he finally located Edie's purse, he had to dig through it to locate her keys. The way they rattled when he finally managed to extract the key ring left him cringing and holding his breath, but Edie didn't emerge from the bedroom to read him the riot act.

Out in the hallway, having carefully pulled the door shut silently behind him, Bob leaned against it and looked around, taking in the fact that he was leaving, and this time he wouldn't be coming back. The side door entrance he had used earlier that morning was locked down overnight, so he had to exit through the main lobby.

"Is something the matter?" Bridget Wagoner asked, looking up from the book she was reading.

"It was a tough day," he said. "I need some fresh air. I thought I'd go for a drive."

"It's late," Bridget said. "Be safe out there."

"I will."

Standing under one of the lights in the parking lot, Bob used the key fob to unlock Edie's Buick, because that was how he thought of it—as Edie's. One of the rules of their married life had to do with never driving one another's vehicles. Whatever sedan Edie was driving at the moment was off-limits as far as Bob was concerned, and the same held true for Edie and Bob's beloved Bronco.

Gingerly Bob crawled into the front seat. He had to grope blindly for the seat adjustment handle before he could fit his legs under the steering wheel. The mirrors in the Bronco were manual. He had to turn on the overhead light to find and decipher the mirror adjustment button. And the fact that he had to push a button to start the car rather than turning the key in the ignition was also unsettling. He had ridden with Edie in this plenty of times, with all these bells and whistles and with the control for the sound system/GPS glowing from the dashboard, but he felt ill at ease behind the wheel. All the newfangled controls left him feeling hopelessly out of date—all the more reason to do what he intended to do.

He drove out of the lot, easing onto the highway. It was after eleven, so there was very little traffic. Within a mile or so he began to feel more confident. And purposeful.

Years earlier, long before IRAs came along, Dan Frazier had stopped by for an appointment, bringing with him a briefcase loaded with a rate book and blank applications. By then Bob and Edie were running the Sugarloaf as equal partners. When Dan had suggested they purchase keyman insurance on him so Edie would be covered in the event of Bob's death, Edie had balked. "What about keywoman insurance?" she had demanded. "Bobby would be in every bit as much of a bind if he lost me as I would be if I lost him."

In the end Bob and Edie had purchased two policies—twenty-year-pay whole life policies for $250,000 each, with the idea being that the cash value inside the policies could be used to augment their retirement. The policies, still in effect, had been paid off long ago, and the suicide exclusion was long since over with as well. Fortunately, the cash values inside both policies—whatever those amounted to—hadn't been handed over to Ocotillo Fund Management. Receiving a $250,000 death benefit from Bob's policy as well as the cash value in her own policy wouldn't make Edie whole from the monies lost to OFM, but the two payouts would amount to almost a quarter of their retirement fund shortfall. Not only that, left on her own, Edie would be paying for only one person at Sedona Shadows rather than two. If need be, she could elect to move into a smaller unit or maybe ask to have a roommate. Either way, she wouldn't have to face the prospect of being summarily booted out of a place where she was comfortable and happy.

Bob stayed on the highway until after the entrance to Tlaquepaque. Turning left, he came to a stop in front of the cattle guard at the entrance to Schnebly Hill Road. The gate beyond the cattle guard wasn't closed. That meant that the county had finally gotten around to grading out the rockslides and washouts that made the road impassible for much of the winter.

Not wanting to call attention to his presence there, Bob turned off the headlights and engine, then he buzzed down the window and sat there thinking about why he was here and what his intentions were. He'd done almost the same thing in front of Dan Frazier's house all those hours earlier. That had been less than twenty-four hours ago, but with everything that had happened in between, it seemed like a lifetime.

There were no headlights or streetlights in view, and gradually his eyes adjusted to the darkness. The moon was up, palely lighting the dirt road ahead until it disappeared over a small rise. Farther beyond that, he could see the narrow pencil line of graded shoulder debris winding its way up the rock face toward the canyon rim far above. His eyes roamed along the path he knew the road followed, in sight and out of it, looking for any signs of headlights or other vehicles. Bob didn't want any unexpected company while he was doing what needed to be done.

He knew he wouldn't have to go far, but he couldn't be sure how the low-slung two-wheel-drive Regal would handle on a surface that, even newly graded, could be challenging in his sure-footed Bronco. Once the road started climbing, he'd only have to manage three or four switch-backs to gain enough altitude to do the job.

Edie would be devastated, of course. That went without saying, but she'd have Ali and B., her son, Chris, and Athena, and the twins all rallying around her. She'd be okay. Eventually, she might even be able to forgive him for not only dying but for wrecking her damned Buick in the process. Ali wouldn't be devastated—she'd be pissed, thinking he'd taken a coward's way out rather than facing up to the problem and accepting the help she and B. had so generously offered.

Bob understood that this was all a matter of pride—his pride. What was that verse Edie was always quoting? "Pride goeth before a fall."

In this case, he told himself, *that's literally true*, and then he laughed aloud at his own dark humor.

Up on the rim, a tiny pinprick of light came into view—a stationary kind of light rather than a moving headlight. Bob had stood on that very spot in the past when he'd been up visiting his "guys," and he had little doubt that he was seeing a camp-fire from the homeless encampment.

How many times had Bob rushed up there to the rescue when someone was in crisis, sitting there in the cold and dark, counseling with people who were ready to give up—people who had nothing left to live for and were ready to do themselves harm?

Bob didn't know the exact number. There had been plenty of them over the years. And what had he told them, sitting by the dying embers of campfires? Trite things, mostly. Clichés. Don't give up without a fight. You have a purpose. There are people somewhere who love you—people who will miss you if you're gone forever. Sometimes Bob had helped place a reconciling phone call to long-estranged loved ones, putting family members back in touch after years of absence. Sometimes he had helped compose the letters they needed to write, and once written, Bob had mailed them himself. Some of the homeless guys had benefits due them, and Bob would help them fight their way through the paperwork jungles.

And why had he gone to all that effort? Because he cared, that's why.

And what was Bob contemplating now? Giving up, that's what—doing exactly what he had begged all those other guys—and they usually were guys—not to do. For the first time in his whole life, Bob Larson could see that what he planned to do would turn him into something he had never been before—a hypocrite. A damned hypocrite!

A new burst of anger shot through his body. Bob Larson would not be the kind of guy who didn't have balls enough to take his own advice. No way THAT was going to happen! Instead, he located the ignition button, restarted the engine, and then moved the gearshift into reverse.

"Time to go home," he told himself aloud. "If you're not going to ship out, then you sure as hell had better shape up."

On the way back to Sedona Shadows, he drove past Safeway and was surprised to see that it was still open. At the next light, he pulled a U-turn and went back. At the floral section he found a single red rose. They had bouquets containing a dozen or more, but he only needed one. As he started to pay for his purchase, he realized his wallet was still missing. Patting his pockets, he was relieved to find a long-forgotten five dollar bill.

That pinprick of campfire up on the Rim had made all the difference, and it also meant that Edie wouldn't have to come to a morgue to do a next-of-kin identification.

With his transaction complete, Bob's loose change tumbled into the container. "Will there be anything else?" the clerk asked.

"As a matter of fact, there is," Bob said. "Do you happen to have any job applications?"

27

When Ali finally went to bed that night, she slept without dreaming or even moving. She awakened at 6:30 to discover that her right arm was numb from the shoulder down and that she and Bella were alone in bed. B., still in his robe, was seated at the small desk in the corner with both an open laptop and an iPad in front of him and a printer spitting out pages in the background.

"You're up early. What are you doing?"

"Printing out a transcript of what your father told us last night."

"A transcript? What transcript?"

B. held up his cell phone. "I recorded it and ran it through voice-to-text. Now I'm printing it. I'm also sending copies to you, Stu, and Dash so you'll all have access to it as needed."

"You recorded everything Dad said? He won't be thrilled when he finds out about that."

"Too bad," B. said. "I wanted to have access to the information he gave to Detectives Drinkwater and Sotomeyer. The only way to do that was to get him to tell us the story. And even though he'd already been through a hellish day, we needed to hear what he had to say while it was still fresh in his mind. Your father's already made his position clear about where he stands on electronic eavesdropping of any kind. Given that, I knew that if I asked permission to record what he was saying, he would have said no on principle. So no, I didn't ask. I recorded the interview anyway, and it turns out that was a good thing."

"Why?"

"Because we now have a way of demonstrating, in real time, that Bob's version of what happened is the real one."

"How is that possible?"

B. grinned. "My ace in the hole. Remember that sophisticated tracking system Stu and Lance put on all of our phones?"

"I remember," Ali said dryly. "I also remember we had to have Mom's help and go behind Dad's back to put it on his while he was showering."

"What's good about this system is that it doesn't just ping off cell sites. It gives actual tracking information. Remember your dad saying that both Hank Sotomeyer and Eric Drinkwater had asked why it took him so long to get from Sedona Shadows to Dan Frazier's place?"

"Yes," Ali replied. "Dad said something about stopping several houses away from Dan's place and sitting there for a while, trying to figure out what he was going to say. Why?"

"I remembered that, too, so I asked Stu to overlay your father's phone's movements over a satellite photo of the whole neighborhood. Take a look at this."

Ali walked over to where B. was sitting and peered at the screen over his shoulder. "Here's where Bob stopped initially," B. explained, pointing. "That's two houses away from Dan Frazier's house. The phone remains stationary in that position for the better part of twenty minutes. Then it travels on up the street, presumably while still inside your dad's Bronco, turns left, and stops here."

Ali leaned in closer to get a better view. "That building has to be Dan Frazier's garage."

"Correct," B. replied. "Bob said he parked close enough to the garage that if Dan had backed out of the garage without looking, he would have slammed into the Bronco. Now look at this. Do you see all these little lines going in and out of the garage and the house?"

"What are they?"

"That's your father going in and out of the garage and in and out of the house. All of those little lines coincide with the timing of Bob's 911 call. After the call ends, the phone moves over to here, somewhere in the vicinity of this tree."

"That's probably where the patrol car was parked, the one where they locked him inside."

"Yes," B. said. "The phone remains in that location for the better part of two hours. When it moves again, you can follow it as it travels directly to Sedona PD, which also tells us exactly how long he was there."

Ali leaned down and kissed the back of B.'s neck. "So all of this backs up Dad's story. Do we drop this information in Eric Drinkwater's lap first thing this morning and tell him to have a nice day?"

"No, we'll let him stew in his own juices for the time being, but we will pass all of the tracking information along to Dash Summers. From the looks of this, your father's situation isn't nearly as dire as we first thought, and we'll let Dash handle that, although working on behalf of your father's defense team gives High Noon carte blanche to stick its nose into any number of things that would be off-limits otherwise."

"So what's the plan?"

"As I said last night, in order to find where McKinzie hid the money, we need to know everything there is to know about him. He's a guy who has devoted a lot of time and effort toward maintaining a large media footprint. Stu's already located a mountain of material that we'll need Edie to collate and sort."

"A large media footprint should make it harder for McKinzie to go dark," Ali suggested.

"It should," B. agreed, "but so far it hasn't seemed to slow him down. Stu is looking in all the usual social media places, including dating Web sites."

"Are we looking into Dan Frazier's media presence, too?" Ali asked.

"That search is already in process," B. said, "but there's far less electronic information out there on him. What we find out about Dan will mostly have to be done the old-fashioned gumshoe way—by talking to friends and associates."

"Do we know who those are?"

"Stu's making a list of all the employees at the office here in town. They should all be interviewed. Someone, namely you, will need to talk to them. Getting an employee list from Ocotillo Fund Management is a little more problematic at the moment."

"You're saying that looking into Dan Frazier's home team is up to me?" Ali asked.

"Looks like."

"In that case, I'd better hit the shower. Once I'm under way, I'll let my folks know that they've been hired as our researchers in chief—Mom for sure, and Dad, too, if she can bring him around. After that I'll see what I can find out about Dan Frazier. In the meantime, you and Bella are on coffee duty."

28

Camille Lee sat at her desk reading through the transcript of Bob Larson's interview B. had e-mailed to her earlier. The day before she'd been actively involved in the search for Bob Larson when he'd gone missing, but today she was benched. When she'd come into the office at seven a.m., she'd asked Stu if there was something he wanted her to do.

Hunched over his keyboard, he'd responded with a snarky growl. "I'm looking for this McKinzie guy, the one who robbed these poor people blind. Leave me alone and let me work."

Cami did just that. When she'd first signed on with High Noon, Mr. Simpson had warned her that Stu could be "a bit prickly." It turned out that on some days he was a veritable porcupine. Rather than be a target for today's temper tantrum, she hid out behind her computer, found her copy of the interview, and read through the whole thing.

In the course of her several months at High Noon, Cami had met both Bob and Edie Larson on occasion—met them and liked them. Bob Larson a murderer? No way! Couldn't be.

When Cami finished reading the interview, she checked out some of the news stories about the incident that were circulating on the Web. There was still no mention of the victims' names—pending notification of next of kin—but a police spokesman had acknowledged that the two people had died of multiple stab wounds.

Multiple stab wounds didn't sound like what Cami knew of Bob Larson, either. Yes, he'd been found with blood all over him, but the man was in his seventies. Did he have the physical strength to overpower two people and then stab them to death? Wielding a knife like that would take effort and endurance. It was easy to dismiss Bob as a hands-on killer, but maybe not as a mastermind. Cami realized that he could have had someone else do the job if he hadn't been physically carrying it out himself.

Looking over at Stu's littered desk, Cami noted the profusion of empty food wrappers and drink containers, not to mention the fact that Stu was still dressed in yesterday's clothes. That told her that he had been at his desk all night long, without so much as walking to the far end of the room and entering his private living space. No wonder he was grumpy, but still, Cami couldn't help wondering what he could have been doing all that time that had kept him chained to his desk.

Turning back to her own computer, Cami opened the list of shared files, scrolled through

Recently Added, and opened the newest of those, one entitled: "Phone Tracker." As soon as she started viewing it, she realized Stu must have spent much of the night working on this one file.

With a time stamp in the corner clicking off seconds and minutes, she watched the tracked movements of a dot labeled "Bob's Cell" overlaid on a satellite view of the area. The tracking began at a spot Cami recognized as the location of Sedona Shadows and eventually entered a neighborhood she recognized as Dan and Millie Frazier's. Then it turned on to a small cul-de-sac labeled "Elberta Drive."

Once on the street it stopped and remained stationary for some time. Cami fast-forwarded through that, but when she slowed the footage down and the label moved again twenty minutes had elapsed on the time stamp. Cami followed the moving cell phone up a long driveway. At the top, there was another short pause before there was a second burst of activity—first into a structure that was evidently a garage, then after another brief pause, into the house, then back to the garage, and finally back out into the yard. It paused again before coming to rest at another location under what appeared to be a large tree. Shortly after the phone entered the garage the first time, Stu had added yet another component to the video—layering in a recording of a concurrent 911 call that came complete with its own matching time stamp.

As far as Cami was concerned, the phone tracker file declared straight out that Bob Larson was innocent. But if he hadn't killed Dan and Millie Frazier, who had? Cami went back to the transcript. The bloody knife—presumably the murder weapon or one of them—had been found in Bob's Bronco. That meant Bob and the killer or killers had been at the Fraziers' residence at the same time. Realizing that sent Cami straight back to her copy of the transcript and to the words "landscaping truck."

So where was the vehicle? Bob claimed he had seen it there when he drove up, but it must have been long gone by the time the cops arrived. Did it belong there or not? Where had it gone and who had been driving? Was the person behind the wheel one of the perpetrators, or was he a potential witness?

Shutting down her computer, Cami grabbed both her iPad and laptop and then pulled her purse out of her desk drawer. She slammed the drawer shut hard enough that Stu looked up and glanced in her direction.

"Where are you going?" he asked.

"Out," she told him.

After all, two could play that game.

29

Haley slept some, but not well. Mostly she tossed and turned. The next morning, still rummy from lack of sleep, she staggered into the kitchen later than usual to start coffee and make breakfast. Most mornings she'd be dressed and ready to go to work by now, but today, with no news from Agent Ferris about when they'd be allowed back into the office, going to work wasn't an option. She had just poured oatmeal into the pot of boiling water when the doorbell rang.

It was 7:40. Having someone turn up unannounced on the front porch at this hour of the morning was very much out of the ordinary. Concerned about waking Gram, Haley hurried to the door before the visitor could ring the bell again. Opening the front door she found a man she recognized standing on the far side of the sturdy security screen.

"Detective Eric Drinkwater, Sedona PD," he said, holding out his ID wallet. "I'd like to speak to you for a few minutes."

"Yes, of course," she said, stepping out onto the porch. "I don't want to awaken my grandmother."

Detective Drinkwater, wearing a suit and tie, left Haley feeling ill at ease and self-conscious in a tank top, shorts, and flip-flops.

"I'm assuming you're aware of the Frazier double homicide?"

Haley nodded. "Yes," she said faintly. "I heard about that."

"I understand you worked for Mr. Frazier for a long time."

"Eighteen years. For part of that time I worked for Millie as well, less so once Dan started working out of the Ocotillo Fund Management headquarters down in Phoenix."

"In other words, you knew him well."

Haley nodded. "Probably better than most."

"Are you aware of anyone who might have wished to harm either one of them?"

Haley sighed. "I don't know of anyone in particular, but after the news about OFM's bankruptcy broke yesterday morning, I'm sure lots of people are understandably upset with him right now. Still, I can't imagine that any of those folks, including Bob Larson, would go so far as to physically attack Dan or Millie."

Drinkwater blinked in surprise at that. "What makes you mention Mr. Larson?"

Haley realized it was time to come clean. "I saw the whole thing," she answered.

"You saw the murders?"

"No, not the murders, but I was nearby during most of the investigation. When cops and aid cars started showing up at Dan's place, the woman who lives across the street, Julia King, came by the office to let me know. She brought me back to her house. I was there from late morning until late afternoon. I saw Mr. Larson's vehicle—his Bronco—parked in Dan's yard, and when one of the cop cars came down the driveway, I'm pretty sure I saw him in the backseat—like he was under arrest or something."

"Bob Larson is someone you recognize on sight?"

"I work in a small business," Haley said. "It's my job to recognize all of our clients on sight, including you, Detective Drinkwater. I believe we carry your homeowners policy. Bob and Edie Larson have been clients for years, too. Dan handled their investment accounts personally, but the office here in Sedona still handles their insurance needs. So, yes, I know Bob personally. I know his wife, and I know both their vehicles, too. By the way, there aren't that many ancient red Broncos driving around here in Sedona, especially ones with old-style plates."

"So if OFM went broke and Bob and Edie lost a ton of money, is it likely that they might have held Dan responsible?"

"I suppose," Haley said, "but the same applies to plenty of other people here in town as well."

"When did you first learn of the Ocotillo bankruptcy issue?"

"I didn't know the first thing about it until a crew of guys from the SEC turned up on Monday afternoon and ordered us to shut down."

"Dan didn't call you or give you any advance warning?"

Haley bit her lip. "No," she said.

"Doesn't that strike you as odd? If you'd worked for him for that long, shouldn't Dan have been the one to let you know things were going south?"

Odd? Haley thought. *It wasn't just odd. It was infuriating!* But she wasn't about to speak ill of the dead or run down the man who had always been her mentor. "He was probably dealing with other pressing issues," she said.

"Were you aware of any clients who were particularly upset when they heard the news about Ocotillo Fund Management going bankrupt?"

Haley thought about Frank Merrick, standing there with his placard and yelling insults at her. "Maybe," she said. Then, after a pause she added, "Probably."

Drinkwater appeared to be gearing up for another question when the screech of a smoke alarm pierced the air. "The oatmeal," Haley moaned, turning on her heels and racing inside. The smell of burned cereal filled the whole house. In the kitchen, Haley grabbed the smoldering pan with a hot pad and flung it into the sink. After turning cold water full blast on the stinking remains, she raced toward the smoke alarm panel and keyed in the code.

By the time Haley returned to the living room, she found Gram, still wearing her nightgown and robe, standing face-to-face with Eric Drinkwater. Haley couldn't tell which had unnerved Gram more—the screeching smoke alarm or finding a strange man in the living room.

"Sorry about that," Haley said to the detective, then to Gram she added, "He's here investigating the murders."

"Well," Gram said. "Since you're already here at this ungodly hour of the morning, are you making any progress?"

Ignoring Gram's question, Eric focused on Haley. "Although people here in town are already well aware of who the victims are, we're still trying to locate their next of kin. I was hoping maybe you could help us with that."

"Dan and Millie have no kids and hence no grandchildren. Dan's folks are both gone, and he was an only child. I believe Millie still has people back in Missouri—an aunt or uncle or two and maybe some cousins," Haley offered. "I still have their Christmas card list on my computer, so I could give you names and addresses, but there's a problem with accessing that list right now."

Bristling at being ignored, Gram went over and sank into her recliner. She didn't suggest that Eric should have a seat—a subtle way of returning the favor and letting him know she hoped he'd be leaving sometime soon. Failing to take the hint, however, he settled onto the sofa.

"I noticed that on both of their phones, you're listed as a person to call in case of an emergency."

"That's true," Haley agreed, "and has been for years. They didn't have anyone else."

"She's also their executrix and will most likely

have to be responsible for arranging Dan and Millie's funerals," Gram interjected. "Which means
she needs to know how soon the bodies will be
released from the morgue."

Drinkwater looked from Gram back to Haley.
"If you're their executrix, are you also a beneficiary
under their wills?"

"Not of their wills. With both of them gone,
most of their joint estate will be going to charity,
although I am the named beneficiary on one of the
life insurance policies. I'll also need to have copies
of the death certificates so I can initiate the death
claims."

There was a sudden shift in Drinkwater's
demeanor. Haley guessed that the possibility of
her receiving some kind of financial gain had just
caused the detective to move her into his suspect
column.

"Why would you be a beneficiary?"

"It's part of a business continuation plan," she
explained. "In the event of Dan's death, it allows
me to purchase my part of the book of business—
the insurance portion—from the estate."

"Is that plan still in effect?" Drinkwater asked.

"Yes," Haley replied.

"Which gives you a certain amount of motiva-
tion as well, doesn't it, Ms. Jackson?"

"I suppose it does," Haley agreed.

"Which means I'll also need a complete listing
of your activities from yesterday—where you went,
when you arrived, and the names of people who
can account for your presence there."

Gram rose from her chair, favoring Detective Drinkwater with a steely-eyed glare. "I am not going to sit here and listen while you grill my granddaughter about something she couldn't possibly have done," she snapped. "Since our oatmeal is obviously burned to a crisp, I'm going to get dressed so we can go somewhere to have a decent breakfast. If you know what's good for you, young man, by the time I'm ready to go, you will be, too."

30

Dressed casually in a pair of jeans, a short-sleeved T-shirt, and sandals, Ali set out for her first stop that morning—Sedona Shadows. She didn't bother calling before she went, and she didn't worry about showing up too early, either. Her mother had always been an early riser, and she still was. When Ali tapped on the door, a fully dressed Edie answered, holding a finger to her lips.

"Your father's still sleeping," she whispered. "I'll get my key, and we can go to the dining hall."

"After everything that happened yesterday, it's not surprising that he didn't sleep much," Ali said when her mother stepped back out of the apartment and they headed down the long, carpeted corridor.

"It's not just a matter of not sleeping," Edie said. "The crazy old coot was out running the streets until all hours—and in my car, too."

"Running the streets?" Ali asked. "What do you mean?"

"Just that," Edie said. "When I woke up this

morning there was a rose on my pillow. I can tell you for sure there was no rose there when I went to sleep. So I checked the trash. Sure enough, the receipt was right there with a time stamp—1:27 a.m. I can't imagine what Bobby was thinking—running off to the store like that in the middle of the night. I liked the rose, though," she added. "That was sweet of him. Now if we just didn't have to worry about Eric Drinkwater shipping him off to jail."

"I don't think you need to worry so much about the jail part," Ali counseled. "I believe B. and Stu have come up with a way to corroborate Dad's version of events about when he arrived at the Fraziers' place and what happened once he got there."

"Really?" Edie wanted to know. "How can they do that?"

"Remember the phone tracking system you helped us put on Dad's phone? It allows us to see exactly when he arrived at the scene, and it lets us follow his movements once he got there."

"Are you serious?" Edie asked.

Ali nodded.

"Oh my goodness!" Edie exclaimed as relief flooded her face. "I just love that husband of yours to pieces. And yes, I do remember the phone tracker incident. I had to smuggle Bobby's phone out of the bedroom while your father was in the shower. Is he going to have to know about it now? Once he finds out, he'll have a fit."

"Maybe so," Ali said, "but seeing as how it's something that should help exonerate him, I doubt he'll be too upset."

"One can always hope," Edie said, but she sounded unconvinced.

Once in the dining hall, Ali got coffee for both of them and then found a table while Edie went to fill a plate from the breakfast buffet.

"You look tired," Ali said when Edie sat down across from her.

"Of course I'm tired," Edie said. "You should have seen the mess those people left behind after that whole search warrant circus. I was up half the night putting things away where they belonged. But about that phone tracker evidence. Does it really mean we'll be able to put this whole homicide nonsense behind us?"

"Not necessarily. Detective Drinkwater may still decide to charge him."

"Does Drinkwater know about the phone tracker?"

"No, at least not so far."

"Since you haven't told the detective, maybe Bobby doesn't need to know about it, either."

Unnoticed by either woman, Bob Larson appeared behind them. "I don't need to know about what?" he asked.

Ali noticed at once that he wasn't quite his old self yet, but he was remarkably better than he had been the day before.

"Busted," Ali answered with a grin. "B. installed a tracking app on your phone that documented your movements at the crime scene yesterday, one that seems to corroborate your version of events."

Bob turned to his wife. "I suppose you knew all about B. doing that?"

"As a matter of fact I did," Edie said. "I even helped him do it."

"Well then," Bob said, "sounds like it's a good thing you did. And now I'm going to go get some breakfast. I'm starving."

As he walked through the buffet area, Ali noticed him nodding and greeting people. So did Edie.

"I can hardly believe it," she said. "He said it was a good thing? Yesterday he said he'd never be able to face coming to the dining room again, and yet here he is. What changed?"

"No idea," Ali said. "Just be glad it did."

When her father returned to the table, Ali explained the tracking results to him.

"So it sounds as though we can breathe easier about the murder charge, but there's still the money situation." He looked at Edie before adding, "I applied for a job last night."

"You did what?"

"When I bought you that rose at Safeway, I filled out a job application. I figure I could work in the produce department or the deli, either one."

To Ali's dismay, her mother burst into tears. "Oh, Bobby," she said. "You shouldn't have."

"Bought you the rose or applied for a job?"

"Both," she blubbered.

He reached across the table and covered her hands with his. "One way or the other, old girl, we'll get through this together," he said. "If we cancel the cruise and cut our expenses, even a part-time job might make enough of a difference."

Ali felt her own eyes mist over. "Speaking of part-time jobs," she began, "that's the real reason I stopped by this morning. To offer you jobs."

"What kind of jobs?" Edie asked suspiciously.

"B. and I have decided that High Noon is going to go after Jason McKinzie. We suspect he's hidden money away somewhere, and we intend to find it."

"I'm all for going after that creep," Edie said, "but aren't the cops the ones who are supposed to do that?"

"The feds will be tracking him down to put him under arrest. Some of our backdoor methods won't work for that, but they'll work just fine for going after his money."

"How do you do that?" Bob wanted to know.

"The first step in any investigation is learning as much about the target as possible. That means we need to know everything there is to learn—from where he went to kindergarten when he was a kid to where he buys his underwear now. We'll be looking into his friends and associates as well as his romantic attachments. That's why Stu Ramey is doing a data-mining job on him."

"A what?"

"Data mining," Ali explained. "That means he's gathering all the online background material he can locate on Mr. McKinzie. Believe me, there's plenty of that. Mounds of it, in fact, and all of it needs to be thoroughly catalogued and analyzed.

Stu, and to a lesser extent Cami, need to stay focused on our paying customers. We can't divert them away from that long enough to do this job justice. We're asking you to do it instead."

"Sort through it, you mean?"

"Yes," Ali replied. "Stu is a wizard when it comes to gathering the material, and he'll ferret out every smidgen of that there is to be found. But he doesn't have the necessary people skills to go through the material, read between the lines, and sort out who Jason McKinzie really is from who he wants people to believe he is. As for Cami? She's too young."

"You're hiring us because you think we're old enough?" Edie asked.

"No," Ali said, "because I think you're wise enough. As you go through the material piece by piece, be on the lookout for anything that doesn't fit."

"We wouldn't be doing anything illegal, would we?" Bob asked. "I'm already in enough trouble with law enforcement."

"No," Ali assured him. "Stu will simply amass everything that's out there either in the public domain or on the Web. It'll be up to you to go through it, looking for needles of information in all that hay."

"Sounds doable to me," Bob said, "especially if it means recovering some of the money."

"Yes," Edie agreed. "You don't have to pay us to do that, but when can we start?"

"Today if you want, but only when you agree that High Noon is paying you."

There was a momentary pause. "All right," Bob

agreed at last. "You drive a hard bargain. Where do we work?"

"You'll need to drive over to Cottonwood. Stu will be accessing the information on our secure server, and we want to keep what he finds secure. We'll set up workstations for you there so the sorting can be done on-site."

Edie frowned. "I've heard talk about secure servers on the news, but I didn't know regular people had them."

"You'd be surprised," Ali said with a smile, "although I'm not sure High Noon counts as regular people."

31

Tanna Romberg's Flights for Life call out had come through on her cell phone just after four a.m.

"We need you," the dispatcher said in her ear. "Terrible car crash south of Hoover Dam—a mini-van carrying a soccer team. Two critical patients have been airlifted to Vegas. Less severely injured are being transported to Kingman. How fast can you be there?"

"In Kingman?"

"Yes."

At that hour of the morning, Tanna estimated there wouldn't be much traffic between her home in Glendale, Arizona, and the Deer Valley Airport just north of the 101 Loop. As a volunteer for Flights for Life, Tanna was responsible for transporting human blood products to cities and towns all over Arizona. Kingman, located in the far northwestern corner of the state, was a place she'd flown into often. To drive there from Phoenix would take close to three hours. Her Piper Cherokee 235 could cut that three-hour trip down to one and a little bit.

"Tell the courier to meet me at Cutter Aviation at the Deer Valley Airport in forty-five," she said, scrambling out of bed and heading for the bathroom. "Since I'm on call, the aircraft is already fully fueled. All I'll need to do is my preflight check."

As predicted, there was zero traffic on I-17 as Tanna headed north. By the time the courier arrived at the FBO and handed her the distinctive cooler box labeled HUMAN BLOOD it was going on five a.m. The flight was smooth and uneventful— dark with glittering stars in a black sky as she flew north and with the sun fully up when she headed back south at 7:30.

Soaring over the mostly brown landscape, Tanna realized that she'd be landing in full rush hour. It would probably take her longer to drive home from the airport than it would take to fly from Kingman to Phoenix.

Her return flight path took her south over Wickenburg and then above Highway 60 before vectoring the aircraft in for an east/west landing at Deer Valley Airport. Tanna was already at a fairly low altitude in her gradual descent as she approached Loop 303. An occasional flight instructor, she'd often flown over this area with students doing touch-and-go landings. Nearby a huge but deserted gravel pit in the middle of nowhere was a recognizable landmark. When sunlight glinted off something down there, it caught her attention.

Peering down she saw a vehicle there—a single vehicle.

Flights loaded with precious cargo—blood flights—were straight up and down affairs, but the trips home were usually much more leisurely, with occasional stops along the way for breakfast or lunch. This time, something about a single vehicle parked in a lonely gravel pit at that hour of the morning bothered her. Maybe it was the Silver Alert she'd seen earlier on her way to the airport—an elderly missing man driving a white Ford F-150 pickup truck.

Shrugging to herself, she turned back and sent the Cherokee into a series of turns around a point, all the while keeping the vehicle in the gravel pit in view. As the plane flew lower and lower, more details came into focus. Yes, it was a pickup truck—a white pickup truck. Then, taking the plane even lower, she saw what looked like two people lying on the ground. They didn't move as the shadow of the plane flew over them, and she knew at once that they were dead.

Pulling back on the yoke, she brought the plane climbing back into the air, calling it in as she went. "I've just spotted two people on the ground in a deserted gravel pit between the 60 and I-17, north of the 303. Can't tell for sure, but I think they're both dead."

32

Haley and Gram lingered over breakfast at the Sugarloaf Café. Gram had her usual, but Haley was happy to have bacon and eggs rather than oatmeal for a change. She was also glad to have someone else doing the cooking.

"How do you suppose she knew?" Gram asked.

The question barely registered. On her side of the table, Haley had been busy creating a mental must-do list: arrange funerals, reopen office, go to the bank, buy new saucepan.

"Who are we talking about?" she asked.

"Jessica Denton," Gram answered. "When she came to the house last night, she already knew Dan and Millie were dead. But Eric Drinkwater just told us that they still haven't released the names."

"She probably talked to one of the girls from the office," Haley said. "It wasn't exactly top secret."

Haley's phone rang just then, with the words "UNKNOWN CALLER" showing on the screen.

"Ms. Jackson?" Agent Ferris inquired.

"Yes."

"I know you're anxious to be back up and running. We've sorted through the paper files and digitally copied and catalogued everything we need from them. We've copied the computer files as well. A truck is on its way back up I-17 right now to bring all your stuff back to you."

"What about a key to the office?" Haley asked. "You changed the locks, remember?"

"The driver will have one for you. You'll need to make copies."

Gee thanks, Haley thought as she ended the call, *and have a nice day to you, too!*

"What?" Gram asked.

"The SEC is returning our files. I'll need to call the girls and have them come in."

"Well, take me home first," Gram said. "With all you'll need to do today, you won't want me in your way."

"I'll take you home on one condition," Haley said.

"What's that?"

"You promise not to try cleaning that burned saucepan. It's wrecked, and I don't want you going after it with scouring pads or sandpaper."

"That's the problem with people these days," Gram grumbled. "They'd rather buy new than work at fixing what they've got."

"Promise?" Haley insisted.

"Oh, all right."

Feeling energized, Haley paid the bill and drove back to Art Barn Road. On the way, she called Carmen. "Call out the troops," she said. "A truck is coming up from Phoenix with our files, and I'd like everyone on hand. Let them know there's no need to dress up. This is going to be more like a moving day than a working day. We'll be in the office, but we won't be open for business. I have a feeling what the SEC is sending back to us won't be nearly as well organized as it was when they hauled it away."

When Haley and Gram entered the house, the smell of charred oatmeal assailed their nostrils despite the fact that Haley had opened all the windows before they left for breakfast. While Haley went to change into something more suitable than shorts and flip-flops, Gram set about going around the house closing the windows.

"Haley," Gram called urgently a minute or so later. "Come look at this."

"What?" Haley asked, zipping up a pair of jeans as she hurried out of the bedroom. She found Gram in the laundry room, standing in front of the window.

"Someone's been here," Gram said. "Look at the screen."

The bottom of the screen had been sliced open right along the frame. Some effort may have been made to push the screen back into place, but it had bowed back out, leaving a visible gap at the bottom.

"Do you think whoever did it is still here?" Gram whispered.

Haley looked out. In order to access the window, someone would have had to use a ladder, and no ladder was visible. The dead bolts on both the front and back doors were still locked. That meant that the intruder must have exited the house the same way he had entered.

"I'm sure they're gone."

"Do we call 911?"

"Let's see if anything is missing first."

Together, they explored the whole house. The few valuables they had were still where they belonged, but Haley could tell that everything in her room had been subjected to a quick but thorough search. Whoever it was had been looking for something specific, but what? And why? The idea of some stranger pawing through her underwear drawer and clothing left Haley feeling queasy.

Her first thought was that maybe it was some kid, playing hooky and doing a little breaking and entering on the side. No, she realized. This was something far more sinister than a youthful lark.

"Come on, Gram," Haley said. "Like it or not, you're spending the day with me at the office. No way I'm leaving you home alone."

"Shouldn't we call the cops?" Gram asked again.

"And tell them what? That someone broke into our home and took nothing? When it comes to attention from law enforcement, breaking and entering is a long way down the list of priorities, especially in terms of a police department suddenly faced with a double homicide."

Haley thought she knew how Eric Drinkwater would react. Something on the order of "If someone broke into your house, searched it, but didn't take anything, what do you suppose they were looking for? And is there a chance that this has something to do with the Frazier homicides?"

"No," she added aloud to Gram. "I don't need another visit from Eric Drinkwater today."

"But," Gram objected, "if I come to your office, I'll miss *Judge Judy* and *Dr. Phil.*"

"No you won't," Haley told her. "There's a TV set in the break room. You can watch on that."

Arriving at the office before the truck or any of the staff, Haley was shaken by what she saw there. The flower arrangements that had been mounded around the front entrance had been knocked over and scattered. The message "Thou Shalt Not Steal!" had been scrawled in vivid red paint and three-foot-tall letters across the entire expanse of the storefront.

Leaving Gram in the Honda for the moment, Haley began cleaning up the mess, salvaging the arrangements that were still relatively intact and dragging the rest to a nearby Dumpster. She wasn't at all surprised that Carmen—always on time and always ready to help—was the first to arrive.

"What do you need me to do?"

Haley went back to the car and pulled her wallet out of her purse. "Go over to the hardware store," she said, handing over several twenties. "Buy a five-gallon bucket, some squeegees, and a gallon or so of graffiti remover. Maybe, before the truck gets here, we can get rid of most of the paint on the windows and walls."

By the time the truck finally arrived, the graffiti had mostly been wiped clean and the flower wreckage had been cleaned up. A two-man crew plus Agent Ferris and a driver had come to Sedona to remove the files. The return trip was accomplished with a crew of one—a surly driver—who didn't take kindly to being told dumping the boxed files out on the sidewalk was unacceptable.

Haley saw at once that her concerns about the state of the returning files were well founded. What had left the office in neatly organized and well-labeled Bankers Boxes came back in a muddled mess. The boxes, many of them missing tops, ended up in teetering, haphazard stacks just inside the front door. Office computers, treated with the same contempt, were left in a pile of hardware that looked more like spilled pieces from a mechanical jigsaw puzzle than they did any kind of working office equipment.

As the driver carried the last box in from the truck, he dropped it from waist height, spilling the contents and sending a spray of files slithering across the tiled floor. Surprisingly enough, Haley couldn't have been more pleased. She recognized the spilled files as ones from her own desk. That meant she'd been spared the effort of going through the boxes searching for that particular one.

"That's it, then," the driver said, dusting off his hands as if relieved to be finished with some distasteful task. He turned to go, but Haley followed on his heels.

"Key, please," she demanded, holding out her hand.

"Oh yeah," he muttered, reaching for his pocket. "That's right. I almost forgot."

Like hell you did, Haley thought, suspecting that his supposed case of forgetfulness had been far more deliberate than accidental. She wanted to slap him, but she didn't.

Instead, she turned and marched back into the building, where Carmen was getting ready to rake up the spilled files.

"Thanks," Haley said. "Don't bother with those. I'll take care of them. They actually came from my desk."

Halfway through picking up the files Haley located the one she needed. It was labeled FINAL DIRECTIVES. Inside she found three envelopes—one for Carol Hotchkiss, one for Dan Frazier, and one for Millie. Carol Hotchkiss was still very much alive. As for Dan and Millie?

Fighting back tears, Haley finished refilling the Bankers Box and carried it back to her desk. Then, slipping the Dan and Millie envelopes into her purse, she headed for the door. Carmen was back at the reception desk, still fielding phone calls and turning away the occasional customer.

"I'm going to be out for a while," Haley said. "Can you look in on my grandmother occasionally?"

"Sure thing."

"As for all those messages? When I get back, I'll start returning those phone calls."

33

When Cami Lee had hired on with High Noon Enterprises, her official title was assistant to Stu Ramey. Most of the time, things were fine between them. She had figured out early on that a big part of Stu's brilliance had to do with Asperger's syndrome. She may have been called his "assistant," but in a very real way he was also her charge.

Early on, too, she realized that trying to steer him away from his steady diet of junk food wasn't a good plan for either of them, so she did what she was asked to do—shadowed Stuart as much as possible; tried her best to learn his skills and techniques; and attempted to smooth the roiling waters when something disturbed him. The man may have been totally at home in front of a keyboard and at ferreting out cyber information, but he was at a loss when it came to ordinary human intercourse.

All of this meant that Cami walked a fine line every day. There were times when his abrupt mood swings were too much even for her to handle, and today was one of those days. The half-hour drive from Cottonwood to Sedona would give Cami a chance to cool off and get her temper back under control.

She called B.'s number. When he didn't answer, she left a message. "I read the transcript you sent and saw the phone tracker clip," she said. "Since Stu's having one of his bad days, I'm ducking out of the office. If you need me, I'm headed to Sedona to see if I can get a line on the landscaping truck Mr. Larson said was at the crime scene. The truck may have nothing to do with it, but I thought we should cover that base anyway, just in case."

During the remainder of the drive, Cami more than half expected Mr. Simpson or Ali would phone back to call her off. After all, she was doing this strictly on her own initiative. No one had asked her or told her to look for the truck, nor was finding it remotely related to her official job description. Still, striking out on her own to do something useful felt pretty damned good. By the time she'd pulled over and stopped at the corner of Elberta Drive and Orchard Lane, put on her lanyard, and grabbed her iPad and purse, she was feeling even better.

Cami Lee had always wanted to be a detective. Now, striding up that first walkway and preparing to ring her first doorbell, she felt as though she was finally doing what she'd been supposed to do the whole time. She might be little more than a self-appointed detective, but she was a detective nonetheless, searching for answers in a double homicide investigation. One thing Cami knew for certain was this: if her parents had the foggiest inkling of what she was doing right then, they would have been appalled.

Her parents lived in the world of academia and engaged in a kind of oppressive snobbishness that drove Cami nuts. Her father, Cheng Lee, had come to the U.S. from Taiwan in the mid-1980s. Now a distinguished professor of robotics at Stanford, he was incredibly proud of having lived up to the name his parents had bestowed on him, as if by giving him the name Cheng, which means "accomplished," they had somehow foreshadowed his future success.

Cami's mother, Sue Ling Lee, came from somewhat more humble beginnings. Her parents, Cami's grandparents, still owned and operated a family restaurant in Chinatown. It was now a second-generation business, and they had fully expected their daughter, Xiu Ling, to follow in their footsteps and make it a third-generation. Much to her parents' dismay, Xiu Ling had zero interest in operating a restaurant. She had won a scholarship to UCLA, where she had majored in French literature, another puzzling choice that had mystified her parents.

Determined to turn away from her roots, the moment Xiu had turned twenty-one, she had gone to court and changed her name from Xiu ("beautiful") Ling to just plain Sue Ling. The following year at an antiwar rally, she met a handsome young graduate student from Taiwan whose student visa was about to run out. The rest, as they say, is history.

Cami sometimes joked that her parents' relationship was a "green card marriage gone bad," in that the two of them had never quite gotten around to getting a divorce. They were both full professors teaching at Stanford. They lived in the same household but operated in different hemispheres. The only thing they had in common was their daughter, which made Cami a constant bone of contention. Cheng had adamantly opposed naming his daughter Camille, but Sue, with her own history as well as her background in French literature, had argued for something that wasn't Chinese but still sounded "exotic." Cheng wanted a traditional daughter—one who was smart and dutiful and did as she was told. Sue wanted a rebel. And then there were Cami's maternal grandparents, who had targeted Cami as the next likely prospect for taking over the restaurant.

For a time it looked as though Cami's father would come out on top in the three-way tug-of-war. Cami was a shy and bookish youngster. Then, at age seven, her life took an abrupt turn with the release of the movie *Crouching Tiger, Hidden Dragon*. Cami was both astonished and enchanted to see a girl who looked just like her doing such amazing things. How was that possible?

As soon as the movie came out on DVD, Cami bought a copy and wore it out with repeated playings. But she did something else as well—she asked her parents if she could study martial arts. Her father and grandparents both said no; her mother not only said yes, she also made it happen by packing Cami off to a gym, where she had exceeded everyone's expectations, including her own, in the art of kung fu. On her first day of high school when a kid on the bus was teasing her about her name and wondering if she was "Chinee or Frenchee," she had simply decked him. She had also gotten detention for the first time ever, but there was no more bullying about her name, ever.

The punch-out on the bus wasn't the absolute end of Cami's being her father's dutiful daughter. No longer shy, she had still been bookish and smart. Her desire to go into law enforcement so she could "help people" was a career choice her parents and grandparents had all derided in unison. It was one of the few instances where Cami could ever remember all of them being in complete agreement.

At age eighteen, taking the line of least resistance, she had more or less acceded to her father's wishes. Rather than enrolling at Stanford, she had gone to her mother's alma mater, UCLA, and come away with double cum laude degrees in computer science and electrical engineering. Upon graduation she had taken the job with High Noon and moved to Arizona—again something neither of her parents wanted. That bit of defiance had been Cami's way of taking control of her own destiny.

On the drive over from Cottonwood, Cami had come up with a suitable cover story. The first time she used it was the worst.

"My name is Camille Lee," she said in a rush, trying not to stammer over the words. "My employer, High Noon Enterprises, is helping the insurance company assess the property damage that occurred at the Frazier residence yesterday. We're hoping to locate possible witnesses the same way the cops are, and we're also hoping to locate information on a landscaping truck that was supposedly seen in the neighborhood around that time."

Mention of a pending insurance claim seemed to help put people at ease. Even so, no one was especially eager to talk. Of course they were shocked by what had happened to Dan and Millie—and in such a safe neighborhood, too. But they were also wary of being sucked into any aspect of the investigation. Everyone denied having seen a stray truck, and if any of them had security cameras on their property, they didn't mention them. Twelve houses later, Cami still had nothing.

Stymied, Cami returned to her car and pondered her options. Should she give up and go back home, or should she keep trying? Due to the date stamp on the phone tracker film she knew exactly when Bob Larson had arrived at the Fraziers' residence. If the landscaping truck had been there when Bob arrived and was gone before the cops showed up, that left only a small window for its departure.

Cami Lee was nothing if not stubborn. Studying her iPad, she located all the possible routes a driver might have taken in leaving the crime scene. Once she had mapped those out, she hit the bricks again. After another hour of diligent canvassing, Cami finally hit pay dirt at the Apple Tree B & B at the corner of Jordan Road and Apple Avenue.

"This is about what happened to Dan and Millie Frazier?" the owner, Martha Brown, asked in response to Cami's bogus insurance claim introduction.

Cami nodded. "A strange vehicle, a pickup, was supposedly spotted near the crime scene," she explained. "I notice you have several security cameras aimed toward the street. It's possible one of them might have captured an image of the truck either coming or going."

"I heard about the murders," Martha said, "and I knew Millie well. If looking at my security footage will help catch the guy who did it, you're more than welcome. Come in and make yourself at home. The monitor's back in the office. You can work there if you like. Would you care for some coffee?"

"Thanks," Cami said. "I'm fine."

Within ten minutes of fast-forwarding through the footage, Cami located the first images of what turned out to be several pickup trucks. The one Cami thought most promising was one that had passed the B & B going southbound at 10:01 a.m. That would be time enough for the vehicle to have driven away from the Fraziers' place while Bob was still on the 911 call inside either the house or garage.

The image wasn't the best. The grainy views of the license plates left a lot to be desired, but Cami thought she saw at least two blurry passengers inside the vehicle.

After downloading the material into her own computer, Cami called Stuart.

"Hey," he said when he answered. "Where'd you go? I thought you were going out for doughnuts or something. You've been gone a long time."

Cami was gratified to hear that Stu had at least noticed she was gone.

"I've actually been tracking the landscape truck from the crime scene," she said. "And I've gotten a bead on it."

"Really? Where?"

"On security camera footage from the Apple Tree B & B on Jordan. I just sent you several clips. The resolution on this monitor is crap. I'm hoping you'll be able to enhance it."

"I'll get right on it, and I'll institute some traffic cam searches, too. On your way back, though, do pick up some doughnuts."

Someone with more people skills might have told her "Great work," but compliments weren't part of Stuart Ramey's skill set, and Cami didn't fault him for it.

"Don't expect those doughnuts anytime soon," she warned him. "I want to go through some earlier footage to see if I can find out when they arrived."

As she finished the sentence, Cami realized that Stuart was long gone. The man may have been big on doughnuts, but he was useless when it came to hanging around for something he regarded as unnecessary chitchat.

34

Homicide detective Dave Holman was in his car headed for Prescott for a routine briefing when the call came in. A private pilot had reported spotting what she thought were two bodies in a gravel pit north of the 303. The location was at the far south end of Yavapai County, but since it was outside any posted city limit, that made whatever it was his department's problem rather than anyone else's.

A single uniformed officer was on the scene when Dave arrived. "Looks like they were shot to shit, sir," the young deputy said. His name was Williams. Since he worked in Yavapai county's southern sector and most likely lived there as well, he wasn't someone Dave had encountered before.

After looking at the two bodies, Dave had to concur. Both victims—one Hispanic and the other Anglo—had been shot once, center mass. The shooter had been dead-on.

"Did you call the ME?"

"Yes, sir," Deputy Williams said. "He's on his way."

"And the truck?"

"I took a look inside. There's some stuff in bags in the back of the crew cab. I wouldn't be surprised if these two don't turn out to be a couple of burglars who've come to grief."

"Did you run the plates?"

"Came back to A.J. Landscaping, Peoria, Arizona. Registered to a guy named Alejandro Joaquín. So far it hasn't been reported missing or stolen."

Dave's first instinct was to go straight to Alejandro and start asking questions, but for right now his job was to stay where he was until after the ME did his preliminary report.

"No missing persons reports?"

"Not so far."

Walking around the bodies, Dave stopped next to the Hispanic guy, who had a handgun clutched in his fist.

"That doesn't fit," Dave told Deputy Williams, who was shadowing the detective's every move.

"What doesn't fit?"

"The gun. When the guy fell backwards, he would have been deadweight—two hundred and fifty pounds of deadweight. He would have hit hard and bounced on the hard gravel. The gun would have flown out of his hands. I'm guessing this will turn out to be our murder weapon, but neither one of these guys pulled the trigger."

Dave scanned the area for tracks and found none. He peered into the truck and agreed that the loot he saw there was probably property stolen from someone else. It took the ME an hour and a half to arrive on the scene from the morgue in Prescott. By then it was late morning and hot as hell. It was only a matter of minutes after that before Dave searched the victims' pockets and found their respective IDs—Alberto Joaquín and Jeffrey Hawkins. He handed them over to Deputy Williams and let him run them.

Williams returned with the names. "Ex-cons," he said, "both out on parole."

"No surprises there," Dave said. "And I'm guessing Alejandro and Alberto are some kind of close relations. Ever done a next of kin notification before, Deputy Williams?"

"No, sir."

"Well, you're about to."

35

Ali was a little out of sorts at having to accompany her parents over to Cottonwood to get them settled in. She had called the office expecting to talk to Cami and had been surprised when Stuart answered.

"Where's Cami?" she asked.

"Beats me. Getting doughnuts, I think."

"And B.?"

"Locked in his office," Stuart said. "Some big crisis in Switzerland. He's been on the phone for more than an hour."

When a call to Cami's phone went straight to voice mail, Ali gave up. She knew full well that anything out of the ordinary was likely to make the wheels come off Stuart's bus, and she didn't want to send her parents into the lion's den without having Cami there to run interference.

She was on her way to Cottonwood when Cami called her back. "Sorry I missed your call," Cami said breathlessly, "but I think I found it."

"Found what?"

"The landscaping truck from the crime scene. Stuart was in one of his moods. Once I looked at the phone tracker video, I knew I had a solid time frame to work with. All I had to do was locate usable security footage."

"And did you?"

"Yes, I just sent some to Stu and asked him to try enhancing it. Now I'm looking for the same truck in earlier footage to see if I can nail down an arrival time. I was talking to him when your call came in. What do you need?"

"Way to go, Cami!" Ali exclaimed. "As for what I thought I needed? Forget it. What I need now is for you to keep on doing exactly what you're doing."

When Ali's parents climbed out of Edie's Buick, they were back to squabbling. "He spent the whole trip backseat driving," Edie complained, "and I'm not driving him back home, either. We're going to rent a car and he can drive his own darned self."

"We can't afford for me to rent a car," Bob objected.

"Believe me," Edie huffed. "We can't afford not to."

"Besides," Bob said, "I don't have my wallet or my license."

"Come on, you two," Ali said. "Quit bickering."

She had intended to tell them about Cami's call, but knowing they'd both be all over Stu and peppering him with dozens of questions, she said nothing. Instead, she escorted them into the building, shuffled them past Stu's closed door, and led them into the office she occasionally used. It took time to set up their respective workstations. She put her father at the desk in front of a computer, helped him log on, and showed him the print routine. Then she located the directory in which Stuart had collected a vast amount of information on Jason McKinzie. Most of it was out there in public, but Ali knew that some of it came from Stu's backdoor methods and that eventually the results of the search would need to go away.

"I think it'll be easier for the two of you to sort all of this if you're doing it with paper copies," Ali explained. "Dad, your job is to go through each of these files and print whatever's applicable."

"What do you mean, 'applicable'?"

"Scan through all the links. Some of them may be ones where the search turned up one person named Jason and another named McKinzie. Delete all of those. Meanwhile, Mom will do the sorting. Once we're done with this material, it'll most likely end up in the shredder."

"But why go to all this trouble?" Bob asked. "Isn't there some kind of computer program that can sort all this stuff?"

"Computers are good at seeing what's there," Ali said. "I'm hoping the two of you will be smart enough to figure out what isn't."

"Yes," Edie chimed in. "She said we're supposed to look for something that doesn't fit."

"Fair enough," Bob said. "We'll do our best."

36

For Cami's next round of fast-forwarding, she started at midnight. At 7:33 a.m., she caught a break—several of them, in fact. For some reason, the northbound camera caught a clear view of the license plate, one that would take only a minimal amount of enhancing. And there was a logo of some kind on the driver's side door, one that had been invisible when the vehicle was traveling the other direction. And this time, there were clearly three passengers inside the truck rather than only two. So who was the third passenger—the one who was missing? Dan Frazier, maybe?

Seconds later, after loading the images and shipping them off to Stuart, Cami called him on the phone.

"I just sent you the first enhancement," he said, "the one of the license plate. I haven't had time to run it, and I'm still waiting for my doughnuts."

"I just sent you some additional footage," Cami said. "There's a logo of some kind on the driver's side door of the pickup. It's probably the name of the landscaping company."

"I suppose this means you want me to enhance this, too, even though we already have the license?"

"That's right," Cami said. "This time focus on the logo and on the passengers. I'm hoping for something we can send through your facial rec program."

"Faces of the killers?" Stuart asked.

Cami could tell from the sudden excitement in Stuart's voice that his black mood had lifted and that, for now, those missing doughnuts were forgotten.

"We can always hope," she said.

"On it," he said. "I'll get right back to you."

"So did that help?" Mrs. Brown asked as Cami took her leave.

"I hope so," Cami said. "But let me ask you something. Has anyone else come by asking about security camera footage?"

Martha shook her head. "No," she said. "You're the first."

"I probably won't be the last," Cami told her.

She was barely back inside her Prius when her iPad dinged with an arriving e-mail and an attached photo. The message on the e-mail said, "Running facial rec now." When Cami opened the photo, she saw a crystal-clear image of the truck with the stenciled words A.J. LANDSCAPING, PEORIA, ARIZONA legible in sharp relief on the driver's side door.

Inside the crew cab, three male faces were visible through the clear glass of the truck's untinted windows. The passenger in the front seat leaned against the window with his eyes closed. He was either asleep or unconscious.

Cami's iPad dinged again. Stuart's subject line told the story: "Front seat passenger, Dan Frazier." The accompanying photo was one of a graying man in his early sixties. The shot had been taken at some black tie event where Dan Frazier had been wearing a tuxedo.

The next e-mail ding brought a message with a different subject line and two attachments, this one for "Alberto Joaquín, driver." The photo was a mug shot and a second attachment was the man's rap sheet along with a summarizing notation from Stuart: "Did six years for grand theft auto. Released on parole six months ago."

The subject line for e-mail number three said: "Jeffrey Hawkins, backseat passenger." Again the attachments contained a mug shot and a rap sheet. Stuart's note added: "Served nine years for second degree murder. Released on good behavior five months ago."

Cami's heart pounded with excitement. She had her phone in hand and was ready to punch Ali's number when it rang with Stu's name in the window.

"What?" she said.

"Remember that plate you asked me to run a little while ago?" Stu asked.

"What about it?"

"I just heard on the scanner. A vehicle with a plate matching that number is now involved in an active homicide investigation somewhere north of Sun City. The Yavapai County Sheriff's Department has officers at the scene."

"Whoa," Cami breathed. "I need to tell Ali."

"Don't bother," Stu said. "She's in talking with B. right now. I'll tell her for both of us."

37

Knowing what her parents were doing would most likely amount to little more than busy-work, Ali felt somewhat guilty. Still, they both seemed happy to be doing something constructive. Leaving them to it, she went looking for B. and found him in his office, on the phone, and making arrangements for an afternoon overseas flight.

"What's going on?"

Raising a finger to indicate she should wait, he motioned her into a chair. "Big security breach in Zurich," he said, mouthing the words, then added into the phone, "Right. I'll hold."

"I left the house a little over an hour ago and you were on your way here. Now you're headed to Zurich. What happened?"

"Basel, actually. Some middle management jerk in our favorite drug conglomerate decided that he didn't have to abide by the security protocols we installed. Shortly after he bypassed them, the company's computers were hacked. Now the formulas for some of their most profitable proprietary drugs are being held for ransom."

"You've got to go?"

"Absolutely. Some things still require a personal presence, and this is one of them."

B. had been on hold the whole time Ali had been in the room. Now whoever he was waiting for came back on the line. "Okay," he said. "Thanks. You've been a huge help. I'll print my boarding pass as soon as it comes in."

"How long will you be gone?" Ali asked.

"Who knows?" B. said, sounding exasperated.

"Which means you're dumping the whole OFM problem in my lap?"

B. nodded. "Sorry about that. And you're going to be shorthanded. Stu is finishing up a couple of things with Cami right now. Then he'll be working full-time on this new crisis. In the meantime, I need to brief you on several items Stu brought to light overnight."

"About?"

"The OFM situation as well as the Frazier homicides."

"I'm all ears."

B. consulted his iPad. "At 2:16 p.m. on Monday afternoon, minutes before the SEC raid commenced, every computer on the OFM network crashed. Employees were still trying to reboot the system when the SEC showed up. Turns out the network didn't just crash. Someone released a powerful worm into the server that overwrote and reformatted every hard drive on their network, took down their cloud storage, and probably any other backup systems that might have been in place. Techs from the SEC attempted to intervene. They were never able to get things back up and running, and they couldn't retrieve any of the data, either."

"Everything is wiped?"

"Yes. That kind of secure delete operation—something that should have taken hours to accomplish—was over and done with in not much more than two. In other words, all of OFM's data—customer information, trading information, everything—went away."

"So it's someone with a whole lot of technical know-how."

"Indeed," B. agreed. "I've called Lance Tucker in on this and have him looking around on the dark web for anyone advertising those kind of services, but having to ferret out the kind of detailed information needed for the bankruptcy proceeding is going to be a monumental undertaking.

"And as long as we're talking bankruptcy," B. continued, "according to news reports, this bankruptcy thing supposedly came as a total surprise to everyone. Not so much. On Friday afternoon of last week, one of the OFM board members, an attorney named Eugene Lowensdahl, was tapped to serve as the CRO."

"What's that?"

"The chief restructuring officer. Think of it as the opposite of CFO, and you don't appoint a CRO unless you're anticipating filing for bankruptcy."

"Let me guess. A CRO is the guy in charge of liquidating assets and initiating clawbacks?"

"Bingo."

"Lowensdahl was appointed by whom?"

"That would be Jason McKinzie, who, as far as we can determine, is truly in the wind. He flew out of Sky Harbor on his way to Mexico City on Friday evening. No one has seen him since."

"He didn't appear for the bankruptcy filing on Monday?"

"Nope. As for the CRO? My guess is that the company is defunct, and there won't be any restructuring—mostly because there won't be sufficient assets for anything other than a complete liquidation."

"What about the building?"

"Funny you should ask. Stu found out just this morning that OFM's corporate headquarters on Central in Phoenix was sold for an undisclosed sum a little over three months ago. Since then, McKinzie has been leasing the space back from the new owners."

"Did anyone else in the company know about that sale?" Ali asked.

"Can't tell," B. replied. "Maybe, maybe not. From what Stu found, McKinzie's name was the only one on the deed."

"Is that even legal?" Ali asked. "In making a decision to liquidate a major asset like that, shouldn't he have had to consult with a board of directors and possibly report the sale to the SEC?"

"You'd think so, but Jason McKinzie hasn't been

coloring inside the lines for a very long time. I managed to get a face-to-face appointment with Eugene Lowensdahl for three o'clock this afternoon. Unfortunately, that ball is now in your court."

"Do we know anything about this Lowensdahl guy?"

"Yes," B. said. "He's a high-end attorney in Phoenix who has served on OFM's board of directors. He's also got something of a reputation as an MCP."

"Male chauvinist pig?" Ali asked with a laugh. "Are you kidding? I haven't heard that term in years."

"It evidently applies here. Years ago, Lowensdahl was sued and settled out of court for attempting to fire one of the female attorneys in his firm, claiming she refused to conform to the company dress code."

"Which was?" Ali asked.

"She evidently had the unmitigated nerve to come to work in a pantsuit."

"Since when doesn't a pantsuit constitute proper business attire?"

"That lawsuit was a couple of decades ago, but the story is still out there on the Internet. Since we need to impress this guy, you should definitely dress for success when you take the meeting."

Ali groaned, looking down at her casual summer-in-Sedona attire. "Heels and hose on a June afternoon in Phoenix? That should be fun. But tell me, what's this face-to-face supposed to accomplish?"

"As CRO, some of Lowensdahl's compensation will be based on a percentage of the money he brings back into play, either from clawbacks or from liquidating assets."

"Yes," Ali said, "with his focus mostly on the low-hanging fruit."

"That's true, but if we convince him that there may be far more low-hanging fruit out there, maybe we can also persuade him that High Noon can help him find it. More money in the pot means more money going back to the investors eventually, but also more money coming to him. Your job is to talk him into hiring High Noon to go looking for OFM's missing funds."

"When you say hiring I take it that's what you mean—hiring us, as in not tackling the job out of the kindness of our hearts?"

"Absolutely not!" B. exclaimed. "Not on your life. You and I both know we'd do it for free in a minute, but if we made that offer, Lowensdahl would never take us seriously. Tell him we want a percentage of whatever we recover."

"How much?"

"Let's say twenty-five percent, for starters."

"Twenty-five?" Ali demanded. "Are you kidding? That's outrageous. This is other people's money, B. It's my parents' money."

B. laughed. "Start high and give Lowensdahl a chance to drive a hard bargain. That's the only way to hook a lawyer, you know. Make him think you're charging an arm and a leg."

Just then Stu burst into the room. "Cami got a line on the vehicle, and I've identified the driver and both passengers."

"What vehicle are we talking about?" B. asked.

"The landscape truck."

"You mean the facial rec worked?" Ali asked.

"Right," Stu answered.

"Wait," B. said to Ali. "You already knew about this?"

"Cami called me about it on my way here. I hadn't had a chance to tell you."

"Tell me now."

Ali quickly recounted Cami's earlier phone call before they both turned back to Stu.

"I ran a facial rec on the passengers in the vehicle as it went north. One of them turns out to be Dan Frazier. The other two are ex-cons with extensive records." He handed Ali and B. two printouts that turned out to be rap sheets.

"These are the guys?" Ali asked. "Alberto Joaquín and Jeffrey Hawkins?"

Stu nodded. "I also ran the plates. Those lead back to an Alejandro Joaquín in Peoria. The thing is, I just heard over my scanner that a vehicle with a matching plate number is now involved in what they're calling an active homicide investigation— a double homicide investigation—north of Sun City."

"Are you kidding? A second double homicide in as many days?" Ali was aghast. "Yavapai County or Maricopa?"

"Yavapai."

Since Dave Holman was the sheriff department's lead homicide investigator, Ali knew the case was bound to have landed in his lap.

"It sounds like we need to talk to both Dave Holman and Eric Drinkwater ASAP."

"Not so fast," B. cautioned. "Don't go off the deep end and talk with Drinkwater until you run it past Dash."

"What about Cami?" Stu asked. "Do you want her to come back here?"

"No," Ali said. "Ask her to try to get in to see Dash Summers and show him what we have. If he gives the okay, Cami and I can stop by Sedona PD and show Detective Drinkwater what the two of you have found. I still need to interview the Frazier Insurance Agency employees. Maybe Cami can help with some of those since apparently I'm on my way to Phoenix for a three o'clock."

"But what about my doughnuts?" Stu objected. "Cami was supposed to pick them up."

Ali hurried around the desk and gave B. a brief good-bye kiss. "Don't worry about Lowensdahl," she told him. "But you'll need to text me the address." Then, on her way past Stu, she added, "As for the doughnuts? My folks are in my office working on the data sort. If I ask her to, I'm sure Mom will be glad to go on a doughnut run."

"Okay, then," Stu allowed grudgingly. "Glazed, not chocolate."

Ali headed out with a smile on her face. As long as strangers came to Stuart Ramey's lair bearing gifts of doughnuts or pizza, maybe they weren't that unwelcome after all. Her smile lasted only as long as it took for her to reach the parking lot, where she ran into the last person on earth she wanted to see right then—Detective Eric Drink-water himself.

"What are you doing here?" she demanded.

"What's your father doing here today?" he asked in return. "I went by Sedona Shadows, and the people there said he was down here working on his case—that you're working on his case. I'm here to remind you, Ms. Reynolds, that this is police business and you need to stay out of it. Interfering with a police investigation into a homicide turns out to be a felony."

"What we're doing has nothing to do with your business and everything to do with ours," Ali said, battling to hold her temper in check. "My father's attorney, Dash Summers, hired our firm, High Noon Enterprises, to do investigative work on behalf of my father's defense team. As a U.S. citizen, my father's allowed that, you know. He's entitled to a robust defense."

"Robust, my ass," Drinkwater growled. "And you know what I think? That you're a rich bitch who believes her money gives her the right to push everybody around."

"And I think you're an overbearing jackass," she returned. "Since this is a free country, we're both entitled to our opinions. But let me remind you, Detective Drinkwater, this is private property. Unless you happen to have a valid arrest warrant in hand, you're trespassing, and if I call the cops here in Cottonwood, the ones who show up won't be coming from Sedona PD. Got it?"

It took real restraint on Ali's part not to nail

him with what Stu and Cami had just learned, but remembering B.'s caution about talking to Dash first, she kept her mouth shut on that score—but not on every score. She already knew that Eric Drinkwater didn't like to be crossed. He was furious now. For a few seconds, Ali half expected that he was going to punch her with a clenched fist. Remembering the way he'd treated her father, she couldn't help herself—she goaded him.

"Go ahead and hit me," she said. "There are security cameras all around this entrance. Anything you do here will be caught on tape—every single move—and the next thing you know, E.D., I'll have your badge."

His eyes bulged in absolute rage. "What did you just call me? Who told you that?"

"You heard what I called you, and it doesn't matter who told me," Ali replied calmly. "Not only that, I meant every word of it. After the way you treated my father yesterday and last night, you should be glad I didn't come up with something a hell of a lot worse."

He glared first at her and then at the overhead cameras. "Bitch," he muttered again before stomping away.

"Good riddance to you, too, Detective Drinkwater," she said under her breath before calling after him. "Have a nice day. Maybe I'll drop by to see you a little later."

38

Leaving the girls—Sheila, Phyllis, Juanita, Susan, Ellen, Pat, and Carmen—to reassemble the office, Haley Jackson set off on a series of difficult errands. Armed with the envelopes from her FINAL DIRECTIVES files, she drove straight to the Whitney Funeral Home in downtown Sedona. Having read the directives she knew now what Dan and Millie had wanted, and she was determined to make that happen. She started with the funeral home mentioned by both Dan and Millie.

When Haley introduced herself, Morgan Whitney, the owner, greeted her somberly.

"I'm here about Dan and Millie Frazier," Haley explained. "I'm in charge of their final arrangements."

"I see," he said, directing Haley to a chair, surprisingly enough without any mention of the obligatory "Sorry for your loss."

Once seated, Haley extracted the two envelopes from her purse, removed the applicable sheets of paper, and passed them along to Mr. Whitney. He read through them before handing them back.

"We lost money, too," he said. "With OFM, I mean. Dan encouraged us to move our 401(k) program over to them, and we did."

As Gram had said, as far as the people of Sedona were concerned, Haley was now the face of Dan Frazier's business. Morgan Whitney wasn't the first to hold Haley responsible for his losses, and he wouldn't be the last.

"I'm sorry," Haley said. "If you'd rather I took the business elsewhere . . ."

"Oh, no," Whitney said. "Nothing like that. Of course we'll handle the arrangements. As it turns out, we need all the business we can get. The wife and I were hoping to retire in a year or two. Now that's not going to happen, so we need to talk about the kinds of services you envision."

"Service," Haley corrected. "A single memorial service for both of them together. No open casket; no viewing; no visitation. I want it small but dignified. As you saw in the letter each of them expected the other to scatter their ashes. With them both gone I'll handle that. What about timing?"

"Have the autopsies been performed?"

"I have no idea."

"I'll have to check with the ME in Prescott. I can't give you an exact date or time until after the bodies are released. What about payment?"

"How much will it be?" Haley asked.

Whitney shrugged. "We'll have to collect the bodies from the ME in Prescott, transport them here for cremation. There's a rental charge for using our chapel facility for the service itself.

There's no extra charge if I officiate, but if you bring in someone else to do that, you'll need to handle their charges. Then, depending on the urns you select, we're probably looking at between five and seven thousand, and require payment in full prior to conducting the services."

That seemed high to Haley but she didn't quibble. "Of course," she said.

Eventually Mr. Whitney led Haley into a softly lit coffin- and urn-lined room to make her selection. Some of the urns were surprisingly expensive. Finally her eye was drawn to a brass one engraved with a simple Greek key design.

"That one," she said.

"Two of them, then?"

"No, just one."

"I'm not sure you understand," Mr. Whitney said reprovingly. "Cremains take up a certain amount of space. The urn you've chosen is large enough for one person but not for two."

"I do understand," Haley said. "Dan and Millie Frazier lived together. They died together, and if I have any say about it, their ashes will be scattered together. I want the ashes mixed together. Load as much of their ashes as will fit into the one urn and feel free to dispose of the rest."

"Of course," he said smoothly. "Whatever you wish."

Haley forced herself to bite back what she really wanted to say. *What I wish is that Dan and Millie weren't dead, and I wasn't here.*

"Thank you," she said, heading for the door.

"Once you have prepared an invoice, give me a call."

She phoned the office as she climbed into her Accord. "How's it going?"

"We're making decent progress," Carmen told her. "I've been sitting here working on reassembling computers while everyone else has been working on the filing mess."

"Let everyone know that I'm ordering pizzas all around," Haley told her. "I'll pick them up and bring them back after I finish at the bank."

As Haley headed back toward the Village of Oak Creek, she noted the bright yellow car driving behind her. She noticed it mostly because she'd always wanted a yellow car of her own. It never occurred to her that someone might be following her. After all, the highway from Sedona to the Village was one long no-passing zone.

39

Ali dialed Dave Holman's cell phone before she exited High Noon's parking lot. "Holman here," he said.

"You wouldn't happen to be working that double homicide down by the 303, would you?" she asked.

"You can't possibly know that," he began, and then stopped. "No, wait. I remember. Stuart Ramey has his police scanner on pretty much 24/7, right?"

"Have you identified your victims yet?"

Dave sighed. "Ali, I know we're friends, and I know you and your family are going through a lot right now, but I . . ."

"Would they happen to be named Alberto Joaquín and Jeffrey Hawkins?"

Dave said nothing for a moment, then he exploded. "My dead guys haven't even made it to the morgue and you already know who they are? How did you do that?"

"I didn't do it," Ali replied. "Cami Lee, Stuart Ramey's new assistant, is the one who figured it out. My father had mentioned seeing a landscaping rig at the scene of the Frazier homicides—a pickup truck loaded with mowers, rakes, and leaf blowers. Unlike Detective Drinkwater, Cami took my father's word as gospel. This morning she went out on her own looking for it. She finally found a set of functioning security cameras blocks from the scene. After she located footage of a landscaping truck coming and going around the time of the crime, she asked Stu to send it through our facial rec program. Three people—Dan Frazier, Alberto Joaquín, and Jeffrey Hawkins went north. Only Joaquín and Hawkins made the return trip."

"So what's the connection between Dan Frazier and my new dead guys?"

"Something you should maybe ask the next of kin."

"I'll do that. First chance I get. This Cami person sounds like my idea of Wonder Woman," Dave said. "How old is she?"

"Twenty-two."

"And have you mentioned any of this to Detective Drinkwater?"

"Not yet, but we will eventually, once we run it by Dash Summers. I expect we'll give good old E.D. the complete package, including video footage, enhanced photos of the bad guys, and copies of their respective rap sheets along with the plate number on the vehicle they were driving."

"Detective Drinkwater isn't going to like having to let go of your father as a suspect, and he won't appreciate having his ass handed to him by a twenty-two-year-old."

"No," Ali said. "I don't suppose he will. I, for one, can hardly wait."

"So what are the chances of getting this Cami person to come to work for the sheriff's department on a permanent basis?" Dave asked. "I could use someone like her on my new double homicide."

"Not gonna happen," Ali said with a laugh. "She's ours."

"But seriously," Dave said. "At this stage of my investigation, knowing that the two cases are related is vital. Thanks for the tip."

"You're welcome," Ali said. "Any theories?"

"Based on what you just told me, I'm thinking Alberto and Jeffrey were hired to take out Dan and Millie, and were rubbed out in turn once the job was done."

"If it's murder for hire," Ali declared, "the person behind all of it is most likely responsible for their deaths, too. My best guess for the guy putting out the contract is Jason McKinzie."

"Maybe so, but good luck finding him. As I said, McKinzie left the country Friday evening before any of these crimes were committed."

"All that means is he must be working with someone else," Ali insisted. "As for him fleeing the country? We'll find him, all right. High Noon is trying to track the money. If we can find that, we'll find him, too."

"Tell you what, then," Dave said, "if I get a line on McKinzie, I'll tell you, as long as you agree to do the same."

"Deal," Ali said at once.

"Okay, I'm here now, doing a next-of-kin. Gotta go inside and talk to Alberto's brother."

Dave hung up. Ali waited less than a minute before calling Stu. "I know B. has you working on something else right now, but could you do me one favor?"

"What do you need?"

"How many evening flights are there from Sky Harbor to Mexico City?"

Ali heard the machine-gun clatter of Stu's keyboard. She considered herself a fast typist, but compared to Stu, she was a piker.

"Two," he said. "Why?"

"Everybody's telling me that Jason McKinzie flew there on Friday evening. I wish there were a way to be sure of that."

"Maybe there is," Stu said. "Let me see what I can do."

"Thanks."

Her next call was to Cami. "Where are you?"

"Finishing lunch."

"On the company's dime, I hope," Ali said. "You sure as hell earned it today. I'm coming to Sedona. Stop by Dash Summers's office and show him what we've got. If he gives the okay, we'll meet at Sedona PD and clue Eric Drinkwater in on what's going on. By the way, don't expect a lot of gratitude."

"That won't bother me in the least," Cami said with a laugh. "I'm used to it. I work with Stuart Ramey, remember?"

40

After Edie's morning doughnut run, she and Bob settled into a rhythm. Working in quiet but purposeful fury, Bob went through the list, checking the links, verifying that the Jason McKinzie mentioned in the item was indeed the correct Jason McKinzie, and then sending the file to the printer. He didn't read through the information or see the photos that showed up on the printouts, but Edie gave him a running commentary as she sorted the material into what Bob regarded as totally arbitrary stacks.

"Look at this," Edie said, holding up pages of an *Architectural Digest* article depicting Jason's "recently reimagined" and very expensive home along the lower flanks of Camelback Mountain.

"Great," Bob grumbled, glancing at the lush interior. "I wonder how much of our money went into that."

There was a profile accompanied by McKinzie's photo from a private jet company's in-house magazine. There were countless photos of him squiring one gorgeously gowned and bejeweled woman after another to innumerable galas. There were articles citing his amazing record as a brilliant investment analyst and his uncanny ability to spot coming trends. Bob listened to the recitations of Jason McKinzie's flamboyant opulence with steadily increasing anger, but being angry was better than being dead, and doing something about it was better than being helpless.

Bob clicked on a file that turned out to be Jason McKinzie's Facebook page. As the computer kicked out page after page of Jason being Jason, Edie plucked them out one by one, studying them as they emerged. Some were duplicates of photos that had appeared elsewhere.

"This whole Facebook thing is weird," she said. "Most of the people I know who are on Facebook or LinkedIn use those sites to stay in touch with old friends or with their kids or grandkids, but McKinzie doesn't have any kids or grandkids, and not that many friends, either, as far as I can tell. So why does he even bother? Most of these show nothing but one woman after another, and seldom the same one twice."

"Must be tough walking around with that kind of arm candy," Bob observed, ignoring the glare Edie sent in his direction.

"There's one notable exception to that. Her name is Ana Stander," Edie continued. "She posts every couple of months or so. I believe she may be from South Africa."

"What makes you think that?"

"Look." Edie handed Bob a page that contained a photo of a single tree with the Kalahari stretching in the background. He thought it was a stock photo of some kind because he was pretty sure he'd seen it before, maybe in *National Geographic*. Below was a caption that said, "Remember when we hiked here?"

"So?" Bob asked.

"The photos are all of places in South Africa, with captions that say 'Wish you were here,' or 'What a great time we had.' But here's what's odd. There are no photos of Ana Stander herself anywhere, and I've looked."

"Maybe Ana's not very pretty," Bob suggested. "Maybe she's seen her competition and knows that her photo would suffer by comparison."

"Still," Edie said, picking up one of her many stacks of paper. "Ali asked me to look for something out of place. Facebook is more for faces than scenery. These photos don't fit. I'm going to go ask Stuart to find out whatever he can on Ana Stander."

It seemed to Bob that Edie was gone for only a moment, and she was fuming when she returned. "He says you need to send him the links. Stuart Ramey is evidently saving the planet. He told me he doesn't 'do' paper."

Bob laughed. "Show me which ones you want him to have."

It took a few moments for him to locate and send the files. While he was doing that, Edie grabbed the next stack of paper from the computer and began shuffling through it.

"Jason McKinzie was part of Ashley Madison?" she demanded.

"Who's Ashley Madison?" Bob asked. "The link came up. I checked it and found Jason McKinzie's name and address, so I know it's the correct Jason McKinzie."

Edie walked over to where Bob was sitting and gave him a quick buss on the cheek. "What's that for?" he asked.

"Ashley Madison is a cheaters' Web site," Edie replied. "The kiss was because you had no idea what it is."

"Jason McKinzie isn't married and, from the looks of things, isn't in a serious relationship," Bob mused. "So why would he join something like that? Isn't this something else that doesn't fit?"

"Probably," Edie said.

"Don't you want to take those into Stu as well?"

"Not on your life," Edie answered. "He about bit my head off just now. Why don't you send him the link and let it go at that?"

"All right," Bob said, "I will."

And he did.

41

Cami called Ali before she made it into town. "Sedona PD it is. I showed Dash the video. He said that since whatever we have will all come out in discovery anyway, I should—quote unquote— knock myself out."

"Let's do it, then," Ali said. "Drinkwater was in Cottonwood a little while ago, but I sent him packing with his tail between his legs. I'm guessing he's back in the office by now licking his wounds. Meet me there."

The previous night when Ali had entered the lobby of Sedona PD, she'd been worried sick about her father. Today, walking inside with Cami at her side and with the evidence clearing her father readily at hand, she felt six feet tall and bulletproof.

It was business hours. The desk by the security door where Sgt. Kronnan had held sway the night before was empty. They turned instead to the counter on the other side of the room, where several office clerks were visible behind a thick shield of glass.

"Ali Reynolds and Camille Lee, of High Noon Enterprises," Ali said through a mouthpiece cut into the glass barrier. "We're here to see Detective Drinkwater."

"May I tell him what this is about?"

"Yes," Ali said. "It's about the Frazier homicides. We'll wait."

Less than a minute later, Eric Drinkwater marched into the lobby. "What are you doing here?" he demanded. "I already told you I won't tolerate any further interference."

"We've uncovered some evidence we thought you should know about," Ali said sweetly, making no reference to their recent altercation. "Our intention is to offer assistance rather than to interfere."

"Who's we?" he demanded, glancing in Cami's direction for the first time. "And what kind of so-called assistance do you have in mind?"

"Let me introduce my associate, Camille Lee," Ali said smoothly. "She's a High Noon operative. She did some investigating on her own earlier this morning, and I think you'll be interested in seeing the results."

Drinkwater shook his head. "All right," he agreed reluctantly, doing a better job of concealing his emotions than Ali would have expected. "Let's get this over with." He glanced back at the clerk. "Is the conference room open?" She nodded, and he set off toward the other end of the lobby, leaving Ali and Cami to follow.

"A conference room rather than an interview

room?" Ali asked. "That counts as a step in the right direction."

She could tell by the stiffening of Detective Drinkwater's shoulders that he had heard the comment. Too bad. The man was a bully, and she was pushing back.

He ushered them into a small conference room next to an office marked CHIEF OF POLICE. Once they were inside, he slammed that door shut behind them and then stood in front of it with his arms folded belligerently across his chest. The agreeable guise he'd worn in the lobby evaporated once they were out of the public eye.

"Show me," he said.

As far as Ali was concerned, this was Cami's show. Ali stayed in the background, allowing Cami to tackle Drinkwater head-on. "You're too tall," she pointed out. "If you want to see what's on my iPad, you'll need to sit down here next to me."

Sighing with frustration, Drinkwater reluctantly took a seat while Cami produced her iPad and called up a file. "This starts with the phone tracker record."

"What's a phone tracker?" Drinkwater asked.

"High Noon is a high-profile company these days," Cami answered. "In order to protect both employees and their families, we see to it that all electronic devices are equipped with the latest in presence technology."

"What technology?"

"Presence," Cami replied. "It allows us to know where an individual is and to follow his or her movements in real time. Those movements are also recorded so they can be accessed later if necessary."

"Look," Drinkwater said impatiently. "How about skipping the engineering lecture and just showing me whatever it is you've got?"

"Yesterday, when Mr. Larson went to the home of Dan and Millie Frazier, his phone was equipped with state-of-the-art tracking. What you're about to see here will show you the record of his movements overlaid on a satellite view of Sedona."

With the iPad on the table in front of her, Cami pressed the arrow to start the video sequence and then pushed it over in front of the detective. "Please notice the time stamp in the upper right-hand corner of the screen. The blue dot is Mr. Larson. At 8:58 a.m. he leaves his unit at Sedona Shadows on foot and follows the corridor to a side entrance. He exits the building and walks to the parking lot, going directly to his designated parking place. Once he's in a moving vehicle, you'll notice that the phone movement speeds up."

"How do I know the blue dot on the screen has anything at all to do with Mr. Larson?"

"Keep watching," Cami advised. "I'm going to fast-forward through the next section while he's driving from Sedona Shadows to the Fraziers' place. You'll have a copy of this, so you'll be able to see for yourself that he makes no stops along the way. This is where he enters Dan and Millie Frazier's neighborhood."

"He didn't just drive to their neighborhood,"

Drinkwater objected, still peering at the scene. "He drove to their house."

"No," she said. "When I said he drove directly to their neighborhood, that's what I meant. See here? The vehicle turns on to Elberta Drive and stops. Notice that the time stamp says 9:29. Again, I'm going to fast-forward, but Mr. Larson's phone and most likely his vehicle remain in that spot near the end of the street for the better part of twenty minutes. Only then does it begin moving again, first continuing up the street and turning in to the Fraziers' driveway. That occurs at 9:50. Now watch what happens next.

"As you can see, the blue dot is hovering over what seems to be a building of some kind—a building that turns out to be the Fraziers' two-car garage. The blue dot remains over the building as long as the phone is inside the building. Now, up in the corner, you'll see a second time stamp. That's from the 911 recording. You'll see the blue dot move as the phone goes from the garage to the house. You should be able to hear the voice-over of the 911 call. Now, as the time stamp on the phone tracker video turns over to 9:52, you'll notice a second time stamp appears on the screen accompanied by the voice-over."

Ali winced when she heard the desperation in her father's cry. "We need help!"

As Cami continued to walk the detective through the video, Ali watched disappointment register on Eric Drinkwater's face as he realized the case he thought he was building against Bob

Larson was going up in smoke along with any chance of his making a quick arrest.

"How did you get a copy of the 911 tape?" he wanted to know.

Cami shrugged. "We asked, and they gave it to us," she said. "So where would you like me to send your copy of the video?"

"I guess you should send me a copy and one to the chief as well," Drinkwater said at last, pausing long enough to write down the necessary addresses for Cami's benefit.

"We'll need to have our experts review the tapes, of course," he added. "For all I know this whole phone tracker story may be completely bogus. What if you made the whole thing up? Now, if show and tell is over . . ."

"Not quite," Cami said calmly. "We should probably take a look at the other videos."

"You have more?" an exasperated Detective Drinkwater demanded.

"Several, as a matter of fact," Cami said with a smile as she queued up the next one. "My understanding is that Mr. Larson indicated to you that he remembered seeing a truck loaded with landscaping equipment parked near the Fraziers' house when he arrived there yesterday morning."

"As I said, we looked into that and found no evidence to suggest that a rig matching that description had been seen anywhere in the surrounding area."

"Maybe you didn't look quite far enough," Cami said. "Here are two sets of time-stamped security footage from the Apple Tree B & B just down from Elberta Drive on Jordan. The first one shows a rig very much like that driving southbound on Jordan past the B & B at 10:01 a.m., which would be while Mr. Larson was still on the phone with the 911 operator. You'll notice that the video resolution on that south-facing camera leaves a lot to be desired, but when I went looking for the same vehicle going northbound here's what I found."

First she ran the enhanced version of the footage time-stamped 7:33 a.m. "You'll notice that at this point there are three passengers inside the truck. What you're seeing now was enhanced several times in order for us to run it through our facial rec program. It turns out Dan Frazier is the man sitting slumped over in the front passenger seat. The other two individuals are ex-cons with extensive rap sheets. The driver is a guy named Alberto Joaquín, and the guy in back is Jeffrey Hawkins. As you can also see, the enhanced version clearly shows a company logo on the door—A.J. Landscaping."

Drinkwater studied the two photos and jotted something in a notebook. "All right, then," he said grudgingly. "I'll look into it."

"Actually," Ali said, "there's one more thing."

"What?"

"About those two suspects—they're both dead."

"What?"

"Earlier today they were found shot to death in a gravel pit north of Sun City. Dave Holman is investigating."

"Why the hell didn't you say so to begin with?"

"Because we wanted you to have the whole story."

"What are the chances your father hired these guys, and then showed up at the crime scene to report the crime in an attempt to throw us off track?"

"You don't give up, do you," Ali said.

"I don't get paid for giving up."

"What about my dad's Bronco? How soon will you be releasing it from the impound lot?"

"I'll have to get back to you on that. We'll be having our experts review all of this. Releasing that vehicle will take some time."

"I'll just bet it will," Ali said sarcastically, then she turned to Cami. "Come on. We're done here."

"In other words," Cami muttered as they made their way back to the lobby, "don't hold your breath about getting that Bronco back anytime soon."

42

There were two matching strip malls, set a block apart, on the west side of Highway 179 in the Village of Oak Creek—Oak Creek Park North and Oak Creek Park South. The office of the Frazier Insurance Agency was located in the one to the south. Among the tenants in the Oak Creek Park North complex were Arizona First Federal Bank and Guido's. First Federal was where the Fraziers had done their banking for as long as Haley could remember. As for Guido's? When it came to quality pizza, it was the only game in town.

Haley turned in at the first Oak Creek Park sidewalk cut-in and stopped directly in front of Guido's. She went there first and ordered three large pizzas for pickup in twenty minutes before she entered the bank.

When she stepped inside, Annette Ogilvie, the manager, rose from her desk and hurried to greet her. "I'm so sorry to hear about Dan and Millie," Annette said quickly. "What an appalling thing. If there's anything—anything at all—that we can do to help, please let me know."

Expressions of sympathy still tended to sap Haley's emotional reserve. "Thanks," she said with an acknowledging nod as she sank into the chair in front of Annette's desk. "I'm going to need access to their safe-deposit box, and I have the letter."

"Of course," Annette said.

Haley drew the two envelopes out of her purse and located the two letters of intent that named Haley Jackson as Dan and Millie's executrix. She handed them across the table to the bank manager, who barely glanced at them before handing them back. After all, Annette herself had notarized them.

"You brought your key?" she asked.

"Yes."

Without saying anything more, Annette ushered Haley into a vault the size of a small bedroom. There she retrieved the box from its slot in the wall, and placed it on the table in front of Haley.

"I'm sure this is going to be tough," Annette said, backing away. "I'll give you some privacy."

Haley was familiar with most of the contents in the box, but she was surprised to see that the postage stamp–sized device Millie had shown her on Friday was the topmost item. Slipping that into the pocket of her jeans, she dug through the rest of the material. She removed the velvet pouch that contained several of Millie's more expensive diamond-encrusted pieces as well as

Dan's father's Rolex watch, which Dan had inherited but never wore. Among the papers she found both Dan's and Millie's birth certificates. Toward the bottom she found the four life insurance policies, including the keyman one she had mentioned earlier to Eric Drinkwater. After jotting down the numbers, she set those aside and picked up the wills themselves.

She knew the documents had been drawn up, but she was unfamiliar with the provisions. Now, as executrix, she needed to know what the wills' insurance policies themselves said and if there were any other named heirs or beneficiaries of whom she was unaware. She also needed to be familiar with all the provisions in the event of any possible lawsuits that might present themselves in the aftermath of the OFM collapse.

The intentions expressed in the wills were straightforward enough. Millie and Dan both named one another as their primary heir and/or beneficiary. Anything remaining in their joint estate after the death of the second to die was destined for a scholarship fund to be established under the name of Daniel and Millie Frazier at Dan's alma mater, Arizona State University.

After reading through the material, Haley put everything back in the box and called for Annette to come let her out.

"Everything's in order then?" Annette asked as she slipped the box back into its designated slot.

"Yes," Haley answered. "As far as I can tell."

It was only as she walked out of the bank that

she remembered the tiny item she had hidden in her pocket. Rather than go back inside to return it to the safe deposit box, she kept right on going. Besides, if Millie had left the drive in a place to which Haley had ready access, whatever was on it couldn't be that big of a secret.

She picked up the pizzas, loaded them into the car, and drove back to the office. In her absence the girls had wrested order from chaos. *My girls now*, Haley reminded herself.

"Time for pizza," she announced, putting the boxes down on the front counter where Carmen continued to be in charge of computer reassembly.

"Let me move this out of the way," Carmen said moving the last of the computers aside.

The computer in question happened to be the one from Dan's private office—an aging Dell desktop that Dan had refused to replace even though it had required constant updating. With Carmen lugging the machine, Haley followed along and waited while Carmen went about plugging it in. This was the first time Haley had set foot inside the back office since Dan died. Once again, Haley's emotions got the best of her. When Carmen left the room, Haley remained. Sitting down in Dan's sagging leather desk chair, she sat quietly for several minutes, studying the sales plaques and framed diplomas and photos that decorated the office's wood-paneled walls. The photos alone turned out to be a gallery of the youth athletic teams Dan had sponsored through the years.

In the privacy of the office, out of sight of her

employees, Haley buried her head in her arms and wept. When the bout of tears finally subsided, she looked up and found herself staring at the blank computer screen. And that's when she remembered the drive once more. With the office door still closed, it occurred to her that maybe this was the time to learn what was on it.

When she tried to retrieve the tiny memory card, she found it had slipped to the very bottom of her pocket. Holding it in one hand, she examined the side of the computer, looking for the proper receptacle. Then she remembered Millie had mentioned something about the card requiring an adapter. Searching through the top drawer of Dan's desk, she found the device stashed among a full supply of dead ball point pens and dull pencils.

After loading the tiny drive into the adapter, she shoved that into the USB port and turned on the computer. The old desktop took forever to boot up. When it finally did, she clicked on the Unnamed File and encountered a screen prompt: PASSWORD REQUIRED.

That wasn't a big deal. Dan had always been hopeless when it came to passwords. If he wrote them down, he lost the piece of paper. Since he was always calling Haley for help in that regard, over time she had learned them all—the passwords for his home computer, his office computer, for his online banking and bill paying programs as well as his Apple accounts. She knew Dan's passwords as well as she knew her own, but when she tried plugging them in here, one at a time, none of them worked.

After the last one failed, Haley sat staring at the machine wondering why Dan had used a different password. Clearly whatever was on the drive had been important to Dan—important enough for Millie to make an unscheduled trip north to take it to the bank. Now with both Dan and Millie gone, what was Haley expected to do? Without knowing what was on the drive, was she supposed to turn it over to the SEC? And what about that homicide cop, Detective Drinkwater, if he came back around asking more questions? Was it possible the drive could have something to do with Dan's murder? And if she failed to turn it over to Detective Drinkwater, would she be guilty of withholding evidence—possible evidence—in a homicide investigation?

Haley was still sitting staring at the words "Password Required" when Carmen knocked on the door and then poked her head inside. "Someone to see you," she said.

"Who?"

"Ali Reynolds from something called High Noon Enterprises."

Haley didn't know Ali Reynolds personally. She knew *of* her, of course, because Ali's parents were Bob and Edie Larson, and they bragged about Ali constantly. Haley could imagine any number of possible unpleasant topics that might be ripe for discussion, but since Carmen had come to get her, Haley couldn't very well dodge the issue by claiming she wasn't in the office.

"Okay," Haley said. "Tell her I'll be right out."

She was about to remove the drive when another thought occurred to her. The SEC had already taken Dan's computer to Phoenix, examined it thoroughly, and presumably copied everything they wanted. Why not keep a copy of whatever was on the unnamed drive right here, hidden in what was essentially plain sight, on a computer that had already undergone official scrutiny?

She scrolled down the directory to the unnamed drive and hit Duplicate. It took longer to copy the files than Haley expected, but eventually the bar on the screen finished filling. When it did, she removed the drive, adapter and all, and went out to see what Bob and Edie Larson's daughter wanted.

43

Jessica sat in her idling car in the far corner of the lot outside the bank, listening in. Once Haley was on the move that morning, Jessica had gone to an auto parts store to buy an AC adapter and to a hardware store for a power strip in order to make her listening station work in the VW. After Haley exchanged a few words with someone who was apparently a bank manager, there had been nothing. When Haley emerged from the bank sometime later and headed into the restaurant next door, Jessica still had no idea if she had the SD card in her possession.

When the restaurant door opened next, Haley appeared, this time carrying a stack of pizza boxes. Other than the cold pizza the night before, Jessica had eaten nothing, and seeing the pizza boxes was a reminder. Still, she wasn't willing to lose sight of her quarry, not even long enough to dodge into a gas station and pick up some coffee.

Haley drove straight back to the insurance office, and Jessica did the same, parking this time among the cars clustered in front of a hardware store at the far end of the strip mall. When Haley went inside the building, Jessica heard a flurry of voices. There was a buzz of talk about using the break room or eating at desks. Haley's purse landed with a thump, and then there was general chatter, but no matter how much Jessica strained to listen, there was no sound of Haley's distinctive voice.

She sat there, listening and worrying. Jason had been completely unnerved by what had happened in the gravel pit, and she couldn't help worrying about leaving him alone at the safe house in Peoria any longer than absolutely necessary. If she didn't get the card back this afternoon, she'd have to give up and trust that the encryption on the card would be enough to hold off all comers. If Jason's complex escape hatch of safe houses and offshore accounts came to light, everything he'd put away would be lost to him and to her as well. Jessica had worked security for many unsavory characters, including some time spent in the employ of the kingpin of a Mexican drug cartel, but this was her first ever chance at a major score, one that, by her estimates, could leave her fixed for life.

There was a sharp rap on the window next to her head, loud enough to cut through the murmur of conversation coming into her earbuds. Startled, Jessica pulled the earphones out and saw an older white-haired woman standing next to the car, motioning for Jessica to roll down her window.

For a breathless instant, Jessica was afraid

Haley had somehow caught on to her, and she almost reached for her weapon. Jessica forced herself to relax before rolling down the window.

"Don't you know that you're not supposed to let your car idle like that?" the woman demanded. "It's bad for the environment."

Jessica almost laughed aloud in relief. "I'm working," she replied. "I need the engine on to keep my equipment powered up."

"You could always go to the library, you know," the woman said. "It's just over there. I'm sure they'd let you plug in whatever you need."

As the busybody stalked off, shaking her head, Jessica caught sight of two new cars pulling up and parking in front of the insurance office. One was an SUV, a silver Cayenne, and the other a bright red Prius. While she'd been sitting there, Jessica had seen one would-be customer after another approach the office and immediately be turned away. The new arrivals, however, a tallish blond woman and a short dark-haired one, went inside and didn't come back out.

Reinserting her earbuds, Jessica went back to listening. "Ali Reynolds," a voice announced. "And Camille Lee. We're with High Noon Enterprises, and we're here to see Ms. Jackson."

"She's in the back right now," someone else said. "I'm not sure if she's up to seeing anyone right now."

Out in the car, Jessica's hair almost stood on end. High Noon Enterprises had been called in on this? She knew High Noon's name as well as their reputation. Lance Tucker, the brilliant young hacker who had successfully infiltrated the dark web, worked for them. Jessica had used the dark web sourcing extensively in putting the safe house network in place. If High Noon somehow gained access to the memory card and broke the encryption . . .

44

The office seemed to be in a state of chaos. Bankers Boxes—some empty and some still brimming with files—littered the room. Two desks had been pushed together to create a worktable, half of which was covered with partially empty pizza boxes. The pizza party seemed to have ended. Most of the people in the room had gone back to work. The only person still seated at the impromptu dining table was a wizened little old lady. Her long white hair was pulled back in a thin ponytail. A snazzy neon-green walker was parked within easy reach directly in front of her chair.

She greeted Ali and Cami with a welcoming smile. "I'm sure she'll be right out," she said. "By the way, I'm Carol Hotchkiss, Haley's grandmother. Help yourselves to some pizza, if you'd like. There's more than enough to go around. And I'm sure someone would be happy to bring you some coffee."

Ali had missed breakfast. By now, just after noon, pizza sounded terrific.

"Thank you," she said, taking a chair and a slice. "Don't mind if I do."

"What about you, Ms. Lee?" Carol asked.

"Call me Cami," she said. "I already had lunch, but I'd love some coffee. Don't have someone go get it. I can see everybody here is busy. Just point me in the right direction. Coffee, Ali?"

"Yes, please."

As Cami went in search of coffee, Carol Hotchkiss turned to Ali. "You maybe don't remember me," she beamed, "but I certainly remember you. At the time when Haley first came to live with me, you were already out of college and no longer waiting tables in your folks' restaurant. Going to the Sugarloaf on the weekends was always a special treat back then, and Haley adored your mother's sweet rolls. As a matter of fact, Haley and I had breakfast there just this morning, although I have to say, the Sugarloaf isn't quite the same without your dad in the kitchen and your mother behind the counter."

Ali smiled. "No," she agreed. "It's not."

"I don't generally come to work with Haley," Carol continued, "but we had a bit of a problem back at the house today, and Haley didn't want to leave me there alone."

"A problem?" Ali asked.

"A break-in, actually," Carol confided. "Not really breaking and entering, I suppose, because nothing was actually broken, but while we were at breakfast, someone came into the house and went through our things."

"Was anything taken?" Ali asked. "Did you report it to the police?"

"Report what to the police?"

Ali looked up to see a late-thirtysomething woman emerge from a private office at the back of the room. There was enough of a family resemblance that Ali recognized at once the new arrival had to be Carol's granddaughter, Haley Jackson. Ali could see that although Haley had gone to some lengths to repair the damage, she had obviously been crying.

"The break-in," Carol Hotchkiss answered.

"I thought we agreed we weren't going to talk about that."

"We agreed that we wouldn't report it," Carol said, "but I didn't know that meant we couldn't talk about it. By the way, this is Ali Reynolds. Her parents used to run the Sugarloaf Café. Ali and her husband, B. Simpson, run a cybersecurity company called High Noon Enterprises."

Haley held out her hand to Ali. "We must have met somewhere along the way, and I do know your parents, of course. And this is?" she asked, looking at Cami.

"My associate, Camille Lee."

Haley took a seat at the table and selected a piece from the dwindling supply of pizza slices still in the boxes. "Sorry about the mess," she said. "Pizza is usually confined to the break room, but today, with all the uproar, I decided to make an exception. Now how can I help you? Is this about your dad?"

"What about my dad?" Ali asked.

Haley shrugged. "I knew that he was taken into custody yesterday because I saw him in the back of a patrol car, but I never in a million years thought he could have done something like that."

"That makes two of us," Carol Hotchkiss sniffed. "How Eric Drinkwater could think your poor father capable of such an appalling thing is more than I can understand."

"Thank you," Ali said. "You're right, they did take him in for questioning, but they released him last night. Originally we thought High Noon would be doing investigative work for Dad's legal defense team, but evidence has surfaced this morning that suggests someone else is responsible."

"Who?"

"I'm not sure. I'm not close enough to the investigation to have that information," Ali said, avoiding Cami's raised eyebrows. "You might ask Detective Drinkwater. He should be able to tell you more. Right now, though, I'm hoping High Noon will be able to help with regard to the Ocotillo Fund Management issue."

"Help how?"

"We have reason to believe that Jason McKinzie has fraudulently siphoned funds away from the company's investors for his own use. There have been reports that he left the country on Friday night and has gone to ground in Mexico City. Before leaving town, he signed all the documents necessary for the bankruptcy proceedings. High Noon's goal is to locate and retrieve as many of those missing monies as possible so they can be returned to the original investors."

"You really think you can retrieve some of those funds?" Haley asked.

Ali nodded. "The last few months High Noon has been working on rounding up monies from a cult-based human trafficking case in Colorado City. We've had considerable success there, by the way. Bad guys think that if they hide money in offshore accounts, no one will be able to find it or seize it. That's often not the case.

"As far as OFM is concerned," she continued, "the way things stand right now, investors will be lucky to get pennies back on each invested dollar. If we can track down McKinzie's hidden assets, we may not be able to make those investors whole again, but we hope to leave them in better shape than they would be otherwise. People are counting on having those retirement funds available."

"That goes for my girls and me, too," Haley said, glancing around the room. "Our 401(k) program is tied up with OFM. That's why I'm sure Dan couldn't possibly have been mixed up with whatever Mr. McKinzie was pulling. Most of us have worked here for years. Dan wouldn't have knowingly betrayed us like that, and if he had seen any of this coming in advance, surely he would have given us a chance to pull our money out of harm's way."

Ali knew that, with bankruptcy clawback provisions in place, early withdrawals from the funds wouldn't have helped. She suspected that Haley had no idea that was the case.

"You seem to think Dan was a good guy."

Haley nodded. "The best."

"What can you tell me about him?"

Ali saw at once that she had touched on a difficult topic. Haley's eyes immediately filled with tears.

"I've worked for both Dan and Millie for the better part of twenty years," she said. "They were far more than just employers. They were the best, and I loved them both. Even though I spent some time this morning working on making funeral arrangements, I still can't believe they're gone."

"Wait," Ali said with a frown, "are you saying you're in charge of their final arrangements?"

Haley nodded. "I'm the executrix of their estates. There's no one else."

"So you must have been very close."

"We were," Haley agreed quietly, "although not so much the last six months or so. OFM hired a new personal assistant for Dan down in Phoenix, and she's been handling most of the day-to-day stuff I used to do."

"What's the new PA's name?" Ali asked. "We should probably talk to her."

"Jessica Denton."

"Do you have any contact information on her?"

"Back at my desk," Haley said. "With the corporate offices closed, her work extension won't be in service anymore and most likely not her company e-mail address, either, but I think I have some of her personal information. Let me go check."

"Jessica Denton isn't exactly my cup of tea," Carol Hotchkiss put in once Haley was out of earshot.

"You know her?" Ali asked.

"She came by the house last night, crying her eyes out because Dan and Millie were dead. If you ask me, Haley had far more reason to cry than Jessica did. Then this morning, when Detective Drinkwater came by the house, he said they were still looking for next of kin. The whole thing just doesn't sit right."

Haley returned with a piece of paper, which she handed over to Ali. "That's all I have for Jessica's nonwork contacts—her e-mail and cell phone. No landline." Haley turned to her grandmother. "What didn't sit right, Gram?"

"The way Jessica Denton came over to the house last night, boohoohing about Dan and Millie. How could she know they were dead when nobody else did?"

Haley gave her grandmother a fond smile. "Come on, Gram," she said. "You're just prejudiced because I've complained about Jessica so much. Maybe she talked to one of the girls here. They all knew because I called and told them."

"Complained why?" Ali asked.

"Because it felt like she was edging me out," Haley answered. "She was doing things for Millie and Dan that I used to do—picking up their prescriptions, dropping off dry cleaning, making restaurant reservations. She's also drop-dead gorgeous, so I guess I was a little jealous. Naturally Gram is in my corner on that score."

Ali nodded. "All right, then," she said. "Let's go back to Monday. Did your computers go down at the same time OFM's did?"

"No. Mr. McKinzie kept suggesting that we should switch over to his network. He said it would save money in the long run, but Dan wasn't interested. That's probably why the SEC needed access to our files and computers."

No, Ali thought, *they wanted your files because they had already figured out that the ones at corporate headquarters had evaporated, and they wouldn't be able to get them back.*

"They came by yesterday, boxed everything up—our files and our computers—and dragged them down to Phoenix," Haley was saying. "They sent them back this morning, so I guess they found whatever they needed. But that's what all this mess is about—trying to put things back away where they belong."

"On Monday," Ali said, "how soon did you know that the network had crashed?"

"Sometime after it happened," Haley answered. "Someone from here—Susan, I think—called down there trying to get information for a client here in town. The office was in an uproar because of the computer snarl. They told Susan to call back later because they were trying to reboot. Before she had a chance to do so, an agent from the SEC showed up here, ordered us out of the office, and locked the place down."

"The agent's name?"

"Ferris," Haley answered at once. "Agent Donald Ferris."

"When he showed up, did he mention what exactly he wanted?"

"You've got to be kidding," Haley said. "Agent Ferris was less than forthcoming. He treated us like a bunch of criminals and warned us that if we tried to smuggle anything out of the office in our purses, it would be confiscated."

"He was worried that you might smuggle something out? That makes it sound as though he was looking for something very specific."

"He mentioned thumb drives, didn't he?" Carol Hotchkiss piped up from the sidelines. "What about that one Millie had—the one she showed you last week?"

Ali caught the withering look Haley shot her grandmother. Ali also noticed the slight flush that colored Haley's cheeks. It was clear something important had just happened, although she wasn't sure what it was.

"What thumb drive?"

For an answer, Haley slid one hand into the pocket of her jeans and pulled out the adapter holding the tiny wafer. As soon as she held it up, Ali recognized it as a microSD card.

"What's on it?" Ali asked.

"I have no idea," Haley answered. "I tried opening it, but it's password protected, and not with one of Dan's passwords, either." With no further prompting she simply handed it over to Ali.

"You're giving it to me?" Ali asked, looking down at it in disbelief.

"That's what High Noon does, isn't it?" Haley asked with a shrug. "Don't you specialize in cyber-security issues?"

"Yes, we do."

"Millie told me on Friday that Dan had insisted she make a special trip home that morning to put this in their safe-deposit box because he didn't want it 'falling into the wrong hands.' I think this memory card may have something to do with the reason Dan and Millie are dead. They put it in the safe-deposit box, one to which they had previously given me access. Since they trusted me with access to the box, that means they also trusted me with whatever was inside it. You already told me that High Noon is trying to retrieve whatever money Jason McKinzie may have stolen. I'd like to believe that's what Dan was doing, too. And maybe that's what this memory card is all about—stopping Jason McKinzie. If so, by giving it to you, I'm hoping I've just kept it out of the wrong hands and placed it in the right ones."

Taken aback, Ali looked down at the tiny memory card and wondered if Haley was right. Did that postage stamp–sized device hidden inside a USB adapter hold the key to all of this, and was it motive enough for four separate murders?

"Thank you," Ali said quietly. "Thank you very

much. If you don't mind, I'll have Cami here rush it to High Noon's campus in Cottonwood. Someone there should be able to unlock it. As I said earlier, High Noon's goal in all this is to go after Jason McKinzie's store of cash. If the memory card contains information that will help us locate his hidden assets, that's how we'll use it—to retrieve assets. On the other hand, if what's here turns out to be connected to the homicides, we'll have to turn the information over to the proper authorities."

"What happens if it's neither?" Haley asked. "What if the information turns out to be strictly personal?"

"Then we'll bring it back to you," Ali answered. "Fair enough?"

"Yes," Haley said. "That's more than fair."

45

The words "memory card" shot through Jessica's consciousness like a bolt of electricity. Listening intently, she realized the old woman had to be the one who had first mentioned the memory card. And now, a piece at a time, she learned the rest of the story.

After copying the files, Dan had handed the memory card over to Millie, who had driven to Sedona and placed it in the safe-deposit box. Even under the threat of death—with Alberto and Jeffrey holding the two of them at knifepoint—neither Millie nor Dan had caved and given up the location of the damned memory card.

Jessica was surprised at that. Shocked, even. She'd worked closely with Dan and Millie for months, all the while despising them. It had never occurred to her that either of them, under the threat of death, could be that tough or display that kind of fortitude. How could she have misjudged them so badly?

Clutching the steering wheel in a white-knuckled

grip, she listened as the situation went from bad to worse.

". . . you don't mind," the woman who called herself Ali was saying, "I'll have Cami here rush it to High Noon's campus in Cottonwood. Someone there should be able to unlock it . . ."

Jessica had been on edge from the moment the new arrivals had mentioned the involvement of High Noon Enterprises. But the idea that the memory card was now in the hands of a High Noon operative was utterly unthinkable. A disaster. A catastrophe. And if the card made it from the Village of Oak Creek to the High Noon office in Cottonwood, Jessica suspected all was lost. Somehow—some way—Jessica Denton had to keep that from happening.

Steeling herself for the challenge, she tuned back in to the voices in her earbuds.

Until that very moment Jessica had had no idea that High Noon was based anywhere nearby. As for Cottonwood? She had heard the town mentioned from time to time, but she was unaware of its exact location. It had to be somewhere nearby, but where?

With the memory card no longer in Haley's possession, Jessica had just lost her eyes and ears. Her planted listening devices were useless now, and so was the GPS tracker on Haley's car. The luxury of following a target from a distance was no longer an option. She briefly considered trying to move the locater from Haley's car to one of the others, but she didn't know for sure which was which. And besides, where the hell was the "High Noon campus"?

Opening her browser, it took her less than a minute to find it. Once she did, she studied how to get there. There were two routes, but if you were in any kind of a hurry to get from the Village of Oak Creek to Cottonwood, there was really only one route that made sense—Highway 179 south and then right onto Beaverhead Flats Road. That way took twenty-eight minutes as opposed to a thirty-eight-minute trip back through Sedona.

Jessica was confident that whoever was carrying the drive would go that way, but she didn't leave the parking lot just then. Much as every fiber of her body ached to take action and move, she watched the office door through a pair of binoculars and forced herself to wait. She needed to know for sure which vehicle was which. It seemed reasonable to think that the lady in the Cayenne was the head honcho and the one in the red Prius the underling, but Jessica didn't dare assume. The stakes were too high. She had to be absolutely certain.

At last, after what seemed like hours of point-less chatter, the two women finally emerged from the office and stood outside on the sidewalk, conferring. The blond woman looked at her watch and said something. The smaller woman, the dark-haired one, nodded and replied before turning to-ward the Prius. That was Jessica's signal to move. Dropping the binoculars, she put the VW in gear. For this to work, she needed to be ahead of her target, not behind her.

When the Cayenne merged into the traffic in the opposite direction on 179, toward Sedona, Jessica headed the other way. The red Prius was the target. As she had anticipated, there were far too many vehicles on the highway for her plan to work. Once she turned on to Beaverhead Flats Road, she hoped it would be a different story. Between that turnoff and the tiny town of Cornville, there appeared to be several miles of relatively deserted highway.

Somewhere between those two critical points, Jessica Denton planned to make her move.

46

Several message announcements had buzzed on Ali's phone during the time they had been inside the Frazier Insurance Agency. Now, driving in slow traffic, in the Cayenne, she checked them. Two were voice mail messages, one from Stu and the other from Dave Holman. The third was a text from B., giving her a street address on Camelback for her 3:00 p.m. appointment with Eugene Lowensdahl.

She knew the number in the 3200 block of Camelback meant that the office had to be in the general neighborhood of Biltmore Fashion Park. Despairingly, she examined the jeans and casual sandals she'd donned early that morning when she had gone to visit her parents at Sedona Shadows. Jeans and sandals may have been fine for whatever she'd done so far today in Sedona and Cottonwood, but her next task was to dazzle a Chief Restructuring Officer. Unfortunately, one of his near neighbors turned out to be none other than a Neiman Marcus store. No, in that kind of upscale enclave, what Ali was wearing right now simply wouldn't cut it.

With a sigh, she headed home to change clothes. Realizing B. was probably on his way to the airport by now, she was about to dial her husband's number when her phone rang with Dave Holman on the line.

"Thanks for throwing me under the bus with E.D.," he said. "He's pissed. You actually called him that to his face?"

"The devil made me do it," Ali answered with a chuckle. "Besides, we solved his cases for him, and that's all the thanks we get?"

"Drinkwater's cases may be solved," Dave replied, "but mine aren't. That's what I need to talk to you about."

"Just to be clear, are we going to be discussing an ongoing case?"

"Apparently," Dave said, "because I've turned up a direct connection between one of my dead guys and Dan Frazier."

"Really?" Ali managed. "You're saying all four cases are connected?"

"Yes. Alberto Joaquín was the yard guy at Dan Frazier's house in Paradise Valley. The owner of the landscaping truck, Alejandro Joaquín, was Alberto's employer, but he's also his brother."

"Our facial rec provided enough identification for you to do a next of kin notification?"

"I don't believe in throwing people under the bus," Dave said pointedly. "I used the victims' driver's license photos for those. Alejandro told me that Alberto didn't show up for work on Tuesday morning, and neither did his company truck. Alejandro didn't report the truck as missing or stolen at the time because he knew a charge like that would violate Alberto's probation and send him straight back to the slammer. Alejandro thought Alberto was out tying one on and that, when he sobered up, both he and the truck would be back."

"Being in jail would have been better than being dead," Ali said.

"I mentioned to Alejandro that there was a possibility Alberto might have been involved in two homicides up in Sedona. As soon as he heard Dan Frazier's name, the poor guy almost had a stroke. Went all pale and short of breath on me. I thought he was going to croak out on the spot. Eventually he came around, though, and that's when he told me. A.J. Landscaping has crews working all over the valley. They've handled the landscaping on Dan's Paradise Valley house for the past three years."

"So, Alberto was part of the work crew?"

"He *was* the work crew."

"But why?" Ali asked. "Why would he turn on his employer like that, to say nothing of betraying his own brother? And what's Jeffrey Hawkins's connection to all this? Did he work for Alejandro, too?"

"No, he didn't," Dave answered. "At one time, Alberto and Jeffrey were cellmates at a private prison up by Kingman. They were both out on parole and evidently hooked up again, maybe just for old times' sake, or maybe for this job. I can't tell.

"At any rate, Alejandro told me that Alberto spent a lot of time at Wheels Inn, one of the rougher biker bars on 43rd Avenue. He liked going there because it was within walking distance of where he lived, three blocks from his rented mobile home. Alejandro said Alberto walked back and forth because he couldn't risk having another DUI on his record.

"I checked with the bar," Dave continued. "The bar manager showed me the security footage for Friday. Turns out Alberto was there most of the evening. Early on it was business as usual, with him just sitting alone at the bar, guzzling one beer after another. Then he left for a while—9:58. When he came back into view at 10:35, guess what happens? All of a sudden, Alberto morphs into Mr. Gotbucks, flashing a fat roll of bills and buying rounds for the house."

"So somebody gave him a fistful of cash," Ali breathed. "Do you think the money was a down payment, and it really was murder for hire?"

"I do indeed," Dave said, "and one with a fairly short timeline. Alberto makes the deal on Friday. On Monday evening, he and his pal Jeffrey somehow gain access to Dan's home in Paradise Valley. According to Paradise Valley PD, there was no sign of forced entry. Evidence suggests that they overpowered Dan. There were signs of a struggle inside the house, and it's clear the place had been ransacked. Maybe it was just a robbery, but the detective I spoke to said that what he saw suggested it was more likely the intruders were looking for something specific."

"Which they must not have found," Ali interjected.

"Correct, at least they didn't find it there. By Tuesday morning I'm thinking the bad guys admit defeat. Since whatever it is they're looking for isn't in the Paradise Valley house, they load Dan into the truck and head off for Sedona, hoping to find it there. According to E.D., there's some evidence of a search there, too, mostly before the deadly altercation in the kitchen. Once that happened, the killers took off in one hell of a hurry—with or without what they wanted—probably because of your dad's unexpected arrival on the scene. By midafternoon that same day Alberto and Jeffrey are shot dead in the gravel pit."

"In other words, as soon as Alberto and Jeffrey made good on the hit, whoever hired them took them out, too."

"Not a lot of evidence to back up that theory so far," Dave said, "but that's how it looks to me."

Ali thought about that. "Did Alberto walk to the bar Friday night?" she asked.

"Yes. The security footage shows him arriving and departing on foot."

"From what you said about the time stamp on the video, he wasn't gone long enough to go very far. Do you think he met up with someone in the parking lot?" Ali asked.

"I think that's likely, but whoever it was parked well beyond the range of the bar's security cameras."

"What about traffic cams?"

"We've asked for help in getting a look at those, but the bar is inside the Phoenix city limits. We're from out of town. In other words, our request isn't exactly a top priority."

"Which traffic cameras are we talking about?"

"The ones at the intersections of 43rd and Mc-Dowell and 43rd and Osborn."

"I'll ask Stu."

"He can access other jurisdictions' traffic cameras?"

Ali knew for a fact it was true, but she didn't want to say that straight-out. "It's possible," she hedged.

"Well, then," Dave said, "any help you guys can give us in the traffic cam department will be greatly appreciated."

Dave had just gifted Ali—and trusted her—with a good deal of confidential information he'd been under no obligation to share. He hadn't asked for anything in return, but she felt she owed him something all the same.

"We found a memory card earlier today that may throw some light on all this," she said quietly.

"Found?" Dave asked.

"We didn't actually find it," Ali allowed. "Haley Jackson, Dan Frazier's office manager in Sedona, found it, and she's the one who gave it to us. According to Haley, Dan sent Millie on a mission to deliver the card to their safe-deposit box in Sedona on Friday morning. Even though they were both coming home to Sedona later that day, he insisted she drop the card off earlier than that, telling Millie that he wanted to 'keep it out of the wrong hands.' Millie evidently stopped by Haley's office on her way to the bank—that's how Haley knew about it. And that's where Haley found the card this morning—at the bank in their safe-deposit box."

"How did she gain access to that?"

"She's Dan and Millie's executrix."

"Tell me about the memory card. What's on it?"

"No idea. Haley tried to look, but she says it's password protected."

"I wonder if that's what Alberto and Jeffrey were after—the memory card," Dave mused. "Where is it now?"

"On its way to High Noon in Cottonwood to see if someone there can hack into it."

"But why would Haley Jackson hand it over to you just like that? Are the two of you friends?"

"Not at all. I think Haley feels responsible because so many people lost their life savings with OFM. I had told her earlier that's what High Noon is all about right now—finding and recovering as much of OFM's missing money as possible. She suspects the card has something to do with the money, and so do I."

"And there's a very good chance that the money has something to do with the murders," Dave added thoughtfully.

"Right."

"So how soon will you know what's on the card?"

"That depends on how long it will take for Cami to hack into it."

"Cami again?"

"What can I say?" Ali returned. "The girl's got talent."

"Are you sure she's not up for grabs?"

"Not on a bet."

"What about the traffic cams?"

"I'll ask Stu to look into that," Ali said. "When it comes to traffic cams, he's the one with the network of contacts."

"Thanks," Dave said. "Appreciate the help."

"You're welcome."

"So how about if we do this?" Dave offered. "If I find something that leads in the direction of the missing money, I'll pass it along to you. And if you run across something that might help me solve my two homicides, you'll do the same. Deal?"

"Didn't we already make that deal?" Ali asked after a pause. "But it still stands. You scratch High Noon's back, we'll scratch yours."

47

Jessica found what she was looking for barely a mile after turning on to Beaverhead Flats Road. There was a slight rise followed by enough of a curve that the two-lane roadway was posted with NO PASSING signs in both directions and divided by two solid yellow lines. Just beyond the curve was a dry wash complete with a culvert and a concrete bridge abutment.

There was no oncoming traffic visible in either direction, so Jessica made a quick U-turn and recrossed the culvert. After yet another U-turn, she parked on the shoulder twenty yards or so on the far side of the abutment. This was old hat to her—an instinctive study in physics and geometry, because she had certainly never set foot in any of those math or science classes back in the old days in El Centro, California.

The school district liked to refer to its schools as welcoming and diverse, but not welcoming if you happened to be a blue-eyed blonde on a campus where Hispanic gangbangers wielded far more authority than any members of the faculty.

Jessica, named Mia Miller back then, had been fourteen years old when her Anglo mother had married a somewhat younger man, a migrant worker, and the two of them had . . . well . . . migrated. The couple had departed in the middle of the night, leaving Jessica alone in the house and totally on her own.

The rent on their two-room shack ran out four days later. A few days after that, the landlord showed up with an eviction notice in hand and a sheriff's deputy in tow. He had brought along a crew of workers who had emptied the place, leaving everything from inside the house—furniture, clothing, canned goods, dead appliances—out on the street, either free to a good home or else for the garbage collectors to pick up, whoever happened to show up first.

Jessica had been there that afternoon, watching the whole process from afar and helpless to stop it. After the crew left, she had raced to the trash heap ahead of the neighborhood vultures and gathered up what belongings she could, stowing them in some stray black plastic garbage bags that had also been left in the pile. Grabbing a grocery cart pilfered from a store two blocks away, she had left the abandoned house behind, pushing the cart with all her worldly goods stacked inside it—a few pieces of clothing, some canned goods that her mother had left behind, a bedroll of no known origin, a lumpy pillow, and a frayed teddy bear that had been her only companion for as long as she could remember.

She slept under a bridge that first night, finding camaraderie among the dozen or so homeless men and women—some older and some younger—who called the bridge home. They took her under their wings, showed her the ropes, and looked after her. They taught her where the soup kitchens were and turned her on to various homeless shelters where she could shower, clean up, and wash a load of clothes without having to answer too many questions. They taught her how to panhandle and made sure she didn't do it on her own without being under someone's watchful and protective gaze.

Where they couldn't look after her was at school—a place where the homeless couldn't go. She was small and apparently defenseless, so they taught her a collection of self-defense moves that toughened her up and made her resilient. The next time the gangbangers came calling, she handled it. Over time, she earned the gangsters' grudging respect along with a nickname, "La Rubia"—"the Blonde"—which she eventually shortened to Ruby.

She went to school every day. She didn't want to run the risk of a truant officer showing up at the address listed in her record only to discover that her family didn't live there anymore. She checked the mailbox every day, on her way back to the camp, deftly intercepting report cards, permission slips, and any other miscellaneous mail the school district happened to send out. She threw the report cards away, and forged her mother's name to the permission slips. She spoke Spanish like nobody's business and signed up for English as a second language, where the grades were easy to come by even though her blond hair and blue eyes raised a few eyebrows.

By the time she was fifteen and with the help of her gangbanger pals from school, she had a fake driver's license and plenty of connections in the world of forged documents—contacts that continued to serve her well all these years later. By age sixteen, she was earning a reasonable living as a car thief. A friend of a friend had hooked her up with a guy running an insurance scam. A guy inside the insurance company targeted high-end cars. Ruby's job was to steal the cars and wreck them in a believable enough fashion that the insurance adjuster (also in on the deal) could total them, and send the mangled remains off to a cooperating wrecking yard.

The whole idea was to leave as many salvageable and undamaged parts as possible. When it came to that, La Rubia was the best. As for grand theft auto? For a minor faced with trying to get by on her own, it paid a hell of a lot better than standing around panhandling on a street corner.

The guy who had pulled her into the racket had taught her the importance of leaving behind no evidence, so she was careful. When she went on jobs, she kept her hair tied back. She always wore latex gloves. And she was fine. Until the day she wasn't. That was the day a guy came running out of his house and caught her in the act of stealing his car.

She had pulled out her 9mm Beretta—a gift from the head honcho of the insurance scam—and plugged the son of a bitch. Then, leaving behind both the dead man and his unstolen vehicle, and unbeknown to her a single stray scrunchie, she had melted into the night. The guys under the bridge—the ones who had looked after her when she was begging at intersections—would have been shocked to learn that their "little girl" had turned into a stone-cold killer.

In the years since, she had left La Rubia far behind. She'd gone by more names than she could remember, but she hadn't forgotten the basic components of grand theft auto. Sitting there on the shoulder of Beaverhead Flats Road, Jessica carefully calculated the times and distances involved. She estimated exactly how fast she'd need to be going when she hit the bridge abutment—fast enough to deploy the air bags, but not fast enough to hurt her. And once the air bags collapsed, she had a fair idea of how much time she'd have in which to draw her weapon and have it at the ready before a certain passing Good Samaritan stopped and came to her aid.

Yes, when the lady in the red Prius stepped forward to see if Jessica needed help, she would be ready and waiting. Her primary goal was re-trieving the card, but as the minutes passed, she realized that taking down a High Noon operative in the process would automatically create a whole

new firestorm of problems. It also meant that her
original plan of lying low in Peoria for a number of
days was out the window. She and Jason needed to
leave the country now. Tonight.

That meant making a whole new set of arrangements on the fly, something Jessica couldn't do on
her own while driving back to Phoenix. She would
need a chauffeur to make that possible, and it so
happened that Ms. Prius was it.

Grabbing the garage door opener off the visor,
Jessica stuffed that inside her computer bag before
fastening the bag shut and belting it securely into
the front passenger seat. Now she could be sure
that she'd be protected by the exploding air bags,
and so would her computer and listening equipment.

She checked her rearview mirror. She was
ready now. She was a little disappointed that she
wouldn't be taking Ms. Prius out immediately, but
for the time being, she could handle a bit of delayed gratification.

48

Pulling away from Haley's office, Cami was over the moon. As far as she was concerned, this was the best day of her life. The investigation she had undertaken all on her own earlier that morning had paid off big-time. Her solo efforts had made it possible to identify Dan Frazier's killers. Well, maybe she hadn't done it entirely on her own. Stu's enhancing techniques and his facial recognition software had put the final nail in the coffin, but without her finding something for him to enhance, none of it would have been possible.

She was still patting herself on the back when her phone rang. Once she saw who was calling, she almost didn't answer. What was it about her mother? She had an uncanny ability to rain on Cami's every parade. In this instance, however, the dutiful daughter won out.

"Hi, Mom," Cami said. "What's up?"

"Your grandfather's birthday is coming up next month. We're having a party at the restaurant. Are you coming or not?"

Yes or no. That was Sue Lee, of course. Nothing at all subtle about the woman. She always came across in full frontal attack mode.

"I haven't worked here long enough to have any vacation time due me," Cami said, hoping to dodge the bullet.

"That's why I told your grandmother the party has to be on the weekend. You do have weekends off, don't you? If not, you need to quit working for those people and find a job with decent benefits."

The truth was, Cami worked around Stu's schedule, and he almost never took any time off. He was more than happy to work 24/7. No one at High Noon had ever implied that Cami was always required to be in attendance when Stu was. She took her days off as needed, always clearing them in advance. But taking time off and flying to San Francisco, where she was bound to be interrogated by a roomful of relatives who collectively disapproved of her career choices, was not something she needed right now. At all.

"He's turning eighty, you know," Sue added pointedly. "There's no telling how many more birthdays he'll have left after this one."

"I'll send flowers, Mom. I promise," Cami said, knowing it wasn't good enough.

"I don't know why you have to be so damned stubborn," Sue said.

Cami stifled an urge to mention that she was a chip off both of her parents' old blocks. She knew from previous discussions like this that her mother was happy to tell everyone within earshot that her husband was impossibly stubborn, while failing to see any trace of her own bullheadedness. Cami, on the other hand, was painfully aware of the presence of streaks of stubbornness on both sides of her DNA.

"And I don't know what's so important about this job of yours that you can't take some time off," Sue Lee continued.

Cami had turned on to Beaverhead Flats Road. Her good mood had evaporated.

"We're taking down bad guys," she said. "Virtual bad guys."

"Well," her mother sniffed. "I hope you're not putting yourself in any danger."

At that point Cami's Prius topped a short rise and rounded a curve. Several hundred yards ahead of her, she saw a yellow car parked on the shoulder of the road. At least that was her first impression—that it was parked. Suddenly it slammed into something, hard. The rear end of the vehicle bucked into the air, and then came down again, hard. A cloud of steam shot skyward.

"Mom," Cami said into the phone. "Someone just got into a wreck. I've got to go."

Ending the call, she pulled over and rammed the Prius into park on the shoulder directly behind the wrecked vehicle. Leaping out onto the pavement, she ran forward in time to see someone—a woman—clawing her way out from under a layer of deployed air bags.

"Are you all right?" Cami demanded, coming up on the driver's side of the vehicle. "Are you hurt? Do I need to call an ambulance?"

And that was when she saw the gun, pointed directly at her. "No ambulance," the woman inside said. "And unless you want a bullet in your gut, you'll do exactly what I say."

Cami froze where she was, staring at the only thing visible in her universe right then—the gaping mouth at the end of a gun barrel. Not a virtual gun barrel by any means, one that was all too real and less than three feet away from her.

"Throw the phone away," the woman ordered. "Now. Toss it out into the brush, as far as you can throw it. Then step away from the car door."

Cami did as she was told. She threw the phone away and moved back onto the pavement, glancing up the highway as she did so. Unfortunately, no vehicles were visible—none at all. She and the woman getting out of the car might well have been the only people on the planet.

"Any other weapons?"

Cami shook her head. That wasn't exactly true. She had a Taser. After the events in Bisbee, Ali had insisted that Cami carry a Taser, but not a handgun. Not yet. She had spent some time at a shooting range, but she didn't feel proficient enough to apply for a concealed carry. As for the Taser? It was in her purse on the floorboard of the Prius, just behind the driver's seat. That meant it was out of reach right now—completely out of reach.

During the confrontation, Cami's limbs somehow had turned to Jell-O. Both her childhood kung fu master and Amir Silberman, her current

Sedona-based coach, who was training her in the art of Krav Maga, an Israeli form of self-defense, would have told her that a lightning-fast kick could disarm her opponent, but not right then—not with Cami's legs trembling and threatening to collapse beneath her. There was no way for her to launch an effective counterattack right that minute.

"We're going to get back in your car," the woman ordered. "You're going to turn around and drive toward Phoenix. You will drive at or beneath the speed limit. If you do anything at all to attract attention, you're dead. Understand?"

Nodding, Cami stumbled toward the Prius. As she did so, she heard the faint ringing of her phone, plaintively calling to her from somewhere off in the brush. She couldn't see the caller ID, but she knew who it was—her mother. That was who it had to be, not that it would do any good. When Cami didn't answer, Sue Lee wouldn't actually do anything about it. She'd just be pissed that Cami had turned off her phone and wasn't picking up.

49

Neither Bella nor Leland Brooks was pleased when Ali showed up at the house and stayed only long enough to change clothes. She came back through the kitchen in a turquoise-blue sleeveless sheath and a pair of matching three-inch heels. The dress showed her figure to good advantage, and the shoes did the same for her legs.

As Bella gave her a baleful look from her bed beside the fridge, Leland handed her a sandwich wrapped in clear plastic.

"Leftover meat loaf," he explained. "I know you. When you're running around like this, you forget to eat."

It wasn't so much what he said as it was the chiding tone behind the words that let her know he was unhappy, probably because his carefully thought-out meal plans for the week had just been thrown out the window.

"Thank you for looking after us," she said. "I'm sorry this week has turned into such an uproar."

"How are your folks doing today?"

"Better than yesterday," she said, "and if I can pull off the appointment in Phoenix, maybe tomorrow will be an improvement, too."

"Good luck," Leland said, seemingly mollified. "But drive carefully."

She left the house. Back on the highway, she was about to dial Stu's number when he beat her to the draw.

"Hey," he said. "Are you on your way to that meeting with Lowensdahl?"

"I am," she said. "Wish me luck and hope there aren't any traffic tie-ups. Otherwise I'm going to be late."

"The traffic cams show everything flowing smoothly right now," he said. "But I'm glad I caught you. I've got some news that you need to have before you go to that meeting, and your parents—both of them—are the ones who've saved the day."

That was the last thing Ali had expected. When his number appeared on her caller ID she had figured he'd be on the warpath about still having Bob and Edie under hand and foot as well as about Cami being among the missing for so long.

"What did they do?"

"Your mom came in here a while ago with a handful of printouts—a dozen or so—that had been copied from posts on Jason McKinzie's Facebook page, all of them signed by someone named Ana Stander. Your mother came in to see me, all hot and bothered because she thought the Stander posts were different from all the others. Once I took a look at them, I had to admit she had a point. Most of the posts on McKinzie's Facebook page have faces on them—usually of Jason and some woman or other. These didn't. They were scenic shots only, accompanied by little notations like 'Wish you were here,' and 'Remember this?'"

"So maybe Ana Stander and McKinzie had been to all those places together?" Ali asked.

"That's what I thought," Stu answered, "but Edie insisted that didn't fit, either. The Ana Stander messages have been coming in for months now—for the better part of two years. Edie insists that when it comes to dating, Jason McKinzie is a 'one and done' kind of guy."

Ali laughed aloud at that. Edie Larson was big on commitment and heartily disapproved of people who routinely "played the field."

"So she comes into my office with a fistful of paper," Stu continued. "I don't do paper. I told her to have your dad send me the links. As soon as I downloaded the first one, I recognized it as a stock photo—the kind of thing people can use without having to pay the photographer a royalty. It turns out that's what they all were—one stock photo after another of scenery from all over South Africa. Seeing them got me to thinking: if McKinzie and Ana had been to all those places together, why didn't they post their own pictures or else pictures of themselves being there?"

"Maybe they're bad photographers?" Ali suggested.

"So I located another copy of one of the photos online, downloaded it, and guess what? The

Ana Stander file was a hell of a lot bigger than the other one."

"Steganography?" Ali asked.

"You've got it. Steganography all the way."

Ali knew a little about steganography. It allowed for the easy encryption of messages by simply concealing the real correspondence within the pixels of a seemingly harmless photo. It was a tool B. and other High Noon employees often used for handling internal communications that had to be sent over easily penetrated public Wi-Fi systems in hotels or airports.

"In other words," Ali said, "you know messages are there, but you can't read them, right?"

"Wrong," Stu replied with a chuckle. He seemed to be in uncommonly high spirits. "It turns out we *can* read them," he added, "and it's all because of your father. Just call it the revenge of the non-nerds."

"My father?" Ali asked. "He doesn't know the first thing about steganography."

"He didn't before today," Stu said, "but now he does. The first time I mentioned steganography, he asked me if it was some kind of dinosaur, but he's on track now. In fact, he's the one who found the password."

"To the encryption? Where?"

"Right there in plain sight in the stuff that came up in my data mining. He was doing just what you told him to do. He and your mom were going through that huge pile of links to find the ones applicable to our particular Jason McKinzie.

Guess what? He found him right there in the middle of one of the downloaded hacks for the Ashley Madison Web site."

"As in *the* Ashley Madison?" Ali asked.

"The very one. Ashley Madison is widely regarded as a cheaters' Web site. A bunch of hackers, armed with a raging case of righteous indignation, tried to blackmail the owners into shutting the site down by threatening to release private information concerning their members. Ashley Madison didn't budge, and neither did the hackers. The information went public on the Web. It includes the clients' Web site names—their Ashley Madison fictional noms de plume—as well as their real names, billing addresses, private e-mail addresses, credit card information, and passwords."

Stu stopped speaking. As silence came over the line Ali wondered briefly if he had hung up. "So?" she asked finally.

"Didn't you hear what I said? The hack download contained everybody's passwords," Stu said forcefully. "Jason McKinzie is one of those arrogant assholes who thinks of himself as the smartest guy in the room, only he's not—not even close. I'm sure he thinks he's got the world's greatest password, and that's the whole problem—all he has is one. He evidently uses it for everything—Facebook, LinkedIn, his private e-mails, probably even his bank accounts, for all I know, right along with Ashley Madison."

Ali knew a little something about this particular topic. Not too long ago she'd been hauled on the carpet and read the riot act by both Stu and B. for not changing her passwords on a regular basis. She did so now, just to keep peace in the family.

"He never changed it?"

"Nope," Stu said gleefully, "not even after the Ashley Madison hack went public. So I tried it on the South African photos and voilà!"

"Voilà what?"

"They opened right up."

"And they are?"

"Receipts for diamonds—hundreds of thousands of dollars' worth—purchased through a Dutch diamond cartel, and not conflict diamonds, either. I asked Lance to look into this, and he got right back to me. The diamonds are purchased through a third party, a money laundering service that operates on the dark web. Once purchased, the diamonds are warehoused at various banking institutions located all over the EU, places McKinzie could stop by anytime and pick up some as needed and turn them into bankable cash."

Ali's jaw dropped. She could barely believe what she was hearing. "So the SOB does have hidden assets," she exclaimed, "and you've found them!"

"We've found some of them," Stu cautioned. "Maybe not all, but a big chunk of them—one large enough to have a lot of zeros on the end of it. By the way, the most recent transaction—and by far the largest so far—happened a little over two months ago, a couple of weeks after the closing date on the sale of OFM's headquarters building."

"Bingo," Ali said.

"Bingo indeed."

"And my parents did this?" Ali asked. "Can I talk to them?"

"Not right now," Stu said. "They're still in the other room and still up to their eyebrows in sorting. Now that we have McKinzie's tried-and-true password, we have access to a lot more material that we never could have seen before."

"Promise me," Ali said, "that the next time you see my mother, you'll give her a hug."

"I'm not exactly a hugging kind of guy," Stu replied.

"In this instance, I think it's worth your making an exception," Ali told him. "What about B.? Does he know about any of this?"

For the first time in the entire conversation, Stu hesitated. "Not exactly," he admitted. "I'm supposed to be working on Basel, and I do have people working on that issue, but this one turned out to be too much fun. I couldn't help myself."

"Don't worry," Ali said with a laugh. "Considering the results, I think B. will give you a pass. And as long as you're not in the Basel loop so far, maybe you could give me a hand with something else."

"What's that?"

"Dave Holman is working his own double homicide, the Sun City one, which we now have reason to believe is directly connected to the Fraziers'. He needs traffic cam information from an area in Phoenix last Friday night. We're looking for a specific vehicle that may or may not have entered the parking lot at a bar called Wheels Inn. It's on 43rd Avenue, somewhere between McDowell and Osborn."

"Okay," Stu said. "I'll call him and verify all the details. In the meantime, what about Cami? Do you have an ETA on when she'll be back here?"

"Cami," Ali said. "I was so caught up in what you were saying, I almost forgot to tell you. She's on her way to you right now, coming from Sedona. A little while ago, Haley Jackson gave us a password-protected memory card that she found in Dan Frazier's safe-deposit box. We need to hack into it to see if it has anything to do with this whole mess."

"Okay," Stu said. "Once it's here, we'll get right on it."

Ali couldn't help smiling. For Stu Ramey, hugging was hard; hacking was easy.

"Right," Ali said. "You do that. In the meantime, I'll call B. and give him the good news."

50

Seated behind the wheel of her Prius, Cami fought to control her breathing. As she did so, her hands steadied. Her limp limbs were once again capable of operating the floor pedals. "Who are you?" she asked. "What do you want?"

"Who I am doesn't matter, but I want the memory card."

"What memory card?"

"Don't play dumb. I know you have it. Ali Reynolds gave it to you. Hand it over."

How could she possibly know that? Cami wondered. Only four people—Haley Jackson, her grandmother, Ali, and Cami—had been involved in the conversation that had ended with Ali handing her the card. Clearly the woman had been listening in on that conversation, but how? Was one of Haley's employees a traitor of some kind?

As for the memory card, was that what this was all about? With no other options, Cami had no choice but to comply. She plucked the tiny memory card and USB adapter out of the pocket of her jeans and handed them over. To Cami's astonishment, the woman immediately buzzed down the window and threw the card, adapter and all, out through the opening, where it disappeared into a sea of dry grass and underbrush.

"Why did you do that?" Cami demanded. "I thought you wanted it."

"As long as no one else has it, I'm good."

Minutes later, they reached the intersection with I-17, and Cami turned south toward Phoenix.

"Remember," the woman warned. "No speeding. Do nothing to attract attention to this vehicle. No flashing your lights or your brakes. If you try any of those tricks, you're dead. And don't think you can crash this car into something and still get away. You can't."

Cami had already arrived at that same conclusion. Ali had used that strategy on a carjacker months earlier, and it had worked. That, however, had been a low-speed crash. The bad guy hadn't been belted in, and the resulting blow had been enough to knock the weapon out of his hand. In this instance, both Cami and her captor were wearing seat belts. Even so, a seventy-five-mph crash was likely to be catastrophic for all concerned. For right now, her best bet was to do as she was told and lull her opponent into a false sense of security. Cami had been caught by surprise earlier. The next time, she'd be ready.

"I suppose you're going to shoot me the same way you shot Alberto Joaquín and Jeffrey Hawkins?"

Out of the corner of her eye, Cami caught the startled look her captor sent in her direction. "My, my," she said. "You're quite the little detective."

"And you work for Jason McKinzie," Cami added.

"Right again. So you know I'm serious. Now shut up and let me work."

Moments later, the woman was speaking into her phone. "It's me," she said without needing to identify herself. "Something's come up. We're going to have to move up our departure. Midnight tonight. Everything else remains the same—same passengers, same location, same destination. . . . Okay, see you then."

They were passing the Cordes Junction exit when Cami saw Ali's Cayenne racing up behind her. Cami was doing seventy-five; Ali, who was known for having a lead foot, was driving in the left lane and going several miles over the limit. As Ali sped past, Cami hoped that Ali would at least glance in her direction, but she didn't. Ali's mouth was moving. Most likely she was talking a mile a minute on her Bluetooth, so there would be no help from that quarter, at least not anytime soon. Not until someone noticed Cami had gone missing.

She understood that Stu Ramey, tucked in among his bank of computers, was the person most likely to find her, but only if he came out of his virtual world long enough to realize she was in trouble. Cami's challenge was to stay alive long enough for that to happen.

At the moment, her captor was under the impression that holding Cami at gunpoint gave her enough of an upper hand. The fact that it had worked to begin with made Cami flush with shame. In the shock of those few first moments while staring down the barrel of a pointed weapon, she had been completely unable to summon her gym-based Krav Maga training.

She had been studying the Israeli form of self-defense ever since the incident in Bisbee where a giant of a man had plucked her out of a vehicle through an open car window and nearly strangled her. Determined never again to be that helpless, she had signed up for Krav Maga.

To her instructor's surprise and to her own as well, she had turned out to be proficient enough that she had already achieved a green belt ranking. Her childhood training in kung fu had served her well in terms of learning the moves, but there was nothing ceremonial or polite about Krav Maga. There was no bowing; no formality; no philosophizing; no rules about not harming your opponent. This was street fighting, plain and simple—kill or be killed.

The problem was, all of Cami's previous Krav Maga training had happened in supervised situations—artificial situations. None of those had been a matter of life and death. This was different.

Cami stood at only four ten. She knew it was easy for other people to look at her and dismiss her and her capabilities based on size alone. That was one of the primary reasons she had signed up for Krav Maga in the first place.

The woman was still on her phone, making one call after the other. She exhibited not the slightest concern that Cami was privy to every word she said. That in itself served as a warning, telling Cami exactly where she stood. By the time those plans went into effect, the woman expected Cami to be out of the picture. It also meant that Cami had to take her captor out first.

She drove steadily onward, doing her best to appear scared and compliant, hoping her opponent didn't catch on. What Cami was really doing, though, was calming her jangled nerves and priming both her mind and body for action. One by one she silently recited the lessons Amir had required that she learn by rote: attack preemptively; establish possible escape routes; do the most damage possible—throat, eyes, fingers, feet.

Yes, she thought, consciously suppressing a smile. Her green belt, although invisible to the naked eye, constituted a concealed weapon. Enough of one, Cami hoped, to give her at least a Krav Maga fighting chance.

51

Ali's next call caught up with B. in the British Airways lounge at Sky Harbor. "On your way to that Phoenix appointment, I trust?" he asked.

"Yes, sir. As requested."

"And what are you wearing?"

"The turquoise silk shantung with matching heels."

"Wish I could be a mouse in the corner," B. murmured. "I've never met the man, but I spend my life dealing with corporate yahoos who think the sun rises and sets in their butts. I'd like to be there to watch the fireworks when you nail his feet to the floor."

"I'm going to, too," Ali said. "Wait until you hear what Stu and my parents found."

It took the better part of ten minutes to bring B. up to date. When she related the story about Facebook, he burst out laughing. "Count on Edie to notice something like that. I've never understood the appeal of Facebook or the need to compulsively look at photos of you and your nearest and dearest in every possible pose. For sure the SEC would go looking back through Jason McKinzie's e-mail history, but I can't imagine them bothering to check out his Facebook entries."

B. listened quietly, waiting until Ali ran out of steam before he spoke again. "It seems to me that Haley Jackson was surprisingly close to Dan and Millie Frazier. What about Dan's other PA, the one down in Phoenix? I wonder if she would know anything about the memory card issue, because it sounds to me as though the card may be an important piece of the puzzle."

"The PA's name is Jessica something. I have her last name in my notes, but I haven't spoken to her. When I finish up with Lowensdahl, if it's not too late, I'll see if I can track her down for a chat."

"What are you going to do about the diamonds?" B. asked. "Are you going to tell Lowensdahl about them or not?"

"I've been thinking about that. Birds of a feather flock together. McKinzie is a crook, and maybe Lowensdahl is, too. Maybe that's the reason McKinzie appointed him as CRO, so he could sway the results one way or another."

"Good call," B. said. "If he hires us to help with the recovery effort, that will be plenty of time to let him in on McKinzie's sizable diamond collection. For right now we're better off keeping that on the q.t."

Ali heard an announcement being broadcast over a public-address system in the background of B.'s voice. "Boarding time," he said.

The next few words of their conversation were entirely predictable. It consisted of nothing other than the sweet nothings people always say to one another when a loved one is setting out on a long journey—travel safe, do what you need to do, don't have too much fun, and come back to me because I'll miss you, and I don't know how I could live without you.

Once the call ended, Ali drove on through the parched desert, realizing that she really meant every one of those words. When her first husband, Dean, had died after a brief but terrible ordeal with glioblastoma, she'd had to find a way and a reason to survive. With a brand-new baby to care for she hadn't been given a choice. When her second husband, the philandering Paul Grayson, had been murdered, on the other hand, it had come as no great loss. His death had revealed the depths of his many betrayals. Those had hurt, but Ali had barely shed a tear for the man himself.

With B., it was different. They were lovers and partners, on the same wavelength, and pulling together in the same direction. If he somehow disappeared from her life, Ali Reynolds truly had no idea how she'd manage to go on without him.

52

Ali exited the 51 at Bethany Home and then, blocks later, turned east on Camelback, which the obnoxious female voice on the GPS insisted on calling Ca-MELL-back. A thermometer on a bank on the corner read 118—one degree worse than she'd been expecting. It had been almost twenty degrees cooler than that when she left Sedona.

Waiting through an exceptionally long stoplight, Ali attempted to strategize on how best to tackle Eugene Lowensdahl. With what she knew of the man's history, she'd either have to handle him with kid gloves or go for the jugular. There probably wouldn't be a lot of middle ground.

When she finally arrived at the Camelback Office Tower, she regarded the name on the ten-story mid-rise as a bit of an overstatement. She parked in a visitor spot on the ground level outside the main entrance. With the AC still on, she sat in her car long enough to extract Dan's PA's last name from her notes. A moment later she sent Stu a text requesting info on Jessica Denton, including her home address. Then, not wanting to have her upcoming meeting disrupted by buzzing message notifications or phone calls, she turned off her phone and opened the car door.

Stepping into Phoenix's heavy summertime heat was like walking into a wall. Inside the welcome cool of the building's main lobby, she studied the posted list of building tenants. Unsurprisingly, the offices of Eugene Lowensdahl, Attorney-at-Law, were located on the top floor.

Ali rode up in the elevator and opened the door to Eugene Lowensdahl's office suite at three p.m. on the dot. The main lobby and corridor had both been pleasantly cool. In her sleeveless dress she found the temperature in Lowensdahl's suite of offices to be downright chilly. The almost frigid air explained why the young receptionist at the front desk was wearing a sweater in the dead of summer, and it also didn't bode well for Ali's pending appointment. She knew the kind of overinflated ego it takes to maintain a steady 68 degrees in your office when the outside temp is a good fifty degrees warmer than that.

"Ali Reynolds," she said, passing her card to the receptionist. "I'm here to see Mr. Lowensdahl."

The young woman glanced at an open appointment book and then, frowning, looked back at Ali's card. "What about Mr. Simpson?" she asked. "I believe he's expected as well."

"He was," Ali said, "but he's been called out of town. He won't be joining us today."

"Right this way, then," the woman said. She

rose and led the way over to a door made of some exotic hardwood, which she held open for Ali to enter.

Ali paused on the threshold and looked around. This was the high-priced spread—a penthouse corner office. Two walls consisted of floor-to-ceiling windows made of slightly smoky glass designed to block out some of the sun. The side of the room that faced north looked out toward Camelback Mountain. The east-facing one showed the McDowell Mountains in the near distance, with the Superstitions towering hazily in the background. The two remaining walls were covered in glossy Formica, one white and one black. The white one held an immense piece of garish black-framed modern art. No doubt it came from a name-brand artist and was hugely expensive, but it looked as though the splashes of blues and magentas had been thrown at the canvas from across the room. Something about the spray of droplets reminded Ali of the blood spatter photo images she had studied in the Arizona Police Academy.

The furniture was mostly white leather on molded stainless steel frames. As for the desk? It consisted of thick pieces of white glass supported by more of the same. The edge of desktop was trimmed with something that looked like onyx. It included a row of built-in electronic receptacles, all but one of them empty. That one held a cord connected to an old-fashioned multiline black phone. The only other item on the pristine desk was a chrome-plated laptop whose user closed the lid abruptly when the receptionist ushered Ali into the room.

A silver-haired gentleman sat in front of the now closed computer, with his back turned pointedly on the view. His dark bespoke suit, made of some featherweight wool, his perfectly knotted yellow-and-blue tie, as well as his French cuffs and jeweled cuff links, were all designed to intimidate. He sat there, saying nothing and staring at Ali with what would have been unnerving scrutiny had she shown up in her blue jeans. Dressed as she was, however, Ali stared right back at him, giving as good as she got.

Finally, she stepped into the room and approached the desk, holding out her hand.

Lowensdahl didn't stand to greet her nor did he accept her proffered hand. "I was under the impression that Mr. Simpson himself would be taking this meeting," he said archly.

During her career as a newscaster, Ali had met plenty of overbearing jerks just like this one, and the best way to deal with them was to go on the offensive and fight fire with fire.

"He was unexpectedly called out of town," she said. Without waiting for an invitation, Ali took a seat on one of the excessively modern and incredibly uncomfortable chairs. "I'm here in his stead."

Lowensdahl dismissed her with a wave of a carefully manicured hand. "My understanding was that Mr. Simpson wished to see me on a matter of some urgency. I don't appreciate having him pawn the meeting off on some underling."

"I can assure you I'm no underling," Ali said with a smile. "I'm actually a full partner in High Noon Enterprises, and I'm here to speak to you about Ocotillo Fund Management. I understand you'll be serving as the CRO in the course of their bankruptcy proceedings."

Lowensdahl blinked and then sighed. "Yes," he said. "That's true."

"My belief is that your first duty as CRO is to determine if it's feasible to restructure the company and help it emerge from bankruptcy. Failing that, you're expected to assemble whatever assets remain and distribute them to creditors, including investors, correct?"

"Yes," Lowensdahl nodded. "That's about the size of it."

"How exactly do you propose to do that?" Ali asked.

Lowensdahl shrugged. "First we inventory all the tangible assets—real estate, bank accounts, automobiles, personal property, whatever—and sell them off to the highest bidder. Whatever funds we're able to obtain from that are used to pay off creditors, including the investors, who receive amounts in proportion to the monies they had previously invested."

"By real estate assets," she said, "I suppose you'd be referring to the equity in OFM's corporate building, for example?"

"Exactly," Lowensdahl said, nodding with a half smile as though encouraging a remedial student who had finally grasped some challenging concept.

"Are you aware Jason McKinzie already sold the building?" Ali asked.

That rocked him. Eugene Lowensdahl's shock and dismay were gratifyingly obvious. "He did?"

"Three months ago," Ali said. "As a member of the board of directors, I'm surprised you were unaware of that."

"This is all news to me," he said, "and something I'll have to verify independently rather than just taking your word for it."

"Of course," Ali said. "So if the equity from the sale of the building has disappeared, what other assets are there?"

"Look," Lowensdahl said. "You can't just walk in here and expect me to discuss confidential client information with you."

"Of course not," Ali agreed, "but High Noon's preliminary analysis of Mr. McKinzie's operation tells us that his customers have millions of dollars invested in Ocotillo Fund Management. That's a lot of money—a lot of other people's money. We also believe he has plenty of it tucked away in out-of-the-way places where he doesn't believe anyone else will be able to find it. He may be resigned to being caught eventually, tried, and even sent to jail, but he also knows that once he's done his time, he'll have access to all that hidden cash, and no one will be able to do a thing about it."

"Ms. Reynolds," Eugene said, trying to regain some ground. "At this point in our investigations, we have no indication that any of the Ocotillo funds have been, as you call it, 'tucked away.' More likely they've simply been badly mismanaged."

"And somehow vanished into thin air," Ali suggested.

"Yes," he said finally. "I suppose you could say vanished."

Ali didn't feel as though she was making much progress, so she decided to give him a glimpse of her high card.

"Supposing I told you that some of that vanished cash may have been turned into South African diamonds?"

"What makes you think that?"

"Without a formal agreement of some kind, I'm not prepared to reveal any of our sources," Ali said. "I'll just say that we're confident that is the case, and we'll be working to verify that information."

"What kind of formal agreement?" Lowensdahl asked.

"We'd like you to hire High Noon to try to retrieve some of those vanished funds," Ali said. "The longer you delay in going looking for them, the less likely you are to find them. Your hands are going to be tied up with red tape. Ours won't be.

"There's been a good deal of publicity recently concerning a group called The Family up by Colorado City," Ali continued. "Are you aware of any of that?"

"You mean that polygamous group that was involved in child trafficking? I suppose I know something about it—whatever was on the news. Why?"

"We know something about the group, too," Ali told him. "High Noon has been actively engaged in tracking down funds that the cult's leader socked away for his own benefit. We've used proprietary techniques that make it possible for us to locate supposedly unfindable funds. I think we could do the same here."

"Come on," Lowensdahl sneered. "You've got to be kidding. You think you can waltz in here with some cock-and-bull story about phony diamonds and expect me to hire you to track down something that may not even exist? No, thank you. I'm not hiring."

"We'd do it on a contingency basis, of course," Ali continued, "say, twenty percent of anything we recover. In other words, if we don't find any concealed assets, we don't get paid. It's as simple as that."

"Not interested," Lowensdahl said.

"What about clawbacks?" Ali asked.

"What about them?" Lowensdahl demanded.

"How are they handled?" Ali asked.

"For those we go to investors who have previously received disbursements and bring those amounts back into the asset side of the ledger. At the conclusion of the bankruptcy proceedings, those funds are returned to all investors on a pro rata basis. That allows us to be fair to all the investors, not just the ones who decided to withdraw funds early on."

"Why are you more interested in retrieving

money from the poor people who've already been victimized than you are in retrieving money from Mr. McKinzie himself?"

Lowensdahl sighed. "Let me remind you, Ms. Reynolds, Mr. McKinzie is nowhere to be found. It's thought that he's left the country."

"And taken the money with him."

"Be that as it may. I'm sure the authorities will find him in good time."

"When it's too late to find the money." Picking up her purse, Ali stood abruptly and laid her business card on the otherwise paper-free desk. "I believe we're done here, Mr. Lowensdahl. Feel free to give us a call if you change your mind about our being of assistance in this matter."

She walked out of his office then, striding away exactly as her mother would have wanted—head held high, shoulders back, and definitely with her knockers up.

53

When Ali opened the car door, the unmistakable smell of twice-cooked meat loaf exploded out of the car. The sandwich Leland had so thoughtfully given her had spent the better part of an hour baking in direct sunlight on the front seat. She settled on the scorching leather seat just long enough to turn on the ignition and activate the AC. Then, with the fan blowing full-blast, she grabbed the sandwich bag and walked it to the nearest trash can. Even so, the steering wheel was still too hot to touch when she returned.

She took a moment to check her phone. There was only one message, from Stu.

Do not go to Jessica Denton's address on Central. Call me.

Cami's still not here and she isn't answering her phone. I'm worried.

Ali dialed Stu's number at once. "Thank God it's you," Stu said when he answered. Stu Ramey wasn't someone to get overly excited about anything. Right now he sounded downright panicked.

"What's wrong?"

"Cami never showed," he said.

"She should have been there hours ago. Where could she be?"

"I got caught up with working on the Basel thing and wasn't paying attention to the time. When I surfaced and noticed she wasn't here, I had just heard on the scanner that the DPS was in the process of towing a vehicle that had crashed on Beaverhead Flats Road."

"Cami left from the Village," Ali said. "That's the quickest route between there and Cottonwood."

"Exactly," Stu said. "I called my dispatcher friend. The wrecked car was a stolen VW Beetle and not Cami's Prius. There were no injuries and the driver had apparently fled. In other words, no extensive investigation was required. Wham-bam thank you ma'am, they hauled it away."

"Was there any sign of Cami at the scene?"

"No, and not of her Prius, either, but that's where we found her phone. Not right at the scene but just north of where the VW crashed. Your folks went out into the brush and found it. Because of the location info, I was able to direct your father right to it. They're bringing it back here now."

"You think she's been kidnapped?"

"What do you think?" Stu replied. "You told me she was bringing me Dan Frazier's memory card. Is it possible that's why she was targeted—because of the card? If so, how would anyone else even know that she had it?"

Ali closed her eyes for a moment, remembering the scene in the office when Haley Jackson had given her the card. There had been only four people present at the time, unless one of Haley's employees had been eavesdropping on the conversation without their being aware of it.

"I was just about to call the cops," Stu said.

"Let's think about this for a minute," Ali said. "Do you have a lock on her car?"

"I do now. It's currently parked inside a garage at a residence on West Par Five Drive in Peoria."

"What do we know about that address?"

"Not much. It's a rental that backs up on a golf course. The landlord won't give me any information on the leasee without having a warrant."

"Cops could get a warrant, but if we bring them in, all hell is going to break loose in that neighborhood. Cami could get hurt and so could innocent people. If the car moves, all bets are off, you should call and report it. In the meantime, text me the address, and I'll head that way. It's rush hour. No telling how long it will take for me to get across town. The last I knew, Dave Holman was still here in Phoenix. I'll give him a call and walk this past him as well. And what about Jessica Denton? Was there something wrong with her address?"

"No, there's something wrong with the person," Stu replied. "The real Jessica Denton, the one with that Social Security number, was born in Laramie,

Wyoming, in 1992 and died three years later. It's probably just some kind of identity theft, but I didn't want you showing up at her door without knowing she wasn't the real deal."

Ali thought about that scene in the office again, with all of them gathered around an impromptu table littered with pizza boxes and coffee cups. She thought about what Carol Hotchkiss had said, something about Jessica stopping by to visit the night before and about something being off about it.

"Text me the address in Peoria, but I'll get back to you. I need to make a call."

Haley Jackson's number wasn't in Ali's contact list, so it took her a moment to look it up and make her way past the receptionist who answered the phone.

"Is something the matter?" Haley asked. "Carmen told me you said it was important."

"It is important," Ali said. "Cami Lee never made it to Cottonwood with the memory card. She may have been kidnapped."

"No. How is that possible?"

"That's what I want to know," Ali said. "I think someone may have been listening in on our conversation. You said Jessica Denton was at your house last night, correct?"

"Yes. For a couple of hours at least."

"Has she ever been in your office?"

"A couple of times, but not recently."

"Where's your purse?"

"Right here by my desk, why?"

"Do me a favor. Empty it onto your desk?"

Driving west on Camelback, Ali listened to the sound of items falling out of the purse onto the surface of a desk. Then she heard Haley say, "What the hell? What's this?"

"What's happening?" Ali asked.

"There's something here in my purse that I've never seen before—a little black box that looks like a compact but it won't open. What is it?"

"In all probability it's a listening device," Ali said. "Jessica probably planted it at your house last night when she came to dinner. Pick it up right now. Before you say another word, carry it into that private office, leave it there, and close the door."

"But why?"

"Just do it."

Ali listened to the sound of footsteps moving across a room with voices chatting in the background. Finally a door closed.

"What's this all about?" Haley asked.

"I believe Jessica may have planted the device in your purse when she was at your house last night."

"She's been listening in on me all day?"

"And may still be," Ali warned. "I believe she was trying to get a line on the memory card. What kind of car was she driving?"

"Just a sec. Gram, did you see what kind of car Jessica Denton was driving last night?"

"A little yellow foreign car of some kind," Carol said. "One of those Bug things."

Ali's heart constricted. "That's all I need to know," she said.

"But wait," Haley interjected. "Don't hang up. Does this mean Jessica is mixed up in all this?"

"It certainly does. A yellow VW Beetle was found wrecked this afternoon, between the Village and Cottonwood. Cami's phone was found near the scene. She wasn't there, and neither was her vehicle."

"You're saying Jessica took her?"

"I think so."

"And the card?"

"That's gone, too. I doubt we'll ever see it again, and that means we'll never be able to figure out what was on it."

"Maybe we can," Haley said quietly.

"How?"

"Because before I gave it to you, I copied it onto Dan's desktop in his office."

"You copied it?" Ali asked. "You mean you still have everything that was on the card?"

"Yes, I have it, but I can't open it. Like I said earlier, it's password protected."

"Here's what I want you to do," Ali said. "I want you to pack up that desktop immediately and take it to High Noon's offices in Cottonwood. Take the bug there, too, and give both of them to Stu Ramey."

"All right," Haley agreed. "As soon as we can get the car loaded, Gram and I will be on our way."

"Do me a favor, though," Ali said. "Put the bug in the trunk. We sure as hell don't want anyone listening in on your conversation as you drive there."

Ali was about to hang up, when she thought of something else.

"On second thought," she added, "don't take your car."

"Don't take my car?"

"If Jessica Denton bugged your purse, there's a good chance she bugged your car, too. Instead of wasting time looking for it, take someone else's car."

"Got it," Haley Jackson said. "Will do."

54

The woman directed Cami off the 101 and into a neighborhood of curving streets lined with tile-roofed houses. Once they turned on to Par Five Drive, the spaces between homes offered brief glimpses of improbably green fairways. Twice Cami had to pause briefly to allow foursomes of golfers to make use of marked golf cart crossings.

"Slow down," the woman directed. "It's the one on the right."

Cami slowed as the door on a two-car garage rolled slowly open. A tan minivan with a handicapped license plate was parked inside.

"Park next to the van," the woman ordered as the garage door rolled shut behind them. "And don't try anything. Make no mistake, I will kill you."

But not with that gun and not right now, Cami thought, forcing herself to remain calm as she opened her own door and stepped out of the car. Gunshots in a neighborhood like this on a weekday afternoon would attract far too much unwelcome attention.

A door leading into the house opened and a man stepped out, smiling in welcome. As soon as he spotted Cami, the smile disappeared. "Jessie, what the hell? Who is this? What's she doing here?"

Jessie? Cami thought, hearing her captor's name for the first time. Could that possibly be Jessica Denton, the woman who was supposedly Dan Frazier's personal assistant? Was she involved in all this, including Dan and Millie's murder? As for the silver-haired man in the doorway, his Bermuda shorts and Hawaiian shirt gave him the look of an ordinary sandal-wearing retiree, but the facial features beneath that perfectly combed hairdo didn't quite work.

Dye job, Cami concluded. This has to be Jason McKinzie, in disguise and trying to look decades older than he really is.

"Don't worry about her," the woman called Jessie said to him. "Slight change of plans. Let's get her inside."

Standing on one side of the car, with Jessica and the gun on the other, Cami surveyed her surroundings, looking for either a means of escape or a possible weapon. She found neither. The rolling door was closed. That meant that the only way out right now was either past or through the man. And there were no weapons here. The garage, with taped but unpainted Sheetrock walls and a shiny, perfectly clean concrete floor, was completely empty—no workbench, no tools.

Besides, in this relatively small space, she'd

no doubt have to deal with both of them at once. She might have a better chance inside the house, where she could at least hope to have access to an impromptu weapon. In a larger space, with the possibility of more separation between her and her two opponents, Cami might find an opportunity to deal with them one at a time.

Letting her shoulders droop and bowing her head as if in resignation, Cami walked into the house. She came in via a tidy laundry room and through a narrow kitchen. On the far side of a quartz-topped island lined with barstools was a great room—half living room, half dining room. On one side of the room was a small vestibule leading to the front door. On the other were floor-to-ceiling glass sliders, looking out onto a small patio and a lap pool, framed in the distance by a stretch of green fairway. A seemingly unnecessary wheelchair was parked in front of the expanse of windows, with a laptop open on the table in front of it.

"Sit," Jessie ordered Cami, motioning with the barrel of her still-drawn weapon toward the barstools.

Barstools were Cami's nemesis. They were almost impossible for her to clamber up onto. Once there, her legs were usually too short to reach the crossbar, leaving them dangling in midair. That was the case now, too, but she did as she was told. Then she sat quietly, continuing to examine her surroundings, listening in all the while as Jason and Jessie argued back and forth.

Looking around, Cami realized that this wasn't a place where someone had lived for any amount of time. The interior was done in a designer-enforced, relentlessly Southwestern style that reminded Cami of her parents' time-share in Palm Springs. A troop of Kokopellis, made of hammered copper, marched single-file along one wall. A tasteful arrangement of red clay ollas spilled across the hearth at one corner of a gas log fireplace. A flat-screen TV hung over the fireplace, flanked on either side by framed prints of people who most likely represented Native Americans, although they looked more like beanbags than people.

The only likely weapons currently in view, other than the clay pots, consisted of a set of knives in a knife block on the kitchen counter next to the sink. Unfortunately, the counter was on the far side of the island from where Cami was sitting. Too far away, she judged. A partially empty beer bottle sat next to the computer on the dining room table. Also too far away and too close to McKinzie. Other than those, Cami saw nothing useful.

"What change of plans?" Jason asked.

"We're leaving tonight. Same deal as before. Meet up with the borrowed turboprop our crop duster friend has at his hangar in Casa Grande at eight. He ferries us as far as Cananea. Our friends take over from there and transport us on to Belize."

"But tonight? Are you kidding? It's too soon. There's still far too much interest out there—too many people paying attention."

"Too bad," Jessica replied. "The conditions on the ground have changed. I'm not sure how it happened, but a cybersecurity company called High Noon Enterprises is now involved."

"So?"

"Believe me, they're bad news for us—very bad news. They've got ways to penetrate the dark web that could lead straight back to us."

"What about the card? Did you get it?"

"Of course I got it," she told him. "I wouldn't be here now if I hadn't."

"Where is it?"

"I threw it out."

"Where?"

"In the desert on the way here. Trust me, no one is ever going to find it. And as long as we have the computer, we don't need—"

She stopped short. "What's that doing out?" she demanded, waggling the barrel of the gun in the general direction of the open laptop. "And why are you not in the wheelchair? What if one of the neighbors spots you?"

"The front blinds are closed. In this weather, nobody in his right mind would be out in his backyard, and the people on the golf course couldn't care less. Besides," he added, "the local news is worthless. I was just trying to get an idea about what's really going on."

"You're surfing the Web? For God's sake, Jason, how dumb are you? Shut it down. Now!"

He said nothing. Like a sulking teenager, he sauntered over to the table, touched a couple of keys, and then slammed the lid shut on the computer.

"What about her?" he asked, nodding in Cami's direction. "What happens to her?"

"I'll handle it," Jessica said.

"Right," he said. "The same way you handled Alberto Joaquín and Jeffrey Hawkins?"

Jessica turned a frosty look in his direction. "It got the job done, didn't it?"

Sitting on the barstool, Cami fought to suppress any visible reaction. She had suspected as much, but hearing the confirmation was chilling. If Jessica and Jason were responsible for killing Alberto and Jeffrey, that meant they were also ultimately responsible for the murders of Dan and Millie Frazier, too.

Jessica sighed. "Look," she said. "I'm done for. I need a shower and some clean clothes before we leave, but it's a long way to Casa Grande in rush hour traffic. We should probably head out fairly soon. Better to be early than late. Can you keep an eye on our little friend for a while?" As she spoke, she laid her weapon on the table, near enough to Jason to be within easy reach.

Cami held her breath. She knew that someone wielding a knife—assuming she could lay hands on one of those—could cross a room and plunge a blade into someone before he'd have time to draw his weapon, aim, and fire. In this case, before McKinzie could pick it up off the table. But that was if she could actually lay hands on a knife, and if the gun remained in the same position.

To Cami's immense relief, McKinzie pushed the gun aside. "I won't need that," he said. "I'm not exactly helpless, you know."

"Really?" Jessica said. "Okay, have it your way." Picking up the weapon and returning it to a small-of-the-back holster, she turned and left the room.

55

Jason McKinzie slumped in his wheelchair and did a slow burn. How dare the bitch talk to him like that? How dare she come in here and start ordering him around like he was some sort of underling? Who was paying the freight here? It was one thing for her to do her damned job, but it was something else for her to decide she was running the show. She wasn't, by God. He was! She was the hired help, and he was in charge.

Then he glanced at the girl. That's all she was, really a little girl—barely out of high school from the looks of her. Sitting there on the barstool with her legs dangling in midair, she looked more like a baby in a high chair than she did an adult. And Jessica thought he should be scared of *her*? Like hell.

"I need to go to the bathroom," she said.

She spoke so quietly and he was so lost in thought that he almost didn't hear her. "Sure," he said, waving. "Help yourself. The powder room's right over there."

56

Ali Reynolds, stuck in a massive traffic jam, used the time to phone Peoria PD. A fatality hit-and-run on the 60 had shifted most of the near west side's north/south rush hour traffic onto I-17. Unfortunately, Dave Holman was already almost back in Prescott before Ali managed to reach him. His advice had been short and sweet.

"Call 911."

She had done so, immediately, speaking to an operator who regarded this as some kind of prank call. Eventually Ali got kicked up to a supervisor, where she had to repeat the story from the beginning.

"A possible hostage situation?" the supervisor repeated. "I'll put you in touch with the Peoria PD watch commander."

"Who are you, again?" Watch Commander Harold Martinson asked after Ali again laid out the situation. "What's your connection to all this? You're saying a possible kidnapping, but this sounds like a straight-out missing persons case to me—a Yavapai County missing person, at that. And what makes you think this so-called kidnapping victim is being held in my jurisdiction?"

Ali wanted to scream out of pure frustration. "My name is Ali Reynolds, with High Noon Enterprises," she said as civilly as she could manage. "Camille Lee is our employee. Early this afternoon she and her car both vanished while she was on her way from the Village of Oak Creek back to our offices in Cottonwood. A wrecked VW Beetle was later found along that same stretch of highway, the one she would have used."

"Yes," Martinson said. "I've got that. I have the report right here—stolen vehicle, wrecked with no injuries, and no trace of the driver. You do understand, Ms. Reynolds, that this incident may be entirely unrelated to your missing employee."

"Cami's phone was found nearby," Ali countered. "It had been tossed off into the brush near the roadway not far from the wrecked vehicle."

"And yet you were able to find it?"

Ali sighed. "Yes," she said. "I didn't find it personally. My people did."

"And now you're claiming that Ms. Lee's missing vehicle, a red Prius, is currently located inside the garage of the residence at 15540 West Par Five Drive here in Peoria?"

"Correct."

"You know this how?"

"As I told you, Cami works for us—for my husband and me," Ali insisted. "Because we're concerned about our employees' safety, we've installed

GPS locating devices on all of their vehicles, Cami's included."

"I'm not sure that kind of spying on your employees' private lives is even legal," Martinson said, "and it makes me glad that I'm not one of them. That said, what you're giving me is pretty thin. You're asking me to send in a SWAT team based on what you've told me so far. Ms. Lee is an adult, right?"

"Right."

"She's not related to you, there's been no official missing persons report filed anywhere, and she's been off the radar for a total of what, five hours?"

"Four."

"So what happens if my guys bust into a house on your say-so—a house in a very nice neighborhood, by the way—and find Ms. Lee tucked in bed with her boyfriend—or girlfriend, as the case may be? What happens then? Who comes off looking like a first-class fool? Not gonna happen, Ms. Reynolds. Not on my watch."

"Thanks loads," Ali said, not bothering to stifle her sarcasm. Ending the call, she inched over to the exit at Glendale and continued north and west, traveling on backed-up surface streets. Then she dialed Stuart Ramey.

"Peoria PD basically told me to go piss up a rope," Ali said. "I'm stuck in traffic, and heading for Par Five Drive as fast as I can."

"You're going there without backup?" Stuart said. "You can't. Don't do it. B. will kill me."

"I don't have a choice," Ali said. "What's going on at your end?"

"One of Jason McKinzie's e-mail accounts is active again. He's been online searching the Net for . . . wait for it . . . information about Jason Mc-Kinzie. The computer he's using is one that—as far as I can tell—has never been on the Internet before. The activity seems to be coming from—guess where?—Par Five Drive in Peoria, at the same location where Cami's Prius is still stationary."

"Where the local cop shop has just declined to participate."

"Maybe we need to call the FBI."

"Maybe so," Ali said, "but I'm worried about that. If we alert them based on information you've lifted by hacking into Jason McKinzie's life, it might invalidate his arrest. I don't want any of our actions to end up jeopardizing a later conviction. Like it or not, Stu, I'm going to that address, but I'm not stupid. I'll take a look around and then I'll leave."

"I still don't like it," Stuart said. "But hold on a minute. I've got something else for you. Haley Jackson showed up a little while ago with a monstrosity of a computer. Not steam-driven, but close. It took three men and a boy—well, your father and me, anyway—to carry the damned thing inside. It takes up most of a desk all by itself, and your dad just finished getting it plugged in. Once we have it up and running, we'll be able to see what was on that drive without having to run the risk of loading the information into one of our computers. No telling where those files have been, and considering the power of the worm that wiped out OFM's files . . ."

He paused. "Okay. It's finally done booting up, and here's the unnamed drive." In the background Ali heard the distinctive key clicks of an old-fashioned keyboard.

"Haley says it's password protected," Ali said.

"It is indeed," Stuart replied, "but I'm taking a wild guess here. Dan stole the files, he's dead, and Jason McKinzie is currently on the lam. Let's try Mr. McKinzie's one-size-fits-all password, which, thanks to your parents, I happen to have right here." A second machine gun blast of key clicks came through Ali's phone, followed by another pause. "Yup," Stuart said. "There you go. Got it."

"Got what?"

"Abracadabra. The drive opened."

Ali could barely contain her excitement. "What's on it?"

"I'm looking. A huge database, for one thing—hundreds of names. That one looks like it might be an OFM client list. There are several that appear to be accounting programs. Those are all accessible, by the way. In addition, there are several much smaller files. Those are encrypted."

"Is it maybe the same encryption key that unlocked the South African photos?"

"Nope. All it took to unlock those was McKinzie's password," Stuart said. "I just tried that one on these, and it didn't work."

"Keep trying," Ali said, and then she added, "Okay, I'm here now. I'm just pulling up."

"Ali," Stuart pleaded. "I beg you. Please do not go near that house without backup."

"But I do have backup," she said, "and you're it. Stay on the line, Stu. There's a local municipal election coming up—a special election. I just saw a yard sign for someone named Lois Rogers who's running for city council. I'm going to go up to the door, ring the bell, and pretend I'm one of Lois's campaign workers. If someone opens the door, I'll try to peek inside. I may be able to get a glimpse of what's going on."

"What if things go south?" Stu asked.

"If that happens, it's your job to run up the flag."

57

Once Cami heard the shower running, she knew this was her moment. If ever she was going to act, it had to happen now, while Jessica was in one room and McKinzie in another; while it would be one-on-one rather than two-on-one. As for which one she should take down first? No question. Jason McKinzie was "it."

Jason had made his opinion of Cami Lee blazingly clear. He regarded her as little more than a fly on the wall—a minor irritation. He had no idea Cami posed any threat at all, much less a serious one. Not keeping the gun had been his first mistake. As for mistake number two? That was his complete lack of hesitation in allowing Cami to use the restroom.

Yes, Cami told herself. She'd take on Jason first. Once he was down, she'd try to make a break for it, out through the back patio and onto the golf course. There would be people out there she could ask for help. And if Jessica happened to finish her shower before Cami had a chance to get away? Well, she'd cross that bridge when she had to.

On her way to the powder room and still searching for potential weapons, Cami found herself staring at a collection of likely looking prospects. On a glass coffee table set between two large upholstered sofas stood three Kokopelli statues. She hadn't seen them before because, due to the high backs on the oversized sofas, the statues had previously been out of Cami's line of sight.

Like the ones on the wall, these Kokopelli figures, too, were made of thin sheets of hammered copper. Each one was attached to a marble base by a single brass strut. Cami could tell just by looking that the two taller ones would be too large and heavy for her to wield effectively. The smallest one, however, appeared to be a good fit.

She'd been telling the truth when she'd said she needed to use the bathroom. Once inside, she was happy to relieve herself. Studying her face in the mirror while washing her hands, she recalled a time when she'd lost a student body election by a single vote. She'd done what everyone always said you were supposed to do. She'd been told that she should always "play fair" and "be a good sport" and not put herself first. Abiding by those dictums, she had voted for her opponent rather than for herself. Had the election ended in a tie, the principal would have had to choose between the two candidates. With Cami's rule-abiding vote for the other girl, Cami had taken the decision out of the principal's hands and made the choice for him.

Still standing in front of the mirror, Cami straightened her shoulders. Sitting on the barstool with her feet dangling helplessly in the air, she'd been as much a victim inside the house as she had been in the car with a loaded gun pointed in her direction. That was over. She was no longer helpless. Now she was angry.

No rules, she vowed to her image in the mirror. *Not this time.*

She came out of the powder room fully prepared to do battle with Jason McKinzie, only to find that he wasn't there. He was no longer seated at the dining room table. He was gone and so was his computer. Thinking he must have joined Jessica in the bedroom, Cami hesitated. If the two of them had hooked up again, her best bet was to make a break for it right now. She should go somewhere and call the cops. After all, she knew in general where Jessica and McKinzie were going. She also knew which vehicles they'd be driving.

Just then the gauzy sheers over the patio sliders puffed slightly as a hot breeze blew into the room. That was when Cami realized one of the sliders was standing wide open. Looking past the patio and lap pool toward the backyard, she caught a glimpse of McKinzie, computer in hand, ducking through an oleander hedge at the back of the property and then sprinting out across the open fairway.

Before Cami could make a move to follow, Jessie, clad in a robe and with a towel wrapped around her wet hair, appeared in the near end of the bedroom hallway. She and Cami must have seen the open slider at almost the same instant.

"What the hell?" Jessica demanded.

Bathrobe means no holster, Cami told herself. *No holster means no gun and no rules.*

Jessica was still staring at the open patio door when Cami launched her attack. Grasping the smallest statue by its supporting rod and holding the base in front of her like a mini battering ram, Cami threw herself toward Jessie, aiming for the throat. Somehow, out of the corner of her eye, Jessie must have seen Cami coming. She spun around and tried to dodge back down the hall, moving fast enough to deflect the incoming blow without avoiding it completely. Rather than hitting Jessie full in the throat, the marble base slammed into the side of her face, slicing open her cheek and sending her reeling.

Unfortunately, Cami wasn't exactly left un-scathed. Carried forward by her own momentum, she smashed into the wall next to the hallway, knocking the breath out of her lungs and the statue out of her hands. Standing together on the coffee table the statues had seemed substantial enough. In reality they were nothing but cheap knockoffs. Cami's so-called weapon landed on the tile floor and exploded into pieces. The faux marble base shattered. The rod, separated from the copper figure, rolled in one direction, while the Kokopelli itself slid out of sight under one of the sofas.

By the time Cami regained her equilibrium,

Jessie had done the same. The next time Cami saw her opponent, Jessie was on her feet and stark naked. The robe was gone and so was the towel. She vaulted toward Cami with a length of material stretched between her hands.

After being momentarily stunned, it took almost too long for Cami's brain to register the words "bathrobe tie" and to understand the threat. If Jessie's plan was strangulation, Cami needed a countermeasure, and she needed it now.

Pivoting away, Cami lunged for the next usable weapon—one of the knives from the block on the kitchen counter. Knowing the larger ones would be unwieldy in close combat, she opted for two small paring knives as she darted past before positioning herself at the far end of the island.

The two women stood still at opposite ends of the quartz counter, each silently assessing the other. Cami noticed that even though Jessica had deflected Cami's initial blow, she had nonetheless suffered some damage. There was a jagged, bleeding wound on her cheek. A steady stream of the blood ran unchecked down her neck and dribbled off her breast.

Measuring from the top of the island, Cami estimated Jessie to be at least five six or five seven. She most likely outweighed Cami by a good forty pounds. It looked as though her arms might be long enough to enable her to fend off the short-bladed paring knives in Cami's hands without much difficulty. And so, Cami decided, if the knives weren't going to be the final answer, then that's where Cami needed to keep Jessie's undivided focus—on those two blades.

Still at the end of the island, Cami forced herself to take a deep breath. The element of surprise may have been taken from her, but Amir had shown her how to turn an opponent's supposed advantage in terms of size and weight against them. Cami's next proposed move was designed to do just that.

Jessie took a single challenging step toward the counter, one which also carried her a step nearer the knife block.

"Don't," Cami commanded.

Holding both paring knives in plain sight, she, too, moved out from behind the island and into the small passage between the island and the kitchen countertop. Cami's and Jessie's next long stare-down took place with nothing separating them but five feet or so of open space.

"You'll never get to the knife block," Cami warned. "I'll be all over you before you do."

"Why don't you try it, you little bug?" Jessie sneered, taking another cautious step forward. "I dare you. You have no idea who you're dealing with."

There was a certain familiarity in all of that, a reminder of Cami's old kung fu days, only this time the opponents were trading insults rather than formally polite bows. And then, for a second or so, Cami was back on that long-ago school bus with the bully needling her. *Which are you, Chinee or Frenchee?*

Taking her own forward step, Cami needled right back. "Darers go first," she said, with a smile. "The way I always heard it, the bigger they come, the harder they fall."

Letting the tie drop from her hands, Jessica sprang forward, and Cami launched her own attack in the same instant. Jessica's whole focus was on reaching the knife block and grabbing for a handle. Ducking forward with the blades of her own knives nearly touching the floor, Cami darted in well under the taller woman's outstretched arms and under her radar as well. As they collided full-force, Cami rose to her full height, smashing into the bottom of Jessica's chin with the top of her head.

The blow was solid enough that it left Cami still standing but dizzy and seeing stars. Jessie, however, pitched straight backward, falling all the way to the terrazzo-tiled floor. With nothing to break her fall, her head bounced twice on the unyielding surface. After that she lay still.

Not knowing how long Jessica would be out, Cami didn't hesitate. Dropping the now unnecessary knives, she used all her strength to roll Jessie's considerable deadweight over onto her side. Next she grabbed the fallen bathrobe tie and bound Jessica's hands securely behind her back, finishing by bending Jessica's knees backward and securing her feet to her hands.

Cami was standing upright and admiring her hog-tying handiwork when Jessie started coming around. When she moaned, a small trickle of blood dribbled out of the corner of her mouth. Obviously she had bitten her tongue.

Out of breath with exertion, Cami quickly gathered up all the knives in the room—both the ones she'd dropped as well as the ones in the block. Out of sight behind Jessie's back, she stuffed all of the knives—block and all—onto the top shelf of the freezer, where they were both out of reach and out of sight. Then Cami went to the bedroom and retrieved Jessie's handgun. Returning to the kitchen, she dropped the fallen robe over Jessie's bloodied and naked form.

The woman's eyes burned with helpless fury. "You bith!" she muttered, lisping the word past a painfully swollen tongue. "You little bith!"

"You should actually be saying thank you about now," Cami told her pleasantly. "When the cops show up here, you're going to be glad to have that robe."

58

Ali had a bulletproof vest in the Cayenne, but if she was going to make the campaign worker fiction fly, she couldn't very well show up in a vest. Her silk shantung sheath made no allowance for carrying a Taser, and her very high heels weren't exactly doorbelling-friendly, either. She ventured up the walkway through a xeriscaped front yard, arriving at the front door with her fight-or-flight mode fully engaged.

"All right," she said quietly into the cell phone now stowed strategically in her bra and switched on speaker. "Here goes. Quiet now, everybody. Not a word."

She pressed the bell. A two-toned chime sounded inside the house, but that was all. No one came to the door. No one answered. She rang the bell again.

"I guess nobody's home," she said resignedly to Stu. "You're sure Cami's car is still here?"

"I'm not sure of anything at this point," Stu replied. "The GPS is still there, but the car may not be."

"The blinds on the front of the house are all closed," Ali said. "But there's a gate on the side of the house. I'm going to go around back and see if I can see anything there."

"Don't," Stu cautioned. "Please."

But Ali's mind was already made up. "Stay with me," she told him. "This won't take long."

Walking around the house, she was grateful for the flagstone walkway that led to a side gate. The rough gravel covering the yard would have torn her heels to shreds, and in the scorching late-afternoon heat, walking barefoot wasn't an option.

She stopped at the gate and was tall enough to peer over it. The back of the property consisted of a small flagstone-paved patio, a lap pool, and another tiny bit of graveled yard. At the end of the yard was a thick oleander hedge lining what was evidently a golf course fairway. There was a golf cart parked in the center of the fairway with a golfer lining up to take a shot, but closer at hand, Ali saw no signs of life. There was no one swimming in the pool. There was no one seated at the patio table with its obligatory four chairs and brightly colored umbrella. The place seemed empty and deserted.

"Okay," she said, her voice barely above a whisper. "Can't stand here any longer or a neighbor will report me for trespassing. Going in now."

Because of the pool, Ali knew there would be a state-mandated pool latch on the inside of the gate. She pulled up on it, cringing at how noisy it sounded in the stillness of that scorching afternoon. Carefully setting one foot in front of the other, she inched onto the patio.

The first set of patio sliders evidently led to a bedroom. She could see closed blinds and beyond those another covering of some kind, maybe blackout curtains. She stopped there, though. Holding one ear to the glass, she heard nothing—no one talking; no radio playing background music; no TV set droning away on an afternoon news show. Convinced the bedroom was empty, Ali moved on.

It wasn't until she reached the patio table that she saw that the door space in the next set of sliders was wide open. Again she paused, listened, and again heard nothing. She pulled the phone out of her bra and held it up to her lips.

"Something's haywire here," she whispered, taking the phone off speaker mode. "Nobody's here. Door's open. Going in."

The phone went back on speaker and into her bra without Ali bothering to listen to Stu's latest bark of protest. She edged up to the near end of the wall of windows and peered around the frame. Through a set of sheer curtains she saw a standard modern great-room arrangement—a kitchen with an island that looked out onto a combination living room and dining room. There was a dining table with six chairs; two sofas with matching end tables and lamps; a flat-screen TV set hanging on the wall over a gas log fireplace.

Then, as her eyes adjusted to the difference between the harsh outside sunlight and the more muted interior, Ali saw something else. Broken pieces of glass—or pottery, maybe?—gleamed on the dark area rug beneath the two sofas.

Something broken, Ali told herself. Did that mean there had been an altercation of some kind? A struggle? Was Cami hurt? Dead?

She hesitated for a cautious moment longer. Still there were no signs of movement inside the house and no signs of life, either. In the distant background she heard faint strains of approaching sirens, but she was too worried about Cami to give them much thought. Instead, she eased herself silently into the room and moved quickly to the spot on the carpet where she had seen what she assumed to be broken glassware. She bent down close enough to examine one of the pieces, peering at it closely without actually touching it. A glance was enough to convince her that it was a hunk of something that looked like carved marble. The base of something, perhaps—a lamp, maybe?

That's when she spotted blood. There were drops of it on the white-tiled floor and some on one of the broken pieces, too. Suddenly she heard a rustling sound coming from somewhere behind her.

Goose bumps instantly covered her body. A chill ran up her spine. Standing and spinning, she fully expected to find an armed attacker directly behind her. No one was there, but the sound came again, louder this time. A thrashing, bumping noise that seemed to be coming from somewhere in the kitchen, from the far side of the quartz-topped island.

Heart in her throat, Ali stepped toward the sound. A moment later she saw a naked woman, tied hand and foot, struggling desperately to free herself. Ali was about to reach out and offer to help her when she heard a fierce pounding on the front door.

"Police! Open up! We're coming in!"

The front door splintered under the weight of a battering ram. A troop of uniformed officers, all wearing SWAT vests and helmets and carrying automatic weapons, burst into the house—through the shattered front door and through the open slider from the patio as well.

"On your knees," one of them shouted, grabbing Ali by the arm and flinging her roughly to the floor. "On your knees and don't move!"

59

Cami was halfway across the first fairway when a golf cart with a red sign marked MARSHAL in the front window came bearing down on her.

"Hey, lady," the old guy in the cart yelled at her. "You can't be here. This is a golf course. I've had unauthorized people out here running around like crazy today. One of you is going to get beaned on the head by a golf ball and end up dead."

"Where'd he go?" Cami asked.

"Where'd who go?"

"The other guy on the course. He came this way, too. I saw him. He was dressed in a Hawaiian shirt and sandals."

"Who isn't dressed in Hawaiian shirts?"

"And he was carrying a computer."

"Oh," the marshal said. "That guy. I have no idea where he went. People called to complain that he was out here screwing up their game. When I came looking for him, guess who I ended up finding? You."

"You've got to call the cops."

"Crossing a fairway is a bad idea, but it's not exactly a federal offense. Come on, sweetheart. Get on board here. Let's get you out of the way so the people waiting to play this hole can at least tee off."

"You don't understand," Cami insisted. "The man's a crook, and he's about to get away. He and his girlfriend have been holding me at gunpoint. She's back there in the house. I left her tied up, but I don't know how good my knots are. She might be able to get loose."

The marshal already had a phone out of his pocket. "Here," he said, handing it to her. "If you want to call the cops, you dial."

Once the phone was in Cami's hand, it was all she could do to hold on to it as the speeding cart bounced through a narrow line of gravel-lined rough and onto another fairway.

"911. What is your emergency?"

"My name is Camille Lee. I was kidnapped earlier this afternoon, by two people who held me prisoner at a house in Peoria—15540 West Par Five Drive. I managed to get away. The man took off, but the woman is still at the house. I tied her up before I left, but I'm worried she may get loose. Her name is Jessie—Jessica Denton, I believe. The man is someone you're looking for—Jason McKinzie. He ran off across a golf course . . ." She held the phone away and looked at the guy driving the cart. "What course?"

"Rancho Vista," he said. Cami quickly relayed that bit of information into the phone.

"Are you hurt?" the emergency operator was asking. "Do you require medical assistance?"

"I don't need anything but some help in catching the bad guy. Help catching both of them. They're planning to leave the country tonight. If we don't stop them, they'll get away. Please, please hurry."

She hung up, saying thank you as she handed the phone back to her driver.

"My name's Larry," he said, stuffing the phone back into his pocket. "I'm taking you to the office, by the way," he added. "I'll need to write up a report about this. Residents aren't allowed on the course unless they're actually playing a round."

The speeding cart rounded a sharp corner and careened onto a cart path, aiming for a long, low building with umbrella-dotted dining decks on one end and a pro shop and club drop-off at the other. Larry drove around to the front of the building, stopping the cart near where a mob of excited people were milling around the front entrance next to a valet parking stand.

"What's going on?" Larry asked one of the uniformed valets.

"Somebody stole Mr. Norton's car," he complained. "We'd brought it up from the lot and had it here idling so it could cool off. All of a sudden, some asshole walks up here, big as you please, climbs inside, and drives off, stealing the damned thing right out from under our noses. I've never seen anything like it."

"Has anybody called the cops?" Larry asked.

"You bet. They're coming."

"I'm sure they are," said Larry, looking at Cami, "and for more than one reason."

Cami shook her head. "He's going to get away," she said despairingly. "We'll never catch him."

"Don't you believe it," Larry grinned. "Mr. Norton's one of those guys who likes to have all the upgrades. If I'm not mistaken, he's got one of those thingamajigs—I can't remember what it's called—that will shut that Buick of his down whenever he hits the button."

"Right," the valet said. "He's on the phone with both OnStar and the local cops right now. They're trying to figure out where's the best place to take him down."

"Be sure to let the officers know that McKinzie isn't just a car thief," Cami said. "He and his girlfriend are responsible for at least four deaths that I know of."

"Is he armed?"

"I don't think so," Cami said, "but he might be."

"I'll go pass that information along."

"Thank God," Cami murmured, watching him walk away. Then, after thinking a minute, she turned back to Larry. "Can I use your phone again: There are people up in Cottonwood who are probably worried sick about me. I need to let them know I'm all right."

He handed the phone over at once. Cami dialed Stu's direct number and was startled when someone else answered. "I need to speak to Stuart Ramey," she said. "Who's this?"

"I'm Edie—Edie Larson. Stu's pretty tied up right now. Our daughter is in some kind of difficulty down in Phoenix. Is there something I can do to help?"

"This is Cami," she said forcefully. "I don't care what's going on. I need to speak to Stu. Now."

"Oh, thank goodness," Edie breathed. "I'm so glad you're safe."

A moment later Stu came on the line. "Cami, is it you? Really?" he demanded. "Are you all right?"

"She said something's going on with Ali. What?"

"We traced your car to a residence in Peoria. Ali went there, hoping to find you. A neighbor saw her and reported a burglary in progress. The cops showed up, put Ali in cuffs, took away her phone, and threw her in a patrol car. They think it's some kind of home invasion case. They believe she assaulted some poor woman and tied her up."

"That 'poor' woman, as you call her," Cami said, "turns out to be named Jessie—Jessica Denton I believe. She's in league with Jason McKinzie. They killed Alberto Joaquín and Jeffrey Hawkins, and I suspect they're responsible for Dan's and Millie's deaths as well. They were planning to fly out of Casa Grande later tonight, heading for Mexico. Right now McKinzie's driving a stolen vehicle, but it's equipped with OnStar. They're hoping to shut the vehicle down someplace where the cops will be able to take him into custody."

There was a pause while Stu reported that information to someone else, and Cami could hear cheering in the background.

"What's happening with Ali right now?" Cami asked.

"I don't know. Like I said, they took her phone away. I've tried calling back, but nobody answers. Where are you?"

"I'm in a golf cart," Cami answered. "But Larry here, my knight in shining armor, is about to take me back across two fairways to the house. If the cops there won't talk to you, maybe they'll listen to me."

60

Sitting in the idling patrol car, Ali couldn't help but see the irony in her situation. A day and a half after the same thing had happened to her father, here was Ali. The car's AC was doing its best to cool the vehicle but it wasn't making much headway in the face of the fierce late-afternoon heat.

Ali was drenched in perspiration. There were sweat lines in the bright blue silk of her dress that would most likely never come out. As an officer hustled her out of the house, one of her heels had caught in a crack in the driveway pavement and broken completely off.

At least she wasn't in cuffs. That meant that her hands were fully visible, complete with one bare nail. The bright red acrylic, so carefully applied at Priscilla Holman's nail salon two days earlier, had slammed into the kitchen countertop and disappeared completely as the cop had thrown her to the floor.

The officers here hadn't listened to her any

more than the ones in Sedona had listened to her father. Her protestations that the naked, bleeding woman on the floor was anything but a helpless victim went unheeded. Ali seethed to think that the woman who was most likely Cami's kidnapper had been hauled away in an ambulance, probably to some overcrowded ER where she was likely to change into someone's scrubs and walk away from the hospital with no one any the wiser.

As for Ali's suggestion that her employee, Cami Lee, might have been imprisoned right there in that same residence? Had anyone even bothered to listen to her and go out to the garage to check the registrations of the cars parked there? If so, no one had come outside and mentioned it to Ali.

Just then a burly uniformed officer emerged from the house. Trotting along beside him and barely reaching his elbow was Cami Lee. They came straight to the patrol car, where the officer pulled open the back door and held out a hand to help Ali emerge.

Sliding off the seat, Ali stood up and swayed drunkenly on the broken heel while pulling Cami into a heartfelt embrace. "I can't believe it's you," she murmured. "I can't believe you're safe. How did you do it? How did you get away? Where were you, somewhere in the house?"

Behind them, the officer cleared his throat. "Excuse me," he said. "I believe I need to introduce myself, and I also need to apologize. I'm Watch Commander Martinson," he said. "I'm so sorry about all this. The story you told me before seemed completely improbable, but obviously, as Cami here has just been telling me, all of it was true."

Ali let go of Cami. As soon as she did so, she tottered on her uneven heels and almost fell.

"What's wrong?" Cami asked. "Are you hurt?"

"I'm fine. I broke the heel off my shoe is all, and that makes it almost impossible to stand. I have a spare pair of tennis shoes in the car, but it's locked, and someone took my keys."

"Of course," Watch Commander Martinson said. "I'll go get them and be right back."

Ali turned to Cami. "What happened? Who did this?"

"Jason McKinzie and someone named Jessie."

"Jessica Denton?" Ali asked.

"I think so," Cami answered. "They were desperate to get that memory card back. She staged the wreck and took me at gunpoint for no other reason than to lay hands on it. Then, once she had it, she tossed it out of the car like it was nothing before we ever made it to the interstate. What's with that?"

"We don't know everything on the memory card, but we know some of it," Ali said. "Fortunately, Haley Jackson made a copy of it on Dan's office computer before she gave the memory card to us. Stu has accessed some of the information and is probably working to learn more even as we speak."

"They're killers, Ali," Cami added. "Both of them."

"How do you know that?"

"Because I heard them talking. McKinzie said that Jessie killed Alberto and Jeffrey. They were planning on leaving the country tonight, and I'm sure Jessie had every intention of killing me, too, before they left."

Ali shook her head. "When I asked you to deliver the memory card, it never occurred to me that I was putting you in such danger."

"How did they know about that?" Cami asked.

"There was a bug in Haley Jackson's purse. Jessica evidently listened in on everything we said. But if they murdered Alberto and Jeffrey, does that mean they're responsible for Dan's and Millie's deaths as well?"

Cami nodded. "That's how it looks to me."

Commander Martinson emerged from the house just then, carrying Ali's bag and grinning from ear to ear. "I'm happy to report that Mr. McKinzie is now in custody," he said, handing Ali her purse. "OnStar shut him down in the middle of an intersection as he was making a left-hand turn onto the 101. Our officers were Johnny-on-the-spot to take him down. And I've sent someone to the hospital to keep an eye on Ms. Denton for us, with orders to take her into custody the moment she's released. They've stitched up the hole in her cheek, but she also has a concussion. She may end up being hospitalized overnight."

He looked at Cami. "Did you do that?"

She nodded. "I hit her in the chin with the top of my head."

"Wow," Martinson said admiringly. "Just plain

wow! You may be a tiny little thing, but you've got to be tough as nails."

After digging in her purse, Ali found her key ring and handed that over to Cami. As she did so, her phone, now in Martinson's hands, began to ring.

"Thank God," Stu said when he gave it to her. "If they're letting you use your phone, Cami must have knocked some sense into them."

Ali glanced at the beefy watch commander and smiled. "You could say that," she said.

"Have you seen my texts?"

"Not yet. I just now touched the phone."

"Until we find out everything Jason McKinzie and Jessica Denton have been up to, I thought it might be helpful for you to have copies of the birth and death certificates for the real Jessica Denton. You're welcome to pass them along to the cops. If they can't hold Jessica on anything else, they can charge her with identity theft for right now."

"Thanks, Stu," Ali said. "I'll hand over this information immediately, but you should know that, as of now, Jason McKinzie and Jessica are both in police custody."

"Both of them?"

"Both."

"Let me tell Bob and Edie."

Ali heard a joyous uproar in the background of Stu's phone. "They're thrilled," Stu said a moment later. "And your mom wants to know what time you'll be home."

"Probably not until much later," Ali said. "I have

a feeling this whole situation is going to take hours to resolve, and I have no intention of leaving Cami on her own until it is. In the meantime, you should probably give Dave Holman a call and Eric Drinkwater, too. Cami said McKinzie indicated Jessica was responsible for murdering Alberto and Jeffrey."

"Dan and Millie, too?"

"Maybe," Ali said. "Time will tell, but both detectives may want to be down here so they can be in on the interviews should the need arise."

Cami returned with Ali's tennis shoes. Gratefully, she sank back down in the patrol car and slipped them on.

"Better?" Martinson asked.

"Much."

Standing back up and finally steady on her feet, Ali opened the first text from Stu and passed her phone to Martinson. "You need to look at these. I have no idea who Jessica Denton really is, but this is who she's pretending to be. The first one is a birth certificate. The second is a death certificate."

Martinson pulled out a pair of reading glasses to examine the documents, then he handed the phone back. "Very interesting," he said. "Now, if you two ladies would be so kind, I'd like to give you both a ride down to the department. I have some detectives who are very eager to talk to you."

"What about our cars?" Ali asked.

"I'll bring you back to yours," he said to Ali. "As for Ms. Lee's Prius? That will probably need to be impounded long enough for us to gather evidence about the kidnapping."

"What about my purse?" Cami asked. "It's behind the driver's seat."

"I'll go get that for you right away, Ms. Lee," Martinson said, and shambled off.

Watching him go, Ali realized that he was being solicitous now because he'd been so completely wrong about the situation earlier in the day.

Oh well, she thought, better late than never.

61

Ali's interview with a Peoria PD investigator took almost no time at all. He wanted to know what had brought her to the residence—the locator beacon on Cami's Prius—and all her movements once she arrived. She was asked no questions about anything that had occurred outside the city limits, and she was in and out in less than an hour.

She was in the waiting room—waiting—when first Dave Holman and later Eric Drinkwater arrived. She and Dave spoke briefly before he hurried off to the interview room.

"Before you talk with McKinzie," she told him, "there are a few things you need to know. He mentioned in front of Cami that Jessica 'handled' Alberto and Jeffrey."

"Did he say anything about Dan and Millie?"

"Not that I know of, but he's also been buying diamonds, right and left. There may be more money out there besides the amount he's invested in diamonds—we're still tracking on that—but you can let him know that whatever happens, he's going to be missing out on some of those extra funds he was counting on to fund his future lifestyle."

"I'll keep all that in mind," Dave said. "Thanks."

When Eric Drinkwater came through the room, he glanced briefly in Ali's direction and then went past without a word of acknowledgment.

Same to you, Ali thought.

At loose ends, she meandered over to a corner of the room and tried to settle into a stiff wooden chair, hoping to have a chance to doze off for a moment. Had she been carrying James Joyce's *Finnegans Wake* along with her, that wouldn't have been a problem. The emotional turmoil of the past two days had left her beyond weary.

When her phone rang at 8:50, she wasn't surprised to see Stu's direct number in her caller ID. "I guess you're still working," she said.

"Have you seen Dave?"

"Yup. He's in an interview room right now."

"You might want to get word to him. My traffic cam guy came through. We've got video of Jessica Denton at the intersection of 43rd and McDowell shortly after the time Alberto Joaquín walked back inside Wheels Inn. She was driving a rental, rented under the name of Barbara Toomey. The vehicle was later found abandoned at a shopping center within walking distance of the house on Par Five Drive."

"Good work," Ali said. "He'll need to go through channels to get this, but I'll let him know."

"Wait," Stu said. "That's not the best of it. Just

wait until you hear." Stu was so excited, he could barely contain himself.

"What?"

"We've got him! We've got lines on McKinzie's money—all of it—or at least on whatever's left."

"How?"

"Your parents found it, or at least they figured it out."

"Found what out?" Stu was so wound up that he was talking in circles.

"They cracked the encryption code. Or, rather, your mother did."

"Are you serious? How?"

"When we tried to open one of the encrypted files, there was a hint for the code—you know, something to prod your memory in case the user has forgotten it. The hint said Lincoln, GA."

"Lincoln, Georgia?" Ali asked.

"I tried that," Stu said. "I found a place called Lincolnton in Georgia and a Lincoln County there as well, but neither of those seemed to help. Then your mom remembered something she read late this afternoon. Jason McKinzie came from humble beginnings, something he didn't care to bandy about. He grew up dirt poor in Morenci, Arizona. The Arizona Historical Society has spent millions of dollars digitizing all the state's hometown papers to make them accessible. One of the links I sent to your dad was from the *Morenci Miner*. Your dad located it and printed it, but your mother is the one who sorted it, and she doesn't just sort them—she reads them as well."

"And?"

"When Jason McKinzie was in the seventh grade, he won a fifty-dollar prize in a Chamber of Commerce–sponsored oratorical contest for reciting the Gettysburg Address. Sure enough, 'Four score and seven years ago' does the trick. And what's in those encrypted files? Banking information—names, locations, amounts, account numbers. And a complete listing of leased properties—condos and houses—including the one on Par Five Drive."

"This is amazing. Does B. know about any of this?"

"He's sleeping right now," Stu said. "I'll let him know in the morning. Or you can."

"Where are my folks?"

"On their way home. Your mother gave Bob a choice. Either he promised not to backseat drive or she was leaving him here with me. I'm sure she was kidding about that. They were both over the moon about finding the money, and I don't blame them. I am, too. Jason McKinzie may have robbed them blind, but they worked their butts off today, trying to get back some of their own."

"And they did," Ali said. "And not just for themselves, either. A lot of other people will benefit as well."

Call-waiting buzzed with an unknown number showing on the caller ID screen. "Sorry, Stu," she said. "I've got another call. With everything that's going on, I'd better take this."

She switched over to the other line. "Please hold the line for a call from Eugene Lowensdahl."

It was late—after nine by then—but Ali recognized the voice of the sweater-wearing receptionist from Eugene Lowensdahl's office. The fact that Lowendahl was calling her was unexpected, but the fact that he couldn't be bothered to use his own fingers to punch in her number was not.

"All right," Ali said. "I'll hold."

He came on the phone sounding only slightly less arrogant than he had earlier in the afternoon. "Ms. Reynolds?"

"Yes."

"It has just been brought to my attention that all data was removed from the OFM computers in the hours preceding the bankruptcy filing."

"I was aware of that," Ali said.

"You were?"

"Yes," Ali said. "The hard drives were wiped by some kind of worm. I didn't mention it because I was sure you already knew about it."

"Well, I didn't," he said. "I had no idea. There are paper files, of course. Everyone is required to maintain those, but scanning and searching through that much paper just to do the accounting will be an impossible task. Not only that, I don't even have a complete listing of the clients."

Thanks to the stolen memory card, Ali was quite sure High Noon was already in possession of such a list. And a whole lot more besides—direct trails to Jason McKinzie's embezzled funds. She also knew how painful it was for someone like Lowensdahl to ask for help, but she didn't make it easy for him. She wanted him to spit it out.

"So what's the purpose of this call, Mr. Lowensdahl?" Ali asked.

"Is your offer of trying to recover funds still on the table?"

"I suppose," Ali said, "at our standard fee of twenty percent."

"Absolutely," he said. "That's more than fair."

Of course, Ali thought, *it's easy to strike that kind of deal when you're busy spending other people's money.*

"Very well," Lowensdahl said. "I'll have my office draw up a suitable agreement tomorrow. Is it safe to assume that you're one of High Noon's principals?"

"Yes," she said. "B. and I are full partners in this endeavor. He happens to be in Switzerland at the moment, but I can sign a letter of agreement just as well as he can."

"All right, then," he said. "We'll be in touch."

Ali pumped air and gave herself an audible "YES!"

A clerk seated on the far side of the room glanced up from her computer keyboard with a wary look. She probably thought Ali was having some kind of spasm, but Ali didn't care.

Bob and Edie Larson were winning. Jason McKinzie and Jessica Denton were losing. What could be better than that?

62

"Turn in here," Bob said, directing Edie into a grocery store parking lot.

"You promised you wouldn't backseat drive," she said. "And why a grocery store? We already ate dinner with Stu."

"Sharing pizza with Stuart Ramey isn't exactly what I'd call fine dining, but just let me out. You can stay in the car. I'll only be a minute, but I'll need to borrow your wallet."

It was after nine. The store was practically deserted. He was back out in less than five minutes carrying a paper bag with a rather distinctive shape.

"You bought booze?" Edie asked.

"Not booze," he said. "Champagne. You and I are going to go home, watch the news, and celebrate."

Back at Sedona Shadows, Bob got down the ice bucket and cooled the champagne while Edie polished off the dust that had accumulated on a pair of seldom used champagne glasses. By the time the local news came on at ten, they were in their respective recliners and holding their respective flutes brimming with chilled champagne.

The first story on *Headline News* was about the arrest of fugitive financier Jason McKinzie, CEO of the failed investment firm Ocotillo Fund Management. Also arrested was his accomplice, former OFM employee Jessica Denton. McKinzie was found driving a stolen vehicle while trying to flee. A local crop-duster pilot from Casa Grande is being questioned in regard to his part in the plot to spirit the pair out of the country in order to escape prosecution.

"Peoria Police Department is releasing no further information about the arrests at this time due to the ongoing nature of the investigation. An anonymous source close to the investigation indicated that, in addition to stolen vehicle charges, there is some speculation that the two suspects may have been involved in a possible kidnapping. Details on that are sketchy at this time. We'll be following this story throughout this newscast. As more information becomes available, we'll be sure to pass it along."

"The details are sketchy, all right," Edie sniffed. "What about their implication in four homicides? When is someone going to mention that?"

"Soon enough," Bob said. "They'll figure it out."

"Are you including Eric Drinkwater in that 'they'?" Edie asked.

"I guess," Bob said, picking up the remote and turning off the TV set. "But that's not what I want to talk about tonight." He raised his glass and they toasted. "Here's to you and me, babe. Turns out the two of us are pretty damned smart, smarter than the average bear."

"How smart are bears?" Edie asked. "Ali told me this morning that they needed our help because we're 'wise.' I think what she really meant is that we're old."

"Old or not, we gave Stu a run for his money today. He never would have come up with the Gettysburg Address, never in a million years."

"That was fun," she agreed.

"But now let's talk about us. Yesterday when I saw the news that our money was gone, I really thought our lives were over. Whether we get all of it back or none of it, I learned a big lesson. You and I are in this together."

"Hear, hear," Edie said with a smile.

"So I've been thinking about those life insurance policies we have on each other."

"The ones we bought from Dan?"

Bob nodded.

"What about them?"

"I think we should take some of the money out of those and spend it on us," he said. "We've made a deposit on this fall's cruise, and I think we should go regardless. I want to bet on us and on the belief that some of the money we lost is going to come back to us. And if it doesn't, we may be poor as church mice, but we'll be church mice together who've just come back from a cruise."

Edie studied him for a second or two, then she

raised her glass and smiled. "Amen to that," she said.

"And I also wanted to say thank you."

"For what?"

"For being there for me when I was at my lowest ebb. I don't know how I would have gotten through this without you and my guys."

"Your guys?" Edie asked. "What did they have to do with anything?"

"They lit a light for me last night. Just when I needed it most, they lit a light that got me to straighten up and fly right."

The phone rang then, their landline, interrupting their conversation and startling them both. Edie put down her glass to answer. A moment later the smile on her face dissolved into a frown. "He's here? Now? All right, we'll be right down."

"Who's here?"

"That was Bridget. She says Detective Drinkwater is down at the desk."

Bob rose from his chair.

"Shouldn't I go with you?" Edie asked.

"No," Bob said. "You stay here. You've done enough for one day. Whatever it is, I'll handle it. Besides, given your opinion of Eric Drinkwater, I'm afraid you might just rip into him."

It was a long walk from their unit at the end of the corridor to the front lobby. Eric Drinkwater stood with his hands in his pockets, staring out through the glass front door toward the parking lot.

"You wanted to see me?" Bob asked.

Drinkwater turned. When he did, Bob saw that

the distinctive Bronco's key ring was dangling from the detective's fingers. "You heard about what went on down in Phoenix tonight?"

Bob nodded. "Some," he said.

Thanks to Stu Ramey, Bob knew a good deal more about the investigation than "some," and far more than he should have, but he didn't let on.

"Two more people are dead besides Dan and Millie Frazier and two suspects are currently in custody," Drinkwater continued, "including Jason McKinzie. He and a female accomplice are being transported to the Yavapai County Jail in Prescott, where Dave Holman and I will be conducting our interviews with them tomorrow morning. The two dead victims found shot to death north of Sun City early this morning are thought to be the doers in the Frazier homicides. A vehicle found nearby, a truck belonging to a Phoenix-based landscaping company, contained items believed to have been stolen from the Fraziers' home in Paradise Valley."

"The Sun City victims were hitmen hired to murder Dan and Millie?"

"That's a reasonable assumption," Drinkwater said. "And once they finished the job, they were murdered by the people who hired them. Which means, sir, that you're no longer a suspect, and I owe you an apology. I also owe you these." He held out the key ring and dropped it into Bob's outstretched hand. "I had a guy from the impound lot drive the Bronco over. It's waiting out front."

Bob took a moment to digest those words. Dan and Millie Frazier were both still dead, but thanks to B. and Ali and Stu Ramey and Cami Lee, Bob's part in that nightmare was over. He looked at the keys for a long moment before slipping them into his pocket, then Bob Larson held out his hand.

"Okay," he said. "Apology accepted."

63

Haley Jackson was standing in the shower when she remembered the mess in the kitchen. By the time she and Gram had finally made it home late last night after yesterday's very long day, she hadn't been able to face it. Now, rather than do the cleanup in her work clothes, she hurried into the kitchen, only to find that Gram was already there and the coffee was almost done.

"Surprise," Gram said with a grin, pointing toward the stove, where a brand-new set of shiny pots and pans sat on display.

Haley stopped and stared. There was no evidence of the old charred pan anywhere in the room. "How did you manage these?" she asked.

"I asked that very nice Carmen Rios—she's a treasure, you know—to go pick them up from the hardware store while we were in Cottonwood. I had told her about the mess, and she offered to come by after work, drop these off, and get rid of the dead one. Because of all the stinky smoke, I asked her to put several of those plug-in air fresheners throughout the house. Look what she found behind our couch."

Gram picked up a small black object from the table and handed it to Haley. She studied the item—something small and electronic. "A listening device?" Haley asked. "Another bug?"

Gram nodded. "That would be my guess. Remember how, just as Jessica was leaving the house, something happened—like she tripped over something and spilled her purse? All of that happened on the far side of the couch. I'm willing to bet the whole thing was a ruse so she could plug this in without our noticing."

"Well," Haley said, reaching for the pan that would work best for oatmeal and giving it a fast soapy wash under running water. "I just heard on the news that both Jessica Denton and Jason McKinzie are currently being held in the Yavapai County Jail in Prescott."

"Good riddance," Gram said pleasantly. "May they both rot in hell."

Once Haley got to work, it was a relatively quiet day. Admittedly, a few still-irate customers came in to formally cancel their policies. Haley spent the better part of an hour on the phone with Morgan Whitney. Dan and Millie's bodies had been released to the funeral home, so the arrangements could be finalized. By the time the call was over, the paid-in-full service was set for 2:00 p.m. on Friday afternoon. She was finishing that call when an anxious Carmen appeared in front of her desk.

"What's wrong?" Haley asked.

"That Agent Ferris is here again," Carmen said. "He's asking to speak to you."

Haley shook her head in resignation. "All right," she said. "I'll speak to him in Dan's office. Bring him there in a few minutes."

Haley stood outside the door for a moment, preparing herself to enter the office. At some point, she supposed, this would become hers. For right now, though, it was still Dan's. By the time Carmen ushered Agent Ferris in, Haley was seated behind the desk.

She rose and held out her hand. "Good morning, Agent Ferris. What seems to be the problem this morning?"

"No problem," he said. "I came to express my apologies and also my condolences."

Haley sank back into the chair and studied the man. "Apologies for what?" she asked.

"For the way you and your people were treated. Dan Frazier was a good guy, Ms. Jackson. He approached our department two months ago, concerned about the solvency of OFM. We asked him to gather evidence for us. In the process of doing so, he told us that he thought someone was spying on him. He believed it was someone in the corporate offices down in Phoenix. I suggested it might be someone close to him up here—you, for example."

"Me?"

"Dan wouldn't hear of it, of course. But that's why we took the files and the computers. The files were cover. What we really wanted was access to employee e-mails to see if someone here had turned on him."

"And we hadn't."

"No."

"Dan had learned that Jason had a laptop that he was absolutely hyper about keeping apart from the company's network. Dan felt sure there was critical information stored on that, and he didn't want us to make a move against McKinzie until he managed to duplicate the files. He downloaded them onto a memory card sometime overnight on Thursday and called on Friday to let us know that he had them. I thought we should move in immediately, but no one would authorize a full weekend of overtime. The raid was moved to Monday. Dan died on Tuesday. So far we've not found any trace of the file."

"I have it," Haley said. "Or at least a copy of what was on the card. The drive itself was left in Dan and Millie's safe-deposit box. I found it there. When I realized it was encrypted, I turned it over to a company called High Noon Enterprises."

She tore off a sheet from a note pad, consulted her phone, wrote down a number, and passed the paper to him. "Ali Reynolds is one of the owners," Haley said. "You should probably speak to her."

Agent Ferris looked at the note and then slipped it into his pocket. "About the funerals . . . ," he said.

"There will be one service only," Haley said. "A memorial service at two p.m. on Friday afternoon at the Whitney Funeral Home here in town."

"Since I feel personally responsible for what's

happened," Agent Ferris said, "I'd like to send some flowers and perhaps even attend, but only if you think that would be appropriate."

"Of course, Agent Ferris," Haley Jackson told him. "You'd be more than welcome to join us."

64

It was two thirty in the morning before Ali dropped Cami off at her apartment in Cottonwood and made it back home to Sedona. The phone awakened her five hours later at seven thirty. Through sleep-blurred eyes, she saw Dave Holman's number in the caller ID screen.

"You're up early," she croaked.

"Up early and on my way to the jail in Prescott, but I wanted to run something past you. During the interviews in Peoria last night, Eric Drinkwater and I were present but benched. We were able to watch the proceedings but didn't participate. My assessment says Jason McKinzie is scared witless while Jessica Denton is one cool customer. So here's my idea—the oldest trick in the book."

"A plea deal?" Ali asked.

"Right, and, the first one to talk gets the death sentence taken off the table."

"But—" Ali began.

"Wait a second," Dave said. "Let me finish. I was talking to Stu a little while ago about the Phoenix traffic cam issue. He mentioned something about unlocking some kind of encryption codes and finding out that McKinzie has secreted sums of money in hidey-hole banks, institutions, and property scattered across the entire planet."

"That's true," Ali said, "and thanks to Haley Jackson I believe we've got a line on those, chapter and verse—not only the account numbers but also recent balances. I haven't put it all together, but the total is going to be sizable. High Noon is about to sign on to help recover those monies. We should have confirming paperwork on that later today."

"I may be able to help with that," Dave said. "I'll be meeting with the county attorney as soon as I get to Prescott. I'm going to suggest that we offer Jason McKinzie a deal, first rattle out of the box. He gives us a full confession—not only on all four murders but also on the OFM swindle. He has to give us everything and agree to testify against Jessica Denton. In addition, he has to grant access to all of his offshore accounts and agree to return the money, which is to be brought back to this country and placed in an escrow account for the benefit of OFM's creditors and investors. Otherwise we charge him with four counts of murder in the first degree, death sentence included."

"What if he asks for a lawyer?"

"He hadn't as of late last night, and that's why I'm suggesting we make the offer before we ask him anything else. That way he won't have a chance."

"Good luck with that," Ali said. "If you can make

it work, it might bring about the best of all possible outcomes. Keep me posted."

Ali dragged herself out of bed, threw on her robe, let Bella out briefly, and then wandered into the kitchen to pour herself a cup of coffee.

"Good morning," Leland said. "And what would you like for breakfast today?" he asked.

Ali answered without a moment's worth of hesitation. "I can't think of anything I'd like better," she said, "than several cups of coffee and one of your meat loaf sandwiches."

65

B. Simpson and Ali Reynolds to see Mr. Lowens-dahl," B. said, laying a business card on the receptionist's desk. Ali happened to be wearing a linen pantsuit that day—a deliberate wardrobe choice on her part. The receptionist was wearing another sweater.

It was a full week after Ali had signed the paperwork designating High Noon as recovery agents working on behalf of the chief restructuring officer for Ocotillo Fund Management. By now there was no question about the company's being "restructured." The bankruptcy proceedings were now focused strictly on dissolution.

Ali and B. had talked long and hard about what they were about to do. Was it moral? Maybe not. Was it right? Absolutely. And now it was time to lower the boom on Eugene Lowensdahl, with Ali doing the heavy lifting. Their planned strategy was partially a bluff, but they knew enough about the timelines involved to believe it might work.

Investigators searching Jason McKinzie's pri-

vate office had uncovered a private security monitor, one that was in no way connected to the one
covering the remainder of the building. On that
they had found footage of Dan Frazier's surrepti-
tious entrance during which he had downloaded
the memory file. Naturally that week's footage had
been taken in as evidence in the Frazier homicide,
a bit of information Dave had been kind enough to
pass along to Ali.

"Could I see it?" she had asked.

"You'll have to ask Eric Drinkwater. That's in
his bailiwick."

"Great," Ali said. "Wish me luck."

To her surprise, when she showed up at Sedona
PD and asked to see it, the detective had agreed
with very little argument. "I don't see why not," he
said. "You'll be able to view the file footage but not
edit it."

Ali's father had told her that he and Detective
Drinkwater had buried the hatchet. Evidently the
peace treaty between the two men extended as far
as Ali.

Drinkwater showed her into a small, poorly
air-conditioned room, sat her in front of a computer monitor, and called up a file. Once it started,
Drinkwater left the room, closing the door and
leaving Ali alone. It broke her heart to watch Dan
Frazier sneak into the room, locate McKinzie's
computer, and insert the drive. At the time, he had
thought he was doing something that would help
the SEC finally bring Jason McKinzie down and
see to it that he was held to account. In the long

run, that's exactly what had happened—he was being held to account—but Dan Frazier had died in the process, and that hurt.

Ali started to exit the file, but then for some reason she fast-forwarded through the rest of the Thursday-night footage and on into Friday morning, where she slowed it again. A young woman Ali assumed to be McKinzie's secretary showed up and set a pile of correspondence on the desk along with a hot drink container of some kind. The office was empty for a spell, then Jason McKinzie showed up. He looked at his desk and then, without touching the cup or the correspondence or even sitting down, he opened a drawer in the desk and pulled out a laptop.

For a period of time, he was offscreen entirely. Then he went back to his desk and made several calls. There was no audio. Ali couldn't hear what was being said, but he looked anxious, upset. Ali continued to scroll through the day. Nothing seemed out of the ordinary until sometime well after six, presumably after most of the other employees had left for home.

Just after 6:30 a female, one Ali now recognized as Jessica Denton, entered the office carrying a stack of paper that had the look of some kind of legal documents. She and Jason proceeded to kiss in an entirely inappropriate fashion, then she pushed away and left the room, returning a few minutes later with a second man in tow. Ali's eyes nearly popped out of her head when she realized who he was—Eugene Lowensdahl. He sat down in a visitor's chair. There was some silent back-and-forthing, then, after considerable discussion, McKinzie picked up a pen, centered the document on a blotter on an otherwise clear desk, signed it, and passed it over to Lowensdahl.

"Aha!" Ali said aloud. "Gotcha."

And today she and B. planned to put that "gotcha" moment to good use.

With B. along, Eugene Lowensdahl respectfully rose to his feet, buttoning his jacket as they entered the room. "Back from your travels, I see?" he asked, shaking first B.'s hand and eventually Ali's as well. He motioned them into chairs.

"To what do I owe the pleasure?"

In answer, Ali pulled a single piece of paper out of her purse and slid it across the table. On it was a single column of figures.

"What's this?" he asked.

"That's a list of Jason McKinzie's offshore bank accounts—the ones we've located so far," she said. "It also includes all current balances."

His eyes scrolled down the page. When he reached the bottom line, his eyes widened and he whistled. "That's way more than I thought it would be," he said.

"We've also located a number of properties and several large caches of diamonds," Ali continued. "We're having both the properties and the diamonds appraised."

"We'll be able to sell them?"

"Over time," B. said. "And not for fire-sale pennies on the dollar, either."

Lowensdahl nodded. "But this is incredible," he said. "I had no idea you'd be able to amass so much information in such a short time."

"We have our sources," Ali said.

"It's going to make for a hell of a payday," he said.

"Actually, that's why we're here. Given the circumstances, our twenty percent fee seems out of line. What's your percentage, Mr. Lowensdahl?"

"Twenty," he said.

"We're willing to make our twenty percent go away. We're prepared to change over to an hourly fee, and we think you should, too."

"What are you talking about?" Lowensdahl said. "Why should I?"

"Because this money belongs to someone else. The people who invested it deserve to get their money back without losing another forty percent in the process."

Lowensdahl sat up straight in his chair. "Ms. Reynolds, you're more than welcome to relinquish your share, but you have no right to dictate what I do with mine."

"You knew McKinzie was leaving before he left," Ali said quietly. "You knew that late Friday afternoon when you came by his office to pick up the bankruptcy paperwork. I'm sure the SEC would be interested in knowing that you had advance knowledge of his departure, and that you made no effort to stop him."

"You have no way of knowing that."

"Yes we do," Ali said. "And we also know that there was a witness in the room at the time who might be willing to testify to that effect."

"What is this? It feels like blackmail."

"And your collecting twenty percent of people's hard-won savings seems like highway robbery," Ali replied. "This isn't so much blackmail as it is a plea deal with a little give-and-take. You might even call it a clawback of sorts. We drop our twenty. You drop yours. As an added bonus, we won't speak to the SEC or the State Bar Association of Arizona."

There was a pause. "Okay," he said finally, conceding defeat. "Done."

"What's your hourly fee?"

"Five hundred."

"You should be able to shave quite a bit off that when it comes to doing simple accounting and administrative work," Ali said. "And to help you with that, here's something else."

She pulled out a memory card and slid it across his desk. He caught it just before it slid off the far side.

"What's this?"

"I believe that's a complete listing of OFM's clientele along with all their contact information as well as some helpful accounting info."

"Where did you get this?"

"Does that matter? What really matters is that we have it. That's only a copy by the way."

"All right," Lowensdahl said finally, conceding on the issue of his hourly rate, too. "One fifty."

"Great," Ali said, smiling, rising to her feet, and brushing the wrinkles from the legs of her pantsuit. "Sounds good, Mr. Lowensdahl. I believe we're done here. Do stay in touch."

66

"So this is where you think it happened?" Bob Larson asked.

"That's what Cami said," Stu Ramey answered. "She was starting to slow down to make the turn when Jessica threw the memory card out of the car."

Bob's Bronco was parked on the shoulder of Highway 179 just east of the I-17 entrance ramp. Armed with matching metal detectors, Bob and Stu had waited until late afternoon to tackle the project. Some of the heat was beginning to dissipate, but it was still hot.

"I did some computerized reconstructions on this," Stu said, "trying to estimate speed, weight, and wind factors to come up with possible distances. If Cami's right, and she had already started slowing down, the object wouldn't have traveled as far as it would have if they'd been going fifty-five. We're going to do this in three-foot-wide sections, thirty feet long, on either side of the fence line. Got it?"

Bob looked at the fence line stretching off into the far distance. He looked at the sea of dried grass on either side of the barbed wire. What he really wanted to say was that Stuart Ramey was absolutely, 100 percent nuts. But of course he couldn't say any such thing. He and Edie owed this guy far too much for that.

"Got it," he said.

"Which side of the fence do you want?" Stu asked.

Bob didn't know exactly how much older he was than Stuart, but when it came to climbing over barbed wire fences, he was in far better shape than the younger man. "I'll take the far side," he said.

They worked for the better part of two hours—back and forth, back and forth. The sweat ran into Bob's eyes and down his shirt. His back ached. His legs hurt. But Stu wouldn't give up. He was relentless. He was going to find that damned USB adapter or know the reason why.

And just when Bob was ready to give up—when he was ready to say he couldn't take another damned step—his metal detector alerted. It wasn't an aluminum can this time or a bottle cap, either. It was, in fact, exactly what they were looking for—the USB adapter with the memory card still tucked safely inside.

"I've got it," Bob shouted. "Here it is."

With more speed and agility than Bob would have thought possible, Stu clambered over the intervening fence and covered the distance between them at a dead run.

"Don't touch it, whatever you do!" Stu commanded, panting and out of breath. "We need to take photographs of it. If Jessica Denton's prints are on it, we don't want to lose them."

67

Cami sat in her oversized first-class seat and stared out the window as first the bay and then the airport runways materialized out of the fog. She had relented after all and agreed to come home for Papa's birthday party, but she hadn't caved completely. She was coming for the party only, would spend the night—at a hotel of her choosing—and fly home the next day. She had assured her mother that there was no reason to pick her up at the airport. Cami would get herself back and forth on her own, thank you very much.

In actual fact Ali was the one who had chosen and booked the Four Seasons and had insisted on buying Cami a first-class ticket and had made arrangements for a limo pick-up and drop-off as well. "It's a perk," she had said. "Let's just call it retroactive combat pay."

It was an afternoon party. Papa had agreed to close the restaurant for the afternoon, but not for the evening. The place would be open again for regular dinner service. By the time Cami set out to walk the mile-plus distance between the Four Seasons and the restaurant, the morning fog had burned away completely. She walked well-remembered streets, looking in familiar shopwindows, peering at strangers, watching the traffic. And all the while, her heart was filled with dread.

Her parents would both be there. Cami wasn't sure who had blown the whistle on her, but somehow her mother had learned of Cami's exploits in Peoria weeks earlier, and Sue Ling Lee was not a happy camper. The mere fact that Cami had finally agreed to show up for her grandfather's birthday celebration hadn't done much to improve mother/daughter relations.

Cami had timed her arrival so the party would already be in full swing when she got there. She had planned to slip in through the back door. That would give her a chance to blend in with the crowd and be involved in conversation before either of her parents spotted her. What she hadn't counted on was the fact that the birthday boy himself was no more enamored of the party than she was.

Papa, seated on an upturned lettuce crate and smoking a forbidden cigarette, hailed her as she made for the door. "Meili," he called, patting the top of the crate. "Come and sit with me."

Cami's grandfather had never approved of the name *his* daughter had given *her* daughter. In a way, Cami saw it as an appropriate bit of "what goes around comes around." She had always called her grandfather Papa, and he had always called her Meili—"Beautiful."

Cami sat.

"Your mother would not like it if she knew we were sitting out here in the alley," Papa said.

"No," Cami smiled. "She would not. And Nainai"—"Grandmother"—"would not like it if she knew you were smoking."

Papa smiled at that. "Then we shall not tell them."

He took another drag on the cigarette. "I'm glad you came."

"So am I," Cami said, realizing suddenly that she actually *was* glad.

"Did you know that when I was a boy I wanted to be a doctor?"

Cami was floored. "I had no idea."

Papa nodded. "My father said to me, 'Boy, you are too stupid to be a doctor. You must learn to cook.'" Papa paused and shrugged. "And so I cooked. I have cooked all my life. It is what I do."

It came as a shock to learn that her mother's version of their family history was a total fabrication. To hear Sue Lee tell it, her parents had loved running their restaurant and had insisted that she grow up and become a part of it. Given Papa's history, Cami somehow doubted that was true.

"What do you want to be, Meili?"

"What I am," she answered. "Someone who helps people."

"Like you are helping all those poor people get their money back?"

Cami was floored again. How did Papa know about that?

"George, our new cook, is on the Internet all the time. I asked him to—what do they call it again?—oh yes, google you. He found many articles about you and read them to me. It sounded very exciting." He took another drag on the cigarette. "And then, I'm afraid, I did a very bad thing."

"What's that?"

"I had George send them to your mother."

Suddenly Cami burst out laughing. She couldn't help it. Leaning over, she kissed her grandfather's weathered cheek and hugged his neck.

"Thank you, Papa," she said. "I think this is going to be the best birthday party ever."

68

B. and Ali left for the Brought Back girls' house-warming party early on Saturday afternoon. It was the Fourth of July, and the handwritten invitation, done in someone's recently learned and somewhat awkward cursive, had said: "Plese come to our Inddependence Day celibration. 2:00 PM. Satarday July 4."

"I believe that's the most touching invitation I've ever received," Ali had said, brushing away a tear as she passed the small envelope over to B. "It took real courage to write that."

"Yes, it did," B. agreed.

"Sister Anselm has been in on the planning. It's Fourth of July all the way—hot dogs, hamburgers, watermelon, potato chips, potato salad, coleslaw, and a batch of red-white-and-blue-frosted cupcakes. This is their first ever Fourth of July celebration, and the girls are very excited."

"What are we bringing?"

"S'mores. You should have seen how thrilled they were when they tried potato chips for the first time. I can hardly wait to see how s'mores will go over."

Late on Friday afternoon Dave had called. "Are you ready for some good news?"

"What?"

"They ran Jessica Denton's DNA through CODIS and got a hit to a twenty-year-old unsolved homicide in L.A. Guy comes out, finds someone stealing his car, and the car thief shoots him dead. DNA from a hair from a scrunchie found near the car leads straight to Jessica. Still doesn't tell us who she is or where she's from, but we're getting closer. And once she's been tried and hopefully convicted on our charges, LAPD will be ready to charge her with theirs."

"I'm glad she's off the streets," Ali said.

"I'm glad they're both off the streets," Dave said. "Without Jason's confession and plea arrangement, we might not be able to nail her, but now it looks like a done deal. With any luck they'll both end up serving life without."

That was Ali's hope, too.

"You're very quiet," B. said as they turned northbound on I-17. "Penny for your thoughts."

"I was just thinking about Jessica Denton," Ali said. "She's linked to at least five homicides now, and Cami took her down."

"Cami is one tough cookie," B. agreed. "And are we ever lucky to have her."

They arrived at the house in Flag and stepped out into a perfect summer day—seventy-five degrees and sunny, with a hint of promising rain clouds peeking over the distant horizon. Maybe the monsoons would arrive shortly. It was time.

The house Sister Anselm had snagged and re-habbed looked like it had stepped out of a Norman Rockwell painting from the fifties. What appeared to be a brand-new American flag hung on one of the newly painted porch posts. A picnic table with a Fourth of July–themed paper tablecloth had been set up in the front yard, along with an odd-ball collection of outside furniture that said "yard sale" all the way.

A smiling Enid Tower, carrying Baby Ann in one arm, hurried to greet them. "I'm so glad you could come. Sister Anselm's already here."

"I'll trade you the baby for this," Ali said, hand-ing over a brown paper bag holding the s'more makings. "Something for dessert," she added.

"But we already have a dessert."

"Believe me, you're going to want to give these a try."

In this house of many women, Baby Ann had quickly become accustomed to being passed from one hand to another, and she made no protest at being left in Ali's care. B. gravitated over to the grill, where a guy named David Upton was keeping a close watch on a newly lit fire.

Months earlier, David's car had clipped a run-away Enid Tower as she ran across a darkened highway directly in front of him in a desperate attempt to escape a pursuer determined to return her to The Family's clutches. Horrified to have hit a pedestrian and wanting to help, David had climbed out of his car only to discover that not only was sixteen-year-old Enid Tower injured, she was also going into labor.

David Upton was not Baby Ann's father, but you couldn't tell that by looking. He was a fixture in Enid's and Baby Ann's lives, and in the lives of the other Brought Back girls as well. He was their go-to guy, their handyman, and their plumber, as well as their interpreter and comforter when the complexities of the Outside became too much for them.

"How's it going?" B. asked.

"I think I've got it now, Mr. Simpson," David said. "What can I get you to drink? We're strictly sodas and iced tea here."

"Iced tea sounds great. That's what I'll have and Ali, too."

As David went to fetch drinks, Sister Anselm appeared on the front porch and then came down to join them in the yard. Just then a small commotion occurred out on the street. When Ali saw the roof of a silver Sprinter pull over and stop outside the fence, she turned back to Sister Anselm.

"You had them invite the governor?"

"Yes, I did," Sister Anselm beamed. "And here she is. I'd better go get the girls."

Governor Virginia Dunham waved off her security detail and came into the yard wearing jeans, a cowboy shirt, boots, and a white Stetson. She looked nothing like a governor. Grinning from ear to ear, she walked over to Ali, holding out her arms. "My turn with the baby," she said.

"I can't believe you're here," Ali said.

"My scheduler couldn't believe it, either," Governor Dunham said with a laugh. "She had a fit when I told her I wasn't doing any public appearances for the Fourth of July. This is way more fun. I wouldn't have missed it for the world."

One by one the Brought Back girls came down the steps to greet their guests. They had met Governor Dunham before, but that was in the very beginning, before they had enough exposure to the world to understand that she was someone important. Now they did, and they approached her shyly. One by one, she pulled them into a one-armed embrace.

"Now who's going to show me the house?" Governor Dunham asked Enid. "That's what I really came to see."

As the governor allowed herself to be led inside, B. turned to David. "Are you ever going to get around to asking that girl to marry you?"

David nodded. "She turns seventeen at the end of the month. I thought I'd ask her then."

"Well done," Sister Anselm exclaimed, clapping her hands in delight. "It's about time."

It turned out to be a terrific party. As expected, the s'mores were a huge hit. Ali was tired and happy as they headed back down to Sedona. High Noon had chalked up some big wins in the last few months. With the amount of money in the OFM escrow account, there was a good chance that many of the smaller investors would actually be made whole. The long-term financial outlook for the refugees from The Family was also looking up.

Then, as if B. could read her mind, he asked, "Has anyone ever mentioned that you and Sister Anselm do good work?"

Ali reached over and squeezed his hand. "Thank you," she said. "So do you."

Turn the page for a sneak peek at
J.A. Jance's thrilling new novel

MAN OVERBOARD

As the cruise ship rocked and rolled in open water, Roger McGeary stood in front of the mirror and tried for the fourteenth time to tie his damned bow tie. He had looked up the directions on the Internet and watched the demo through to the end, but that wasn't much help.

He knew for sure it was his fourteenth attempt because that was something Roger always did—always *had* to do—he counted things. His arms ached. His hands shook. Beads of sweat had popped out on his brow, and the underarms on his freshly starched and pressed dress shirt were soaked through as well. A glance at the clock told him he was already ten minutes late to meet up with the girls in the bar for a predinner beverage.

When the doorbell to his stateroom buzzed, he gave up, dropped the ends of the still untied tie, and pounded the dresser top in frustration. The blow sent one of his cufflinks skittering across the polished wood surface and onto the carpeted floor, where it immediately disappeared from view under the bed. Roger was on his hands and knees searching for the missing cufflink when Reynaldo, his cabin butler, stuck his head around the doorjamb.

"Turndown service," he announced. "Or would you rather I came back at another time?"

"No," Roger said. "Now's fine."

"Can I help you with something?" Reynaldo asked solicitously.

"I've lost my damned cufflink, and I can't for the life of me tie my damned tie."

Crouching at the foot of the bed, Reynaldo quickly retrieved the missing cufflink and dropped it into Roger's meaty fist. Leaning on the bed, Roger heaved himself upright. "Thanks," he said. "Appreciate it." And he did.

"As for the tie," Reynaldo offered, "I'd be happy to help with that and with the cufflinks as well."

Feeling embarrassed and self-conscious at his own obvious incompetence, Roger surrendered himself to Reynaldo's ministrations. It took only a matter of seconds and a few deft movements on Reynaldo's part before the tie was properly tied.

The butler stood back for a moment to admire his handiwork. "Cufflinks next," he said, and Roger handed them over. Once the cufflinks were fastened, Reynaldo retrieved the jacket from the bed and held it up so Roger could slip into it. The jacket settled smoothly onto Roger's massive shoulders as though it had been made for him—because it had. Aunt Julia had seen to that.

"You're going on a cruise, Rog," she had told him. "You need a tux for formal nights on board, and by God you're going to have one." A lifetime's worth of experience had taught Roger that arguing with Aunt Julia was a losing battle. He'd gone straight out and ordered the tux. At Aunt Julia's urging he'd also invested in a new sports jacket and some Big and Tall dress shirts as well.

"After all," Aunt Julia had counseled, "it's a two-week cruise. You can't go down to the dining room in the same thing night after night."

The Big and Tall shirts were necessary because Roger was a big man. Standing next to him, Reynaldo was tiny by comparison. Once the jacket was properly in place, the butler reached up and dusted off a tiny speck of lint before giving Roger an approving nod.

"Very good, sir," Reynaldo said. "Take a look in the mirror."

Turning back to face the mirror where he'd spent the better part of forty-five minutes battling with the tie, Roger McGeary was startled to see the reflection staring back at him. He looked . . . well . . . good.

He'd never worn a tux before. Members of the Dungeons & Dragons Club back in high school weren't the kinds of kids who went to proms or homecoming dances. And if they did somehow get around to getting married eventually, they evidently didn't do so with a full contingent of bridesmaids and groomsmen. If there had been geeky weddings in Roger's circle of acquaintances, he himself had never been called upon to perform bridal party duties. And so, at the ripe old age of forty-and-a-half, he was astonished to see that the tux made all the difference.

Of course, his shoulder-length hair—still mostly brown but beginning to go gray—was maybe a bit incongruous with the tux, but it was too late to do anything about that now. Besides, Roger had worn his hair that way from the moment he turned twelve and realized that having a son with shoulder-length hair was something that drove his father nuts. Anything that bugged the hell out of James McGeary was exactly what his son would do.

Roger grinned at Reynaldo. "Thanks for your help," he said.

"Don't mention it, sir," the butler replied. "That's why I'm here."

That was something else his old D&D pals would find astonishing—Roger McGeary on a cruise? In a stateroom with a damned butler? Get out!

Feeling somewhat jaunty, Roger stopped long enough to pull his cell phone off the charger and slip it into his jacket pocket. Earlier when he'd been looking for directions on the tie, he'd noticed that the charge was lower than it should have been, and he'd plugged it in while he was showering and shaving. If it was losing its ability to hold a charge, he'd need to go looking for a new one once he got back home.

Roger took the phone along with him to dinner now more out of force of habit rather than because he was expecting any calls. After all, he was on vacation, and his office in San Jose, California, was many time zones away. Letting himself out of the cabin, he started toward the elevator lobby. He'd taken only a few steps when a sudden pitch sent him bouncing off first one wall and then the other.

It's the English Channel, after all, he told himself. *What do you expect?*

His stateroom was fairly well aft. As he tottered down the long hallway, he couldn't help thinking again of the kids he'd hung out with back in high school. The only one he still stayed in touch with—sometimes by text and occasionally by running into each other at cybersecurity conferences—was Stu Ramey, the guy who had once been Roger's best friend. They had met up in Adams Junior High—junior prison, as they called it.

Smart, overweight, and both wearing glasses, Roger and Stu had bonded immediately. From junior high on, the nerdy outsiders had been bullied and disparagingly referred to by their classmates as Tweedledum and Tweedledee. That was in Phoenix, where at least he'd had a friend or two. Once his mother pulled up stakes, moved him to LA, and dumped him into the zoo that was Sepulveda High School for his senior year, he'd had no friends at all, and he had been utterly lost.

It was hardly surprising that Roger had never attended any of his high school class reunions. He'd still been locked up in Napa for his tenth. As for the twentieth? Thanks to Aunt Julia, he'd been back on his feet by then, and had actually received an invitation to the one in LA, but he'd had no interest in attending. He didn't remember anyone from Sepulveda High, and he doubted anyone there remembered him, either. As for South Phoenix High? Kids who'd come there via Special Ed hadn't exactly been welcomed with open arms. He supposed he could have crashed that one, but since his only friend at the time had been Stuart, there wasn't much point.

As for Roger? Years of therapy hadn't fixed his damaged self-esteem issues or his overweening insecurities, either, although seeing himself in the mirror in his tux was maybe a start. And the next time he saw Stu, he'd have to ask him about the reunion situation. Maybe Stuart Ramey had more balls than Roger did. Maybe he'd gone back and braved the ravening horde—arrogant jocks, perky cheerleaders, and all.

In the elevator lobby, Roger stepped aside for a couple heading back the way he'd come. The woman had a decidedly green cast to her skin, and she clung to her companion's arm with something close to a death grip. Roger thanked his lucky stars that he wasn't prone to motion sickness and wondered if any of the girls were, either.

Calling his prospective companions for the evening "girls" was a bit of a misnomer. For one thing, they were all north of sixty—possibly even north of seventy—but very well preserved. In the dining room the previous evening, the first night of the cruise, their four-top table had been next to his two-top by the window. As the wine flowed and plates of food came and went, they noticed that he was on his own. The next thing Roger knew, the three women had drawn him into conversation, asking where he was from, was he on his own, what did he think of the cruise so far? By the time dinner was over, they had commandeered him to accompany them to the bar for an after-dinner drink, and before the evening ended—sometime after midnight—he had agreed to join them for the following night's formal dinner.

Aunt Julia would have called them "classy old broads." They were well dressed, well manicured, and no doubt well-heeled. Roger had no doubt that the bits of jewelry on display were the real thing—diamonds as opposed to zirconium. So, although he was happy to have been included in their circle, he knew he was completely out of his element.

He didn't mention to them or to anyone else onboard that the two-week cruise, complete with his two-room suite and the butler, was a freebie. Roger had detected and successfully prevented a massive data breach that would have thrown the cruise ship line into a nightmare and disrupted their entire reservations system. Not only had he preempted the attack, he'd also managed to catch the culprit—a disgruntled former employee. As far as Northern Star Cruise Lines was concerned, Roger McGeary was a hero, and they were prepared to treat him as such.

When Roger stepped off the elevator on deck five, he stood for a moment, staring in through the open doors of the Starlight Lounge. The place was crowded. The "girls"—Angie, Millie, and Dot—had managed to snag seats at the bar and were evidently holding a spot for him. The barman, a cheerful guy named Xavier, caught Roger's eye as he stood in the hall, nodded, and immediately turned to prepare Roger's preferred beverage—Campari and soda—which was poured and in position in front of the single open stool before Roger made it across the room.

This was only the second night of the cruise, Roger noted, so how was it possible that Xavier recognized individual customers on sight and had already memorized their preferred beverage? Roger was entirely at home in the cyberworld in front of keyboards and glowing computer screens, but Xavier's people skills—his easy humor and pleasant gift of gab—were completely absent from Roger's skill set. He'd never be able to be a bartender, never in a million years.

Dorothy Hollister, aka Dot, was a divorcée with a thick southern accent. A little slip of a thing, with brightly hennaed red hair and a slick black sheath dress, she was also the self-proclaimed ringleader of the group. Dot launched herself off her stool and tackled Roger, greeting him with an enthusiastic hug.

"My goodness gracious," she said, looking him up and down. "If you don't clean up nice."

"Why, thank you, ma'am," Roger replied, trying to match her accent with a sort of ersatz cowboy gallantry and then flushing in embarrassment because he felt like he'd already made a jackass of himself.

"You're not just having Campari and soda, are you?" she demanded. "Shouldn't you have something with a little more firepower than that? How about joining us in a Kir Royale?"

That's what "the girls" had been drinking at the bar the previous night, and that's what they were having tonight as well. Roger wasn't much of a drinker, and he didn't do drugs, either—any kind of drugs other than his doctor-prescribed antidepressants—but he'd allowed himself to be persuaded. Once he'd made it back to the room the previous night, he'd looked up Kir Royale, which turned out to be a heady combo of champagne and crème de cassis. Roger had attempted to tell them that he couldn't dance—wouldn't dance. With a couple of Kir Royales under his belt, they had managed to cajole him onto the dance floor, sometimes with all three of them at once. By the time the girls had bade him goodnight, everybody had all been flying high—Roger included.

"See you tomorrow," Dot had admonished him, shaking a finger in his face on her way out. "Drinks in the bar at seven; dinner at seven-forty-five. Don't be late."

Xavier had watched the three women leave the bar and head tipsily for the elevator. Shaking his head in mock sympathy, he turned to Roger. "I believe you have your hands full, sir. Would you care for a refill?"

"Those were a little stiff for me," Roger told him. "I'd better not."

Now in the predinner cocktail hour, canapés came and went, and so did first a second Campari and soda and finally a third. When seating at the bar proved too noisy for conversation, Dot corralled a nearby table. In the ensuing conversation, Roger began to learn a bit about his companions. The three women were old college chums who had all attended Wellesley and had stuck together through thick and thin ever since, including taking two-week cruises each and every year.

Roger didn't know exactly where Wellesley was, but he was pretty sure going there was pricey. And knowing how much the cruise cost on the open market, he estimated there had been a whole lot more thick in their lives than there had been thin. Dot had a cabin—a Star Suite like his—all to herself, while Angie and Millie bunked together in a Veranda Stateroom. In the bar and again when they moved into the dining room, Roger listened to their harmless dinnertime chatter, feeling as though he was being given a window into another world, one he'd never even imagined.

Somewhere between courses three and four, between the mixed green salad and the pappardelle pasta, Roger came to the realization that these women had most likely been contemporaries of his late mother, may she rot in hell. Unlike Eloise McGeary, however, the "girls" actually seemed to like him.

Sometime between the surf-and-turf main course—prime rib and lobster—and dessert—a delectable flan topped with a layer of crisp caramel and three perfect raspberries—Roger felt the buzz of an incoming text. But the wine had been flowing—white followed by red—and he was on vacation. If someone from work wanted to be in touch, they could damned well wait. And if it was Aunt Julia? Well, then, she could wait, too. It was probably midmorning or so in Payson, Arizona, and she'd be out looking after her horses. Taking the phone out of his pocket but without bothering to look at the screen, he powered it off.

Once dinner was over, the group migrated back to the bar, where a piano player accompanied a singer who did everything from Patsy Cline to the Beatles. The passengers were mostly of that vintage, Roger noted, and so was the music.

More than a little booze passed Roger's lips in the next little while—and it was definitely of the high-test variety. Halfway through his third Courvoisier, he realized that Millie and Angie had both disappeared from the picture, and he was left with an increasingly aggressive Dot, who was feeling him up in a most insistent and suggestive fashion. Roger was just drunk enough to find it laughable that this very spry older woman was hitting on him, but once she mentioned, not so coyly, that he was the "only fresh meat" to be found onboard, it didn't seem so funny anymore.

Excusing himself to go to "the little boys' room,"

he fled the bar, ducked into the elevator, and made his way back to his deck. The ship was rocking and rolling underfoot, but this time it wasn't just the roiling sea that sent him staggering back and forth from wall to wall all the way down the corridor. He was drunk—as drunk as he'd ever been in his life. He tried his key in the wrong door to begin with. When it didn't work, he finally tumbled to the fact that he was trying to enter the wrong suite.

Once he finally got inside, he felt like he was going to puke. Closer to his lanai than the bathroom, Roger fought his way through blackout curtains, pulled open the slider, stumbled over to the rail, and cut loose. Then, incredibly grateful that he had made it in time, he stood for a long time savoring the wind and the sea and the pounding rain and pulling himself together. He didn't care if his tux got wet at that point because it would for sure have to go to the cleaners anyway. He was almost ready to go back inside when his phone buzzed again.

How could that be? Hadn't he turned it off during dinner? Swaying back and forth next to the rail, he fumbled the phone out of his pocket and scowled down at the screen in frowning puzzlement. What he saw there wasn't really a text—at least it didn't look like a standard text. The words appeared one at a time, scrolling past as though a very fast typist was typing them in real time.

He had read through only a sentence or two before he recognized what he was reading. The words on the screen were all too familiar, and standing there in the wind and the rain, he could almost hear his mother's voice, berating him in the car as they drove to his high school commencement:

What on earth did I do to deserve such an incredible little shit? You're just like your father, Roger McGeary, utterly and totally worthless, and you'll never amount to a hill of beans. What have you got to show for that supposedly high IQ of yours? You barely graduated, for cripes' sake. Your GPA isn't good enough to get into college, and what the hell would you do if you got there? Screw around the same way you did in high school? If you think I'm going to let you sit around the house on your lazy ass, buster, you have another think coming. James McGeary, that worthless father of yours, finally had the good grace enough to do the world a favor and off himself. With any kind of luck, you will, too.

Roger recognized the words—Eloise McGeary's words. A few months earlier, during the course of treatment, he had recalled them all and written them down verbatim in a document for his therapist, Dr. Amelia Cannon. She had assured him that writing out exactly what his mother had said was a mental health exercise—a way of recognizing his mother's meanness and spite for what it was as well as a way of negating Eloise's powerful hold over him.

At the beginning of Roger's senior year in high school, Eloise had uprooted her son and moved to LA. Lost in the new situation—overwhelmed and unable to cope— he'd barely managed to graduate. A little over a week after commencement, Roger McGeary had attempted suicide. Deeming him a danger to himself and others, Eloise had made it her business to have her son locked away in a mental institution for the next ten years of his life. It was only in the past few months, at Aunt Julia's urging, that he'd finally gone for counseling. It had been in the course of his supposedly confidential sessions with Dr. Cannon that Roger had written down these very words—the ones that now seemed to have developed a life of their own on the screen of his cell phone.

Roger's hands trembled. If the words he had written for Dr. Cannon could surface here, that meant they could surface in other places as well. They were out in the world somewhere, most likely all over the Internet, where eventually they were bound to be used against him. Somewhere down the line, some boss—somewhere up the chain of command—would bring those words to bear and use them to imply that Roger was unstable somehow; that, if he was undergoing therapy, he most likely couldn't be trusted with the kinds of security clearance levels necessary to perform his duties. He'd be done for—out of a job—unemployed and unemployable.

And in that moment, on the night that should have counted as a social triumph, Roger found himself sliding back into the same kind of blinding despair that had kept him in a state of mental paralysis for the better part of ten years. He wouldn't go there. He wouldn't. He couldn't. He had fought so hard to climb out of that snake pit of unending darkness that he couldn't stand to fall back into it again. Could. Not. Stand. It.

The words stopped scrolling. The screen went completely blank, as though the phone wasn't even turned on. He punched the power button and the phone came to life, starting over from scratch as though it had been completely powered off. When the start-up sequence finished, Roger went straight to the texting app, looking for the message he'd just seen, but it wasn't there.

There was no sign of it at all—not his text file or his mail file or even his document file.

So where had the words come from, then? If he hadn't seen them—if he'd just imagined them—maybe he really had gone nuts. Again. And that was something he could not endure. Would not endure.

By then he was soaked to the skin, but that didn't matter. Making up his mind, he put the phone down on the lanai's patio table and then pulled one of the deck chairs over to the railing. He clambered up onto the chair and then stood for a moment—hearing the words again—not as they had appeared on the screen but as he had heard them more than two decades ago, in his mother's shrill voice. He was still hearing them as he plunged over the side of the ship and into the black water far below, with no one onboard the ship any the wiser. It was only then, as the icy sea closed over him, that Roger McGeary finally moved beyond the reach of his mother's earthly torment.

Five minutes or so after being placed on the patio table on deck seven, Roger McGeary's telephone flashed to life once more. It remained there, glowing in the dark for some time, before shutting down.

It was Reynaldo, coming the next morning to deliver Roger's breakfast, who found the sliding door open and the carpeting inside the stateroom soaked by lashing rain. Out on the lanai, a spray-soaked cell phone lay faceup on the table. The butler immediately tossed a life vest over the rail and then sounded the alarm: Man Overboard.

By then, of course, it was far too late.

Half a world away, in a basement lined with dozens of racks filled with hundreds of computer blades, a man sat hunched over a single screen. Alive with anticipation, he watched the action and listened to the dialogue. This was his show, after all. He was the director, producer, sound engineer, and cameraman, if not the star. He didn't consider himself a cyberbully. He was more a cybergod. He liked to think of himself as Odin, and Frigg was his all-knowing artificial intelligence sidekick and companion.

He was jacked up on coffee and uppers. That was what it took to stay awake and alert when you were tuned into a life that was spinning toward the drainpipe seven or eight time zones ahead of you. Odin had chosen to let the game play out tonight—on the night of the cruise ship's formal dinner. For a time, listening in through the remote access malware he'd inserted into Roger's phone, Odin had worried that one of the women might opt to go back to Roger's room with him or, worse, that he'd go to hers. Luckily that hadn't happened. Odin was aware that if things didn't come to a head tonight, the ship's data throttling capability might come into play and make him have to give up on the project altogether for the time being. It was also possible that if Roger noticed the unexpected power drain on his phone, he might suspect there was a problem.

Odin remembered being told once that it was always the shoemaker's kids who didn't have new shoes. With Roger McGeary a rock star in terms of corporate cybersecurity, his phone should have been completely impenetrable. Odin had had zero luck in accessing his work accounts, but the security procedures on Roger's personal cell phone had left the device vulnerable to attack.

Odin had paid a small fortune to procure malware that had been developed in Israel. Once installed on a smart device of any kind, it allowed full access to everything on it—keystrokes, e-mails, texts, cameras, and

GPS locations, as well as recording devices. Customers paid a hefty six-figure installation fee for the software and then continuing fees based on the number of people being monitored by the program.

Theoretically the system was only sold to properly vetted entities—usually government agencies of some kind. Searching the Dark Web, Odin had found a disenchanted software engineer, one the software developers had fired for cause, who had been more than willing to sell him a black-market copy. Since Frigg was available and fully capable of handling all necessary monitoring requirements, Odin was able to keep the whole operation in-house without incurring any ongoing fees.

Tuning back into the distant conversation—the laughter and the clinking of glasses—Odin heard Roger excuse himself to go to the restroom, except he hadn't. The next sounds he heard had nothing to do with someone taking a piss or washing his hands. There was the distinctive ding of an arriving elevator followed by a recorded voice saying, "You are on deck seven." After that, Odin heard a strange series of thumps followed eventually by the slamming of a door. Moments after that, there was a scraping sound of some kind and hurried footsteps pounding on a metal surface. The footsteps ended with the noise of someone heaving his guts out.

The noises made sense then. Roger, probably drunker than he had ever been in his life, had rushed headlong into his cabin, unlatched the lock on the slider, and then made for the rail and was mostly over it before being sick. All of which meant that Roger McGeary was exactly where Odin had wanted and needed him to be for this final chapter—outside and alone on the cabin's balcony.

Odin gave Roger a minute to recover his wits before launching the attack. While the texted words scrolled silently across the screen, Odin watched the pallid face, captured by the cell phone's camera, as it registered first astonishment followed by hopelessness and finally utter despair.

Odin couldn't help smiling at that. It was exactly what happened to weak people when their darkest secrets were exposed to the light of day . . . or, as in this case, the light of night.

Odin felt his own heartbeat quicken. He may have been the one holding the gun, but the final decision was really up to Roger. Would he pull the trigger or not? Waiting for the man to choose seemed to take forever. Later, reviewing the film, Odin measured the elapsed time with his stopwatch—fifteen seconds was all it took from beginning to end, although it seemed much longer. At second number sixteen, Roger set the phone down on something. He did so carefully and with drunken deliberation. Odin couldn't see exactly where the phone had been placed, but fortunately it was still faceup—on a patio table, maybe? From Odin's vantage point, all he could see was a light-colored overhead surface of some kind—probably the ceiling area of Roger's balcony, formed by the floor of the one above his.

Odin leaned closer to his computer and upped the volume. There was a lot of noise in the background. His view of the ceiling didn't show what the weather was like outside the ship, but he suspected it was stormy with plenty of wind and rain. After a few moments, Odin heard some kind of grating noise—wood on metal, maybe?—followed by a grunt of exertion followed by nothing—nothing at all.

Odin felt vaguely disappointed. He had wanted to witness firsthand Roger's despairing headlong plunge into the sea, but the unfortunate camera angle on the cell phone robbed him of that. Oh, well.

Just to be on the safe side, Odin gave it five minutes—five long minutes of wind and rain and nothing else. There was no way to know for sure if it had worked—either it had or it hadn't. Either Roger McGeary had thrown himself off the ship or he had not, and that meant it was far too soon for Odin to gloat over a job well done. Hours from now someone would notice if Roger McGeary was really missing. In the meantime, Odin saved the film file for his private collection and then waited for his remotely installed malware to perform its self-deleting exit program.

Once the purge was complete, Odin stood up, stretched, and looked around. It was five o'clock in the afternoon. He'd been up for close to twenty-four hours. Even so, he needed to shower and dress for dinner. His mother was fine with him spending his days and nights behind the locked doors of the computer lab inside his spacious basement apartment. Irene didn't seem to mind what her son did during the day as long as he showed up promptly each evening just as dinner was being served.

As far as Odin was concerned, spending an hour and a half each day with his annoying mother was a small price to pay for having virtually unlimited funds as well as unlimited freedom. Besides, he didn't need to be there in the lab personally keeping watch. He'd done his part. The rest was up to Frigg. If and when the man overboard alarm went out onboard the *Whispering Star,* either now or hours from now, Frigg would be among the first to know, and once Frigg knew, so would Odin.

In the months leading up to this night, Odin, with Frigg's very capable help, had learned everything there was to know about Roger McGeary, including all the telling details necessary to pull the underpinnings out from under him. Odin would wait until morning. Once

Roger's death was confirmed, it would be time for Odin and Frigg to go hunting again.

Odin had every confidence another victim was out there just waiting to be found—someone who, with the benefit of enough information and a little encouragement on his part, would be more than willing to end it all with Odin on hand to watch the performance to the bitter end. If that wasn't the perfect way to commit murder, Owen Hansen didn't know what was.